A MICHIGAN YANKEE

MARCHES with SHERMAN

a Union Soldier's Spiritual Journey

CATHERINE RHODES HAHN

Copyright © 2014 by Catherine Rhodes Hahn

Published by
Sheliday Publishing Company
Grand Rapids, Michigan USA

ISBN-10: 0692289364
ISBN-13: 978-0692289365

Edited by Robert Banning
Cover and interior design by Matt Plescher
Cover photo courtesy of James Rogers/Big Rapids Pioneer

This novel is sincerely dedicated to all American servicemen and women who have left home and family to answer the call of their country.

CONTENTS

Acknowledgements   xi

1 *September 1864, Casnovia, Michigan*   *1*
Final Day at Home

2 *Casnovia to Grand Rapids, Michigan*   *13*
Leaving Home ~ Mustering In

3 *Camp Blair and Indianapolis*   *23*
Homesickness ~ Rough Beginnings ~ A First Letter

4 *Chattanooga, Tennessee*   *31*
Thirteenth Michigan Regiment ~ Recommitments – Meeting Joey

5 *Rome, Georgia*   *47*
North Meets South: A Gentle Encounter

6 *Kingston, Georgia*   *67*
Joining General Sherman's Army

7 *Atlanta*   *75*
Preparing to March ~ A City in Flames

8 *Leaving Atlanta*   *83*
The March to the Sea Begins ~ Sherman's Neckties

9 *Covington*   *95*
First Sight of Slaves ~ Heavy Weather ~ Sparing the Poor

10 *Milledgeville*   *107*
Thanksgiving Day ~ Losing a Comrade

11 *Sandersville*   *117*
   Skirmishes ⁓ Picking Up Orphans

12 *Davisboro, Louisville*   *123*
   Bathing in the Woods ⁓ A New Messmate

13 *Buckhead Creek, Lumpkin's Station, Sister's Ferry*   *131*
   Saved by Tramp ⁓ A Troubling Discovery ⁓ Lost and Found

14 *Ebenezer Creek*   *141*
   Death in the Creek ⁓ Bad Weather and Tough Going

15 *Siege Line outside Savannah*   *153*
   A Long Wait and Sudden Victory: Praise God! We Made it!

16 *Christmas 1864 in Savannah*   *169*
   Sherman's Christmas Gift to President Lincoln ⁓ Seeing the City

17 *Casnovia, January 1865*   *187*
   Lonesome Letters from the Front

18 *Casnovia*   *201*
   A Birthday Party without Papa

19 *South Carolina and Casnovia*   *213*
   Sloshing through Rainy Lowlands ⁓ Illness ⁓ Snowy Memories

20 *North Carolina*   *229*
   A Bumpy Ambulance ⁓ Gentle Deserters ⁓ Costly Battles

21 *Goldsboro, North Carolina*   *245*
   A Sad Loss ⁓ Typhoid Fever in a Field Hospital ⁓ General Sherman's Visit

22 *Davids Island, New York*   *257*
   In Transit ⁓ De Camp General Hospital

23 *Casnovia*   *265*
   Happy Memories — An Ominous Letter

24 *Casnovia to Grand Rapids*   *281*
   Sad Memories — Getting Underway

25 *Grand Rapids to Brooklyn, New York*   *297*
   A Long but Hopeful Trip

26 *De Camp Hospital, Davids Island*   *309*
   The End of the Journey — Crossing Safely

27 *Cypress Hills Cemetery, Brooklyn*   *319*
   Safe in God's Arms — United in Peace

Author's Notes   *329*

Original Christmas Letter   *331*

Atlanta to Savannah Map   *337*

Acknowledgements

I WISH TO EXPRESS my deepest gratitude to Professor Wallace Bratt, who spent many hours meticulously editing my book, and to my daughter, Melissa, who did all the typing, and without whose advice and encouragement this novel would not have been written. I would also like to thank Irene Bolthouse for her excellent job of proofreading. I am grateful to my husband, Wes, for his prayer support. And most of all, I thank my heavenly Father for his goodness and his faithfulness to me. My prayer is that this story will glorify his holy name.

During the seven years I spent in writing and researching my novel, I had the pleasure of consulting people, mostly by telephone or email, from both the North and the South. I found them to be equally gracious and helpful. The information each supplied is truly appreciated.

I want to thank the following people: Sally Veurink, Hart, Michigan, and Frank and Mary Seaman, Grant, Michigan, for contributing to the Seaman genealogy; Lynn Beuerle, Scottsdale, Arizona, for furnishing copies of seven of Rufus's Civil War letters; Maurice C. York, J. Y. Joyner Library, Manuscripts and Rare Books Department, East Carolina University, Greenville, North Carolina, for locating the name of the ship and its captain that, in all probability, carried Rufus to De Camp General Hospital in New York Harbor; Lynn Hahn for providing the information on his great-great-grandfather, Simon Foster; the congenial librarians in the Genealogy Department of the Grand Rapids Public Library for providing views of 1864–65 newspaper copies of the *Grand Rapids Daily Eagle*, as well as views of maps of Grand Rapids in the 1800s.

I am also grateful to First Baptist Church, Rome, Georgia, for information concerning their church building during the Union occupation from May to November 1864; to Cypress Hills Cemetery, Brooklyn, New York, for data about Confederate soldiers being buried near Union soldiers; to the National Archives for providing military and medical records of Rufus's service in the Union Army; and to The History Channel.

The Internet provided much important information for this project: Walkley genealogy, Wallace Ewing www.familypursuit.com; *History of Muskegon County*, "Casnovia Township" Chicago, H. R. Page and Co. 1882, www.rootsweb.ancestry.com; The Civil War Diary of James Laughlin Orr, 1838–1919, Second Division, Fourteenth Corps (covers Sherman's march to the sea) www.crossmyt.com; "Diary of a Union Soldier Crossing Sampson County, 1865," (printed in the September 1986 issue of the *Huckleberry Historian*), Charles Sawyer, One Hundred Forty-first New York Infantry, Twentieth Corps, information provided by great-grandson Richard Fowler, Norman, Oklahoma, 2012, www.clintonnc.com; The Battle of Bentonville: *Caring for Casualties of the Civil War*, Reading 3: "The Wounded on the Field of Battle," compiled from Lt. M. W. Bates, (Twenty-first Michigan Volunteer Infantry, First Division, Fourteenth Corps), Glimpses of the Nation's Struggle: Papers Read Before the Minnesota Commandery of the Military Order of the Loyal Legion of the United States, 1897-1902 (St. Paul, MN: Review Publishing Company, 1903), 146-151; David's Island and Fort Slocum: Some Overviews (DeCamp General Hospital) found at http://home.earthlink.net/michaelacavanaugh/id2.html; Spanish Moss, found at http://en.wikipedia.org; The Salzburgers, the Georgia Salzburger Society, www.georgiasalzburgs.com; and information concerning the oath of allegiance to the Union Army.

I also consulted the following books: *The Story of Grand Rapids* (Grand Rapids, MI: Kregel Publications, 1966); William T. Sherman, *Sherman's Memoirs*, Library of America (New York: Literary Classics of the United States, Inc., 1990); *The March to the Sea and Beyond* (Baton Rouge: Louisiana State University Press, 1995); *To The Sea* (Nashville: Rutledge Hill Press, 1989); *Marching with Sherman* (Reno: University of Nebraska Press, 1995); *Sherman's March*, Vintage Books, (a division of Random House) 1988; *Army of the Cumberland* (Bloomington: Indiana University Press, 1959); *A Shield and Hiding Place* (Macon, GA: Mercer University Press, 1987).

1

September 1864, Casnovia, Michigan
Final Day at Home

"Please, God," Sarah whispered, "help me stay strong for Rufus." She knew from the start that no one could halt the dawning of tomorrow, the dreaded day of her husband's departure. How quickly the time had flown by since he received his unexpected draft notice. Rufus had spent those precious days making provision for the difficult time when he would be far away and unable to care for his family. In the morning, he would leave to report to the Union forces.

In Michigan, September announces the start of the fall harvest season. Rufus, a good provider, wanted his small family to have a well-stocked root cellar to supply them with food throughout the long winter.

Standing at the large open kitchen window, Sarah saw Rufus at work in their potato patch out back. Her heart already ached with loneliness. She felt glued to the window as she continued to watch the tender scene unfold before her misty eyes.

The late afternoon sun gave the soil of the potato patch a rosy glow. Dorothy and Lucy tagged along after their busy papa as he picked up newly dug potatoes and put them into crates to be stored in the root cellar, along with the other vegetables, canned and dried fruits, and berries. Though not a big man, standing only five feet, seven inches, Rufus still accomplished much hard work. Four-year-old Dorothy picked up potatoes with her tiny hands as best she could. The girls' loving father never expected his young children to work, but he always enjoyed their companionship—especially today.

A proud Rufus smiled down at Dorothy. "You're Papa's helper, Dorothy."

This praise aroused jealousy in two-year-old Lucy. Lips pursed, she bent down, picked up one potato with both hands, toddled over, and dropped it into the crate.

"Lucy's Papa's 'elper, too," she declared.

"Of course you are," Rufus chuckled. He stooped down and gathered both children in his arms. Carefully he examined each child's dear, familiar face—faces that reflected their mother's, with their light brown curly hair and blue eyes. He studied each feature to stamp their sweet images upon his memory so he could carry them with him. It frightened him to think how quickly they would change. It tore even more at his heart to think how quickly they could forget him.

Blinded by tears, Sarah pulled herself away from the window. Lifting up the bottom of her apron, she quickly dried her eyes. She picked up the whistling teakettle from the stove and went out onto the back porch. After pouring the hot water into an enamel washbasin, she walked over and rang the dinner bell. The clang interrupted Rufus's melancholy thoughts.

"Mama has supper ready, girls. Let's be on our way."

Boosting Lucy onto his sturdy shoulders and taking Dorothy by the hand, he started down the dirt path to the house, a humble home nestled in a grove of mostly pine trees. Rufus had planned to make the homestead larger, but now those plans would have to wait.

As they hurried along, they heard a honk overhead.

"Look, Papa!" Dorothy cried, pointing upward to the flock of geese flying in a V-formation.

"They're flyin' south to warmer weather," Papa explained. "They know cold weather's comin'. God's given the geese the know-how when to fly south."

"Why now, Papa?" Dorothy asked. "It's warm."

"We've been enjoyin' warm Indian summer weather, but it shan't stay this way much longer," Papa continued. "Our chilly nights speak of fall.

The leaves will start turnin' beautiful colors of red, yellow, and orange in just a couple of weeks."

Rufus felt tightness in his chest as he spoke to Dorothy and Lucy about the leaves turning colors. He loved those fall colors, but he knew he wouldn't be here to see them this year. He especially admired the red maple leaves. His eyes wandered to the big maple next to their house. When he and Sarah built their four-room home eight years ago, Rufus took special precautions to make sure nothing disturbed that stately tree.

As he and the girls neared the back porch, faithful Buster, their old Shepherd dog, lumbered down the steps to greet them. He walked stiffly over and licked little Lucy in the face.

"Papa, Buster's kissin' me," she squealed.

"That's cuz he likes ya," Papa told her. "Come up on the porch so I can wash your face and hands. You come, too, Dorothy."

During summer the family kept a dented basin on a washstand on the back porch where Rufus could wash up after working in the fields. Today, with the unseasonably mild weather, he led the girls over to use that washbasin now filled with warm water.

They laughed as they splashed each other and Papa, who eagerly joined in their antics. "I'm gonna get you, Dorothy! And you, too, Lucy," he threatened. He stomped his feet, pretending to chase them. Barking Buster joined in the fun. Their faces and hands washed, the giggling merrymakers, along with Buster, slipped into the house. The aroma of freshly baked johnnycake wafted through the open door to whet Rufus's appetite.

Rufus crept into the kitchen, where Sarah was dishing up the special meal she had prepared for him on this, his last day at home. Tiptoeing behind her, he teasingly untied her yellow apron. She whirled around and found herself wrapped in a big bear hug. "Rufus!" she scolded. "You're always untying my apron." She pretended to be angry, but he noticed how tightly she returned his embrace. He swallowed the big lump that rose in his dry throat as he drew her closer. How could he leave her and the children alone?

Sarah put both trembling hands on Rufus's shoulders and stepped back. Her sorrowful eyes caressed his dear face, from the blue eyes that twinkled when he looked at her to the gentle smile that had stolen her young girl's heart ten years ago.

She reached out with one hand to smooth his unruly blond hair. "Everything's ready to eat. Let's sit down." The catch in Sarah's voice revealed her emotions. At the table, the little "helpers" sat with bowed heads and folded hands, waiting for Papa to say grace. Papa and Mama quickly sat down to join them.

A gay, red-and-white-checked tablecloth adorned the round table covered with steaming dishes of ham, sweet potatoes, squash, corn on the cob, applesauce, and johnnycake—and for dessert, pumpkin pie with whipped cream. Nearly all their food was raised and grown on their farm. Michigan's wide variety of fruit trees and berry bushes helped provide the family with a healthy diet.

Papa bowed his head to pray the blessing. "Dear Lord, we thank thee for this food, and we pray thy blessing upon it. And today, Father, I pray a special prayer for my family. I pray for thy divine protection and care over them. Please cover them with the blood of the Lamb. I also pray for the troops in this War of the Rebellion. May thou watch over both sides, Union and Confederate, and bring peace to our nation. Amen."

Dorothy and Lucy each responded with a resounding "Amen!"

Though surprised by Rufus's prayer, Sarah didn't say a word. She hadn't heard him pray aloud that much in a long time. But she, too, prayed for God's help today.

Warmed by the crackling fire in the wood range, the small kitchen felt cozy.

Dorothy, wide-eyed, stared at all the food. "Mama! It's just like Christmas!"

The parents' eyes met. There would be no family Christmas dinner this year.

"Mama's made a wonderful supper," Rufus agreed. He smiled his gratitude at Sarah.

"Thank you, Rufus. You're more than welcome."

"And oh, before I forget," Rufus said, "Edwin will haul the potato crates and put them in the root cellar. We talked about that last week. He'll use his buckboard. They're too heavy for me to carry that distance."

The cheerful chatter of Dorothy and Lucy at the table kept the mood from being subdued. The children had been spared the knowledge of the sad changes about to occur in their once happy family.

After the tasty meal, Rufus rose to go to the barn to milk Queenie, the one cow they had left. All other livestock, except for some chickens, their driving horse "Colonel," and a sow, now were being kept at a neighbor's farm, where he could look after them. The neighbor would keep the milk produced in exchange for boarding the cattle. Rufus kept Queenie at their farm to supply the dairy needs for Sarah and the girls. Colonel would pull their buggy and sleigh, and the sow could be bred next year after Rufus came home, or Sarah could sell it, if she needed money.

"I want to go with Papa to the barn," stated Dorothy.

"Me too!" piped up Lucy.

Sarah sadly smiled at her daughters, knowing it would be a long time before they could accompany their beloved Papa to the barn again. She took down their lightweight coats that hung on pegs at the back door and slipped their arms into them. With unsteady hands she buttoned them up.

Rufus took the oil lantern from another peg. He opened the back door and the trio stepped out into the chilly September evening. With the fall season upon them, the days were growing shorter. Dusk greeted them.

Sounds of evening fell on their ears as they followed the well-worn path that led to the large, weather-beaten gray barn. The tall grass lining both sides of the path had already turned brown. Crickets chirped, and a lone whippoorwill whistled from the woods nearby. Soon its voice would no longer be heard, since whippoorwills would fly to a warmer climate before many days had passed.

The hooting of an owl echoed the whippoorwill's call.

"I hear Hootie, Papa," Dorothy exclaimed. "I hear Hootie."

"Me, too, Papa!" agreed Lucy. "I hear Hootie, too."

"Hootie sleeps durin' the day. He's just gettin' up," Papa replied.

The owl had lived in their woods for several months. The girls loved to hear him hoot, so they had named him "Hootie."

Before they entered the darkened barn, Rufus lit the lantern. Once inside, he hung the flickering light from a hook on an overhead beam. Colonel, their chestnut gelding, whinnied. The girls ran over to his stall to pet the gentle horse on his velvety nose. Rufus picked up the milk pail along with the milking stool and walked over to Queenie in the box stall. He tied the Guernsey cow to a post, ready for milking.

"Who wants to be first?" he inquired.

"I do, Papa!" begged Lucy, jumping up and down.

"I'll go last, Papa," Dorothy kindly offered.

Papa picked up Lucy and set her on the gentle cow. Queenie had become a dear pet of the family.

"Sit nice and still, Lucy, and don't kick Queenie," Papa cautioned. "When the milk pail is half full, it'll be Dorothy's turn."

Papa perched on the milk stool and started milking. Dorothy kept peeking over his shoulder to watch the pail filling up.

"Find the cats' dish, Dorothy," Papa told her. "They'll want their warm milk."

Dorothy searched until she located the cats' metal dish sticking out from under some straw. She felt something bump against her legs as she picked it up. All three barn cats were rubbing against her, purring in anticipation of their warm supper. She bent down and petted them—two short-haired tabbies and one long-haired tortie.

"Dorothy," Papa called. "It's your turn now."

Dorothy then took her place on Queenie, calmly sitting there while Papa finished milking and Lucy sat on some nearby straw, cuddling the cats.

That chore done, Papa filled the cats' dish with warm, frothy milk. He walked over to the pigpen, poured milk into the sow's feeding trough, and tossed her some corncobs. He untied Queenie and put one forkful of hay in her manger and another in Colonel's. From the pump near the box stall he pumped three fresh pails of water, one for Queenie, one for Colonel, and a third for the sow. Finally he bedded the box stall and the horse's stall with fresh straw before hanging the pitchfork back up and taking down the lantern.

"Come girls," Papa called. "We're through with chores. Let's go to the house."

Both girls gave each cat, as well as Queenie and Colonel, a farewell petting before they were ready to leave.

Papa opened the barn door and secured it behind them, as they stepped out into a beautiful, brightly lit night. The large harvest moon hanging low in the sky made the lantern unnecessary as they walked the path to the house.

"See the man in the moon?" Papa asked the girls, his eyes twinkling with mischief.

"Aw, Papa," answered Dorothy. "You know there's no man in the moon, really."

"I see him, Papa! I see him!" shouted Lucy.

Papa laughed. "No, Lucy. Dorothy is right. There is no man in the moon. I was just funnin' ya."

"Lucy race you, Papa," she challenged. "Beat ya Dorothy!" Lucy started toddling as fast as she could toward the house.

Dorothy, always Papa's helper, stayed beside him, with her hands next to his on the milk pail's handle. She thought she needed to help him carry the milk, and Papa let her think so.

While Rufus and the children were in the barn, Sarah had cleared the table and washed the dishes. She tenderly touched the cup Rufus had used. She stroked its handle, thinking how long it would be before they all sat at the table again. It would be a lonely year.

Sarah wondered how a man so meek and sensitive could be a soldier. But she understood how staunchly Rufus opposed slavery. He also took great pride in his country and didn't want to see it divided. Ever since he was a boy he had been hearing the story about how his own grandfather had carried messages for General Washington during Howe's invasion of New York City in 1776 and 1777.

Lucy burst into the house triumphantly. "I beat Papa and Dorothy, Mama," she boasted.

Papa and Dorothy followed Lucy shortly. By their secret smiles, Mama knew they had allowed Lucy to win. Anyway, Papa and Dorothy couldn't run very fast, since they were carrying the full pail of milk. Having set the pail down, Papa hung the lantern back on its peg on the wall, and Sarah covered the milk with a clean strip of cheesecloth. Rufus then carried it outside and put it in the well to keep it cool. Later, Sarah would skim the cream off to churn into butter—but not tonight. Sarah took the girls' coats off and hung them back on their pegs.

The barn chores done and the kitchen all tidy, the little family gathered in their sitting room, an inviting place graced with easy chairs, rockers, a sideboard, tables, and oil lamps.

Sarah's crocheted doilies, displayed on different pieces of furniture, added to the room's charm. A Franklin potbellied stove set in the center of the inside wall heated the room and two adjoining bedrooms. On the wall over the sideboard the clock ticked away the hours much too quickly.

Suddenly it struck eight chimes, a cruel reminder that the day would soon be over. Their one luxury, the piano, stood proud and tall in the corner. Rufus brought an extra lamp from the kitchen and placed it on the piano. Earlier, Sarah had lit the lamps in the sitting room.

Lucy ran up to the piano, lifted the lid, and started plunking on the keys.

"Play, Mama, play," she pleaded.

Sarah usually played the piano every evening. A petite woman, she could barely reach the pedals. She found great joy in playing popular songs of the day, especially Stephen Foster tunes, while her family sang along. Tonight made no exception.

Sarah gently began to play Foster's "Beautiful Dreamer." Rufus's and Dorothy's sweet voices joined in singing the familiar lyrics. Lucy hummed along, able to get a word in now and again.

"What would you like me to play next?" Mama asked, as she finished the haunting melody.

"Alooya, Mama, alooya," chimed in Lucy.

"Which one's that?" inquired Mama.

"She means that new song we received from my relatives in New York," Rufus explained. "Remember? The chorus has 'glory hallelujah' in it."

"Oh, now I know. 'The Battle Hymn of the Republic,'" she replied.

Sarah pulled out the sheet music and forcefully started playing. Rufus stood behind her and peeked over her shoulder, his baritone voice resounding on the last verse, "As He died to make men holy, let us die to make men free, His truth is marching on."

After Lucy had enthusiastically sung a few hallelujah choruses, Sarah sadly covered the piano keys. She thought the song beautiful, but couldn't appreciate it right now. It only added to the burden of her heart.

"Bedtime, girls," she told them. "It's time to get in bed and say your prayers."

"Trot me, Papa," Lucy teased. Papa picked her up and trotted her on his knee.

Dorothy's turn came next. Papa usually gave both girls a ride on his knee before their bedtime.

Rufus and Sarah slipped the girls into their flannel nightgowns. Together, Dorothy and Lucy knelt beside their bed and prayed with simple, childlike faith. Rufus helped Sarah tuck them in. He kissed each girl and left the room. Dorothy and Lucy thought Papa had kissed them just good-night, but Papa knew he had kissed his darling daughters goodbye. When they got up tomorrow, he would be gone.

Sarah followed him, knowing how heavily his final goodbye to Dorothy and Lucy weighed on his heart.

Rufus sat in his favorite rocker, head in hands. Sarah put her hand on his shoulder. He looked up and smiled. Lips trembling, she smiled back. Emotions held down all day for the children's sake now rose. Rufus pulled her onto his lap.

"Do you want Papa to trot you on his knee, too?" he joked, trying to comfort her.

She laid her head on his shoulder.

"No, I want Papa to always be here. I'll miss you so," she sobbed.

"Oh! How I'll miss you and the girls," groaned Rufus.

"I—I keep thinking of Martin and what happened to him," Sarah stammered.

Rufus's younger brother had enlisted in the Union Cavalry at Grand Rapids on August 12, 1862, and died serving his country on February 2, 1863.

Rufus held her closer and kissed the top of her curly head. As they clung to each other, he noticed tears beaded up on her long eyelashes. The lavender fragrance she always wore seemed to close them in, shutting out the war far away.

"You'll never know how much I hate to leave you and the children," murmured Rufus. "But as we talked it over before, they drew my name in the lottery for this area, so I feel it's my duty to go. Maybe I coulda' borrowed money on the farm and hired a substitute to go in my place, but I don't believe that's right. The government shouldn't have allowed it. It's not a fair draft law."

Sarah sat up and admired him. Slowly she quieted down. As much as she didn't want him to go, she couldn't help but be proud of the stand he took on the draft law.

"I think everything you'll need has been taken care of," Rufus assured her. "The wood's cut for the stoves, and if you run out, my brothers will cut more. The root cellar is full, and I've made arrangements with Warren to pay you money each month."

Rufus felt he could depend upon his brother Warren, who ran a general store in Casnovia.

"Even though you are well provided for here, I still want ya to move closer to your folks," Rufus advised. "Your pa told me he would be glad to help ya. I'm sorry I didn't have time to move ya before I leave, but ya can take most of the supplies with ya."

Slowly, Sarah stood up. They needed to go to bed, but she hated to see this last day end.

"Morning will come earlier than usual. Isn't Pa picking you up at dawn?" Sarah asked.

"Yah, he is," Rufus answered. Sarah's pa had offered to drive Rufus into Grand Rapids with his buckboard and team of Morgan horses. "I wish ya could go with me as far as the Rapids, but it would be too hard a trip for ya. It's rough ridin' so far in the buckboard."

Rufus picked up the lamp, and they reluctantly went to bed, ending his last full day at home with his family.

The next morning Sarah got up early after a sleepless night. Rufus had risen before her and had a fire blazing in the kitchen stove. She fixed a big breakfast of eggs, bacon, fried potatoes, and oatmeal. The aroma of coffee perking on the stove filled their cozy home.

Rufus came in from the barn, where he had done the morning chores. He carried another full pail of milk to be covered with cheesecloth and set in the well.

"Ya didn't sleep much, did ya?" he asked.

"No," she answered, "and you didn't either, did you?"

"No, I didn't. Mmm, everything smells great. I'll sure miss your cookin'."

Breakfast ready, they sat down together at the kitchen table. They bowed their heads as Rufus prayed a short blessing. They ate in silence. Both had so much they wanted to say to each other, but they didn't know how to begin. Sarah mostly picked at her food, but she was happy to see Rufus eat heartily. She had packed him a big lunch to take for the journey as well.

Having finished, Rufus rose. "It turned a lot colder overnight. There's frost on the ground this mornin'. I'd better have my heavy jacket with me." Taking it down from a peg, he laid it next to the lunch sack.

He then took Sarah into his arms and kissed her goodbye. Both were too overcome to talk. They knew they loved one another, and that left nothing more to say. Rufus turned abruptly and walked softly to the children's bedroom door. Cautiously he cracked the door to take one last peek at the two curly heads asleep on their pillows. "I love ya," he whispered. "God bless ya both." Hearing wagon wheels rumbling down the road, he carefully closed the door, returned to the kitchen, and picked up his coat and lunch.

Sarah put on a warm shawl. Together they went out onto the porch and down the steps. Without saying a word, they walked hand in hand to the road, oblivious to the beautiful sunrise. They could see the horses' breath as the buckboard pulled alongside and Pa called out a greeting.

"Good mornin', Rufus. Good mornin', Sarah."

"Good mornin', Pa," they both replied.

Rufus quickly kissed Sarah. "Goodbye, Sarah. I love ya."

"I love you, too, Rufus. Goodbye."

Rufus jumped onto the buckboard. He sat down in the rear with his legs dangling over the back.

"I'll check on ya soon, honey," Pa promised.

"Thank you, Pa."

Pa made a clucking sound, and the pair of beautiful bay Morgans started clip-clopping down the bumpy road.

Sarah stood motionless, gusts of wind blowing her skirts around her ankles. She drew the shawl more tightly around her shoulders. She couldn't keep from shivering, which she knew didn't come from the cold alone. Still, she never took her eyes off the buckboard carrying Rufus away.

And Rufus kept his eyes on her, until his Sarah was only a dot on the hazy horizon—standing alone.

After watching the buckboard disappear, Sarah pulled her wool shawl still more tightly around her. Slowly she returned to the lonely house. Buster ambled up from the barn and greeted her on the porch. He looked up at her with mournful eyes and whined, his tail drooping. She bent down and put her arms around him.

"I know, boy, you hate to see him go, too." She buried her face in his soft fur and released her pent-up tears. But soon she stood up and dried her eyes with a handkerchief, feeling somewhat better from letting the tears flow. Together, she and Buster walked inside.

In the quiet house she checked on Dorothy and Lucy to see if they were still sleeping. Pleased to find that they had not awakened, she took a cup down from the kitchen cupboard, poured coffee from the large granite pot on the hot range, and took the steaming cup into the family parlor to Rufus's cozy rocker. In his special chair she felt closer to him.

The cup warmed her hands as she sipped. She slowly rocked while waiting for her daughters to awaken. A quick glance at the clock on the wall, whose ticking kept company with the creaking of the rocker, told her it would soon be time for the girls to wake up—and find their Papa gone.

"What can I say to them?" Sarah wondered. "How can I share with such little ones the heartbreaking news of their Papa leaving for the army?"

The sound of giggles and the patter of small feet broke the early morning stillness. Sarah set her coffee down on a nearby table and gripped both arms of the rocker. "I must not cry when I tell them," she whispered to herself. "They mustn't know of the danger involved in going to war."

Her knees felt weak as she pushed herself to her feet to face her unpleasant task—a duty left to her alone.

2

Casnovia to Grand Rapids, Michigan
Leaving Home ~ Mustering In

After Sarah's lonely figure had faded completely from view, Rufus wiped his eyes with the back of his glove and turned around. He crawled on his hands and knees the length of the buckboard, over feed sacks, buckets, and other paraphernalia, to sit beside his father-in-law on the front seat.

Out of the corner of his eye, Pa anxiously stole a glance at Rufus's downcast face. He knew Rufus and Sarah were unusually close to one another and to their children. This separation would be a cruel hardship for them all.

"Sarah and the children will be all right, Rufus. I'll keep checkin' on 'em," Pa assured his son-in-law.

"I know you'll help, and I'm grateful. I just wish I could've moved her nearer to you, where she wouldn't be so lonesome. I don't like leavin' her and the children alone out on the farm," Rufus answered.

"We'll get her moved," promised Pa. "First chance we get."

"My brothers will help her move, too," added Rufus.

The rumbling buckboard hit a rut in the bumpy dirt road, jarring them. Pa laughed. "It's still a lot easier goin' than when you first came here, eh Rufus? You'd been happy for any road then."

"That's for sure," agreed Rufus. "I shan't forget the choppin' it took to make a trail to Town 10."

The narrow road they now traveled had been cut through dense pine woods. In 1852, when the Seaman family came by oxcart from Hillsdale, Michigan, to the Casnovia area, few roads existed north from Grand Rapids in the direction of Casnovia. There had been none at all for the last five miles, making it necessary for them to chop their own crude trail to their destination: Town 10 North, Range 14 West. Forests still bordered the road on both sides. They had purchased their deep wilderness farmland with war scrip given as pensions to soldiers who had served in the War of 1812. The family had located their tract of land by following government survey stakes.

"At least, comin' here to Casnovia didn't take us as long as the trip from New York to Hillsdale," Rufus said. "The New York trip must have been hard on my ma. With us ten children we made quite a caravan. I remember the little ones, Lafayette and Silence, ridin' on Ma's lap in the oxcart. How she ever managed to keep a watchful eye on the rest of us—makin' sure we took turns ridin', too, so we wouldn't get too tired—I'll never know. She had a hard time keepin' us in the cart for very long. We much preferred to walk so we could run and play."

In 1842, before coming to Casnovia, the adventuresome Seaman family had migrated from New York State to the Hillsdale area. The Seamans descended from Captain John Seaman, born in England, who received a grant of land at Hempstead Plains, New York, in 1637 from Charles I. All ten of the children were born in New York State. The older children received most of their education in Hillsdale. Later, their Grandpa and Grandma Seaman died in Hillsdale and were buried in Dow Cemetery. Grandpa Seaman, because of his services to George Washington during the Revolutionary War, was qualified to be buried in the area of the cemetery reserved for veterans.

The sun rising in the cloudless sky soon melted the silvery frost on the trees and ground, though the breeze still kept its nip. The cooler weather made the horses friskier. They carried their smartly braided tails straight out behind them and trotted briskly as long as the road remained smooth enough. Often, however, long stretches of rough, bumpy roads made it impossible for the faithful horses to go faster than a walk.

Suddenly Pa gently pulled back on the reins, slowing the shying team.

"Whoa, boys. Easy there." Pa spoke calmly to the startled horses, settling them down from being spooked by movement ahead. A family of deer had burst out of the woods on their right, crossed the road in front of them, and sprinted into the trees on their left. A beautiful doe led the column of three, followed by a spotted fawn nudged along by an eight-point buck serving as the rear guard. Many deer lived in the forest.

Rufus chuckled. "I wonder if they're part of the deer that ate in my corn field."

"Did they destroy much of your crop?"

"No, I had a pretty good corn crop this year. I don't begrudge them what little they ate. Besides, as ya know, I usually did a little deer huntin' when it got cold enough to keep venison in the well pit. But I never killed more than we could eat."

Rufus had become a crack shot from his hunting experiences. As a younger man, he had the privilege of hunting with his father to provide meat for the family. He never enjoyed killing, but he loved the companionship they shared during those special times.

The excitement caused by the deer over, Pa relaxed his grip on the reins and allowed the horses to return to an easy trot. The road had become smoother.

About halfway to their destination, Pa began watching for a familiar bubbling brook flowing just a few feet from the road. Shortly he noticed it.

"This makes a nice place to feed and water the horses," he said. "I've stopped here before on trips to Grand Rapids." He slowly guided the team to a stop at the side of the lightly traveled road.

Both men nimbly hopped down from their seats. Pa, a wiry man of small stature, unharnessed the team, while Rufus took the two buckets and the burlap bag of grain from the bed of the buckboard. He opened the sack and scooped grain into each bucket.

With the thirsty horses relieved of their harnesses, Pa led them by their bridles over to the clear, rapidly flowing stream to drink. When they had drunk their fill, he tethered them to the side of the wagon and fed them the buckets of grain. Both horses nickered their "thank you" at the sight of their meal.

"Would ya like some lunch, Pa Walkley?" Rufus asked, as they climbed back onto their seats. "I think I'll have a bite to eat."

"That sounds good to me, too. Much obliged."

Before Rufus took the brown paper off the large lunch that lay on the seat beside him, both men bowed their heads, and Pa gave thanks for the food.

Rufus handed Pa a thick ham sandwich made with homemade bread and butter and took one himself. He unscrewed the lid from the quart jar of cool buttermilk Sarah had packed and set it on the seat between them.

"Help yourself," Rufus told Pa, nodding toward the jar.

"Thanks." Pa took a long, cool drink.

They slowly ate their lunch in the quiet solitude, free of rumbling wagon wheels. A concert of lilting songs from a variety of birds serenaded them from the thick pine trees. Corn-fed crows cawed overhead, while a fox squirrel scurried across the road and up a tall tree. A blue jay, acting his role as sentinel, gave a cry of warning as he spotted Pa and Rufus—intruders in the wilderness.

"Mm, this sandwich is good. Sarah must have fixed ya wonderful victuals last night," Pa declared.

Rufus chuckled. "Yeah, she did that all right. It reminded Dorothy of Christmas dinner."

His sandwich finished, Rufus brought out a generous piece of johnny-cake for each of them.

"My ma sure fixed a great meal last Sunday after church, too. No one can make chicken and biscuits like Ma," boasted Rufus. "I so appreciate my family all gettin' together like that."

"Your ma and pa wanted the family together. They are quite worried about ya goin' because of losin' Martin," Pa told him. Pa knew Rufus's parents well.

"I know," answered Rufus. "Sarah worries more about me because of what happened to Martin, too."

"Your pa told me that your ma still has trouble acceptin' that Martin isn't ever comin' home," Pa Walkley added. "When there isn't a body or a funeral, it's easy to think that maybe they made a mistake and he'll still be showin' up."

Rufus nodded. "I understand how Ma feels. I feel that way sometimes myself. Martin loved his family so much and always wanted the best for them. It's hard to accept that he's . . . that he's dead." Rufus's voice trailed off in stifled emotion as he sat silent, remembering his loss. "I hate to put the folks through this a second time," he mumbled.

"It's not your fault," Pa assured him. "You're doin' the right thing. At least you're not hidin' from the draft, as many draftees do. I'm just concerned over how you'll be treated. I hear the volunteers don't cotton to draftees."

"Yeah, I've heard that, too. I'll just have to wait and see," Rufus concluded. "Would you like more lunch? We have a lot more."

"Oh my, no, thank you, Rufus. I'm stuffed. We had better be on our way if we want to arrive in Grand Rapids on time."

Pa reached in the back of the buckboard and picked up two currycombs and two brushes. He handed a set to Rufus, and each man started brushing and currying one of the dusty horses.

"I love your horses, Pa," Rufus remarked, as he gently brushed King. "They're the finest team I know. I hope to have a team this nice someday. They sure are a royal pair."

"That they are, Rufus, that they are," agreed Pa, putting the finishing strokes to Prince's flowing ebony mane.

Pa had named his horses King and Prince and jokingly referred to them as his Royal Pair. The Morgans had come all the way from New England, where Pa had at one time lived. While in Connecticut, he learned all about the Morgan breed they had in Vermont and knew they would be the horses for him. Though smaller in stature, the breed had great endurance and performed equally well under saddle or in harness.

"When Martin first joined the service, he wrote home that the Union Army used Morgans for some of their cavalry troops," remembered Rufus.

"Yeah, I recall you sayin' that. And they certainly couldn't go wrong with that choice."

"That's for sure," echoed Rufus. "I know Martin really trusted the Morgan mount assigned to him."

Rufus's complimentary remark about the Morgans brought a wide smile to Pa's red-bearded face and a twinkle to his blue eyes. He loved his horses and took great pride in their appearance and conduct. It made him especially proud to have Rufus praise his team, because Rufus shared his love of horses and always knew good horseflesh when he saw it.

Brushed, with coats glistening, the gentle pair stood quietly to have their harnesses put back on and to be hitched once again to the familiar buckboard. Pa regained his seat and Rufus joined him. He untied the reins and resumed driving the beautiful bays on the latter half of their journey.

Closer to Grand Rapids, the forest gave way to fields cleared for farming, just as Rufus had cleared his eighty-acre farmland.

"The wind is really sharp, now that we've left the protection of the forest," noted Rufus, tightening his jacket and pulling his hat down more firmly. It seemed cold for late September. They passed several fields of newly picked yellow corn stalks standing neatly in rows and being gently tossed by the breeze—stalks that would soon be chopped to make fodder for the cattle. Farm buildings now dotted the landscape. Friendly puffs of white smoke spiraling upward into the blue sky from chimneys kept the farmhouses from looking bleak and lonely. In one barnyard, Holstein cows cavorted happily in the fresh air, while their farmer mucked out the barn after milking.

Whenever the two passed another horse-drawn wagon, the drivers exchanged friendly waves and greetings, as each continued traveling toward his own destination.

Pa and Rufus soon noticed a small flock of wild turkeys on the ground in an open field next to the road. The rumbling of the wagon wheels frightened the heavy birds into awkward flight, causing them to swoop back over the fence to their home in the forest.

"We'll stay on the Newaygo State Road until we come to Stocking Street, then we'll take Stocking to Bridge Street," Pa explained, as he drove the team across Leonard Street.

Traffic picked up as they entered Grand Rapids. They passed many differently styled buggies and buckboards with various breeds of horses pulling them. None seemed as fine to Pa and Rufus as Pa's Morgans. "We've really made good time," Rufus commented.

"It's because of Prince and King," Pa boasted. Rufus smiled and nodded.

Reaching Stocking Street, they angled southeast. Stocking took them to Bridge Street and to the latticed bridge, where, after paying their toll fee, they crossed the Grand River. They then turned onto Canal Street and followed it to Monroe Avenue.

"Look at that!" they exclaimed in unison. Their eyes had been caught by a wide banner stretched high across Monroe promoting "Lincoln for President."

"I certainly hope Mr. Lincoln is elected again," Pa commented to Rufus.

"I do, too," answered Rufus. "We need him to stay in charge durin' this war." Monroe brought them to the plank road that connected Grand Rapids with Kalamazoo, Michigan. Before train travel came to Grand Rapids in 1858, the stagecoach made daily trips between the two cities over this road. Pa's team shied as their hooves left cobble-stoned Monroe Avenue and stepped onto the wooden planks leading out of town.

"Easy, boys, easy," Pa said, calming them down.

"It's only a couple of miles farther to the Kent County Fair Ground, where Cantonment Anderson is located," Pa told Rufus.

"Yeah, you're right. It's on Hall," agreed Rufus.

"Do ya know any of the new recruits goin' with ya, Rufus?" Pa asked.

"Yeah, I'm acquainted with some of 'em. Quite a few of the men are from Casnovia. I don't know whether they are draftees or volunteers."

Pa turned and looked at Rufus. "I just want to take this opportunity to tell ya how proud I am of ya, Rufus. Ya coulda' paid a substitute to go in your place, but ya didn't. I've heard that only a very small percentage of men drafted show up to be mustered in like ya are doin' today. And as a draftee, ya won't qualify for any of the benefits the volunteers receive. I'm happy to call ya my son-in-law. I know ya love my daughter and have always been a wonderful husband to her and a good father to your children."

"Thanks, Pa," Rufus whispered.

Pa's praise blessed Rufus. He knew the pride Pa felt for his own two sons in the Union Forces, Edwin Walkley with Company C, First Regiment, United States Sharpshooters, and Wyllys Walkley with the Twenty-Third Infantry, Company C. Both had shown valor in the service of their country. And now, for his father-in-law to be proud of him as well warmed his heart.

"Here's Hall Street now." Pa guided the buckboard left toward the fair grounds. They could see new recruits arriving. Pa pulled up alongside the rigs in front of Cantonment Anderson. He pulled out his watch.

"We're in plenty of time," he noticed. "It's only four o'clock." Mustering time had been set for five o'clock.

"Write to us, Rufus," Pa requested. "And give everything to the Lord." It concerned Pa that Sarah and Rufus weren't serving the Lord now the way they once had. At one time, they faithfully attended both church services on Sunday and never missed the Wednesday night prayer meeting. Now they came to church on Sunday morning only occasionally and never to prayer meeting on Wednesday night.

"I can't promise, but I'll try and write," Rufus answered. "Please look after Sarah and the children."

"We will. Edwin is home now, and he'll be able to help her," Pa reminded Rufus.

"Yeah, I know Ed will be a big help to her on the farm." Edwin Walkley had served his three-year enlistment with the sharpshooters and had been discharged only last month.

Rufus jumped down from the buckboard and turned to shake Pa's hand. "Goodbye, Pa. Thanks for bringin' me. Please take care of Sarah and the children," he said once more.

"I will," Pa promised. "Goodbye, Rufus."

Rufus walked toward the cantonment as Pa headed back to town. He planned to put the horses in one of the livery stables near Ionia Avenue and stay overnight at the National Hotel.

Rufus approached the encampment, where a sentinel paced to and fro before the gate. In a grove of trees just within the enclosure, guards stood near a blazing campfire. One noticed Rufus, smiled, and pointed to where he should go.

Upon entering the wooden building, Rufus saw other new recruits gathered in small groups of three or four, standing around, talking and joking. He recognized his townspeople from Casnovia and walked over to join them in the back of the room.

"Hello, Rufus." His neighbor Frank cordially greeted him. "This is the big day, eh?"

"How are ya, Frank?" Rufus asked, as he shook the burly man's hand. "Yeah, I guess it is the big day. Are we supposed to wait here to be mustered in?"

"Yeah, that's what someone told us. It'll happen at five o'clock. Not everyone is here yet."

Farmers made up many of the new recruits, so that much of their conversation centered on how well their crops had fared this season.

Finally, right at five o'clock, the big moment arrived. Captain Bailey, accompanied by a sergeant, entered the room carrying a roster.

"Line up over here, men," Captain Bailey ordered. Though he was a younger man and small in stature, the captain's booming voice made up for his size. The men scrambled to line up in three straight rows.

Captain Bailey called out each name written on the paper in his hand. All men present and accounted for answered the muster roll.

"Raise your right hand." Captain Bailey then read the oath of allegiance to their country, each man repeating it after him.

> I, Rufus Seaman, do solemnly swear that I will support and defend the Constitution and government of the United States against all enemies whether domestic or foreign; that I will bear true and faithful allegiance to the same, any ordinance, resolution, or law of any State, convention, legislature, or order or organization, secret or otherwise, to the contrary not withstanding; that I do this with a full determination, pledge, and purpose, without any mental

reservation or evasion whatsoever, and especially that I have not by word or deed or in any manner whatever given countenance, aid, comfort or encouragement to the present rebellion or to those who have been or are now engaged in the conspiracy against the government of the United States, so help me God.

"Now that you are mustered in, men, you are to stay here in the barracks for tonight," Captain Bailey told them. "Tomorrow you'll leave on the train for Jackson, where you will stay at Camp Blair. Sergeant Boon, take them over to the barracks."

Rufus, along with the others, followed the sergeant to a nearby building. Inside, wooden bunks lined the wall in tiers of three. Both Rufus and Frank took a lower bunk. They sat down on the tic mattress that covered the hard boards—a mattress that had been, like the others, furnished by the Ladies of Valley City.

"I don't think we'll sleep much tonight, Rufus," Frank remarked.

"I don't think so either, Frank. I wish I'd brought a quilt or a blanket."

"Me, too."

Many of the men played cards to pass the time. Soon all of them received orders to go into the mess hall next door for supper.

Later, back in the barracks, nine o'clock meant bedtime.

"Put out the lamps, boys," the sergeant ordered. Groans could be heard as the recruits lay down on their hard bunks for the night.

Rufus was so tired that he soon fell asleep.

They arose early the next morning. After being served a hearty breakfast, they lined up outside in preparation for their march to the railroad station.

Captain Bailey called the muster roll. Every man answered, "Present."

"All right, men; we are going to march through town to the railroad station. Fall in behind me," he instructed them.

Captain Bailey, marching at the front, then led them out of the camp onto Hall Street. They would take the same route that the Third Michigan Volunteers Infantry had taken on June 13, 1861, except that no ovation greeted these recruits, a detachment of draftee and volunteer substitutes who would be forwarded to various regiments after they reached Camp Blair. No bands played, and no flags waved, as they had for the Third Michigan when they marched to the station. Yet Grand Rapids' citizens were still intensely patriotic, believing that the Union must be preserved at all costs. So if they had known about these recruits leaving today, they would have honored them as well.

The group started down the plank road and marched to the depot at Leonard and Plainfield. Many of them felt stiff from sleeping on the hard bunks, but they moved forward with their shoulders back and their heads held high. A beautiful fall day made the march more tolerable.

At the depot, the Detroit and Milwaukee train sat hissing on the tracks, letting off steam while waiting for the new recruits to get aboard. Rufus and Frank boarded and took a seat together. The Detroit and Milwaukee Railroad would take them as far as the Detroit Station, where they would change trains and take the Michigan Central Railroad the rest of the way to Jackson. At an average speed of twenty miles per hour, it would be only a few hours before they arrived in Jackson.

Rufus and Frank talked with each other about their families. All the recruits from Casnovia enjoyed camaraderie; Rufus liked Frank's company and felt pleased they would be together.

3

Camp Blair and Indianapolis
Homesickness ~ Rough Beginnings ~ A First Letter

The ride to Jackson proved uneventful, the train arriving safely and on time. Two noncommissioned officers from Camp Blair, Sergeant Loomis and Corporal Bond, met the new soldiers at the station. Sergeant Loomis, a veteran with vast experience, ordered them to fall in and begin their march to Camp Blair. His worn face and set jaw told the story of the many campaigns he had been in. Corporal Bond, newly promoted to his rank, lacked the sergeant's assurance.

After sitting for several hours, the men were glad to be on their feet. Once again they marched with straight shoulders and heads erect, a valiant group of recruits.

When they arrived at Camp Blair, Corporal Bond led the men to a row of small barracks. Inside they found cots lining both sides of the room. An army blanket lay folded at the foot of each bed.

"Let's take these two bunks," Frank suggested. "That way we'll be beside each other. Let's try to stay together."

"Yeah, I'd like that, too," Rufus replied, as he took possession of the cot next to Frank's. "I notice we have blankets here."

Tired from marching, many of the recruits lay down on the bunks to rest. But soon Sergeant Loomis entered and ordered the men to follow him to the quartermaster's building next door. There he randomly outfitted the men in the Union's wool blue uniforms and leather boots, with little regard for size and shape. Each man also drew a knapsack, a canteen, a tin cup on a belt, a musket, and a cartridge box that held forty rounds of ammunition.

Back in their barracks and amid much horseplay, the recruits traded clothing with one another until most of them enjoyed a better fit.

Three weeks had passed at Camp Blair when, at the sound of reveille, Rufus awoke with a sore throat and runny nose. Each of the preceding days the men had drilled from morning to night, training for combat. Rufus hadn't even had a moment to write to Sarah. Every time he thought of home, a lump came into his throat. This morning, as usual, the men hurriedly dressed to line up outside for roll call. Sergeant Loomis boomed out each man's name, and all answered, "Present!"

"We have received orders as to which outfit each of you will be assigned to. You will fill the vacancies left in different companies and regiments," the sergeant told them. In other words, they would take the places of those who had died, been wounded, or been furloughed.

Upon learning that he had been placed in the Thirteenth Michigan, Company G, Rufus checked with the other men from Casnovia to see who would be with him.

"Frank, were you assigned to the Thirteenth Michigan?"

"No. Is that the company you're goin' to? I was hopin' we'd be together."

"Me, too. I'm disappointed."

On questioning the other recruits from Casnovia, Rufus sadly discovered that he alone had been put into the Thirteenth Michigan. He decided to ask if he couldn't be reassigned to be with some of the others from his hometown.

The captain was sitting at a small writing table at the front of the barracks containing the officers' quarters. As Rufus approached, the captain looked up and smiled. Rufus clumsily saluted and cleared his sore throat.

"Yes, private, may I help you?" the captain asked.

"I was wondering, sir, if I could be put in an outfit with some of the other men I know," Rufus inquired. "I'm the only one from our group in the Thirteenth."

The captain's smile instantly faded and a stern expression replaced it. "I should say not," he growled. "You'll stay where you've been assigned. You're dismissed!" The captain then turned his attention back to the papers on his table.

Rufus stood still a moment. His eyes noted the captain's set jaw. He knew it would be useless to keep trying. He would have to go wherever they sent him.

The next day, Rufus found himself traveling on the train moving through southern Michigan into Indiana. This time he couldn't enjoy the fellowship of his friend Frank or the other comrades he knew from Casnovia. He never had felt so alone. Sitting next to the window, he watched the unfamiliar countryside slide by. The leaves on the trees along the track had started to change color. The bright red, orange, and yellow hues of maple, oak, and poplar trees dotted the landscape.

The changing colors reminded him of how much Dorothy and Lucy always enjoyed playing in the fallen leaves. The girls thought it great fun to lie down and have their papa bury them in a pile. The little rascals would then suddenly jump up amidst squeals of laughter. To recall their pleasure brought a bittersweet smile to Rufus's lips. He regretted he wouldn't be repeating these games with them this season.

"But I'll be home next year," he told himself. "I'll be gone a year, but next autumn I'll be home when the leaves fall. I'll play with 'em next year."

His moist eyes blurred the colors visible through the window. He knew he needed to look ahead to his homecoming, and not dwell on the lonely year of service for his country that stretched out before him.

Each turn of the train's wheels took him farther from Sarah and home, as did the click, click, click of the tracks. The repartee between the other soldiers in the coach only made him feel more alone. Many swore as they talked. Rufus did not like to hear that kind of language. He missed the boys from his hometown and wondered where they might be traveling now. If only they could have stayed together! The bad cold he had caught in Jackson added to his melancholy. His raspy throat hurt when he swallowed, and his nose continued to run. Occasionally he suffered a coughing spell.

He kept staring out the train window until the shadows of night falling made it impossible to see clearly. A full moon slowly rose. The conductor lit some lanterns hanging in the coach. The chattering of the men gradually died down to silence. Rufus wrapped himself in the blanket he had been issued and laid his head back in the hope he could get some rest.

He woke with a start at the squealing of the train's wheels coming to a halt. The troops had arrived at their destination, Indianapolis, Indiana. Rufus knew by the kink in his neck that he had slept long. He rose and picked up his gear to depart the train. The coach aisle was soon crowded with hungry soldiers pushing toward the exit. After several hours without eating, they hoped for warm food at their destination. Hungry himself, Rufus joined the throng.

Much to everyone's disappointment, however, no fine meal awaited them. Instead, they received government issue hardtack and coffee. Rufus did find a few minutes to write a short letter to Sarah; writing to her brought him more comfort than food could.

* * * * *

Back home, Sarah peeked out the parlor window upon hearing the rumble of buckboard wheels in her driveway. Recognizing her brother Ed's team, she hurried to the kitchen door. Before dropping by to see her, each of her family members went to the Casnovia post office for any mail she might have gotten. Sarah longed to hear from Rufus. She had gotten no mail in the five weeks since he had left, and she felt alone and sad.

Ed bounded up the back porch steps and into the kitchen with a broad smile on his handsome face. He reached into his pocket and pulled out a letter.

"Here you are, Sarah, a letter from Rufus. I told you he'd write when he could. It's not easy to find time to write in the army."

"Thank you, Ed." Her hand trembled as she reached out for the letter. Ed followed her as she slowly walked into the sitting room and sat in Rufus's rocker. As she opened the envelope, her eyes hungrily scanned the familiar handwriting.

"Rufus wrote this letter October 15—just four days ago!" she exclaimed.

"It was postmarked 'Indiana,' not all that far from here. That must be why it didn't take longer."

Sarah silently began to read her first letter from Rufus.

Indianapolis, October 15, 1864

Dear Wife,

I take this time to let you know where I am at present. I arrived here last Saturday and expect to leave this afternoon and where I don't know, but the report is that we are going to Atlanta but may heaven protect thee and the children. May God have mercy on you, Sarah. See to things for if you don't there is nobody that will. Have the wagon and sleds put in the barn and let nobody have them for I want something when I get home for they that are at home are better able to buy than I will be when I get home so I want you to prepare for the worst and keep what we have. When Ed thrashes the wheat, have him put it in that big box and don't sell any of it. I have not much time to write so you will have to excuse me this time but will prove true to you Sarah as long as my life is spared. May heaven protect us in this world and the world to come. Sarah I can't think of home without tears. Sarah, this is from your affectionate husband

Rufus W. Seaman

Ed watched her read the letter. He resembled his sister, with the same light brown hair and deep blue eyes, but whereas Sarah had a woman's petite figure, he had a man's tall, muscular build. After serving three years in the sharpshooters, he knew how much it meant to receive mail from a loved one far away. Sarah read the letter twice before looking up and handing it to Ed.

"You may read it, Ed. He says . . . he says the report is they are going to Atlanta." Sarah's eyes moistened. She knew what that could mean. They had read about the Atlanta campaign in the *Grand Rapids Daily Eagle*.

Ed patted Sarah's shoulder as he took the letter from her hand. He read it, trying not to look concerned. "If Rufus goes to Atlanta, chances are he will be with General Sherman's command," he told her, as he handed back the letter. "The general's a good man to serve under. I've heard that he never asks his troops to fight unless it's absolutely necessary. He cares about his men. And I'll do as Rufus wants about the wheat," Ed assured her, trying to change the topic from the subject of Atlanta. "I understand how he feels. He wants to be able to take up farming where he left off. I'll also help you put the wagon and sleds in the barn."

"Uncle Ed! Uncle Ed!" Just up from their afternoon nap, Dorothy and Lucy raced out of their bedroom into their uncle's arms. Ed bent down and embraced his nieces.

"Girls, your mother has something special to share with you," he told them.

"Yes, come over here," Sarah asked them. "We have a letter from Papa."

Both children jumped up and down. "A letter from Papa. A letter from Papa," they chanted as they climbed up on their mother's lap. They quietly listened with rapt attention as their Mama read their Papa's letter to them. When she finished, their faces showed the disappointment they felt. A tear rolled down Dorothy's cheek.

"But, Mama, isn't Papa comin' home?" she wanted to know. "He didn't say he was. Papa said he was goin' to Atlanta. Where's Atlanta?"

"No, honey, Papa isn't coming home yet. He's going to be gone a year. Atlanta is a city way down South."

Dorothy didn't realize how long a year could be. She only knew it took a long time from one Christmas to the next one.

Sarah felt a lump rising in her own throat. She wanted him to come home, too.

"But your Papa's all right. Isn't that wonderful?" Ed tried to cheer all three of them. "Yes, it is." Sarah smiled. "I'll write Rufus tonight and let him know how happy his letter has made us. And I must let Rufus's ma and pa know we finally heard from him. They have been anxious, too. He doesn't write to them, because they can't read or write."

"Of course. If I run into any of the Seamans, I'll let them know you've received a letter."

Ed sat down in a nearby chair. "Who would like to be trotted?" he asked.

Lucy ran over and jumped on his knee. She giggled, as he trotted her up and down. With her ride over, he looked at Dorothy. "Don't you want a ride, honey?"

"No," she answered. "I only want my Papa to trot me."

Ed smiled at her. "I understand, Dorothy; we all want your papa home."

Sarah sat in Rufus's rocker long after Edwin had left for home. Her brother helped her in every way he could, but he had his own farm and family to care for. The main responsibility for the farm lay on Sarah's small shoulders. She sighed as she rose, anxious to start churning butter before doing the evening chores. After chores she would write Rufus, now waiting to move on to Atlanta. "Yes, may God have mercy on us."

4

Chattanooga, Tennessee
Thirteenth Michigan Regiment ~ Recommitments ~ Meeting Joey

A few days later, Rufus, along with the other recruits, boarded the train again. Regulars coming back from furlough joined them, as well as paymasters and commissioners. Paymasters came to pay off the men before their departure to a new sphere of action, and commissioners came from several states to take the men's votes for the presidential election.

At noon on October 19, 1864, the troop train from the North chugged into Chattanooga, Tennessee, its stack puffing smoke that hung in the blue sky over the Appalachian Mountains.

"Everyone out," the sergeant bellowed. Rufus grabbed his gear and joined the exiting line in the aisle, falling in behind the returning furloughed men, who knew their way. The paymasters and commissioners left the train first. The regulars followed close behind, with the new recruits bringing up the rear.

"Don't worry, recruits," the sergeant snapped. "We'll tell you where to go. Just follow me." He marched them for several minutes until they came to a field of tents pitched along the Tennessee River. Some of the tents consisted of a log base with a canvas top, while others had been made only with canvas. "Grab an unoccupied tent, and put your gear in there. This is where the Thirteenth Michigan is camped."

Each recruit chose a tent at random. After a day and a half without eating, they just wanted food.

At eight the next morning, Rufus sat on his blanket, penning a short letter to Sarah. As yet, no one had been fed. He had barely finished the letter when the first sergeant burst onto the field and called the roll. This done, he shouted, "All troops follow me," then led them to a large tent, where at last they sat down at a long, hewn-out table to eat breakfast.

As soon as the troops had finished, the commissioners let them vote for president. Rufus cast his ballot for Abraham Lincoln, as did the majority of Sherman's army. Most of these battle-worn veterans believed only Lincoln would bring about the kind of peace they had been fighting to achieve, unconditional surrender by the Confederate forces.

After the voting, the sergeant took the new recruits to the infirmary tent, where the attending physician gave each a physical.

"But Doc, we've already been checked over," one recruit complained. He was right: all of them had.

"I know you have," answered the doctor. "But you've been ordered to be examined again. They want only the healthiest soldiers for where you're going."

This bit of news caused a stir among the men. "Where are we goin', Doc," one dared to ask. "Are we goin' to Atlanta?"

"That's what I'm told," the doctor murmured. "At least Atlanta will be on the route to your new unit."

Rufus's turn came next. "How is your health, private? Have you been exposed to measles or chicken pox?"

"No, I've had a bad cold, sir, otherwise I'm fine," Rufus answered.

The doctor spoke to Rufus after quietly examining him. "I think your cold is about gone now. You're in good shape."

Those who didn't pass their physicals would not continue on this journey. They would be sent to other areas of need.

Physicals over, the sergeant marched the recruits who had passed their examinations out onto the field for more training. They drilled in two-hour sessions, with as many as five sessions a day. Each man learned to fire his weapon and execute various maneuvers.

At night, sitting around their tents, the men discussed where they might be going and why only those in excellent physical condition were needed. Their rough language and profanity kept Rufus from joining this group of strangers or feeling a part of them. For someone who had always had many friends, feeling outside of the group made everything more difficult.

He wished again that he could be with his hometown boys. However, determined to do his best, he promptly obeyed any and all orders they gave him, drilling from sunup to sundown every day without complaining.

* * * * *

"Cover me, Mama, cover me," Dorothy begged.

"Cover me, Mama, cover me," Lucy echoed. Both girls lay expectantly on the ground, their bodies shaking with giggles. The bright sunshine kept the fall day from feeling too chilly. Sarah swept the leaves from under the old maple tree into a pile to cover the girls. She knew they missed their papa doing this—but then, they missed Papa in everything they did.

Sarah picked up an armful of leaves to cover Dorothy, and then another armful to cover Lucy. Their merry laughter did much to ease the loneliness in her heart.

"Hello, Sarah," a voice said. Sarah looked up to see her father walking toward her. Amidst the playfulness, she hadn't heard his buckboard come into her driveway.

"Hello, Pa," she answered. As he came alongside Sarah, his quick eye noticed the two rustling mounds on the ground. "Where are my granddaughters?" he asked. "Don't they want to see their grandpa?" He winked at Sarah, playing along with their game.

With squeals of delight, Dorothy and Lucy jumped up from their hiding places and threw themselves into Grandpa's arms. After giving both girls a big bear hug, their grandpa reached into his pocket and pulled out a letter. "I think this is something you'll be happy to see," he told Sarah. He handed her a letter from Rufus.

"Thank you, Pa," Sarah exclaimed. Grandpa led his granddaughters over to their swing and pushed them high, first one and then the other.

Hurrying to the porch steps, Sarah sat down and ripped open the envelope. The sun was warm.

Chattanooga, October 20

Dear Wife,
I have time to write a few lines to let you know that I am here in the 13 Michigan VV Infantry Company G. I reached here yesterday

noon and have not drawn anything to eat for two days and it is eight o'clock today and no signs yet. And my belly cries, "cupboard" and the way we have fared ever since we left the Rapids is worse than any hogs for we are only half fed and misused. I came here and will make the best of it. Oh Sarah, don't forget me for if it wasn't for you I would choose death rather than life.

Sarah, write often and let me know how you get along and I will do the same. I have to buy piece meals and on my knee and as soon as I can get time, I will write more and the particulars of the way here. May God have mercy. So no more at present but remain, Sarah, your affectionate husband.

Rufus W. Seaman

Please send me five dollars direct to Company G 13 Michigan VV Infantry,

Chattanooga, Tennessee.

Sarah scanned the letter. She knew immediately she couldn't read all of its contents to Dorothy and Lucy. They would never understand about their papa being hungry. She didn't want them to know what Rufus was suffering.

While Sarah read and reread Rufus's letter, Pa looked over and saw her grim face. He stopped pushing the girls and approached the porch. "Is everythin' all right with Rufus?" he softly inquired, as he sat on the step below her.

Sarah shook her head and handed him the letter. "He's not being fed well, Pa. He hadn't eaten for two days when he wrote this. Of course, he'd been traveling. He's in Chattanooga, Tennessee, now. He's in the Thirteenth Michigan Infantry, Company G. Also, he's not getting the letters I write him. I've written every week. He must be terribly anxious about us."

"Grandpa! Grandpa! Come push us," Dorothy and Lucy called. Sarah patted the step next to her, beckoning the girls to come and sit down. Both girls scampered to their mother's side and sat, one on either side.

"Let's read what your papa wrote," she told them, as they snuggled up close. She read to them the parts of the letter that would not upset them.

Dorothy and Lucy never took their eyes off their mama's face until she finished reading to them.

"Papa didn't write a very long letter, did he, Mama?" Dorothy asked.

"Papa's very busy, honey," Sarah explained. "But he promised us in this letter he'd write often."

"Yes, I know he did," sighed Dorothy. "That makes me happy."

"Me, too," Lucy chimed in.

Dorothy took Lucy's hand, and together they skipped back over to play on the swing.

"I wouldn't worry about Rufus goin' hungry, Sarah. I'm sure it's because they were travelin' on the train," Pa said. "And some of your letters will reach him eventually."

Unnoticed, the sun had vanished behind a cloud, depriving the porch of its warmth. Sarah shivered. "Would you like a cup of coffee, Pa? I baked some johnnycake this morning."

Pa looked up at the dark clouds forming. A sudden wind started blowing the pile of leaves.

"No, honey, I think I need to start for home. It looks like it may rain."

He caught the sadness in Sarah's voice. "If the weather is all right, I'll try to bring Ma for a visit tomorrow. Save us some johnnycake."

Sarah smiled. She would enjoy a visit from her understanding mother.

Pa reached in his pocket and pulled out two lumps of sugar.

"Dorothy! Lucy! Do you want to give a treat to King and Prince before Grandpa leaves?"

The girls answered by running up to their grandpa as fast as their little legs could carry them. He gave each girl a cube of sugar.

"Remember to hold your hand flat," he cautioned them.

Dorothy gave her treat to King, and Lucy gave hers to Prince.

"I'm going home, now, so give me a hug goodbye." Grandpa bent down to get his hugs. Sarah and her daughters watched as the buckboard slowly moved out of sight.

"I hope he can bring Ma tomorrow," Sarah thought.

* * * * *

At the sound of the bugler blowing taps, Rufus eased his weary body down onto his hard bunk. It had been a pleasant day, but now the night mountain air felt cold. He wrapped himself in his blanket.

With eyes closed, he listened to the night sounds. If he listened real closely, he could hear the ripple of the Tennessee River flowing next to the camp. A dog barked far away. The song of a killdeer floated on the night air. One by one, many of the soldiers began to snore, worn out from drilling day after day. Then he heard someone weeping softly in the tent next to his. "Maybe it's the young boy," he thought. He didn't fault the lad; he felt only sympathy.

He found himself praying more fervently than he had in some time. At one time, Rufus and Sarah had lived close to God, but in the last two years they had fallen away. Now Rufus knew he needed to get back to the fellowship he once enjoyed. In his loneliness, he came to realize that God had a purpose in allowing the two of them to be separated like this. He believed God loved them so much that he wanted them to return to him in an intimate relationship. Rufus wanted that for himself—and for Sarah, as well. He wanted the two of them to walk in righteousness and in the fear of the Lord.

Tomorrow being Sunday, maybe he would find time to write to Sarah. He would tell her what God had shown him. He gradually fell asleep with more inner peace than he had felt since joining the army.

The next morning after breakfast Rufus hurried back to his tent, anxious to write his letter. He felt happy to have a Sunday off. Usually, Sunday would be just another day of drill.

Sitting cross-legged on his bunk, he held in his hand three long sheets of stationery that he folded so that each would have four pages. Next to him on the cot lay his portfolio, with a small inkbottle balanced on it. He had just dipped his pen and begun to write when the sergeant entered his tent, carrying some of the officers' militia knives.

"Polish these, private," he ordered Rufus.

"Yes, sir." Rufus jumped to his feet, took the knives, and set to work. Later, the knives all polished, Rufus poured out his lonely heart to his precious Sarah. He wanted her to share in his rededication to the Lord.

The following week the daily drill continued for all troops, the new recruits as well as seasoned veterans. They marched up and down the field, two hours at a time, with only short breaks. Rufus knew the army wanted to prepare all of them for any hard campaign that might lie ahead.

The weather remained pleasant until Thursday, when a cloudburst with high winds set in. While it rained, some of the troops played cards on the floors of their tents. Others tried to nap, but the pounding rain on the canvas roof made sleep almost impossible.

Rufus stood looking out of the doorway of his tent, not feeling a part of what was going on around him. He had not heard from Sarah since he left home. After each mail call, he felt more discouraged. He knew she was writing to him, but her letters weren't arriving.

In the tent next to his he noticed a young recruit sitting by himself on his bunk. The boy's uniform was too large, with a cap too small to protect his curly red hair. Rufus suspected he might be the same young man he had heard crying in the night.

Realizing how alone the boy must feel, Rufus made his way through the wind and rain to the boy's tent.

"Hello, I'm Rufus Seaman." He put out his hand as he ducked inside.

"'Lo, I'm Joey Thorpe," the boy replied, shaking Rufus's hand.

"I thought I saw ya at Jackson," Rufus remarked.

"Yeah. Me and my two brothers joined up together, but they separated us at Jackson."

"I'm sorry. My friends from my hometown and I were separated at Jackson, too. It makes it pretty lonely."

"Ma didn't want me to join the army, but I did anyway, 'cause I wanted to be with my brothers. I sorta ran off with 'em, and now I ain't even with 'em."

"Be sure you write to your ma. She'll be worried," Rufus kindly encouraged him.

"I know. I feel bad about it, but I ain't got no writin' paper."

"I have paper; I'll give you some." But before Rufus could go back to his tent to get it, the sergeant once again burst onto the scene.

"Everyone outside. Drill time," he ordered.

The rain had let up, and the fierce wind had abated, leaving the ground speckled with puddles. The troops would get soaked, but march they would nonetheless.

Back in their tents that evening, Rufus brought Joey two sheets of writing paper and a loan of pen and ink.

"Thanks." Joey smiled shyly at Rufus.

"You're welcome," Rufus assured him. Rufus liked Joey, because he didn't use bad language. He also admired the way the youth struggled to keep up with the rest of the men during drills, never shirking his duty.

"Where are you from in Michigan, Joey?" he asked.

"I'm from a farm near Kalamazoo." Joey kept his eyes riveted on the stationery in his lap. "Ma and my sister live there alone now. Ma can't read or write, but my sister will read my letter to her."

He raised his head to look at Rufus. "Where are ya from?"

"I own a farm near Casnovia."

"Where's Casnovia? I never heard of it."

"It's a small town a few miles north of Grand Rapids. My wife and two daughters are livin' alone there." He then added, "I'll leave ya, so ya can write your letter." As Rufus went back to his own tent, Joey understood the sadness in his older friend's voice when he spoke of his wife and children.

In a few minutes, taps sounded the end of another grueling day.

Back home, raindrops pelting the roof made Sarah feel sad, too. Last week Pa had promised to bring Ma for a visit if it didn't rain, but three days of inclement rain had spoiled that plan. Torrents kept pouring down, overflowing the rain barrel under the eave by the back door, while miniature rivulets ran down the sandy driveway. No one could travel on such muddy, washed-out roads.

Sarah sighed. Maybe a cup of coffee would lift her spirits. She rose from the rocker to go into the kitchen. Dorothy and Lucy had been sitting on the floor near her, dressing their rag dolls. Dorothy suddenly stopped playing and cocked her head, listening, as though she heard something. She quickly put her doll down and dashed over to the window.

"Grandpa and Grandma!" she cried. "I thought I heard them. They came! They came!"

Sarah hurried to the window to peek out. They had actually come in this terrible weather. She whirled around to greet them at the back door.

Ma left her open umbrella in the corner on the back porch, while Pa drove his team and buggy out of the rain onto the upper barn floor by the hayloft. He then tethered King and Prince, unhitched them, and began to rub them down before giving them their feedbags and water.

Ma stepped into the kitchen and wiped her wet shoes on the colorful rag rug just inside the door. Sarah took her damp coat and hung it up.

"I'm surprised to see you out in this weather," she exclaimed. Ma patted her arm. "I know, honey, but Pa had to go into Casnovia to a board meeting, and of course, while he was there he went to the post office to get your mail. You have another letter from Rufus." Her face beamed as she slipped the letter from under her sweater, where she had kept it dry. Sarah clasped it tightly before laying it on the table, saying, "I'll put the coffee on before I read it."

She took the blue granite pot from the back of the stove and made a fresh brew. The four of them sat around the kitchen table near the cozy range. Dorothy and Lucy climbed onto their grandma's lap as Sarah opened the letter and started to read silently.

Chattanooga, October 23, 1864

> *Sarah, I have the most time to write today that I have had since I left home. Today is Sunday and the first Sunday I have had since I left home and there is everything going on today. I made my brag too soon. I had to stop and polish, just now, militia knives. Nothing about Sunday.*
>
> *Sarah, I would like to see you and tell you all about things here instead of writing, but I can't at present but hope the time will come when I can tell you all about it.*
>
> *Sarah, keep up good courage and true to me and forsake me not in this trying hour. I hope we will meet again on this side of time, but Sarah, if we should not, pray for me that I may overcome the evil of this world so we can meet in Heaven.*
>
> *I sometimes think it is a good thing for me that I had to come down here for I feel the need of religion. I see so much sin and profane language, most of the men swear awful and it makes me sick. I feel the need of Him who said He came into the world to save poor sinners. May the Lord forgive me, Sarah, pray for me that I may get in the straight and narrow way.*
>
> *Sarah, return to the Lord thy God. Remember me in thy prayers. Sarah, it may be the best thing for us that ever happened for I feel as if it was the Lord's will. I feel as if it was a blessing to me and I hope it will prove true, for I feel I can live a better life than I have done and if the Lord sees fit to spare my life so I can return home, I hope*

when I come home that I may find you rejoicing in the Lord thy God so we can travel one road together rejoicing and live more happy than ever than before.

Sarah, if we seek the Lord and find His face and have our sins forgiven, we may feel thankful that it is as it is. The Lord seen fit to separate us but it is for our benefit. Sarah, return to thy Lord and be faithful unto the end.

Sarah, be kind to the children and take good care of them. Sarah, I would like to see you but as it is I cannot but I trust the time will come. Sarah, write often. I would like to hear that you are seeking the Lord thy God. Sarah, write and let me know where Makins is. I don't know where he is. Sarah, we don't get any news here. Sew a long string for I would like to have something to amuse me.

Sarah, I have neglected one thing in writing as to my health. It is middling good at present. I have been a little unwell. I caught cold at Jackson and have not been very well since but am on the gain. So no more tis from

Rufus W. Seaman
To Sarah E. Seaman

Co. G 13th Mich.
VV Infantry 14th ac
Chattanooga

Sarah, this is the last postage stamp and that I have only five cents to buy more with. I would like to have you send me one or two if you can. I don't get any letters from you and don't know why. All I know that they don't come.

Sarah finished Rufus's letter and glanced up. Ma noticed that her blue eyes glistened with unshed tears. She reached over and covered Sarah's hand with hers.

"Is something wrong, honey? Is Rufus all right?"

"Yes, he's all right. There's nothing wrong." Sarah smiled. She stood up and held out Rufus's letter to her mother.

"Here, Ma—you read it to the girls while I set the table. They always love to hear from their papa."

"Oh yes, Grandma, please read us Papa's letter," exclaimed Dorothy.

"Yes," begged Lucy.

Ma reached out to take the beloved letter. Softly she read aloud. Before she finished the first page, her voice had dropped to a hoarse whisper. Reading of Rufus's rededication to serve God more faithfully, she felt a tear roll down. She brushed it away. She and Pa had prayed for this.

"Now, Lord," she silently prayed, "I pray Sarah will do as Rufus has done."

The back door opened just as Ma finished the letter. Pa entered the kitchen in his stocking feet, having left his wet boots on the porch. His disheveled red hair stuck out in strands beneath his soaked wool dress hat. He took off his wet hat and his coat and hung them on a peg, then went to the kitchen sink and, using the dipper from the pail, poured water into the washbasin to scrub his hands. Quickly drying them on a towel, he sat down at the table, with a granddaughter on each knee.

"Mmm, that coffee sure smells good, Sarah. Did you save me some johnnycake?"

Sarah laughed. "Yes, but I only make johnnycake for you, Pa, and for Ed, when he stops by." Sadly, she added, "With Rufus gone, I couldn't get rid of it otherwise."

She poured three cups of strong coffee, along with two glasses of milk for the girls, and then put a plate of the promised johnnycake on the table. Pa said grace before they had their refreshments.

"How's Rufus, Sarah? Where's he now?" Pa inquired, taking a piece of the johnnycake.

Sarah set her cup down. "Rufus is fine, Pa. He's still at Chattanooga. I really appreciate you fetching my mail in this weather."

"You're welcome, honey. Glad to do it. Rufus has sent you three letters in little more than a week."

"I know. I just wish he'd get my letters the way I get his."

The sun peeked through the window, making the kitchen glow yellow. The rain had ceased. Sarah blew out the oil lamp she had lit earlier because of the dark day.

"Before too long, instead of fall rains like today, we'll be havin' winter blizzards. If it had been snow today instead of rain, we would be snowbound,"

Pa commented. "I wish you'd move closer to us, Sarah. I hate to think of ya here alone this winter. I know Rufus doesn't want that either."

Sarah rose to put more wood in the kitchen range. She picked up the coffee pot and poured refills.

"I know, Pa, but I want to stay here. This is Rufus's and my home. I feel closer to him here."

"I can understand that. We'll try to look after ya, then. We need to get the rope up leadin' from the house to the barn, so ya can find your way in a blizzard. It may be early, but I don't want to take any chances with my girl." Pa grinned at her.

Ma spoke up. "If you and the girls would ever like to come and stay with us, you are more than welcome. We'd love having you. Your brother and sisters would enjoy Dorothy and Lucy living at our house with them, too."

All too soon, Ma and Pa stood up, ready to head home. Pa hitched up the team, and they left amidst many hugs and promises to return soon. As they drove away, Sarah and the girls stood on the porch, admiring the rainbow. Sarah smiled to herself, for she knew Ma would be telling Pa all about the letter. They would both rejoice.

After Ma and Pa had vanished from sight, Sarah led the girls back inside.

"Time for your nap, girls," she told them.

"But I'm not tired, Mama," Lucy tried to say through a big yawn.

Sarah laughed. "I'm afraid your yawn gave you away, Lucy. Let's get your shoes off, girls."

"All right, Mama," Dorothy promised.

With the girls all tucked in, Sarah turned to leave.

Dorothy called her back. "Mama."

"Yes, Dorothy. What is it, Sweetie?"

"I want to stay right here, like you said. I don't want to move. I feel closer to Papa here, too."

Sarah bent down and kissed her daughter's cheek, then went into the kitchen to clear the table and do the dishes. The work done, she entered the parlor to sit for a while in Rufus's rocker.

Her eyes fell on the family Bible that rested on the maple end table next to where she sat. A cherished heirloom, the well-worn Bible had been handed down to her on her wedding day by her Grandma Walkley.

A devout Christian, her grandma had been a godly influence on Sarah, leading her, at ten years of age, to accept Jesus as her Savior.

At one time, whenever Sarah and Rufus needed comfort, they always went to the Lord together. A tragedy they suffered two years ago had changed both of them. The Lord had been faithful to walk them through their deep sorrow, but their great loss and the cares of the world gradually caused them to fall away. They still loved God and wanted to live a Christian life, and at times they even cried out to the Lord, but they no longer had any joy in doing so, or sought the Lord as they once had. Sarah knew she and Rufus had lost their first love, but now she realized, with deep regret, that she had been angry with God. She agreed with Rufus: they needed to get back to God. She slipped out of the rocker onto her knees to pray, humbly asking God to forgive her.

Her fervent prayer finished, Sarah sat quietly in the chair while waiting for Dorothy and Lucy to wake up. Slowly rocking, she recalled earlier, carefree times with Rufus . . .

. . . She couldn't have been more than five years old when her parents moved to Hillsdale, Michigan, from Connecticut and lived across the road from the Seamans. Little did she realize then how Rufus would become an important part of her life and how dearly she would come to love him. Sitting alone in her quiet chair now, the girls still in bed, she recalled the night he gave his life to Christ.

It was in 1850 in the Baptist church in Hillsdale attended by both the Walkleys and the Seamans. The last meeting in a weeklong revival was to begin at 7:00 p.m.

A packed church was waiting expectantly to hear the anointed evangelist preach one more time. Accompanied by the pump organ, the congregation sang three hymns. After the last note had stilled, a hush settled over the sanctuary. The man they came to hear, a small, bald speaker with gold-rimmed glasses, stepped up to the pulpit. And he didn't disappoint them, but gave yet another inspiring message from the Bible. Afterward, he walked down from the platform to stand in front of the pews and gave the altar call.

Rufus, almost a man at seventeen, and his younger brother Martin answered the call to accept Jesus as their own Savior. Unabashed at the tears coursing down his cheeks, Rufus humbly walked down the aisle as the pump organ played the invitational hymn:

> Just as I am, without one plea,
> But that Thy blood was shed for me,
> And that Thou bidd'st me come to Thee,
> O Lamb of God, I come! I come!

Sarah, seated in the pew beside her Grandma Walkley, didn't understand why Rufus would do that. He never did bad things. She only knew him to be good and kind. He helped people all the time. He teased a lot, but did nothing bad. Sarah already had the beginnings of a crush on him.

She looked at her grandma and knew by the pleased expression on her kind face that she thought Rufus needed to be saved.

Her father and mother had given Sarah permission to spend the night with her grandparents, and after they got home from church, she questioned her grandma about it.

"Grandma, why did Rufus do that tonight?" she asked.

"Do what, honey?"

"You know—walk down the aisle like that. He isn't bad."

"No, but he's a sinner. The Bible says we all are. Because of that, we all have to repent of our sins and accept Jesus into our hearts as our own Savior. Only the blood of Jesus can wash away our sins. That's why Rufus did what he did tonight," Grandma explained, as she reached for her big, well-worn Bible. She opened it, turned to Romans 3:23, and read aloud, "For all have sinned, and come short of the glory of God."

"Oh," Sarah murmured, quickly turning her head so her grandma wouldn't see the tears welling up in her eyes. She suddenly felt convicted and wished she could do what Rufus had done.

She hadn't turned her head quickly enough. Out of the corner of her eye her observant grandma had noticed Sarah's sudden tears. She gently laid her hand on her granddaughter's quivering shoulder.

"What is it, Sarah?" she softly asked.

"I, I, I just want Jesus in my heart," Sarah stammered.

"Why, honey, you can do that right now." Grandma turned to Romans 10:9–10 and read to Sarah, "'That if thou shalt confess with thy mouth the Lord Jesus, and shalt believe in thine heart that God hath raised Him from the dead, thou shalt be saved. For with the heart man believeth unto righteousness; and with the mouth confession is made unto salvation.' Come, let's kneel, and I'll lead you in the sinner's prayer."

Together they knelt by Grandma's old rocker, where Grandma led Sarah in the sinner's prayer and to a personal relationship with the Lord.

5

Rome, Georgia
North Meets South: A Gentle Encounter

The next morning, reveille sounded an hour earlier than usual. After an early breakfast, the troops assembled on the drill grounds.

The sergeant stepped in front of them. He took off his cap with his right hand and smoothed his greasy brown hair with his left before putting it back on. An unlit cigar hung from the corner of his mouth.

"This is it, men! We have orders to march." His voice never quavered once as he spoke. "Take only what ya really need. Don't even take a change of uniform—only the clothes on your back. Leave everything else here."

"Will we be back here, Sarge?" One soldier asked.

"No, we won't be comin' back here to Chattanooga. We're marchin' to Atlanta."

He dismissed the troops, and they went back to their tents to choose clothes. Each picked his finest uniform shirt and pants, along with his best suit of underwear and best pair of socks.

A beautiful orange sun rose in the east as the Thirteenth Michigan Regiment headed south. The troops marched all day, with only a half-hour break at noon for a quick meal of corn.

At the outset, the men talked and joked with one another. Birds singing in magnolia trees and the pleasant weather helped lift their spirits. By midafternoon, however, much of the banter ceased. With the sun beating down relentlessly, their bodies wearied. They often lifted canteens to their parched lips for a quick sip. Despite its metallic taste, the water briefly quenched their thirst. At dusk they halted for the day.

"We'll bivouac here," the sergeant ordered the tired men. "You new recruits, be careful of snakes. You're in the South now, ya know. Many snakes down here are real poisonous."

Soon small tents, with room for only one or perhaps two men, dotted the landscape next to the dusty road. Lookout Mountain loomed on the horizon—beautiful with its lavender cast in the sunset.

After another quick, scanty meal of corn, the tired and somewhat disgruntled soldiers crawled into their canvas shelters to sleep. Joey approached Rufus.

"Would ya care if I slept in here with ya?"

"Of course not, Joey, I'd be happy for the company."

Both men fell asleep the moment they laid their heads down.

For two more days the Thirteenth Michigan continued southward, marching from dawn to dusk, with few rests in between.

On the windy morning of November 1 they crossed the bridge over the Etowah River into Rome, Georgia, where they were to join their unit, the Second Brigade, First Division of the Fourteenth Corps. General Sherman had made Rome his headquarters for a short time, but planned to move to the more centrally located Kingston tomorrow, November 2.

As the weary troops approached the Union encampment site, they could see the tattered flaps of its many rows of tents fluttering in the breeze.

"Soldiers, try to find an empty tent in one of the back rows. You may need to double up," the sergeant told them. "The officers' quarters are in front."

Rufus and Joey discovered a vacant tent big enough for two men in a back row. Most of the camp's tents already housed troops destined for the upcoming campaign.

All troops quartered, the sergeant ordered them to line up. He took the cigar out of his mouth and spat on the ground. "We'll soon receive orders to march to Atlanta. We may leave in the mornin', so be ready. Ya are to destroy all personal belongin's, including your portfolios, letters, and the like. Destroy everythin'. Take only what ya have on your back."

After the sergeant dismissed them, Rufus and Joey went back to their tent.

"If I need to get rid of my portfolio, I'm gonna write one more letter to Sarah. Ya should write home, too," Rufus told Joey.

"Yeah, I should," Joey agreed.

Their letters written, Rufus and Joey ripped up the portfolio and destroyed any personal items they wouldn't need. They kept just a few sheets of paper and a pencil in their pocket. Some troops burned their letters and portfolios.

That evening, just before taps, Joey entered the tent, frowning.

"The men are talkin' 'bout why we had to destroy all personal items and why we all hafta be in such good health. They said they sent all sick and unfit men back to Chattanooga on the train after they fixed the damage the Rebs did. Whaddya think, Rufus?"

Rufus looked up into the teenager's worried brown eyes. "Well, I don't think it's because of any harsh battle comin' soon. Rumors keep comin' about us marchin' to the sea. If that's the case, they don't want the wagons filled with sick men. They want us all to have the endurance to march the distance."

Joey's face brightened. "Oh, yeah, that makes sense." He grinned sheepishly. "Are ya ever afraid, Rufus?"

"Yeah, I'm afraid, but not for myself so much. I'm afraid of what will become of my family, if somethin' happens to me. But I give that to God. I believe He'll take care of 'em."

"'Night, Rufus."

"Good night, Joey."

A cold, nasty rain fell all day on the second and third of November. On the third, the Thirteenth Michigan made its way to Tilton, Georgia. Under the command of Major W. G. Eaton, they then received orders to return to Rome. The expected call to march to Atlanta and on to Savannah didn't arrive all that week. The soldiers spent their time drilling, gathering firewood, and cleaning the camp area. Some gambled at cards to escape the tedium of camp life.

Saturday morning, after the usual drill, Rufus and Joey sat in their tent. Rufus wanted to tour Rome—to stroll down its streets to see if he could find a church that might allow a Yankee to attend this Sunday's morning service. He decided to invite Joey to come along.

"Did you go to church at home, Joey?" Rufus asked.

"Yeah, I had to take my ma. She's real religious. She was always after me to become a Christian."

"Then did ya accept Jesus as your Savior, Joey?"

"Naw, I thought it seemed kind of sissy like."

"What's sissy about it? Do ya think Someone Who gave His life willingly on a cross is a sissy?"

"No, I guess not." Joey looked down at his feet. "You're a Christian, ain't ya, Rufus?" He spoke in almost a whisper.

"Yeah, I am. I would like to find a church to go to this Sunday mornin'. Would ya like to go with me?"

"Sure, I'll come along," Joey answered with a big smile, happy that Rufus included him. They received permission from the sergeant to briefly leave the encampment, which lay in a grove of pine trees on the edge of Rome.

The two entered the quaint town and started down Broad Street, which was lined with trees down the middle—trees that provided shade for the horses tethered there.

"How big's Rome?" Joey asked.

"I don't know. I did overhear some of the men sayin' that before the war, Rome was a busy town. They said steamboats even sailed these rivers, bringin' much trade to Rome. And the boats carried passengers, too."

"Steamboats? Wow! But there ain't no people around now."

"You're right. That's because most of 'em left last May when our troops occupied Rome."

They noticed on the other side of the street a tall, handsome Union soldier promenading down the walk with a lovely Southern lady on his arm, the two of them chatting and laughing softly. They made an impressive-looking couple, he in his uniform with shiny brass buttons, and she in her wool suit, with matching hat and muff to protect her from the piercing fall wind blowing off the waters.

Rufus and Joey exchanged puzzled looks. Rufus had seen the soldier off and on since he left Jackson, but he didn't know anything about him.

Continuing down the broad street, they turned a corner. Rufus abruptly stopped in front of a brick building with a white, wooden bell tower. It was the First Baptist Church. Rufus, a Baptist himself, felt a profound need to worship in God's house. He longed to sing his praises from the old hymnals.

Now he felt only disappointment. He could tell there would be no service this Sunday. The church building had been set up for use as a hospital to care for the wounded. He and Joey could also see that Union officers had stabled their horses in the basement.

"It's too bad the church basement is bein' used as a stable," complained Joey. "After all, it is a church."

"Well, Joey, you know it's the church buildin', and it should be shown respect as God's house," replied Rufus. "But the real church is the people who worshiped here. I'm sure they are still worshipin', wherever they have gone. The real church itself is still all right."

"You're right there, private," agreed a friendly voice from behind them.

Rufus whirled around to face the same Union soldier they had seen walking with the Southern lady.

"I agree with what you said about the worshipers bein' the church," he explained. He put out his hand and introduced himself. "I'm Tom Shafer."

Rufus shook his hand. "I'm Rufus Seaman, and this is Joey Thorpe." Joey shook Tom's hand.

"I know somethin' about this church," Tom went on. "My aunt and uncle attended here, also my cousin. You see, even though I'm from Michigan, I have relatives here in Rome. We don't agree on our politics, but we're still family. Even if this church hadn't been set up as a hospital, there aren't enough people left in town to hold services. And the church is bein' used for a good cause. Hospitals have been set up in several of Rome's churches. There is a great need for 'em, because many of the wounded, both Union and Confederate, are brought into Rome to be tended in these very hospitals."

"I see what you mean. It is a good cause. I just kept hopin' I could find a meetin' to attend this Sunday. Bein' in the army has made me feel more the need for God."

"Yeah, me too. We're in the army, where there is a lot of vice, as there is in most armies—gamblin', drinkin', and cursin'. We need to stay close to God. Maybe you'd like to meet with some of us Christians in the

Thirteenth. We get together for Bible study and a time of prayer. And maybe we could have our own time of devotions together when we're on the march. We could try to camp together."

"I'd like that very much," Rufus answered, surprised to hear about the Christians among the troops.

Then Tom turned to Joey. "And you're welcome, too."

Joey mumbled, "Thank you." He shuffled his feet, feeling awkward.

"We usually meet around a campfire, if it isn't rainin'," Tom explained. "Sometimes we even have coffee, if we can find some. You know how we Union boys love our coffee." Tom smiled, showing a mouth full of straight white teeth below his dark mustache.

"I sure do. The Bible study and the coffee sound mighty good."

"Where is your tent, Rufus?"

"Joey and I share a tent at the rear of the encampment on the west side. Are you a new recruit, Tom?" Rufus asked.

"No, I'm not a replacement. I went home to Kalamazoo, Michigan, on furlough. I arrived here just a few days ago. I rejoined my company, the Thirteenth Michigan, in Chattanooga. I'm in Company G."

"I'm assigned to the Thirteenth Michigan, and I'm in Company G, too!" Rufus exclaimed. "I think we traveled on the train together. You musta' gotten on at Kalamazoo. I remember seein' ya. I'm glad to know you're a Christian."

"Did ya enlist?" Tom asked, as the three headed back toward the encampment.

"No, I was drafted as a replacement troop."

"Oh. Most draftees don't show up."

"Yeah, I've heard that. I've also heard that we aren't received too well when we do show up."

"I don't feel that way. I'm glad to know ya. The Thirteenth Michigan is a good outfit. You'll do fine with 'em."

"Joey's from near Kalamazoo, where you live."

Tom turned toward Joey. "We're probably neighbors, Joey. I live on a farm near Kalamazoo."

Joey smiled. "Yeah."

Tom led them on a path along the river back to the encampment. Joey picked up a pebble and skimmed it across the water.

"I'll see ya later," Tom told them when they reached the camp. He took a few steps, hesitated, and then turned back toward Rufus and Joey.

"Say, how would the two of ya like to go with me tomorrow to visit my aunt and uncle? That is, if we can get permission to leave camp."

"I think I'd like that. Thank ya for invitin' us," Rufus answered. He looked at Joey. "Wouldn't ya like to go, too?"

Joey nodded.

"Then I'll see ya tomorrow," Tom said, as they parted ways.

Rufus and Joey hurried to their tent, Joey leading the way.

Once they were inside, Rufus turned and faced Joey. "What's wrong, Joey? I have a feelin' somethin' is botherin' you."

"Yeah, you're right. I feel bad I paid no attention to my ma when she wanted me to be a Christian. Now it's too late."

"It's not too late. If ya really want to accept Jesus as your Savior, ya can do that right now. It's never too late."

Joey's eyes lit up. "You mean I don't hafta be in a church and answer the altar call to be saved?"

"No. That is one way to accept Jesus, but not the only way."

"Then if I can do that now, I want to. Will ya show me how, Rufus?"

"Sure. Ya need to confess in prayer that you're a sinner and ask Jesus to forgive ya. Ya need to invite him to come into your heart. Would ya like me to say the sinner's prayer with ya?"

"Yeah, I would."

"Let's kneel by your bed."

They knelt, side by side.

"Repeat this prayer after me," Rufus began. "'Lord Jesus, I know Thou art the Son of God and the Savior of the world. Thou didst die on the cross for our sins and arose on the third day. I confess I am a sinner. I pray Thou wilt cleanse me with Thy blood and come into my heart. I want to live my life for Thee. I love Thee. I thank Thee for saving me. Amen.'"

Joey solemnly repeated the prayer for salvation after Rufus.

"Now you're saved—you're a Christian," Rufus assured Joey, whose eyes brimmed with tears. Rufus put his arm around Joey's shoulder. "Now ya should write your ma and tell her you've become a Christian," he suggested. "She'd want to know."

"Yeah, I know she would. I'll write her yet today," Joey promised.

The clanging of the dinner bell interrupted the tender scene. Rufus and Joey, happy they had had time to finish praying, got to their feet. They knew if they wanted to be fed their noon meal they needed to go to the mess tent without delay. Later that afternoon Joey wrote a letter to his mother, telling her the good news.

The next morning after drill, Tom stopped by their tent. The sky looked somewhat threatening. "I talked to the sergeant, and he said we can have passes for this afternoon . . . if the weather holds." He looked up at the clouds. "Let's leave after we've eaten our noon mess. Otherwise, my aunt and uncle will try to feed us, and they don't have that much food."

"Mail call," the sergeant barked. All the men eagerly gathered around. Rufus stood to the side, listening for his name, but once again, he didn't hear it. He couldn't understand why nothing came from Sarah. He ached to get a letter, to know how she and the children were getting along. With slumped shoulders, he shuffled away.

Joey watched Rufus and saw the sad expression in his eyes. "If he would only get a letter," Joey thought.

By midmorning the day cleared, although it was somewhat cool and windy.

After mess, the three Union soldiers ambled down Broad Street until they came to a tree-lined avenue.

"We turn here," Tom told them. "They live in the third house down this street." Tom stopped in front of a square white house. A gated picket fence enclosed the yard. He opened the swinging gate and led his friends up the boardwalk to the porch, where they mounted the wooden steps leading to the front entrance.

Tom's gentle rap brought to the door a lovely young woman with golden hair and blue eyes that matched the blue of her dress. Tom introduced her to Rufus and Joey as his cousin Nellie Shafer.

"I'm happy to meet you both," she drawled. The smile on her face revealed no animosity toward the Union soldiers.

"We're happy to meet ya, too, ma'am," Rufus and Joey replied.

"Please come in."

Nellie ushered them into the parlor. Bright sunlight filtered through the white curtains hanging at the four tall windows. Tiger, the family cat, lazily cuffed the lacey design reflected on the carpet.

The room held several fine pieces of furniture, including a cherished upright piano standing in the corner. A fire crackled in the fireplace, adding cheerful warmth. On the polished wooden mantel was a picture of a handsome young man dressed in a Confederate uniform.

Tom's aunt and uncle, Fred and Irene Shafer, stood to greet them. After cordial introductions, Aunt Irene moved toward the doorway. "I'll make some coffee, and I have some freshly baked molasses cookies. Do you like them?" she asked. All three guests assured her that they loved molasses cookies.

"Do you like music?" asked Nellie. "We could sing around the piano. I know Tom enjoys that." Nellie shyly glanced at Tom.

"I do, too," Rufus said. "My wife, daughters, and I always gathered around the piano to sing in the evening."

Nellie sat down at the piano and uncovered the keys. After rifling through some music, she selected a piece. Uncle Fred settled in his easy chair to read the newspaper and enjoy the singing.

"This is a song that is dearly loved by our troops," she explained. "And I think you will like it as well. It's called 'Lorena.' I'll play it through once, so you'll know the tune."

The three stood behind her, peeking over her shoulder at the music, ready to sing the words. Rufus and Tom started singing when Nellie began to play the song the second time. Nellie's soprano joined their voices, and Tom sang the harmony. Joey, feeling shy, softly sang only a word now and then at first, but by the second verse he sang with gusto.

> Oh the years creep slowly by, Lorena,
> The snow is on the ground again;
> The sun's low down the sky, Lorena,
> The frost gleams where the flowers have been.
> But my heart beats on as warmly now
> As when the summer days were nigh;
> Oh the sun can never dip so low
> A-down affection's cloudless sky.
>
> A hundred months have passed, Lorena,
> Since last I held that hand in mine,
> And felt the pulse beat fast, Lorena,
> Though mine beat faster far than thine.

A hundred months, 'twas flowery May
When up the hilly slope we climbed,
To watch the dying of the day,
And hear the distant church bells chime.

We loved each other then, Lorena,
For more than we ever dared to tell;
And what we might have been, Lorena,
Had but our loving prospered well.
But then, 'tis past, the years are gone,
I'll not call up their shadowy forms,
I'll say to them, "Lost years, sleep on!
Sleep on! Nor heed life's pelting storms."

The story of that past, Lorena,
Alas! I care not to repeat,
The hopes that could not last, Lorena,
They lived, but only lived to cheat.
I would not cause e'en one regret
To rankle in your bosom now;
For "if we try, we may forget,"
Were words of thine long years ago.

Yes, these were words of thine, Lorena,
They burn within my memory yet,
They touched some tender chords, Lorena,
Which thrill and tremble with regret.
'Twas not thy woman's heart that spoke,
Thy heart was always true to me,
A duty, stern and pressing, broke
The tie which linked my soul with thee.

It matters little now, Lorena,
The past is in the eternal past,
Our heads will soon lie low, Lorena,
Life's tide is ebbing out so fast.
There is a Future! O, thank God!

> Of life this is so small a part!
> 'Tis dust to dust beneath the sod,
> But there, up there, 'tis heart to heart.

"That is a beautiful song," Rufus agreed. "I can see why your troops love it. So do I."

Tom bent over and whispered in Nellie's ear. Nellie blushed. "Tom—Tom wants to sing 'When I Saw Sweet Nellie Home,'" she stammered.

"That's my favorite," Tom chuckled as he looked over at Rufus. Nellie played the introduction to the familiar tune and they all joined in.

> In the sky the bright stars glittered,
> On the grass the moonlight fell;
> Hush'd the sound of daylight bustle
> Closed the pink-eyed pimpernel,
> As down the moss-grown wood path
> Where the cattle love to roam,
> From the August evening party
> I was seeing Nellie home.
>
> Chorus:
> In the sky the bright stars glittered
> On the grass the moonlight shone;
> From an August evening party
> I was seeing Nellie home.
>
> When the autumn tinged the greenwood,
> Turning all its leaves to the gold,
> In the lawn by elders shaded
> I my love to Nellie told.
> As we stood together gazing
> On the star-bespangled dome,
> How I blessed the August evening,
> When I saw sweet Nellie home.
>
> White hairs mingled with my tresses,
> Furrows steal upon my brow,

But a love smile cheers and blesses
Life's declining moments now.
Matron in the snowy kerchief
Closer to my bosom come;
Tell me, dost thou still remember
When I saw sweet Nellie home?

Just as they finished a rousing last chorus of "When I Saw Sweet Nellie Home," Tom's Aunt Irene entered the room, carrying a tray with a coffee pot and a plate of cookies she placed on an end table. "Everyone come and help yourself," she said. Nellie rose and crossed the room to assist her mother with pouring the coffee. Each person accepted a steaming cup, along with a cookie, before sitting down. Nellie distributed yellow napkins to make the coffee hour complete.

"Let's all bow our heads in a short word of prayer, giving thanks for the refreshments," Mr. Shafer said.

"Dear Lord," he began, "we thank Thee for this food and for the blessings Thou hast bestowed upon us. Please keep our Johnny safe, wherever he is, and protect Tom and his friends from harm as well. In Jesus' name we pray. Amen."

After the prayer was concluded and before sitting down in the chair next to the cozy fire, Rufus, taking a sip of his hot coffee, quietly asked, "Is that a picture of your Johnny on the mantel?"

"Yes, it is," answered Mrs. Shafer, who sat in the matching wingback chair on the other side of the fireplace. "We're very proud of him."

"I'm sure you are," Rufus responded. "He's a fine-looking man."

"I don't believe in slavery, but I do believe in states' rights," Mr. Shafer said, though his gentle tone held nothing argumentative. "I believe in states' rights just as you, like Tom, I presume, believe in the Union." A small man with brown eyes and thinning light brown hair, Mr. Shafer did not appear intimidating.

"Yes, sir, I do," Rufus politely answered.

"Well, there is one thing I think we all can agree on: we want an end to this war," Mr. Shafer declared, concluding that part of the discussion.

Everyone agreed.

"What part of Michigan are you from, Rufus?" Mr. Shafer asked. "I'm originally from Michigan myself."

"I'm from Casnovia, sir. That's a small town north of Grand Rapids."

"Yes, I believe I know about where that would be. But isn't there mostly pine forest north of Grand Rapids?"

"It was that way in the beginnin'. We had to chop a trail to where my parents' farm is now. But much of the land has been cleared for farmin', and there are other towns north of Grand Rapids."

"What part of Michigan are you from, Joey?" Mr. Shafer asked.

Joey quickly gulped the last bite of his second molasses cookie before answering. "I come from a farm near Kalamazoo."

"Joey and I are neighbors," Tom told his Uncle Fred.

"Do you have a family, Joey?" Mrs. Shafer asked.

"Yeah, I have my ma back home. I run away and enlisted with my older brothers, but we was separated," Joey replied.

"That's too bad, Joey, I'm sorry to hear that."

Mrs. Shafer turned toward Rufus. "What about you, Rufus? Do you have a family back home?"

"Yes, ma'am. I have a wife, Sarah, and two daughters—Dorothy, who is four, and Lucy, who is two," Rufus replied. "They live alone out on our farm."

Nellie rose to pick up the coffee server and proceeded to refill her guests' cups.

"When did you leave Michigan, Mr. Shafer?" Rufus asked.

"I left Michigan about twenty-two years ago. I came south to visit, and, after I met a certain lovely lady, I settled here." He looked over at his wife with a special tenderness. Her flaxen hair and blue eyes still moved him. "I've never been sorry." He spoke in almost a whisper.

The grandfather clock in the hall chimed the half hour; it was now 2:30 and time to go back to the encampment.

Tom and Rufus looked at one another. They knew they should get back, even though they both felt reluctant to leave after enjoying themselves so. The atmosphere at the Shafer home seemed like an oasis, compared to their crude army life in tents.

Tom was the first to rise.

"Thank you, Aunt Irene and Uncle Fred, for this wonderful afternoon.

Thank you, too, Nellie." When he spoke to Nellie, his cheeks dimpled into a broad smile. "I'm afraid we need to get back to camp."

Rufus and Joey thanked Mr. and Mrs. Shafer, and both shook hands with Mr. Shafer. "Thank you for havin' us, sir; I really appreciate your kindness," Rufus said.

"My nephew Tom is always welcome in this home, and that goes for his friends, too."

"That was fun at the piano, Nellie," Rufus remarked. "Only it made me homesick."

After thanking their Southern hosts for their hospitality a final time, the three Union troops prepared to leave. Nellie walked them to the door and stood on the porch, waving until they disappeared from sight.

General Sherman's four corps, the Fifteenth, the Seventeenth, the Fourteenth, and the Twentieth, as well as one division of cavalry under General Kilpatrick, lay spread all along the way from Rome to Atlanta.

On the seventh of November came the expected order from headquarters to march to Kingston. This included Rufus and all the Michigan Thirteenth Regiment at Rome, which was destined for the campaign. They grabbed only the bare essentials, wrapped them in their ponchos, and threw them over their shoulders.

Rufus marched alongside Joey and Tom. Because of their Christian faith, they enjoyed a special camaraderie. A few of the residents of Rome stood quietly along the street, most of them glad to see their Union enemies leave. But not everyone felt happy.

Tom's cousin Nellie stood among the small group of spectators. As they passed by, Tom broke from the marching ranks to embrace Nellie for a final goodbye. A few other troops also broke ranks, wishing to say their goodbyes to some of the ladies they had come to know. Tears flowed amid promises to come back someday after the war.

Joey, observing what was happening, turned to Rufus.

"Do ya think it will ever work out between 'em? Do ya think they'll come back?"

"If they really love one another, it can work out. Yeah, they may come back and even choose to live in the South. I'm sure Tom will come back."

Rufus realized Tom loved Nellie more deeply than only as a cousin.

Not all of the Union troops from the encampment marched out of Rome. General Corse, with a few of his soldiers, stayed behind, awaiting orders from General Sherman.

* * * * *

Back home, Pa and Ma Walkley were sitting at Sarah's kitchen table with their granddaughters, Dorothy and Lucy. They were waiting eagerly for Sarah to open the letter from Rufus they had picked up at the post office that morning.

Sarah poured steaming cups of coffee from the familiar pot for each of her parents and prepared frothy cups of cocoa for her daughters. The warmth of the fire in the wood range made the kitchen pleasant on this cold, bleak November day.

After she had served the hot beverages, Sarah joined her family at the table. She took the letter from her apron pocket and opened it almost cautiously, as though she feared what it might contain. She clasped the pages to her heart for a moment before she started to read them to herself.

Georgia
Rome November the first in 1864

Dear Wife,

I approve this chance to write to you. We arrived here this morning after three days march and the word is that we leave here in the morning for Savannah some two hundred miles and if it is true, I know not when I can write again but will write first chance and every chance.

Sarah, you have no idea how soldiers fare and what hardships they have to undergo and I know but little about it but I have lived two days on corn.

Sarah don't worry about me but see to the things and take good care of the children. Tell them that I would like to kiss them but Sarah I can't and you must kiss them for me. Sarah, if I could feel thy hand once more but I hope the time will come. Trust in the Lord thy God and pray to Him for my deliverance.

I would like to write more. Sarah, write often for my heart aches to hear from you.

Sarah, write and let me know what company and what regiment Wyllys is in for I have forgotten. I haven't seen anyone that I know since I left Jackson. I tried to get in with the boys from our town but could not. So I am here among strangers. So this will have to do for this time.

Good bye Sarah

From Rufus W. Seaman
To Sarah E. Seaman

Dorothy and Lucy watched Mama's face as she perused their papa's letter. They carefully sipped their hot cocoa until Mama, after silently reading it twice, looked over at them.

"Come here, Dorothy and Lucy. Papa wants me to give you something." She smiled.

Excited, both girls raced to their mother. Sarah hugged and kissed each daughter.

"That is from Papa," she told them. "He wrote me to kiss you for him. He loves you and misses you very much."

"I love Papa, too," Dorothy said. "But when is he comin' home? I miss him."

"Me, too," Lucy joined in.

"Papa will come home as soon as he can, but he can't right now," Mama explained.

"Where is Rufus now, honey?" Pa inquired.

"He's at Rome, Georgia. He thinks they'll soon start for Savannah. Here, you may read his letter."

Pa knew by the expression on Sarah's face that she didn't want to talk about the letter in front of the girls and didn't intend to read it to them. As he scanned it, he understood why.

Just then the rumble of buckboard wheels sounded in the driveway. The old dog, Buster, asleep on a rug in front of the range, woke and lumbered over to the back door, his tail wagging a welcome.

Those in the house soon heard footsteps stomping up onto the porch.

The back door burst open to reveal Edwin Walkley's smiling face. He wrapped his arms around himself. "Brrr, it's cold out there." Seeing Buster, he bent over to scratch his ears.

"Uncle Ed! Uncle Ed!" Dorothy and Lucy scrambled from the table to greet their uncle. Ed stooped down to give his nieces their usual hugs. He stood back up with a giggling girl in each arm. Buster lumbered back over to lie in front of the stove again.

"Mmm, do I smell coffee?" Ed asked. He looked at his father. "Did you leave me any cookies, Pa?" he teased. He plopped down at the table with both girls on his lap.

Sarah rose from the table to get a cup for her brother. Then she remembered the cookies. She quickly filled a plate and set it in front of him.

"I ate the first plateful," Pa joked, "so Sarah had to fill another plate for you."

Sarah laughed. "I'm afraid I forgot to serve any cookies. I kept thinking about Rufus's letter. Pa hasn't had his cookies, either." She picked up the pot and refilled their cups. All enjoyed molasses cookies with their second round of coffee.

"So you got another letter, sis?" Ed asked, as she sat beside him.

"Yes, Ma and Pa brought it out to me this morning."

"What did Rufus have to say? Has he joined up with Sherman yet?" Ed reached for a second cookie.

"Apparently. He wrote the letter I received today on November 1 from Rome, Georgia. He thinks they'll soon be going to Savannah." Sadly, she added, "If they do, he doesn't know when he'll be able to write."

"You know he'll write, if he can. He's proved that. You've done quite well in getting his letters lately. Let me see . . . today is the twelfth, so it took about eleven days for this letter to get here. That's pretty good for comin' that far." He reached over and patted Sarah's hand.

In her heart she agreed with her brother. She had gotten four letters from Rufus in the last couple of weeks. She didn't want his mail to her to stop.

It blessed Ma Walkley to see Edwin willing to talk to Sarah about Rufus. When he first came home from serving his three years with the sharpshooters, he seemed reluctant to talk about the war at all. The family understood that and did not question him, but he always tried to encourage his sister about Rufus.

"I hate to break this up, but I stopped by to clean the barn." Ed pushed back his chair and got to his feet. "I think I had better get at it."

"I'll help you, son," Pa offered, as he, too, left the table. "It'll go twice as fast that way." Father and son put on their coats and headed for the barn.

Ma and Sarah chatted while they cleared the table. They put the dirty dishes in the dishpan. Sarah lifted the lid of the range to lay three more sticks of wood on the fire. She filled the teakettle at the kitchen pump and placed it on the stove. Soon the water would be hot enough to do the dishes.

"Let's sit in the parlor, Ma." Sarah led the way, and Ma followed; Dorothy and Lucy were back on the parlor floor, playing again with their dolls. Ma picked up her knitting bag from the easy chair where she had put it when they arrived, and then sat down, while Sarah chose to sit in Rufus's rocker.

The knitting needles danced in a constant rhythm as Ma knitted a blue sweater to give to Lucy for Christmas. She planned to knit a matching sweater for Lucy's doll as part of the gift. Dorothy would receive the same type of sweater set.

"Thanksgiving is only two weeks away," Ma reminded Sarah. "Pa and I would like the family gathering at our house. Would that be all right with you, Sarah?"

"Of course, Ma, what would you like me to bring?" Sarah had no desire to hold the Thanksgiving gathering at her house without Rufus.

"I thought I would fix the turkey, dressing, gravy, mashed potatoes, and baked squash. The other family members could bring baked beans and desserts. Oh, and I'll furnish the rolls, too," Ma added.

Some time later Pa and Ed entered the kitchen. "We're all through at the barn. I think we should start for home, Ma," Pa suggested. "I have some township work to do."

Pa, an elected justice of the peace, performed the duties of his office earnestly.

"I need to get on home, myself," Ed stated. He crossed the room to hug his mother and sister goodbye.

"Thanks, Ed, and you, too, Pa. I'm really grateful to both of you," Sarah said.

Dorothy and Lucy jumped up and lifted their arms to receive goodbye hugs. Uncle Ed squeezed the two curly heads. "I'll stop around to help out in a day or two, sis." Goodbyes spoken and hugs given all around, Ed left.

"We plan on attending church on Thanksgiving Day, Sarah. Shall we pick you up?" Ma asked, as they walked toward the door, arm in arm.

"Oh, yes, please do. I want to go."

"We'll see ya again in a few days," Pa promised. "We can make more plans about Thanksgiving then."

"Thank you for bringing me the letter."

"You're always welcome, honey. We know how much they mean to ya," Pa answered.

After one last hug from Dorothy and Lucy, Ma and Pa left for home.

6

Kingston, Georgia
Joining General Sherman's Army

That evening at twilight, as shadows lengthened, the Thirteenth Michigan Regiment, along with the other troops that left Rome, marched into Kingston to join General Sherman and his army.

After a late supper of lukewarm soup, Rufus, Tom, and Joey pitched their tent in the large encampment. Tired from their all-day march, they longed to go to bed.

"When do ya think we'll march to Atlanta?" Joey asked, stifling a weary yawn with his hand.

Rufus and Tom looked at Joey. They shrugged. "We don't know, Joey," answered Tom, "but I'm sure it'll be quite soon."

The next afternoon, on November 8, the troops followed the first sergeant's order to fall in. Major Eaton wanted to address the Thirteenth Michigan Regiment. The major stood before them, a tall, handsome man with a full beard and blue eyes, cool and composed, showing the demeanor of an officer. Only traces of his boyish grin kept him from appearing stern.

"All troops below Chattanooga who are designated for this campaign shall now receive their orders to march to Atlanta. Since you men of the Thirteenth Michigan Regiment are assigned to the Second Brigade, First Division, Fourteenth Corps, you are under those orders," he told them.

Holding up a sheaf of papers for everyone to see, he continued, "General Sherman just issued these orders pertaining to the march. I shall not read them verbatim, but they are essentially as follows: General Sherman wants to inform you men of the four corps that he has organized you into an army for a special purpose that will involve a long and difficult march. All he asks of you is that you display the same discipline, courage, and patience you have shown in the past. He hopes you will strike a blow at the enemy that will produce his complete overthrow. He wants to impress upon you that during marches, and even in camp, you must keep your places and must not scatter about and risk being picked up by hostile persons. Also, our wagons should not be loaded with anything but provisions and ammunition. All servants, other noncombatants, and refugees should now go to the rear so as not to hinder our march. At some future time we will be able to provide for the poor whites and blacks who seek to escape the bondage they are now suffering."

Major Eaton looked up from the papers in his hand. "Those are basically the orders General Sherman issued earlier today. Do you all understand them?" The men nodded. "Then you may be dismissed."

After dismissal, the men walked away in silence, each deep in his own thoughts about being a "special army." What did General Sherman have in mind? The seasoned veterans were not alarmed; they trusted "Uncle Billy," as they called him, completely and would follow him anywhere. But new recruits, like Rufus and Joey, wondered what he meant.

"Tom, what do ya think General Sherman intended by callin' us a special army?" Rufus asked, as the three comrades walked back to their tents.

"I can't say for sure, but I think he believes he's organized an army that will bring this horrible war to an end and thereby save lives on both sides," Tom replied. "That, after all, is his goal."

"What'll we eat on such a long march?" Joey asked.

Rufus laughed. "That's a good question, Joey. I've been hungry more than once since enterin' the army. At times I've lived on nothin' but corn."

"Oh, I'm sure we'll soon receive further orders, and then we'll know what to expect on the march," Tom assured them.

Tom proved right. The next morning, on November 9, General Sherman issued additional orders. The afternoon of the same day Major Eaton addressed the Thirteenth Michigan Regiment once more. He cleared his throat, raised his voice, and said, "General Sherman issued further orders this morning. Again, I won't read them word for word, but basically they are as follows:

1. The army is to be divided into two wings. The Fifteenth and Seventeenth Corps will compose the right wing commanded by Major General O. O. Howard. The Fourteenth and the Twentieth Corps will compose the left wing commanded by Major General H. W. Slocum.
2. The four corps shall march in columns on four parallel roads as much as possible. They will converge at certain points as ordered.
3. One wagon and one ambulance shall follow each regiment, and accordingly, an appropriate proportion of ammunition wagons, provision wagons, and ambulances shall follow each brigade. The separate columns will routinely start at 7:00 a.m. and march about fifteen miles a day.
4. Foraging parties will be sent out to gather all provisions. Soldiers are not to enter any inhabited dwelling. They should attempt to leave an amount of provision adequate for each family's needs.
5. The power to destroy mills, houses, cotton gins, etc. is entrusted to corps commanders alone. This general principle is laid down for them: Where the army is unmolested, no destruction of property should be permitted. But when the march is molested, you may retaliate in kind.
6. Cavalry, artillery, and foragers may appropriate horses, mules, wagons, etc. where needed. In all foraging, the party shall refrain from abusive or threatening language. Foragers should attempt to discriminate between the hostile rich and the poor and industrious, who are usually neutral or friendly.
7. Able-bodied Negroes who can be of service may be taken along, if supplies are adequate.
8. An organization of a pioneer battalion for each corps should be attended to. Negroes could be used here. This battalion should repair roads and widen them if possible, so the columns will not be delayed when reaching difficult places. Army commanders should give the artillery and wagons the right of way,

with their troops marching on one side. Troops should assist wagons at steep hills or when crossing streams.
9. Captain Poe, chief engineer, will assign each wing of the army a pontoon train that is fully equipped and organized."

The papers with General Sherman's orders rustled in Major Eaton's hands, for it was a windy day. "These orders are quite lengthy," he continued, "but I have read all of their main points. If there is anything you don't understand and would like to know more about, you're welcome to come to my tent. You're dismissed."

Before taps, Rufus, Tom, and Joey always tried to take time to have devotions together, something that meant a great deal to all three of them. During their devotions they shared their concerns with one another and prayed for each other. Tonight they also discussed General Sherman's orders and the march, as all three men sat cross-legged on the ground inside the tent—three men in whose lives God came first, family second, and country third.

"Well, Joey, we now know how we're gonna eat on the march," Rufus teased. "We're to live off the land. Only I don't think that will be as easy as it sounds."

"I think you're right, Rufus. It's gonna to be difficult," Tom agreed.

"Who will be the for . . . for . . . whatever they're called?" Joey asked.

"Foragers," Tom told him. "They'll probably be assigned their duties in Atlanta."

Rufus sat with his head bowed. "This march doesn't worry me anywhere near as much as not hearin' from Sarah," he quietly said. His heart ached to hear from home. "And there won't be any mail durin' the march to the sea," he added.

Tom reached over and laid his arm on Rufus's shoulder. "We're gonna keep prayin' you'll hear from Sarah, and I believe you will."

Rufus raised his head. "I believe I will, too. We're also gonna keep prayin', Tom, that you'll hear from Nellie." Rufus knew that Tom wanted to hear from Nellie as much as he, Rufus, wanted to hear from Sarah.

"And Joey, you'll hear from your ma. She'll be proud of ya. You've grown so in the Lord," Rufus told him.

Joey blushed. It pleased him to have Rufus commend him like that. He respected Rufus and Tom and wanted to be like them.

"I think we should pray now, before we hear taps," Tom suggested.

Rufus and Joey agreed. They first prayed for their own family, then for one another. Finally, the three of them together prayed for peace.

On the morning of November 10 General Corse received telegraphed orders from General Sherman stating that, before evacuating his post, Corse was to burn all structures in Rome that could be useful to the Confederate war effort. Included in the order were all forts, mills, iron works, and the Nobel Factory, as well as two railroad depots. Churches, including those housing hospital facilities, were not to be destroyed.

Corse and his troops carried out these orders the night of November 10 and joined Sherman at Kingston the following day.

One day later, on November 12, Major Eaton called an assembly of the Thirteenth Michigan Regiment. After the first sergeant had called the roll, Eaton stepped before the men.

"The order we have been waiting for has been given. We are to march for Atlanta in fifteen minutes. Your orders from General Sherman include breaking up the railway between here and Atlanta as soon as the last of our trains going from Atlanta to Chattanooga passes over. You are also ordered to destroy anything that could be useful to the Confederate war effort. Any questions?" he asked, as he looked over the troops.

One private nodded and partially raised his hand.

"Yes, private?" Eaton gently responded.

"What d'ya mean by sayin' we are to destroy anything useful to the Rebs?" he asked. "What kinds of things should we destroy?"

"We are to destroy railroad depots, bridges, factories, mills, forts, and anything the enemy could use in fighting us. This will mostly be done by fire." The major paused to see if anyone else had a question. No one did.

"Be prepared to march in fifteen minutes. Be out here and fall in your ranks. That's all, men. Dismissed!"

Back in their tents, each man grabbed what meager possessions he could carry. Rufus, Tom, and Joey hurriedly picked up their knapsacks and a few personal belongings before scurrying to join their unit.

The twelfth of November also saw the last of all railroad and telegraph communications, leaving the army standing alone to fend for itself. The same day General Sherman and his full staff left Kingston for Atlanta, taking the troops with them. Marching orders went out for all detachments, strung the length of Georgia, to start for Atlanta without delay, breaking up the railroad on their way and destroying anything that could prove useful to the enemy. A total of forty-five thousand Union troops in northwest Georgia responded to General Sherman's order that day, as did all of the troops at Kingston.

Marching in the column beside Tom, Rufus noticed that he appeared upset. When they arrived at the railroad, Rufus took a moment to talk to him before they started tearing up the tracks.

"What's wrong, Tom?"

"Some of the boys just told me about Rome. I'm concerned about Nellie and my aunt and uncle."

"What did ya hear about Rome?" No one had told Rufus what happened there.

"General Corse burned a good deal of Rome a couple days ago, before he evacuated the city. I wish I could get back there to check on 'em."

"But weren't they only supposed to burn buildings that would be useful to the enemy?"

"Yeah, that's right, but once you start burnin' buildings, anything can happen. One building you set on fire can have sparks that can easily set the structure next to it on fire, even if it is a building that shouldn't be burned. They said the business street is burned, and remember how close their home was to that area?"

"If ya want to go there, I'll go with ya," Joey spoke up.

"You and Tom can't go there, Joey. You'd be shot by some local residents," Rufus told him.

Providentially, a trooper, one of General Corse's men, then walked up. "I've been trying to find you, Tom. On our way out of Rome I rode around by your uncle's house. They are all okay. The fire didn't touch them. I knew you'd want to know."

"Thanks, Will, I really appreciate that. I've been worried."

"What about the Baptist Church?" Rufus interrupted.

"We didn't burn it," Will quickly replied.

Tom turned toward Rufus. "I don't believe you've met my friend, Will Withers. Will, these are my friends, Rufus Seaman and Joey Thorpe." They all shook hands.

"Let's get to work!" the sergeant bellowed.

At that point, and continuing all the way to Atlanta, they worked with their regiment, ripping up the tracks of the Western and Atlantic Railroad. After they had started blazing fires with the ties, they laid the rails on the flames. When the center of a rail became red hot, the boys picked it up by its ends and wrapped it around a tree, rendering it useless to the enemy.

Other soldiers destroyed a variety of additional structures that would be potentially helpful to the Confederate cause. Needless to say, more than a few towns between Chattanooga and Atlanta suffered the same unhappy fate as Rome.

7

Atlanta
Preparing to March ~ A City in Flames

By the afternoon of November 14 all detachments had reached Atlanta and discovered a city bustling with Union troops, wagons, horses, and mules—with everyone charging in different directions in haste to prepare for the march. An aura of expectancy was obvious among the soldiers.

The Thirteenth Michigan Regiment pitched their tents beside the thousands of other tents already in the huge encampment located approximately a mile outside of the city. Captain George Roe then ordered his master sergeant to have the men fall in so he could address them. As soon as they had lined up in their customary ranks, the captain, eager to get on with the day's agenda, immediately exited a nearby tent and stepped to the front of the troops. Roe enjoyed a fine reputation as an officer. A medium-sized man with rather handsome, rugged features, he never gave an order to his men that he himself wouldn't be willing to execute. A veteran of many major battles, he looked older than his thirty years.

Roe paused a moment to look over the troops before speaking. "As you know, men," he began, "General Sherman has grouped the four corps into wings, a left wing and a right wing. Our corps, the Fourteenth, commanded by General Jeff Davis, is now a part of the left wing commanded by General H. W. Slocum. As you've already been informed, the four corps will march in four columns on parallel roads, about twenty to forty miles apart, whenever that's possible. Troops will march on the side of the road and will give the wagon trains the right of way. Our regiment will have one supply wagon and one ambulance wagon following us, each drawn by a single team of horses. Other wagon trains with heavier loads, such as those carrying ammunition, will be drawn by teams of six mules and will travel behind the brigades. Our corps will need drivers for these wagons; we'll also need foragers to gather food.

"Each of you will carry forty rounds of ammunition, a poncho, and one blanket. Travel as light as you possibly can."

"We are now cut off from all outside communication and must be ready to march in a few hours. The other three corps, the Twentieth, the Fifteenth and the Seventeenth, have most of their wagons loaded. They'll move out in the morning, along with General Kilpatrick's cavalry of five thousand mounted soldiers. The Fourteenth still has wagons to load. That's where you men can help. The sergeant will show you what to do. Dismissed!"

In order to facilitate the loading process, the sergeant broke the regiment into smaller groups and led them to a large area crowded with empty wagons waiting for their cargo.

Rufus loved horses and was captivated by the tremendous assortment of them standing in the loading area. Along with a number of mules, they were tethered nearby, waiting to be hitched to the loaded wagons.

"I brought you some help," the sergeant told the corporal in charge.

"We can use it," blurted one rough private, busy with cartons of supplies.

After the corporal explained exactly how each wagon should be stacked, all the men of the Thirteenth Michigan Regiment, including Rufus, Tom, and Joey, pitched in to help. They toiled silently, except for an occasional grunt as a trooper heaved a weighty box of ammunition onto the wagon bed. Although they worked steadily until the evening mess, the Fourteenth Corp's wagon trains still weren't equipped to move out with the other corps in the morning.

"They've collected some fine horse flesh, that's for sure," Rufus remarked to Tom and Joey on the way back to their tent. "I sure would like the chance to look 'em over. I'm certain I spotted Morgans among 'em."

"I'd like to see 'em myself," answered Tom. "We should be able to find time to look at 'em more carefully before we leave. Do ya like horses, Joey?"

"Yeah, I like 'em okay, but not like Rufus. I don't know one breed of horse from another."

That evening, following their nightly devotions, Tom, Rufus, and Joey sat by the fire outside the tent the three of them now shared. Thousands of flickering flames from campfires were sprinkled across the landscape and lit up the starless sky. Many different sounds drifted over the clear night air—singing soldiers harmonizing in songs about home and girlfriends, gambling soldiers yelling over the roll of dice, and drinking soldiers imbibing forbidden liquor.

"I love to hear the men sing, only it makes me feel more lonesome," Rufus commented.

"Yeah, I enjoy hearing the men sing, too," replied Tom, with sadness in his eyes. "It reminds me of Nellie. But I don't like the way a few of the men found liquor. That could mean trouble."

"You're right," agreed Rufus. "Liquor spells trouble."

"Joey, why are ya so quiet?" Rufus asked.

"I just been thinkin' I would like to be a forager."

Rufus and Tom exchanged looks. Neither friend wanted to see that happen; they thought foraging would be too dangerous.

"You'll have to wait and see if they put ya in that detail," Rufus kindly informed him. "Mornin' comes early," he continued. "We'd better go to bed." He put more wood on the fire for the night—just as taps sounded.

Reveille sounded earlier than usual the next morning. After roll call and a hasty breakfast, the sergeant ordered the Thirteenth Michigan Regiment back to loading the wagons of the Fourteenth Corps. As they hurried over to resume the task, the other three corps began their march out of the encampment. With their columns stretched out long, it would be hours before the last wagon left the camp.

The soldiers assigned to continue their loading once again took up the heavy task of stowing boxes of supplies onto the wagons. Except for a break at noon, they stayed with it until they finished their work late in the day.

The wagons loaded and ready, Rufus, Tom, and Joey wandered over to look at the horses that soon would be hitched to them. They saw animals of every color and size—mostly draft horses, but also a few saddle broncos for some of the troops to ride. There were dappled grays, roans, sorrels, and many that were bay-colored, as well as a few all black and all white steeds, most of them having flowing manes to match. Each horse had its own personality—some standing quietly with their eyes drooping in sleep, others pawing at the dirt, anxious for action. Rufus's eye caught sight of a nicely matched bay team.

"There's a team of Morgans!" he exclaimed. "Wouldn't I love to drive 'em!"

Nearby, Captain Roe sat on his mount, observing the three men's interest in the horses. He overheard Rufus's remark and rode over to him. "Would you really like to drive a team like that, private?" he asked. "Do you have any experience at that sort of thing?"

Rufus answered "Yes" to both questions, as he saluted the officer. "As a farmer, I drove teams a lot, sir. I needed to drive 'em to do my plowin', cultivatin', harvestin', and many kinds of odd jobs."

"What is your name?" asked Captain Roe.

"Rufus Seaman, sir," he answered.

"We'll see what we can do about you driving the Morgan team, Rufus, but I can't promise anything."

"Thank you, sir."

As the captain turned to ride away, the noisy boom of shells and exploding gunpowder alarmed the serene encampment. Troops came running from every direction, all eyes turned toward Atlanta, which was a mile away on the horizon.

Tongues of flames lapped at the black smoke spiraling into the sky and covering part of the city.

"It's all right, men," Captain Roe assured the soldiers. "It must be that General Sherman gave the order to destroy any structure useful to the enemy. We knew he planned to do that." He spurred his horse and rode at a gallop for Atlanta.

Captain Roe's explanation proved true. General Sherman had authorized fires to be set that afternoon to destroy any building that could be of use to the Confederate Army. Since the city was a major Rebel supply center, many captured guns and wagons were marked "Atlanta." Sherman also had instructed soldiers on provost duty to protect all structures not designated for destruction. Troops started torching the iron foundry first, followed by the oil refinery and warehouse and depot area. When they set fire to the rest of General Hood's arsenal, shells burst, showering hazardous wreckage upon the city. As the wind increased in velocity, fires roared unchecked and ignited other buildings.

Atlanta's population was lower at this time than it previously had been. After its fall in September, General Sherman ordered the city to be evacuated by everyone except the Union Army. He could not protect its residents from hostilities, nor did he want the burden of feeding and guarding those civilians who remained. All would have to leave. Some chose to be sent north, but most wanted to be delivered to Confederate lines at Lovejoy. General Hood accepted a truce that provided for the transfer of Atlanta's civilians, and Federal trains and six-mule-team wagons transported them to their destination.

The night wore on, but the soldiers in the encampment found it hard to turn in. They sat quietly, each sunk in his own private thoughts, as they watched the spectacle taking place in Atlanta. The putrid smell of oily smoke from fires permeated the fall air even as far as a mile away. As they watched, angry flames billowed up and then fell back, only to rise again in another area of the city.

Sitting at their campfire, Rufus, Tom, and Joey shared their feelings with one another and joined in earnest prayer for the people of Atlanta.

"I can't help but feel terrible sorry for any women and children still livin' in Atlanta," confessed Rufus. "I keep thinkin' about my Sarah and our children—what if they lived there?"

"I know how ya feel," answered Tom. "I feel that way, too. I keep thinkin' about Nellie and my aunt and uncle, and what they went through at Rome. But even so, I still believe in what General Sherman is tryin' to accomplish through all this—to bring this terrible war to an end. You're a new recruit, Rufus, and I realize what a devastatin' picture the burnin' of Atlanta is to ya, even watchin' it from this far away. I agree; it really is a heart-wrenchin' sight. But most of the soldiers in this army have seen much worse."

Tom studied the ground as he continued: "Many of the troops are seasoned veterans who have seen their best friends blown away from right beside them. They've seen battlefields strewn with the wounded and dead from both sides. They have heard the moans of Union and Confederate soldiers callin' out for help—or just for a drink of water—but there was no help for 'em, for most of 'em had fatal injuries. The only wounds they might recover from were those to their arms and legs, and that meant amputation. If they were wounded anywhere else in their body, they usually died, with death sometimes taking long, agonizing hours. So ya see, to these veterans, myself included, the destruction of buildings and structures don't compare to the destruction of human lives on a battlefield."

Rufus didn't question what Tom said. He knew he was talking about what he himself had witnessed, and that he had lived through these scenes of death.

"I like to think that what we're doin' will end the war sooner and save lives on both sides," Tom explained. "Who knows—maybe even some soldiers from Atlanta will come safely home, if the war is ended soon—boys that may be killed if the war continues much longer." Tom looked up at Rufus. "That is why I believe in followin' General Sherman. His goal is to end the war."

"Oh, I agree. The war must be ended for the sake of both sides. I'm for that. Aren't ya, Joey?"

"Yeah, but I'm pretty homesick," Joey replied. "I wanna go home."

In the midst of all this chaos, they suddenly heard the music of a harmonica coming from a campsite a few tents over. The melody sounded soft and gentle. As Rufus continued to listen, his heart swelled with joy. He knew the song being played—an old favorite hymn.

One by one, strong male voices joined in, singing along with the harmonica as it played the familiar melody. From campsite to campsite, their voices harmonized. Rufus, Tom, and Joey also joined the impromptu choir. When the harmonica player finished several verses of the first hymn, he slipped smoothly into a second, also well known. The men's voices kept harmonizing with every hymn he played. The hymn sing continued until taps sounded, during which a lone tenor sang the words along with the bugler.

> Day is done,
> gone the sun,
> from the lakes
> from the hills
> from the sky,
> all is well,

safely rest,
God is near.

Their singing lifted up God and country and did not have any connection with the burning of Atlanta. They didn't sing to any Union triumph over that city; they sang to Jesus' triumph on the cross.

Inside the tent, as they got ready for bed, Rufus spoke to Tom and Joey about the reverence with which the soldiers had sung.

"I don't understand how the men sang like that. It was like they really knew Jesus as their Savior—like Christians."

"They probably are Christians, Rufus. There are quite a few of them in this army, but it's always the wild, rowdy men who curse, gamble, and drink that everyone notices," answered Tom. "But I'm acquainted with other Christians here. In fact, some of the soldiers who were stationed in Atlanta before the march were telling how there had been several weeks of nightly revival meetings held there by a chaplain from the Sixty-Ninth Ohio. They said many of our troops eagerly attended the services."

"Oh, that's great to hear!" exclaimed Rufus. "Wasn't it wonderful to sing like that tonight?"

"Yeah, I enjoyed it, too," Tom replied.

Joey agreed with both of them.

After raging for hours, the fire finally died down around midnight, leaving a third of Atlanta burned to the ground.

8

Leaving Atlanta
The March to the Sea Begins ~ Sherman's Neckties

November 16, 1864
Weather: Fair

In the east the early light of dawn struggled to peek through the dense smoke hovering over Atlanta. Up for hours already, the entire camp worked together, lining up the columns of the Fourteenth Corps. Captain Roe assigned all drivers and foragers, telling them their duties. Joey obtained what he requested, being appointed a forager, but Rufus was not assigned to drive the Morgans. Though disappointed, he understood; after all, the captain had said he couldn't promise him that assignment. Most of the soldiers would simply proceed on foot and give assistance where needed. That included Rufus and Tom, who chose to march together, so they could be messmates. Captain Roe, along with Major Eaton and other officers, rode up and down the columns on horseback, encouraging the foot soldiers before they started.

"The wagons have the right of way," he reminded the drivers. "The marching soldiers are to help you up hills and across any water."

He then turned and spoke to the foragers. "Remember that you are to avoid using abusive or threatening language and to leave each family enough food for their use."

Tom edged his way over to where Rufus stood, awaiting orders to move out. His poncho and rifle lay at his feet.

"I've just been talkin' to Captain Roe," Tom said in a hushed tone. "He told me that last night in Atlanta they torched some buildin's that weren't designated targets. It seems that when the authorized fires started to die down near midnight, drunken soldiers and lawless arsonists descended on the city's residential area, lootin' and settin' fires."

"I wondered why Atlanta was still smolderin' this mornin'," remarked Rufus. "When we went to bed last night, the fires were beginnin' to die down."

"Captain Roe said General Sherman and some of his engineers took to the streets to line up help to put out the fires he hadn't authorized, but they were burnin' beyond control, partly because of the wind."

"Did he actually say General Sherman himself went out on the streets to stop the fires?" an awed Rufus inquired.

"Yeah, Captain Roe said Uncle Billy spent most of the night tryin' to save private homes and churches. I'm sure he didn't get much sleep."

"Well, we know he never intended to destroy the residential area. It's a disgrace those few troops didn't obey orders."

"Yeah, that's exactly what some of the officers are sayin'—that it's a disgrace."

Tom looked around. "Where's Joey?" he asked.

"He's over with a group of foragers. They'll have to start lookin' for food and supplies as soon as we get underway. I hope he'll be all right."

"So do I. I'll march beside ya. We'll probably be assigned to destroy the railroad tracks," Tom surmised. "We can work together."

"I'll like that." Rufus picked up his poncho and rifle.

Tom backed away from Rufus as he saw the sergeant approach.

"All right, men, time to fall in. Let's move out," barked the sergeant.

7:00 A.M. THE MARCH BEGINS

When Rufus heard the order, he quickly fell in step beside Tom as the troops marched out, four abreast, in the Left Wing Column of the Fourteenth Corps. He now was one of sixty thousand Union soldiers embarking on an action swooping across miles of hostile territory, with the intent to destroy anything of value to the Confederacy, thereby defeating their cause. The Fourteenth Corps moved at a steady, rapid pace, leaving Atlanta on the Decatur road.

A weary General Sherman rode alongside them on his favorite mount, Sam. He wore a large, black, battered hat with no officer's braid and continually chomped on a cigar he held between his teeth. The weather was beautifully sunny and the air was brisk.

Each soldier carried a rifle with forty rounds of ammunition, a blanket, a canteen, a haversack or knapsack with food, eating utensils, and a canvas fly tent. A tin cup hung at each man's waist. Rufus wrapped everything but his rifle in the rubber poncho he flung over his shoulder.

As they moved onward, a regimental band started to play the "Hallelujah Chorus" of the "Battle Hymn of the Republic." The cheerful soldiers soon harmonized, singing the song with gusto. When Rufus heard them, a lump rose in his throat. It took him back to his last night at home, when his little family had gathered around the piano and Lucy wanted to sing the "'allelujah" song. He just couldn't join in with the other troops this time.

On the outskirts of the city, General Sherman stopped on a hill to look back. Atlanta, a representative and symbol of Southern resistance, lay behind them. Smoke now hung in a thin veil over the city. Just before the last Union wagons and soldiers had left Atlanta, drunken Union troops, along with Confederate deserters, had rushed to pillage the city. Now, with Sherman's troops gone, Southern looters driving wagons from as far away as fifty to a hundred miles came to Atlanta and joined the deserters in scavenging their own people.

After a brief pause to look back at the city, Sherman turned his horse, and the columns moved east toward Decatur, traveling through Georgia's beautiful countryside, tramping over rolling, wooded areas. Marching along, they repeatedly stopped briefly to set fire to authorized mills and gins and anything that could be of value to the enemy. Unfortunately, a few undisciplined soldiers also torched some unauthorized structures. Tom guessed right when he told Rufus the two of them would probably be assigned to destroy the railroad tracks, for their regiment soon received orders to be part of that demolition team. They would move into action wherever their crew had tracks to rip up.

After much starting and stopping, they reached Decatur about noon. For the columns, noon meant time for dinner. Rufus stretched his back, flexing his shoulders, then grabbed two buckets from the pack mule. The company mules carried most of the messmates' cooking supplies.

"I'll fetch some water for ya," he told Tom. "I'll get water for the mule, too."

Tom nodded and sat down on a nearby log, resting only a minute before gathering wood to start a fire. The army usually marched for fifty to sixty minutes and then rested for ten minutes. It had now been over an hour since their last stop.

Rufus strapped his rifle onto his shoulder. Carrying a bucket in each hand, he trudged up a grassy knoll in search of water. He kept a keen lookout not only for streams, but also for men in gray. He remembered the warning the troops had received about not straying too far from the columns. Wheeler's Confederate cavalry, or sometimes Rebel guerrillas, often took isolated stragglers as prisoners—or killed them.

When Rufus got back to camp, he found Tom sitting by a blazing fire, waiting for the water to arrive so he could boil sweet potatoes and corn for their dinner. A coffee pot and kettle from the pack mule were at his feet. By the time Rufus had fed and watered the mule, the aroma of Tom's coffee wafted on the air. Sharing all duties, the messmates worked as a team, with each man doing his job.

"That smells good." Rufus sniffed the air. "Especially the coffee."

"Where did ya find the water?" Tom asked. "It didn't take ya long to get it." Tom knew it was dangerous to go into the countryside.

"I was fortunate," Rufus answered. "I found a flowin' brook not too far from that knoll. That's why it didn't take me long."

Both men unrolled their ponchos and took out their eating utensils. Each unhooked his tin cup from his waist and filled it with steaming coffee. Tom sweetened his with sugar he took out of his knapsack, but Rufus drank his black.

Tom took a sip from his steaming cup. "The potatoes will soon be done," he said. "I cut them up smaller so they would cook faster. After they're done, I'll drop the corn in. The corn won't take but a minute."

"I suppose when Joey and the foragers get back, we'll have meat with our potatoes," Rufus said hopefully.

"Yeah, I think so. I wonder how Joey is doin'." Tom stood up to serve the potatoes. He then dropped two ears of corn into the boiling water.

"I keep prayin' Joey is okay. I'm a little worried about him," Rufus confessed.

"Yeah, me too."

They bowed their heads and said the blessing before eating their dinner.

After their meal, each man cleaned his own dishes, wrapped his utensils back in his poncho, and hung the cup back on his belt. Rufus cleaned the coffee pot and kettle before putting them back on the company pack mule. He wrapped up the coffee grounds and stored them in his knapsack, to be used again at supper. Both buckets still contained a fair amount of water. After refilling their canteens, they emptied what was left on the campfire to put it safely out.

Mealtime over, Captain Roe rode down the column, ordering the soldiers to fall in and begin marching again. All along the unit, the other groups of messmates quickly extinguished what was left of their campfires and lined up.

Rufus and Tom, each throwing his packed poncho over one shoulder and his rifle over the other, joined the soldiers in line. They needed to get back to demolishing the railroad as they resumed their march. The column moved out, hoping to reach General Sherman's goal of fifteen miles a day.

At Decatur, the Twentieth Corps and the Fourteenth Corps took separate roads to later rendezvous at Georgia's capital, Milledgeville. The Twentieth moved northeast to Madison and then south through Eatonton. The Fourteenth Corps took a more direct route to the capital, continuing their march through Decatur until they received orders to bivouac a few miles beyond the town, near Lithonia. They had covered ten miles that day.

Wagons were parked along the road where the troops were to set up their camp, but the wagons contained only the small amount of food brought back by foragers. Messmates gathered what they could find for their supper that night and for their breakfast in the morning.

Joey stood next to the wagons, looking rather solemn. Both Rufus and Tom felt relieved to see him back safely.

"Hi, Joey, how'd it go?" Rufus called.

"Okay, I guess." Together they picked out food for their supper and breakfast.

Each messmate did his part in preparing for the evening meal and the night. Rufus again took two buckets. "I better fetch water so ya can wash your face, Tom. It's all black."

"Yeah, I guess it is, if it looks anythin' like yours, Rufus." Tom and Joey burst out laughing. The pinewood ties burned like pitch, with the smoke blackening the faces and hands of the soldiers as they tore up the rails, the most difficult job of all.

Rufus went in search of water, thankful for the remaining daylight. Tom started plucking a chicken to roast for their supper, while Joey took their fly tents and buttoned two of them together to make one larger tent. He then found stakes for the tent and pine needles for their beds; their knapsacks would serve as pillows. Each man had a blanket of his own. Joey set up the combined tent so it would face the campfire, hanging the third tent over the open end to keep out mosquitoes and other bugs.

Rufus, Tom, and Joey relished a tasty supper of roasted chicken, sweet potatoes, and corn, and their favorite beverage, coffee. Then they cleaned up their utensils and sat around the campfire a moment, wishing they had time to enjoy their devotions. But the soldiers assigned to destroy tracks would work late into the night tearing up the Augusta railroad, and Rufus and Tom needed to join them.

"Wow, look at all the bonfires!" Joey exclaimed, as he stared at the many small pockets of flames that were visible for miles. "Is that all rail ties burnin'?"

"Yeah, it is," Rufus answered. "Tom and I have been doin' that all day. You remember how we did the same thing between Kingston and Atlanta?"

"I sure do. I ain't forgot that. We laid the middle of the iron rails across the fire until they were heated enough to bend. Then we picked 'em up at both ends and wrapped them around a telegraph pole or a tree."

"That's right," added Tom. "Hard work, but I believe it's necessary."

Rufus nodded. "I do, too."

"So do I," piped up Joey. He laughed. "We called the bent pieces of rail 'Sherman's neckties.'"

Rufus was glad to hear Joey laugh. He had been quite solemn since getting back from foraging today. Rufus wondered why.

Changing the subject, he asked, "What do ya think of Stone Mountain, Joey?"

The mountain was visible from their camp; it was a gray, granite mass silhouetted against the night sky. The bonfires set by the soldiers illuminated its lofty features.

"Oh! That sure's some sight. The fellas was talkin' about it. It's all gran . . . gran . . . granite they said. Is that so?"

"That's what they claim," replied Rufus. "It's a mass of granite. We know it's a very special mountain."

"You'll have much to tell your ma about, Joey," Tom told him.

Rufus and Tom stood up to go.

"I'm sorry, but Tom and I have to get back to work."

Rufus bent over and ruffled Joey's red hair as he walked by. "We're under orders to destroy the tracks up to a certain point tonight," Rufus explained. "Then tomorrow we'll start from that point. See ya in the mornin'."

The regiment was forced to continue its work by the light of the bonfires and lanterns. The moon helped illuminate the scene, but kept hiding behind the clouds. Not until the wee hours of the morning did Rufus and Tom return to camp. They crawled into the tent where Joey lay sleeping. Rufus smiled to himself, as did Tom, at what they saw. Joey had taken Rufus's and Tom's ponchos and laid them over the pine needles, with each one's blanket folded at the foot, and had put their knapsacks down for pillows. Their young messmate had made their beds ready for occupancy. Thankful for Joey's thoughtfulness, both men lay down fully clothed and immediately fell asleep from exhaustion.

November 17, 1864
Weather: Fair

Reveille sounded at 6:00 a.m., and Rufus, Tom, and Joey jumped out of bed. Each man hurried to do his chore: Rufus went for water, Tom built a fire for making breakfast, and Joey packed up the tent.

In a short time the three of them sat on the ground, eating their early morning meal.

"How'd ya like foragin', Joey?" Rufus inquired. "I didn't get a chance to ask ya yesterday."

"I . . . wanted to talk to ya about that. I guess I'm not a good forager." Joey's face looked solemn, as he kept his eyes on his plate.

"Why do ya say that?" Tom asked. "What happened?"

"Well, we came to this farm where they were really poor. I mean really poor—the poorest people I ever seen. I just couldn't take anythin' from 'em. I told one of the other men about how I felt, and he said I wasn't a good forager. Was I wrong?"

"Ya did right, Joey. Ya aren't supposed to take from the real poor, unless ya can leave enough for their need," Rufus told him.

"That's right," Tom joined in. "Ya did what was right."

Joey's freckled face broke into a wide grin. It made him happy to know Rufus and Tom thought he had done right.

After their quick breakfast, they gathered their belongings. Before Joey left to go forage, they stood in a circle and repeated the Twenty-third Psalm together.

> The Lord is my shepherd; I shall not want.
> He maketh me to lie down in green pastures:
>   he leadeth me beside the still waters.
>
> He restoreth my soul: he leadeth me
>   in the paths of righteousness
>   for his name's sake.
>
> Yea, though I walk through the valley
>   of the shadow of death,
> I will fear no evil: for thou are with me;
>   thy rod and thy staff they comfort me.
>
> Thou preparest a table before me
>   in the presence of mine enemies:
> Thou anointest my head with oil;
>   my cup runneth over.
>
> Surely goodness and mercy shall follow me
>   all the days of my life:
> And I will dwell in the house of the Lord forever.

They concluded, "Amen."

"Do what ya think God would want ya to do, Joey," Rufus told him.

"I will, Rufus," he promised.

"And be careful," Tom cautioned. "Take care of yourself."

"I will, Tom. Goodbye."

"Goodbye, Joey," Rufus and Tom answered.

Shortly after Joey left, they received the call to assembly, where the adjutant would read their marching orders and any other instructions. The order of march changed every day; regiments, brigades, and divisions all rotated within the corps.

Rufus and Tom smiled knowingly at each other when the adjutant read the order that put their First Division at the front of the column today. They already knew their regiment had received orders the night before to continue the work of destroying the tracks this morning.

Marched 7:00 a.m.

After dismissal, the troops marched to the work that awaited them. The officer in charge gave Rufus the job of helping to dig up the ties and then carrying them over to the fire. The grueling, slow labor was not made easier by the heat of the flames.

Rufus had just finished laying a load of ties on the fire when he heard a voice behind him and felt a hand on his shoulder.

"Good job, private. We need to keep these fires hot."

Rufus turned around to look into the fatigued face of General Sherman, who was standing with his cigar in his right hand. "I'm really interested in the destruction of this railroad. I feel it's really necessary to our cause," the General explained.

"So do I, sir," Rufus agreed, saluting.

The general's eyes brightened. It pleased him that Rufus understood, and didn't just obey orders blindly.

"What is your name, private?"

"Rufus Seaman, sir."

"Is everything going all right with you, Rufus?"

"Yes, sir, only I would like a letter from home."

"So would I, Rufus. I'm counting the days until we hear from home again. Are you married? Do you have children?"

"Yes, sir, I have a wife and two daughters."

"I see. I understand how you feel. I haven't seen my own wife for nearly a year, and we've had a baby boy born since I left. I really want to see him."

"I understand, sir."

"But remember, we'll probably get more than one letter when we do hear again."

"I hope so, sir."

"Keep up the good work, Rufus. I hope to see you again."

The general nodded, put his cigar back in his mouth, and turned and walked away. Rufus watched him leave—a scruffy-looking man in a slouch hat, making his way among the troops, encouraging each one as he passed by. So much responsibility lay on his shoulders. Rufus knew now why General Sherman's men all loved him. Uncle Billy would just as soon stop and talk with a private as with an officer. He cared about all his soldiers.

With the good weather, all went well. The First Division had the advance. Starting through Lithonia, a town with a population of about three hundred, they marched twenty miles to Conyers, helping to destroy three miles of the Augusta railroad along their route. Now, in the late afternoon, they pulled over to bivouac.

"There's Joey!" cried Rufus. Tom and he were walking along the columns, seeking their young messmate. They found him standing next to the foragers' wagon, waiting for them to come by. Another trooper a little older than Joey waited with him.

"Hey Rufus, Tom, over here," Joey called, waving to them. All three were happy to be united again. Rufus and Tom always felt relieved when they saw Joey safely back.

"I'd like ya to meet my friend," Joey told them. "This here's Simon Foster. He's a forager, too." All three men shook hands as Joey presented his new friend.

Acknowledging the introduction, Rufus and Tom said, "We're happy to meet ya, Simon."

"I wonder if Simon could be one of our messmates?" inquired Joey. "Many of the troops have four messmates. Simon could share a tent with me, and ya would have more room in your tent that way."

Rufus and Tom had to admit that having three in their tent made it crowded.

"It's fine with us, if it's all right with Simon." Rufus knew Simon must be someone who did not use profanity; else Joey would not have invited him to be a messmate. Bad language was something all three detested. "Don't ya have your own messmates, Simon?" Rufus asked, for he didn't want to separate messmates who got along well.

"Yeah, but I really don't have much in common with 'em," Simon replied.

"Then welcome aboard, Simon," Rufus said, and gave him a big smile. "Where shall we pitch our tents for tonight?"

"Right over there," Tom suggested, pointing to a vacant area large enough for two tents. Situated among the pines, it would make a great campsite.

Early that evening, with tents pitched and supper over, the four sat around their flickering campfire. The scent of pine knots permeated the clear night air. Hundreds of such campsites dotted acres of Georgia's knolls and valleys. Different sounds drifted from these sites: Northern voices hashed over the day's march; raucous laughter bellowed out over card games; singing accompanied harmonicas. Cursing peppered the language everywhere as, sadly, many of the men could not speak one sentence without using profanity.

"Where in Michigan are ya from, Simon?" asked Rufus. "Were ya a farmer, like most of us?"

"I'm from near Breedsville, a small town northwest of Kalamazoo. I farmed with my Pa before I joined up three years ago."

"Then you're a seasoned veteran, like Tom. Joey and me are new recruits," explained Rufus, playfully tapping Joey on the knee. "Tom has been in the Thirteenth Michigan Regiment for three years, too. You've probably seen each other before."

Tom looked closely at Simon, taking in the details of his appearance. He noted his full head of brown hair, brown eyes, and the beginning of an almost black beard. Most troopers on the march were letting their whiskers grow, including Tom, Rufus, and Joey.

"I can't remember seeing ya before, Simon. Ya don't look familiar to me," Tom remarked. "I guess our paths just never crossed."

Simon laughed. "I think I can explain that. Most of the time I was assigned to the Pioneer Brigade."

"Pioneer Brigade? What's that?" Joey wanted to know.

"I've heard about 'em. They're a brigade made up of handpicked soldiers with special construction skills," Tom answered. "They build roads, bridges, railways, forts, and supply depots for the army. You can be mighty proud you were picked, Simon."

Simon kept his eyes averted, feeling ill at ease over the praise and attention.

Tom noticed his discomfort and changed the subject by bringing out his pocket Bible. "We didn't have a chance to hold devotions last night like we planned to do on the march. Does anyone have a favorite chapter he'd like to read tonight?"

No one spoke at first. "I'll read Romans 8, if that's all right," Rufus offered. "It's one of my favorites."

"I think that's a favorite with everyone," Tom commented, handing the Bible to Rufus.

Rufus finished reading the chapter and looked up. "I'm fond of this whole chapter, but two or three verses really speak to me and bring me much comfort. One of 'em is verse 28: 'And we know that all things work together for good to them that love God, to them who are the called according to his purpose.'

"I feel this is true in my own life. I believe God allowed me to be drafted for it to work for my good. Since bein' in the army, I've drawn much closer to him because of my need for him. My wife and I had a very close walk with God once, but because of circumstances, our relationship to him gradually grew colder. Even though we still loved God very much, we had lost our first love for him and our joy. Now I have 'em back, and I thank God for it. There's no price too great to pay to be right with God. I pray I'll never be out of fellowship with him again."

"Rufus, all I can add to that is, Amen," Tom told him. Joey and Simon nodded their heads in agreement.

"I think we'd better pray before they sound taps," suggested Rufus. He looked at Simon. "We pray for our families and any needs we might have. You may join us if you feel comfortable, or we'd be happy to include your family in our prayers."

"I'd like to join ya," answered Simon. "I especially want to pray for my brother Jonathon, who is also in the Union Army. He's in the Nineteenth Michigan Regiment, Company G, and must be somewhere here with the Twentieth Corps."

"That's wonderful. Joey prays for his ma and for his three brothers in the Union Army. Tom prays for his family back home, as well as for his cousin in the Confederate Army and for his cousin's family in Rome, Georgia. I pray for my wife and daughters back home in Casnovia, Michigan."

The four troopers bowed their heads and took turns praying for their own families and for the families of one another. They also asked God for wisdom and health for General Sherman and for the war to be ended.

Taps sounded just as they said their last "Amen."

9

Covington
First Sight of Slaves ~ Heavy Weather ~ Sparing the Poor

November 18, 1864
Weather: Fair

Marched 6:00 a.m.

All columns moved out together, the First Division still marching in the advance. The troops enjoyed perfect weather and excellent roads. They were delayed at Yellow River as they waited for a herd of cattle to cross safely. Caution was necessary, since cows might become nervous and panic as they walked on the pontoon bridge.

After crossing the river, the columns continued toward Covington, a beautiful village nestled in a vicinity known for large plantations. Entering Covington, the soldiers closed ranks and unfurled their flags. Their bands played patriotic songs as Sherman's army proudly marched down the street. White people boldly came out on the porches of their neat houses to look with scorn on the hated invaders, but the town's joyous Negroes thought the Day of Jubilee had come. They crowded around General Sherman's horse, shouting and praying with ecstasy, referring to the general as the "Angel of the Lord."

While at Covington, Rufus's regiment, along with other units, went back to work on the destruction of the railroad, tearing up four more miles of track. After leaving Covington, the columns crossed another river called the Ulcofauhachee. Late in the afternoon the First Division halted to make camp on a tributary of the Yellow River.

They had covered fifteen miles that day.

The day's march completed, Rufus and Tom soon located Joey and Simon waiting for them by the forage wagons. Foragers left on foot early in the morning, often before daybreak, and traveled five or six miles ahead of their brigade. They worked in groups of fifty, supervised by two mounted officers who had been briefed about the day's route and who thus could eventually guide the foragers back to their lines. They usually returned with a confiscated mule or horse pulling a seized wagon or carriage loaded with food of every kind. Typically, they joined the main road ahead of their train.

After picking their campsite, each messmate performed his usual chores. Rufus took the buckets to fetch water, and Tom built a fire to start supper, while Joey and Simon pitched the two tents.

When Rufus returned with the pails filled, Tom quickly got up to make a pot of coffee before the two of them scrubbed the black, smoky pitch off their faces and arms. Once they were fairly clean, they joined Joey and Simon already sitting by the fire, waiting for supper to be ready.

"How'd it go?" Rufus asked them. "It looked like ya found a lot more forage this trip." Today they had brought back enough food to fully load the wagons.

"We did find a lot more food. Ya should just see the big houses and farms," Joey exclaimed. He lowered his voice. "We seen some slaves, too. I . . . I never seen 'em before."

"Ya must've been on some plantations. They'd have slaves." Tom rose to serve the fried ham and roasted sweet potatoes he had prepared, along with the coffee. After he had prayed the blessing, all four dug in with ferocious appetites.

Supper over and utensils cleaned, the four of them helped themselves to a second mug of coffee before sitting back down by the fire. The hum of male voices could be heard around the campfires tonight. Sherman's troops had first encountered Negro slaves on today's march.

"How'd ya feel about the slaves, Joey?" Rufus asked him.

"I felt real sorry for 'em. I saw this one man that had scars all across his back. He'd been whipped!"

Rufus and Tom exchanged looks. "That's horrible!" Tom spoke with disgust, and Rufus nodded his head in agreement.

"Did ya see the man with the scarred back, too, Simon?" Rufus inquired.

"No, I didn't. I visited a different plantation than Joey. I saw slaves, but only at a distance. But I still felt sorry for 'em," answered Simon.

"The slaves I saw today blessed me," Rufus confessed. "As we were marchin' through Covington, they ran out into the street, singin' and prayin'. They prayed like someone who had a close relationship with God. Their faith inspired me."

"I was impressed by 'em, too," Tom admitted.

"I wonder who told 'em about Jesus," Rufus mused. "Their spirits were so free."

"When you speak of their spirits being free," Tom said, "I'm reminded of 2 Corinthians 3:17." He then quoted that verse: "Now the Lord is that Spirit: and where the Spirit of the Lord is, there is liberty."

"I like that verse, Tom. It's a shame the Negroes are slaves, and against their will. But many people are slaves by their own choice. They're slaves to sin," Rufus pointed out.

"Yeah, Rufus, and that is the worst slavery of all," Tom hastened to say, "because then Satan is your master."

"That's why we all need the Spirit of the Lord and to know Jesus as our Savior," declared Rufus.

"We need ta be Jesus' slaves," Joey blurted out, with Simon agreeing.

"You're right, Joey and Simon. We do need to be His slaves."

"Now, I think it's time for us to pray for our families," Rufus suggested, bowing his head. All agreed, and each reverently prayed a special prayer for his loved ones.

Their prayers finished, the bugler blew taps. All four stood up, and Tom added more wood to the fire. They bade each other good night as they lay on their bed of pine needles. Reveille would come early.

November 19, 1864
Weather: Rain

When reveille sounded, Rufus awakened in the dark to hear raindrops beating on the side of his fly tent. He knew what that meant for the march—mud. All four messmates responded to the call without delay. They grabbed their ponchos, slipped them over their heads, and donned slouch hats to fend off the rain. Without grumbling, each one set to work at his specific chore. At the break of dawn, and with breakfast over, Joey and Simon left with the other foragers. Now that the rain forced the soldiers to wear their ponchos, they wrapped their belongings in their blankets, which they threw over their shoulders.

Marched 6:00 a.m.

Rufus and Tom joined the ranks of their First Division, now following the Second Division, which had obtained the advance. From Covington, the Fourteenth Corps turned right toward Milledgeville, where they would rendezvous with the Twentieth Corps. The columns marched through a windblown rain down the ridge between Little River and Murder Creek, covering fifteen miles despite the weather and mud.

At day's end, they stopped to bivouac near Newborn, a small, nondescript village of three hundred citizens. The Second Division would halt to camp first, while the First Division marched beyond them and camped farther down the road.

When they came to the forage wagons, Rufus and Tom didn't immediately see Joey and Simon. "Here we are—under here," Joey called. The two sat hunched beneath one of the wagons, trying to keep out of the rain. They held a day's ration of food in their arms.

"It's nice that you're waitin' for us with food, but we have to march past the Second Division before we can make camp," Rufus explained.

Joey and Simon fell in beside Rufus and Tom, and the four of them soon arrived at the place where the First Division would spend the night. Joey and Simon chose a campsite on a knoll, hoping it would give some protection from flooding. Rufus left to get water, as usual, while Tom searched for wood dry enough to burn. Locating some, he shortly had a fire blazing and supper started. Joey and Simon pitched both tents as close to the fire as would be safe. They all crawled inside to eat their supper.

After finishing their meal, the four lay in the opening of their tents, soaking up the flickering fire's warmth.

"Did ya get a lot of forage today?" Rufus asked. "We heard that many of the Negro slaves have attached themselves to our column. Since Covington they've been followin' us. The concern is how to feed 'em."

"We didn't know that," Simon answered, "but we did get a lot of forage."

"I really feel sorry for those slaves. There are women and children with 'em," added Rufus.

The cold rain continued to blow in their faces; combined with the mud, it had made today's march extremely difficult. The troops came into camp with their boots and clothing soaked. They couldn't take their boots off for fear they would shrink overnight, making them too small to put on in the morning. No one had a change of clothing.

"Maybe we should pray for our families and go to bed," Tom stated.

Their prayers over, all four fell asleep before taps sounded, as did most of the camp on this rainy night.

November 20
Weather: Rain, foggy and cold

Reveille sounded before dawn. Joey and Simon left right after breakfast. Rufus watched them walk off together to join their band of foragers and noticed the camaraderie the two of them shared. Simon made a fine friend for Joey, and it pleased Rufus.

Marched 6:00 a.m.

The Second Division was still in the advance, with the First Division marching behind them and the Third Division in the rear. The columns marched fifteen miles through a cold, nasty day. At 3:00 p.m. Sherman stopped to bivouac at Eatonton Factory on the Little River.

After Rufus and Tom met up with Joey and Simon by the forage wagons, they soon had their campsite picked and set up. The four sat around a blazing fire of pinewood, trying to get warm. They put some stakes in the ground near the fire and stretched their blankets between them, hoping to get them dry.

"Ain't that a fire over there?" asked Joey.

"Yeah, it is. They're burnin' the factory," replied Tom.

"When I went to fetch the water, I heard some soldiers talkin' about runnin' the mill," Rufus commented. "They spoke as though they were gonna run it all night."

"Are there still Negro slaves followin' the columns?" asked Simon.

"Yeah, more join all the time," Rufus replied. "Some of the troops told today how Sherman paused at a plantation around noon, where some slaves told how their master whipped 'em with saw blades and with paddles with holes cut in 'em. They said their master would then actually rub salt in their wounds. The troops said Sherman got real mad."

"What'd he say to their master?" asked Simon.

"Their master wasn't home right then. Supposedly he had gone to Milledgeville to help with the resistance there," Rufus answered. "General Sherman continually reminds the slaves they aren't to hurt their masters or their families. I can see now why they might want to."

As usual, after supper they held their nightly devotions by the light of the fire.

"Anyone have a scripture he wants to share?" Tom asked.

Joey spoke up. "A Bible verse I know is John 3:16. Ma was always quotin' it to me: 'For God so loved the world that he gave his only begotten Son, that whosoever believeth in him should not perish, but have everlasting life.' That's the only Bible verse I know by heart."

"That's a good scripture to know," Rufus answered. "Your ma wanted you to know the Lord. I'm sure she'll be really happy and proud that you wrote her and told her you accepted Jesus as your Savior."

"Yeah, I know she will."

A cloud passed over Rufus's face. "I wish I could write my family again, but for now we can at least keep prayin' for our loved ones."

"Anyone have anythin' to add?" Tom inquired, as he glanced around the fire at each face. "Simon?"

"I couldn't help but think of my own ma when Joey talked about his ma quotin' John 3:16. My ma did the same thing."

"That must've been a verse many mothers used," agreed Tom.

When they remembered their families in prayer, each one prayed in a special way for his mother.

November 21
Weather: Rain

Marched 6:00 a.m.

The Second Division still marched in the advance, followed by the Third Division, but now the First Division brought up the rear. The First Division commander, Brigadier General C. C. Walcott, positioned the wagon train three-fourths of the way back in the column. Troops marching in the rear of their division drew train-guard duty. Today this included Rufus and Tom. After marching at the front of the columns, tearing up railroads, they now received an assignment to proceed to the wagon trains. Train guards not only protected those wagons, but also pulled them out of the mud in order to keep them moving. Most soldiers hated train-guard duty, preferring to march toward the front of the column, where they could make camp earlier and get first chance at the forage wagons. Soldiers in the rear might not make camp until 11:00 p.m., when those ahead of them had already taken most of the forage.

The columns traveled down the west bank of Little River on Milledgeville Road. Tramping in the cold rain, the troops wallowed their way through Georgia's wet red clay. The weather delayed them often, as wagon wheels repeatedly got mired in the clay. Train guards worked tirelessly, putting their shoulders to the wagons, pushing them out of the deep mud holes.

Some of the teamsters cursed and whipped their horses and mules to get them to pull. It made Rufus angry to see the animals abused that way. One teamster in particular, a burly-looking bearded man, didn't know how to handle or care for his team. His horses had tails and manes caked with mud from a lack of currying. Looking more closely, Rufus recognized the Morgans he had admired in Atlanta, the very team he had wanted to drive. The horses became skittish when their teamster started cursing them again in a raspy, angry tone. As he raised his whip to lash them, Rufus couldn't take it.

"No! Don't do it that way," he shouted to the driver. "Gentle 'em."

The teamster stopped and looked up in surprise with his piercing, steely eyes.

"Gentle 'em? I don't know what ya mean. Suppose ya show me," he challenged Rufus with a sneer, as he spit out a stream of tobacco juice.

Rufus accepted the challenge. He jumped up on the wagon seat and picked up the lines. Gently he flipped them over the horses' backs, never yanking on the bits in their mouths. He spoke to them in a soft voice, calming them down as he coaxed them forward. To the amazement of the watching teamster, the Morgans actually pulled the wagon out of the mud. Rufus then jumped down and handed the team back to their driver.

"I'll try to drive 'em that way from now on," he sheepishly promised.

Rufus smiled, slapped him on the back, and walked away.

After the Second Division had covered twelve miles in the advance, General Davis ordered the Fourteenth Corps column to camp. The First Division, bringing up the rear, kept on marching until they had moved beyond where the Third and Second Divisions had bivouacked. Continuing long after nightfall, they passed hundreds of the two divisions' campsites made visible by their inviting fires.

Onward they marched in the rain, until the officers at the front of their columns could find a suitable vacant area for the First Division to halt for the night. Rufus and Tom continued their work of pushing the wagons along.

When at last the officers in charge had picked a field for the First Division's camp, Rufus and Tom noticed forage wagons parked beside the road. They looked for Joey and Simon, but didn't see them.

"I wonder where they are," asked Rufus.

"I don't know," replied Tom. "The forage wagons are empty. I guess this is what happens when you're last in line. Ya don't eat."

Still wondering where Joey and Simon could be, Rufus and Tom entered the field, looking around for a good campsite. Many pine fires burned already.

"Rufus! Tom! Over here," someone called to them.

They looked in the direction of the familiar voice to see two smiling faces. Joey and Simon motioned for them to come over to where they had a campfire going and their fly tent already pitched. Beside them on the ground lay a sizeable amount of forage. In order to watch for Rufus and Tom, they had positioned their campsite near the road.

"We was through early, so we marched to where we thought you'd be stoppin' tonight and settin' up this campsite," explained Joey.

"We also took a share of the forage before it was gone," added Simon. "There was a lot of it today."

"It's wonderful that ya did this," Rufus told them. "We thought we'd go hungry tonight when we saw the forage wagons empty."

Being late to set up camp, they didn't have time to do more than prepare a quick bite of supper and pitch the other fly tent. They bowed their heads for a few minutes of prayer together before a welcome taps sounded.

November 22
Weather: Cold and windy

Marched 6:00 a.m.

The Third and First Divisions now passed the Second Division, with the Third Division marching in the advance. The Second Division, camped on Cedar Creek, would march in the rear tomorrow.

The weather turned cold and windy overnight. A heavy frost had covered the ground by morning. With no rain, the roads had improved somewhat, but remained difficult for marching. Rufus and Tom still drew duty as train guards. By 4:00 p.m. they had covered twelve miles. General Sherman, riding ahead of the advanced division, halted to bivouac. General Davis stopped his lead column on a ridge where a high, raw wind blew. He chose this cold position partly because of nearby wood and water. General Sherman asked him to allow his rear division to move ahead to a valley farther on, where it would be warmer. That night they camped ten miles from Milledgeville.

Joey and Simon once again waited for Rufus and Tom to march past and joined them when they appeared. The four picked a campsite in the valley, away from the cold wind.

"Brrr, it's cold! I'll get a fire goin' right away." Tom said, and started to gather pinewood in his arms.

"Simon and I'll pitch the tents so they face the fire again. It'll be warmer that way," Joey decided.

Rufus grabbed the buckets off the pack mule. "I'll see if I can find water close by. A cup of coffee sure would taste good." He went over the knoll, crossed the road, and moved into a grove of pine trees, searching for a stream. Walking along, he thought he heard children's voices and stopped to listen. The voices came from the other side of the grove.

Even though he knew it could be dangerous to get too close, he wanted to see the children. Slowly he made his way out from the trees. On the other side, in the clearing, lay a small, run-down farm whose gray, weather-beaten buildings needed painting. In the yard he saw two shabbily dressed children. The tow-headed little boy, around ten, was trying to chop wood, but he didn't have the strength or the size to swing the axe. The little girl, about eight, ran around barefoot, playing with a ball.

Near the back porch, Rufus saw a pump, a good place to get his water. When the children looked up to see him approaching, they ran into the house. Sorry he had frightened them, he decided he'd pump his water and leave as fast as possible, but while pumping, he noticed the pile of wood that needed to be split, and that no smoke was coming from their chimney. They needed a fire in their cookstove on a cold day like today. The father must be away in the Confederate Army. His mind went to Sarah and his own children on a farm in Michigan—alone, just like this family.

After he had pumped the water, he walked over to where the little boy had left the axe. Rufus hurriedly chopped up a large stack of wood. Laying the axe down, he picked up his buckets of water and started to walk away. After a couple steps, he heard the door off the porch open a crack.

"Thanks, Yank," said a woman's voice with a Southern accent.

"You're welcome, ma'am. Thanks for the water. God bless," Rufus answered.

"You're welcome, and God bless you, Yank." The door gently shut.

Back in camp after eating their supper, Rufus and his messmates gathered around the fire. Hot coffee in his hand, Rufus told them about his experience at the farm.

"I'm sorry I was late gettin' back with the water," he apologized.

"That's all right, we just want ya to be safe," answered Tom. "I was startin' to be a little concerned about ya."

"This family reminded me of Sarah and my little girls—all alone on a farm with their men in the army. I wanted to help 'em as much as I could. They seemed so poor. The little girl didn't even have shoes on her feet in this cold weather. And the little boy had outgrown his pants."

"I understand how ya felt," Tom replied. "I think we all feel especially sorry for the children."

"I'm concerned about this family in the mornin', when the foragers take off," Rufus added. "They're too poor to have any extra food."

"I know what we can do," said Simon. "Joey and I could go there first, but not really take anythin'. The other foragers will then go on to someplace else, thinkin' we have this farm. They don't really care for small places that much anyway."

"Yeah, Simon! We can do that!" Joey exclaimed.

"Thanks, fellas. I'm really happy you're willin' to spare that family." With that assurance, Rufus felt so much better.

Before praying together, they shared stories about their own homes and families.

Exhausted, they turned in early. All four crawled into bed and fell asleep, never hearing the nightly bugle.

10

Milledgeville
Thanksgiving Day ~ Losing a Comrade

November 23
Weather: Clear, but cold

Marched 6:00 a.m.

The Third Division marched in the advance, followed by the First Division. The Second Division had the rear position, where the First Division's wagon trains caused delays most of the day. Because of those delays, General Sherman and his staff left the First and Second Divisions behind and rode straight to Milledgeville. They entered the capital city that morning with bands playing and their flags proudly fluttering in the cold breeze. The Third Division marched with dignity down the street behind the bands. The Twentieth Corps of the left wing had just preceded them into the city.

Even with the delays, the First and Second Divisions had managed by evening to march ten miles before halting to bivouac. They camped on the outskirts near Milledgeville, thereby uniting the left wing virtually within sight of Georgia's capital.

As evening fell, the four messmates sat around their campfire once again. Each looked forward to this time when they could talk over the daily news.

"How did it go at the little farm this mornin'?" Rufus asked Joey and Simon.

Both their faces lit up with wide grins. Rufus could tell they were pleased with themselves.

"We did what we said we'd do. We got there first, and the other foragers went on by and left us alone," answered Joey.

"We also helped 'em hide what little food they had," Simon added. "The woman livin' there was a nice lady and really thanked us. She asked us if the kind Union soldier had sent us. We said ya had, and explained to her how ya have a wife and children alone on a farm back home. Her eyes got kind of misty."

"I want to thank both of ya," Rufus told them. "It was very carin' and thoughtful of ya both."

"We were glad to do it," they replied.

"We didn't want their food taken, either," Joey continued. "After all, tomorrow is Thanksgivin'. We found some food for us off one of the wagons."

"I heard some news today about General Kilpatrick's cavalry," Tom informed them. "It seems they had quite a fight with General Wheeler's troops at Lovejoy, where General Kilpatrick whipped 'em." Kilpatrick's mounted troops protected the columns from Wheeler's cavalry, and they skirmished with one another many times.

"Tomorrow the First Division marches in the advance," Tom reminded them. "We're gonna proceed through Milledgeville, where we'll join our other forces to continue the journey to the sea."

"That's right," Rufus agreed, looking at Joey and Simon. "Captain Roe was tellin' Tom and me about it. He said General Sherman rode into the capital this mornin'. That's where he is now."

"Was there any resistance?" asked Simon.

"No, not at all. He said most of the citizens stayed in the city. Only Governor Brown, state officials, and the legislature fled the capital," replied Tom. "In fact, General Sherman is stayin' in the governor's mansion."

"What did the town's residents do?" Simon wanted to know.

"Captain Roe said no white people could be seen, but his men were given a warm welcome by the Negro slaves. He told us the sidewalks were crowded with 'em," Tom replied.

"How large is Milledgeville?" Joey asked.

"They say the population is around two thousand," Rufus answered.

Tom took his worn Bible from his pocket. "Anyone have a favorite verse he'd like to read tonight?" he asked. "I think we have time."

"Well, another favorite of mine is Matthew 6:33: 'But seek ye first the kingdom of God, and his righteousness; and all these things shall be added unto you.'" Rufus didn't need to read the verse; he had it memorized.

"That is a good verse. It's a verse to live by," Tom pointed out. "The key word, I think, is 'seek.' We must really seek the kingdom of God and his righteousness with all our hearts. Never stop seekin'."

"That's right," Rufus hastened to say.

Joey and Simon nodded.

They had just finished praying for their families when taps sounded.

November 24
Weather: Fair
Thanksgiving Day

Marched 10:00 a.m.

Leaving their encampment just short of Milledgeville, the First Division marched in the advance through the city, followed by the Second Division.

Proceeding down Green Street in the middle of the town, the soldiers could see provost guards stationed everywhere to protect the dwellings. Because of those guards, little burning took place. Structures burned in accordance with orders included the arsenal, penitentiary, railroad depot, and bridge. The Union troops spared many fine-looking buildings, such as the state capitol.

After resting a day, General Sherman now renewed the march, riding in front of his troops as they vacated the capital city. Sherman himself accompanied the Twentieth Corps traveling by the Southern Road, while the Fourteenth Corps took the Upper Road.

Moving out of the Milledgeville area, the Union Army marched east across the wooden toll bridge over the Oconee River, burning the structure after all forces had passed over it. The weather was beautiful, with a bright, blue sky. Steep hills near the Oconee proved difficult to climb, but once over them, the soldiers had better marching on more-level sandy roads. Pine trees grew densely on both sides of the roadway. The army also encountered several large farms where the land had been cleared and produced bountiful crops.

Late that afternoon the army halted and camped eight miles east of Milledgeville.

Rufus and Tom found Joey and Simon waiting for them by the forage wagons, as usual.

"Look at all the forage you boys have," remarked Rufus, eyeing the food lying at their feet.

"Yeah, it's Thanksgivin', ain't it?" asked Joey. Joey and Simon chuckled as they picked up their share of the food. The two friends had talked it over earlier and decided they would follow President Lincoln's proclamation and celebrate Thanksgiving.

"Well, bring the food along, and I'll do what I can to see we have a nice Thanksgiving dinner," Tom said amiably.

"Oh, I had forgotten. It *is* Thanksgivin'," replied Rufus, his thoughts suddenly far away with Sarah and his family. He wondered if Sarah would be able to attend church services today. He hoped so.

At the camp, which was set in a grove of fragrant pine trees, each messmate completed his usual task. After Tom had finished preparing a tasty meal, they all sat on the ground around the blazing fire, plates in their hands. The chill in the fall air made the fire welcome. With heads bowed, they went around the circle, as each prayed his own prayer of thanksgiving. They then ate their feast of pork, sweet potatoes, corn, and coffee.

"I'm sure this food tasted good to those poor prisoners," Simon commented.

Tom and Rufus looked at each other. "Prisoners? What prisoners are ya talkin' about?" Tom asked.

"Oh, didn't ya hear about the prisoners? Some of the troops were talkin' about it while we were waitin' for ya at the forage wagons," answered Simon. "They were tellin' how some Union soldiers who had been held prisoner in Andersonville escaped and staggered into our lines. They had traveled over a hundred miles through Rebel territory to make it here. Somehow, they had dug out of the stockade. They were almost dead from starvation."

"I'm glad they made it," Rufus stated. "I'm sure they had a wonderful Thanksgivin' Day."

"Our troops are really angry over the Rebels starvin' the Union prisoners they take. Now that we know Georgia has a bounty of food, they feel it's cruel of 'em to not feed their captives," Simon continued.

"They're right," replied Tom. "I heard General Kilpatrick is gonna' be sent to Millen to try and free our prisoners at Camp Lawton. I hope he's successful."

"So do I," Rufus said as he stood to pour a second cup of coffee for everyone. "We need to include prayer for our prisoners when we pray tonight."

"Yeah, it must be somethin' awful to be a prisoner," Joey commented.

Later that night Tom sat with his Bible in his hand. "I think I'd like to read the Ninety-first Psalm. I feel it's a psalm that gives God's children security. It also comforts and encourages us.

> He that dwelleth in the secret place of the most High
>   shall abide under the shadow of the Almighty.
> I will say of the LORD, He is my refuge and my fortress:
>   my God; in him will I trust.
>
> Surely he shall deliver thee from the snare of the fowler,
>   and from the noisome pestilence.
> He shall cover thee with his feathers, and under his wings
>   shalt thou trust: his truth shall be thy shield and buckler.
>
> Thou shalt not be afraid for the terror by night;
>   nor for the arrow that flieth by day;
>   nor for the pestilence that walketh in darkness;
>   nor for the destruction that wasteth at noonday.
>
> A thousand shall fall at thy side, and ten thousand
>   at thy right hand; but it shall not come nigh thee.
> Only with thine eyes shalt thou behold
>   and see the reward of the wicked.
>
> Because thou hast made the LORD, which is my refuge,
>   even the most High, thy habitation;

There shall no evil befall thee, neither shall any plague
   come nigh thy dwelling.

For he shall give his angels charge over thee,
   to keep thee in all thy ways.
They shall bear thee up in their hands,
   lest thou dash thy foot against a stone.
Thou shalt tread upon the lion and adder: the young lion
   and the dragon shalt thou trample under feet.

Because he hath set his love upon me,
   therefore will I deliver him:
I will set him on high, because
   he hath known my name.

When Tom finished reading the Ninety-first Psalm, he looked up. "What do ya think is the main verse to show us how we can claim the promises of this psalm?" he asked.

Joey looked at his feet for a moment before speaking. "Ain't it that we set our love upon God?" he asked.

"You're right, Joey. We set our love upon him and dwell in the secret place of the Most High," answered Rufus. "We abide in Christ and his word and dwell in God's presence."

"I really like that psalm," Simon told Tom. "I'd like a copy of it."

"I'd be happy to copy it for ya," Tom answered. "Does anyone have paper and pencil?"

"Just a minute, I have some." Rufus rose to look in his knapsack. "Here, I found a couple of sheets and a pencil."

"Tom spent several minutes copying the psalm by the light of the fire. When he was finished, he handed it to Simon, who folded it neatly and put it in his pocket. "Thank ya, Tom, I really appreciate this."

"You're very welcome, Simon. Is everyone ready to pray now?" The four of them spent much time in prayer for their families and the prisoners, concluding just before taps.

November 25
Weather: Fair

Marched 6:00 a.m.

The Second Division now passed the First Division to take the advance. Because Rebel cavalry had burned nine bridges crossing Buffalo Creek, the Fourteenth was forced to delay the march, as they threw over a pontoon bridge on which the troops could cross the narrow, deep stream with its swampy banks. The closer Sherman's army came to Savannah, the more skirmishes occurred between the Confederate cavalry and Federal infantry.

After marching thirteen miles, the divisions received orders to halt and make camp.

When Rufus and Tom continued toward the foragers' wagons, they saw only Joey waiting for them up ahead.

"Hi, Joey, where's Simon?" Rufus called to him.

"I . . . I don't know. We separated as we left this mornin', and I ain't seen him since." Joey's voice trembled as he answered. "He didn't meet us with the other foragers, like he's always done before. We often separate like that, but meet afterwards."

"He'll probably still show up," Tom tried to reassure him.

"I hope so," Joey murmured.

"Let's make camp and wait for him there," suggested Rufus.

"No, I want to wait for him here," Joey firmly insisted.

Rufus put his hand on Joey's shoulder. "That's fine; we'll get the camp set up."

Rufus and Tom picked out a site for their tents in the piney woods. The two of them did their usual chores.

Hiking along in his search for water, Rufus passed other campsites. One trooper, seeing the buckets in his hands, pointed the way to water. "Keep goin' straight, and you'll see a stream on the left," he called to Rufus.

"Thank you," Rufus replied.

Moving in the direction the trooper had indicated, Rufus heard the brook before he saw it. Just up ahead, he noticed Captain Roe's bay horse drinking large gulps of the cool water. The captain stood next to him, holding the reins. As Rufus approached his superior officer, he quickly saluted him.

"Hello, private," Captain Roe said, returning the salute. "If you're looking for water, you've found it."

"Yeah, I'm lookin' for water," Rufus replied.

His horse's thirst quenched, Captain Roe threw the reins over the steed's neck and mounted. Rufus stepped toward him.

"Captain Roe, one of my messmates who's a forager hasn't shown up this afternoon. Have you heard anything about a missing forager?"

A cloud passed over Captain Roe's face. "I'm afraid I have. One of the officers who went out with the foragers this morning says he thinks three of them were captured and taken prisoner. I don't know any of their names or the details. That's all I know. I'm very sorry."

Rufus thanked Captain Roe before the officer rode away. He then filled his buckets in the clear stream.

"How can I tell Joey?" he thought. "Just last night we were talkin' about how terrible it must be to be a prisoner." Numb with sadness, he trudged back to his campsite.

He arrived to find Tom sitting by the fire, cooking supper. Rufus sat down beside him and told what Captain Roe had related about the missing foragers.

Tom shook his head. "How terrible! You've heard the rumors goin' around about what the Rebs have been doin' to our prisoners, haven't ya? They even slit their throats. They did that to two of our prisoners and left them for dead, only they cut too high, so they lived and made it back to our lines."

"Yeah, that's horrible. I heard they've been shootin' our prisoners, too. I think I'd better go and find Joey." Rufus got to his feet. "He needs to be told. Even though they had been together only for a week or so, Simon and he were close friends."

"Yeah, I know they were. It will be hardest for Joey, even though we'll miss Simon, too," Tom answered.

"We'll all miss Simon. I enjoyed him as a messmate." Rufus left.

He found Joey still standing by the foragers' wagon, just as he and Tom had left him.

"Joey," Rufus spoke gently. "Come to our camp."

"No," he spoke in almost a whisper. "I'll keep waitin' here."

"Simon's not comin'." Rufus hated to tell him like this.

"He's not comin'?" Joey asked. "How d'ya know?"

"I saw Captain Roe and asked him if he knew anything about a missin' forager. He said that he heard three foragers were taken prisoner. It looks like Simon must be one of 'em."

Joey looked at the ground, biting his lip. He shoved his hands into his pockets, and with slouched shoulders started shuffling toward their campsite. Rufus didn't say a word, but walked close beside him, pretending not to hear him sniffling.

As they reached the camp, the aroma of coffee greeted them. Rufus poured a mug for Joey, who, deep in thought, sat down to drink his cupful. Finished, he stood.

"Where are your fly tents?" he asked Rufus and Tom. "I'll pitch 'em for ya." His voice sounded strained, but he wanted to do his chore as a messmate. Rufus and Tom passed him their fly tents.

"Ya can put yours over the end," Rufus told him. "We can all sleep together." Joey pitched the tent as Rufus suggested.

Tom fixed a fine supper, but no one had any appetite, especially Joey. Coffee appeared to be all that anyone wanted. Rufus and Tom forced themselves to eat a small portion of the food, but Joey didn't want anything. They saved him some supper and kept the coffee pot hot over the fire for him. Maybe he would eat something later.

"I think we need to pray for Simon," Rufus proposed.

"You're right." Tom took his Bible from his pocket.

"Why?" Joey asked. "Why are ya gonna pray for Simon, when he's dead?"

"Captain Roe didn't say he was dead, Joey. He's been taken prisoner and needs our prayers," Rufus replied.

"It's the same thing. The Rebs kill their prisoners," Joey retorted. "They torture 'em, and they kill 'em."

"Yeah, sometimes they do," agreed Tom. "Although we don't know that he's been killed, we do know he's been taken prisoner and needs our prayers."

"And if he's dead?" Joey wanted to know.

"Then he's safe in the arms of Jesus, Joey," Rufus said softly.

Joey sat almost stunned for a moment. "Yeah, he would be with Jesus, wouldn't he? I mean, if he's dead?"

"That's right, Joey. As a Christian, now is when ya give all your sorrow to God and lean on him," Rufus advised. "Give him the pain you're feelin'—continue to put your trust in him. God knows how ya feel, and he knows where Simon is. Draw close to God. This is not the time to pull away from him," Rufus cautioned, thinking of his own experience.

Joey looked with respect and admiration at Rufus—the person who had led him to the Lord. He knew he would only tell him the truth.

"I know you're right, Rufus. I'm gonna trust God. I'm ready to pray now," Joey replied. "And we'll pray every day for Simon, won't we?" He didn't speak it as a question, but as a statement.

"Yes, we certainly will," Tom assured him.

When taps sounded that night, the full moon fell across a crowded fly tent where three soldiers lay sleeping, side by side—thankful for one another.

11

Sandersville

Skirmishes ~ Picking Up Orphans

November 26
Weather: Foggy

Marched 6:00 a.m.

The Second Division marched in the advance through the fog, followed by the First Division. As the left wing neared Sandersville, they skirmished with Wheeler's cavalry.

The Twentieth Corps chased the Confederates through the town, where Rebel troops fired on them from the second story of the courthouse, as well as from the streets. In the dense fog, the troops found it difficult to distinguish their comrades in blue coats from their enemy in gray. The Fourteenth Corps, entering Sandersville by another route, also encountered skirmishing until Wheeler's troops fled the village.

General Sherman, angry over Rebels using the courthouse as a fortification, ordered it burned, along with the adjoining jail. He spared private dwellings, however, commenting, "I don't war on women and children."

By noon the columns halted to bivouac. They camped on the southeast side of town.

Pleased to be stopping early, Rufus and Tom started looking for Joey among the forage wagons.

"Here I am." Joey sat perched on the side of a wagon, a pile of forage beside him. They helped him carry the food to the bivouac area, where they picked out their campsite. The fog finally lifted to reveal a sunny day.

The camp set up and Rufus back with the water, Tom shortly had dinner ready. After eating, the worn-out trio took long naps for the remainder of the afternoon.

Their evening meal over, they sat around the campfire, discussing the latest news.

"The foragers was talkin' 'bout Captain Belknap and some of his foragers comin' across a couple little girls all alone in a tumbledown log cabin near Sandersville," Joey related. "They was real dirty and hungry. The foragers first fed 'em, then bathed 'em and washed their hair. They tried to find their folks or someone who would take 'em, but no one wanted 'em. They all was too poor to take in more little ones."

"How old were the little girls?" Rufus asked.

"They thought they was about three and five," he replied.

"What did they do with 'em?" Tom asked.

"The foragers kept 'em. They couldn't leave 'em. They're gonna take 'em with 'em to their regiment. They'll take turns carryin' 'em to Savannah. They even stole some clothes for 'em."

"That's kind of the foragers," Rufus remarked, "though it will be a hard task for Captain Belknap to carry 'em so far." Rufus thought of Dorothy and Lucy, and his heart ached for these abandoned little girls.

"Did ya hear that some of our prisoners who escaped from Millen prison made it to our lines?" asked Tom. "They say they were very emaciated, just like the escapees from Andersonville." Tom paused. "We need to pray for Simon."

"Can ya read that part in the Bible Simon liked?" asked Joey.

"You mean Psalm 91?" Tom wanted to know.

"Yeah, that's the one," Joey replied. "I like that one, too."

After Tom had read the Ninety-first Psalm, they spent time praying for their families, Simon, the little girls, and the escaped prisoners.

Taps sounded just before they were finished, but they still went on to give God the burdens that lay on their hearts.

November 27
Weather: Fair

March delayed until 1:00 p.m.

The First Division, ordered to Davisboro, marched in the advance, protecting all trains of the corps. Moving straight toward that destination, they halted to camp outside the town for the night.

As Rufus and Tom marched toward the forage wagons to get their food, they saw Joey waiting up ahead. The foragers, guided by their officers, always managed to come out just ahead of where the columns would bivouac.

"Hey!" Joey called. "Look what I got!" He held up a jar in one hand and a loaf of bread in the other. Coming closer, they could see that Joey clasped a container of peach jam. Rufus frowned when he saw it.

Joey noticed the expression on Rufus's face. "Don't worry. I didn't enter any house and take it. I told ya I don't go in the houses. A woman called me to her back door and gave me the bread and jam. She said, 'A young boy like you should like bread and jam. Most foragers would have come right in and taken it off my table—but you're too nice a boy for that.'"

Joey looked down, feeling a little embarrassed telling them what she had said about him. Rufus put his arm around Joey's shoulder, ashamed that he ever doubted him. "She's right, Joey, ya are too nice to do that."

"And I agree," Tom hastened to add.

"She also said this war shouldn't be fought with children," Joey added.

"She's right again," Rufus told him. "Young boys like ya should still be on the farm." Joey didn't take offense, because he knew Rufus told the truth.

Thick slices of bread slathered with peach jam accompanied their supper that evening.

"Ya know, I could be satisfied with just this bread, jam, and a cup of coffee," commented Tom. "And I'm not a young boy," he laughed, referring to the woman's remark about Joey.

"I'm not young, either," chuckled Rufus, "but I feel the same way."

Joey sat smiling, delighted to see Rufus and Tom enjoying the bread and jam so much.

Later, sitting around the fire with their usual mugs of coffee, the three talked over the events of the day.

"Did ya notice the trees with the hangin' moss?" Tom asked Joey. "Rufus and I saw 'em while we were marchin'."

"Yeah, we sure did," Rufus told Joey. "We marched past some of those trees. Tom pointed 'em out to me. I'd never seen 'em before."

"I saw that, too," answered Joey. "What d'ya call that on the trees?"

"They call it Spanish moss," Tom replied. "My aunt and uncle in Rome told me the folklore about the Spanish moss."

"What's folklore?" asked Joey.

"It's when people tell a story about some happening or event that supposedly occurred at a certain time in the past. It's similar to a fairy tale," answered Tom.

"What's the story about the Spanish moss?" Joey inquired.

"The folklore goes that in the 1700s there was a man who, with his Spanish fiancée, wanted to start a plantation near Charleston, South Carolina. His fiancée was beautiful, with long, raven hair."

"What's raven hair?" Joey asked.

"She had black hair," answered Tom, before continuing the legend.

"One day, as the couple walked over the area where they wanted to have their plantation, they were attacked by Cherokee Indians who did not want to share their land with outsiders. As a warnin' for them to stay away from the Cherokee land, they cut off the dark, long hair of the man's fiancée and threw it up into a nearby live oak tree. As people kept comin' back to look at the tree, they noticed the hair had shriveled and turned gray. It was also spreadin' from tree to tree. Through the years, the moss has spread from South Carolina to Georgia and Florida. And that's the story," Tom concluded, as he leaned back and smiled.

"Wow, is that really true?" asked Joey.

"No," answered Tom. "That's only a tale told about it. But Spanish moss does have its own particular beauty. Only I wouldn't reach my hand into it," Tom warned. "It's been known for rat snakes and bats makin' nests in there."

"The stars are really beautiful tonight." Rufus sighed, studying the sky.

"Can ya see the Big Dipper and Little Dipper?" Joey asked. "I can." He pointed to where he located the Big and Little Dippers, so that Rufus and Tom also could see those constellations.

"How many stars are there?" Joey wondered.

"Only God knows," answered Rufus. "And He even knows their names."

"That's right," agreed Tom. "God's word tells us that." Tom took his Bible out of his pocket and opened to Psalm 147. He read verses 4 and 5.

> He telleth the number of the stars;
> he calleth them all by their names.
> Great is our Lord, and of great power:
> his understanding is infinite.

"We serve a mighty God," he said.

"Yeah, we sure do." Joey spoke in a whisper—awed by the God who made the stars.

"I don't want to forget to always praise and thank him," Rufus remarked.

They all agreed and made it a point to do just that during their evening prayer time before taps.

12

Davisboro, Louisville
Bathing in the Woods ~ A New Messmate

November 28
Weather: Fair

Marched at daylight

The First Division marched into Davisboro, where some of the regiments were assigned to destroy the railroad. All trains of the corps moved through Davisboro, still following under the protection of the First Division. After marching fourteen miles, they camped on the Ogeechee River.

Once the three messmates had set up their campsite, Rufus and Tom wanted hot water and soap. Having been among the troops assigned to destroy the railroad, they needed to clean the oily pitch smoke from their faces and arms.

Soon Rufus brought a bucket of water to heat over the fire Tom had built. By suppertime, Rufus's and Tom's faces glowed above their whiskers. Even their straggly beards appeared clean. After grace they all enjoyed a hot meal.

"Georgia sure has a lotta rivers and swamps," exclaimed Joey, as they sat around their campfire.

"Yeah, and they aren't always easy to cross," lamented Rufus. "The Rebels have burned a total of eight bridges within less than a mile from here. The officers say we'll have to make a road by corduroyin' the swamp with debris from the rails and bridges in order for the trains to pass."

"And that's a lot of work," added Tom. "It will delay us. The Rebs are doin' everythin' they can to stop us."

"We can be thankful we haven't had any skirmishes since leavin' Sandersville," mentioned Rufus. "Some of the troops were sayin' that, while camped near Sandersville, General Sherman had a chance to read a few of the Southern newspapers to find out what they were writin' about us. One paper predicted 'the utter annihilation' of our army. Another actually wrote we are retreatin'," laughed Rufus. "I wonder what the newspapers up North are writin'."

"With no communication, it's hard to say," Tom replied.

He then reached for his Bible. "It's gettin' late. Anyone have somethin' he'd like to say?"

"A hymn has been goin' through my mind all day. Do ya ever have that happen?" Rufus asked.

"All the time," Tom answered.

Joey nodded, too. Even though he had become a Christian only since meeting Rufus, he'd always taken his mother to church and therefore knew many hymns.

"Which one is it?" Tom asked.

"'Amazing Grace,'" answered Rufus. He softly began to sing the beautiful hymn. Tom's baritone joined in, followed by Joey's tenor. The volume gradually increased as they sang with more feeling. Faintly, a distant harmonica from another campsite blended with their voices. The mellow sound grew louder as the soldier playing the harmonica strolled toward the singers. Upon reaching their campfire, he sat down beside them without missing a single note. After they all had finished "Amazing Grace," the harmonica player launched into another hymn. The three singers then accompanied him on "Nearer, My God, to Thee." At the hymn's end, he stopped and introduced himself.

"Hello. I'm Robert Turner. I didn't mean to interrupt, but I couldn't resist joining you on my favorite hymn." Robert smiled as he spoke, revealing a perfect set of white teeth. He had a full head of light-brown hair with whiskers to match. He appeared to be around twenty-five years old.

"We're glad ya did," Rufus told him. "I'm Rufus Seaman, and this is Tom Shafer and Joey Thorpe. You're welcome to join us anytime. We have prayer every night after supper."

Robert's face lit up. "That must be wonderful. After hearing cursing all day, I'd like to get away to pray."

Taps sounded, and Robert had to scurry back to his own campsite.

"I'll try to see you again. You wouldn't like a fourth messmate, would you?" he called over his shoulder as he left.

"Yeah, we would like that," Rufus hollered after him.

Even though taps had sounded, Rufus, Joey, and Tom still prayed a short prayer before they went to bed.

November 29
Weather: Fair

Marched 6:00 a.m.

The columns crossed the Ogeechee River by corduroying the broad swamp to make a road passable for the trains. The divisions marched three miles to Louisville, where they parked the trains and made camp.

When Rufus and Tom met up with Joey at the forage wagons, they found Robert waiting beside him, holding sweet potatoes and corn in his arms.

"Were you serious when you said you wouldn't mind another messmate?" he asked them.

"Yeah, we were serious," Rufus answered, as he turned to look at Tom and Joey. "It's okay with you two, ain't it?" he asked.

"Sure, it's okay," replied Tom.

"Okay with me," agreed Joey.

Once in camp, the four pitched their tents. Joey buttoned his to Robert's, so the two of them could share a combined shelter.

Tonight, as usual, they relaxed around their campfire after supper.

"Where's your home, Robert?" asked Rufus.

"Near Kalamazoo, Michigan," he answered.

"So's mine!" Joey blurted out.

"That's great, Joey!" Robert exclaimed. "We're both from near Kalamazoo, and we're both foragers."

"Is that why ya were waitin' with Joey—you're a forager?" Tom asked.

"Yeah, I am," Robert replied.

"I've seen ya before, Robert," Tom commented, "but I've never met ya."

"Yeah, I've seen all three of you before, too."

"Are ya married, Robert?" Rufus inquired.

"No, I'm still looking," Robert told them. "Are any of you married?"

"I am," replied Rufus. "I have a wife and two little daughters who I miss terrible. My wife's livin' alone with them on our farm in Michigan."

"What'd ya do before ya joined the army?" Tom asked Robert.

"I was studying to be a Baptist pastor, like my father. Meanwhile I worked in a lumberyard," he replied. "And I didn't join the army; I was drafted for a year." He carefully studied the faces of his three messmates. Knowing many troops looked down on draftees, he wondered how they would accept his being one, too. Yet he wanted to be honest with his newly found Christian brothers.

Rufus laughed. "I was drafted, too. I know about the disgrace attached to bein' a draftee. But ya won't feel any prejudice from Tom and Joey."

They all became better acquainted, as each one began to share with Robert about his own family. After Tom told Robert about Nellie and the songs they loved to sing, Robert took his harmonica from his pocket and started to play "Lorena." None of them remembered all of the words, but they enjoyed the music.

"That's a song the Rebs like, although it originated in the North," Robert told them. "Do you have a favorite?"

"Yeah," Tom answered. "Do ya know 'When I Saw Sweet Nellie Home'?"

Robert knew the song and started to play it. This time Tom, Joey, and Rufus could sing the familiar words, especially Tom. It brought back many poignant memories for him.

After playing several popular songs, Robert switched to some hymns, starting with "Amazing Grace." They all sang with deep feeling, from the heart. As the last lines of the final hymn, "Rock of Ages," died out, a peaceful silence settled over the campfire.

"Would ya be willin' to lead us in our devotions?" Tom asked, holding out his Bible to Robert.

"I'd be honored," he answered, taking the Bible from Tom's hand.

"I'd like to read 2 Corinthians 4:7–9. I think these verses are very uplifting." Robert read in a steady voice. "But we have this treasure in earthen vessels, that the excellency of the power may be of God, and not of us. We are troubled on every side, yet not distressed; we are perplexed, but not in despair; persecuted, but not forsaken, cast down, but not destroyed."

He closed the Bible and handed it back to Tom. "I like what these verses promise us," Robert commented. "We are earthen vessels, but because of the treasure within us, we are not defeated. We are conquerors because of God's power and love. When we experience Christ's power in our lives, nothing can defeat us spiritually. When we are at our weakest, he strengthens us with his resources to increase our faith, hope, and strength."

What Robert shared encouraged the others.

"That's good, Robert." Rufus complimented him. "You'll make a wonderful pastor."

Tom and Joey agreed. They all took turns praying and had a blessed time of Christian fellowship with their new messmate before taps ended the evening.

November 30
Weather: Fair

The Fourteenth Corps remained stationary around Louisville.

At daybreak a heavy mist hovered over the encampment. The radiant rising sun soon dissipated the fog, revealing a warm, pleasant day. Most of the troops, including Rufus and his messmates, took advantage of a free day in camp by bathing and washing their hair, since the march allowed little time for personal hygiene. One of the soldiers' biggest woes happened to be head lice. Few escaped infestation, officers and privates alike.

Rufus fetched two extra buckets of water to fill three large kettles they had placed over the fire. It didn't take long for the water to become warm.

"Who wants to go first?" asked Rufus. They had chosen a place hidden by the trees to take sponge baths.

"I'll go," Joey volunteered. Rufus handed him the soap from his knapsack. Joey threw his blanket over his shoulder, picked up a kettle of warm water, and headed for the trees.

"We need to wash our clothes, too, Joey," Rufus called after him.

"Okay," Joey yelled back, as he disappeared behind the pines. Their laundry typically consisted of one pair of drawers, one pair of socks badly in need of darning, and one shirt, along with a blanket for each of them.

In half an hour, Joey reappeared with a shiny, scrubbed, freckled face, and wet red hair neatly combed. Wearing only his trousers, he carried his dirty shirt, drawers, and socks in one hand and his shoes in the other. His bare feet stepped gingerly on the ground littered with pine needles.

"I hope I washed all them varmints outa my hair," he joked.

Rufus, Tom, and Robert each had their turn behind the trees with the kettle of warm water. After all four had bathed, they did their laundry.

"We need to fix a clothesline," Tom noted.

All worked together, putting up a line. Soon their laundry hung on it, gently blowing in the breeze. They sat huddled in their blankets while waiting for their clothes to dry.

"I'd sure like to wash my blanket," Rufus said, as he tried to brush off some of the dirt stuck to it.

"Maybe we can wash our blankets after our clothes get dry," Tom suggested. "On a day like today it shouldn't take long for them to dry."

Tom proved right. Their clothes dried quickly, so they could get dressed in time to wash and dry their blankets before evening.

Following a beautiful sunset, a host of stars filled the Georgia sky. A large yellow moon cast its beams across the campsites nestled in a grove of aromatic pine trees. The troops sat around their fires, drinking in the beauty of the night.

With Robert now one of their messmates, Rufus, Tom, and Joey looked forward to more music.

"Could ya play your harmonica, Robert?" Joey asked, as they sat having a second cup of coffee.

"Sure, Joey." Robert gulped down the rest of his brew and stood. He rinsed his tin mug before hanging it back on his belt. Taking his harmonica from his shirt pocket, he sat back down next to Joey. "What do you want me to play?"

"Lorena," Joey answered.

Robert smiled and nodded. He favored this song, too. He started softly playing the well-loved melody. Rufus, Tom, and Joey harmonized on the lyrics, which they now had come to know more completely. Other voices from nearby campsites soon joined in. Most of the troops liked to sing, and everyone enjoyed another concert of a variety of songs—both popular tunes and well-loved hymns. Finally, Robert stopped playing. "Isn't it time for our Bible reading and prayers?" he asked.

"Yeah, it is. I was just about to mention it," Tom replied.

Taps sounded shortly after they had finished their devotions. It felt good to crawl into a bed with clean blankets.

December 1
Weather: Fair

Marched at 6:00 a.m.

The First Division proceeded down the road that led to the railroad, while the Second and Third Divisions took another route, arriving at noon on the Milledgeville Road. Rufus and Tom joined their First Division in destroying the tracks, covering ten miles.

Their day's work over, a weary Rufus and Tom, their faces blackened by the pitch smoke, wended their way past the loaded forage wagons in search of Joey and Robert. They found them, their arms loaded with food. All four moved to the pine campground.

That evening around the campfire a visitor joined them.

"Where'd he come from?" Joey wondered.

"I don't know," Rufus answered.

"Is he hungry?" Tom asked, scraping together some scraps from their supper. Their visitor sniffed, turned his nose up and left the food untouched.

"Do ya think he belongs to anyone?" Joey asked, scratching the visitor's ears.

"I think he must, Joey, or he would have been hungry," replied Rufus.

"Yeah, s'pose you're right," mumbled Joey. The visitor and Joey had taken a liking to each other.

"Have you seen him before?" Tom asked Robert.

"No, but they're not uncommon in this army," Robert replied. "I've seen others. The soldiers seem to have a variety of pets. Some of them are tamed animals from the wild, such as squirrels."

"Do ya think I could keep 'im, if no one comes for 'im?" Joey inquired.

"I don't know, Joey. He would mean a lot of extra responsibility for ya," Rufus told him. "But as a man in this army, ya have the right to decide that for yourself."

One look at the sparkle in Joey's eyes told what he had determined to do. "Then, if the rest of ya don't mind, I'd like to keep 'im, unless someone claims 'im."

"It's all right with me. I don't mind sharing our boudoir with him," joked Robert.

Rufus and Tom nodded their approval.

"I think I'll name 'im 'Tramp,'" Joey told them. "He's a tramp and we're trampin' to the sea."

Shortly after devotions, taps sounded. Exhausted, Rufus and Tom eased their aching bodies down on their pine-needle beds. In the tent next to them, Tramp curled up between Joey and Robert as though the little curly-haired black dog had always slept there.

13

Buckhead Creek, Lumpkin's Station, Sister's Ferry

Saved by Tramp ~A Troubling Discovery ~ Lost and Found

December 2
Weather: Fair

Marched at 6:00 a.m.

The Second and Third Divisions marched on Millen Road, while the First Division joined them from a road intersecting theirs and took the advance. After proceeding for twelve miles, they camped at Buckhead Creek.

On their way to meet Joey and Robert, Rufus and Tom met Tramp even before they spotted his new master, as the dog came bounding past the line of forage wagons to greet them. His wagging tail shook his whole body when Rufus and Tom bent over to pet him.

"He must remember us from last night," laughed Rufus.

"Yeah, I guess he does." Tom scratched Tramp's ears. "He sure is a nice dog. I'm glad Joey has him.'

"Yeah, I am, too."

That evening during devotions, Joey asked Robert a question.

"Do ya think God could use an animal to protect ya?"

"God is all-powerful. He can use anything," Robert answered.

Joey studied Robert for a moment. "Then do ya think what happened today was God protectin' us?"

"Yeah, I do, Joey. There's no doubt God's hand was in it."

"What happened today, Joey?" Rufus inquired.

Joey looked at Robert, who smiled and nodded for him to go ahead and tell Rufus and Tom their experience.

"Well, ya know how Robert, Tramp, and me left this mornin' before daybreak to go foragin'. We was goin' along just as the sun was comin' up. The sun was in our eyes and we couldn't see too good. All at once, Tramp stopped and snarled. He just stood there and kept growlin' real low and deep. Robert and me looked around to try to figure out why he was growlin'. Then we saw what it was. A group of vigilante Rebels was ridin' down the road and we would've walked right into 'em. I grabbed Tramp and we quick hid behind a big oak tree till they was out of sight. Tramp saved us from bein' captured or even killed." Joey reached over and hugged his little dog.

"I guess he did save ya! God used Tramp to protect ya," Rufus said as he turned to face Joey. "We have much to thank God for tonight."

They all agreed and gave much praise to their Heavenly Father, their Protector, during their time of prayer.

DECEMBER 3
WEATHER: FAIR

MARCHED 7:00 A.M.

The First Division, marching in the advance, had to take another road to make room for the Twentieth Corps traveling on their front. All three divisions of the Fourteenth Corps marched on the Augusta Road ten miles north of Millen. The Confederates, having burned the swamp bridges, made it necessary for the Fourteenth Corps to put down a pontoon bridge. Despite that delay, the troops marched ten miles and camped near Lumpkin's Station.

Meanwhile, the Twentieth Corps, under General Slocum, steadily moved northeast on the road toward Camp Lawton, the prisoner-of-war camp located north of Millen. They firmly marched with one purpose—to rescue the thousands of Union soldiers imprisoned there.

The Fourteenth Corps wished them Godspeed, as they waited anxiously to hear whether the Twentieth Corps had accomplished their mission of mercy. The troops remembered the Union escapees from Camp Lawton who had found their way to the Fourteenth Corps's lines—prisoners ragged and only half alive from being starved.

After supper, voices of the First Division echoed around their campfires, discussing the horrible discovery the Twentieth Corps had made when they reached Camp Lawton. First Division officers had received word of what had occurred through contact with the Twentieth Corps, which was camped nearby, and the word spread rapidly. Loud voices sounded angry, while milder voices sounded sad.

Speaking to Joey and Robert, who didn't know what had happened, Rufus spoke in a low, sad voice. "It makes ya feel really bad to think that when the Twentieth Corps finally burst through the stockades into Camp Lawton, they found it empty. The Rebs had moved our prisoners to prison camps out of Sherman's path, possibly to Andersonville."

"And the evidence of cruelty they saw at the prison only adds to our disappointment and anger. I'm glad the Twentieth Corps burned the stockades and any other part of the prison that would burn," Tom commented. "I don't blame 'em." Tom never approved of any unnecessary burning—none of the messmates did, but torching that stockade and prison was necessary.

"The news from the Twentieth said our prisoners had few huts or shelters. And that the Rebs even stole the clothes off their backs. Our troops actually lived in filthy hovels they dug in the ground." Rufus shook his head in disbelief.

"Yeah, and they also told how they found in a shed several sets of punishment stocks that were well worn from use." Tom spoke with disgust.

"How many prisoners did they say were buried in that mass grave?" Robert asked. "Didn't the board the Rebs placed over the grave say '650 Buried Here'?"

"Yeah, that's right," answered Rufus. "Terrible."

Joey remained silent. His thoughts went to Simon, whom they believed to be a prisoner. "Please, God," he whispered, "take care of Simon."

Robert stood up to put another pine knot on the fire. "I'm concerned over how this is going to affect our troops. I mean we have to guard our hearts, so we don't try to get even by being brutal to the Rebel prisoners."

"I see what ya mean, Robert; we do have to guard our hearts, just like it says in Proverbs 4:23: 'Keep thy heart with all diligence; for out of it are the issues of life.' As Christians, we have a right to fight fair, but we must never return evil for evil," agreed Rufus.

Robert took his Bible out of his knapsack. "Let's read Romans 12:20–21." He flipped the pages of the Holy Book until he came to that passage; then he began to read the following verses: "'Therefore if thine enemy hunger, feed him; if he thirst, give him drink: for in so doing thou shalt heap coals of fire on his head. Be not overcome of evil, but overcome evil with good.'"

"That's what we need to do—overcome evil with good," Tom stated.

Rufus and Robert nodded their heads. They believed that, too.

"What does it mean about coals of fire on his head?" asked Joey.

"It doesn't mean to punish him. The coals of fire are meant to soften his heart and bring him to repentance," Robert explained. "God wants every sinner to repent and accept Jesus as his Savior. God loves sinners, but he doesn't love their deeds. He hates sin."

During their nightly time of prayer, each man prayed for God to guard his heart from bitterness and revenge.

December 4
Weather: Fair

Marched at 5:30 a.m.

The First Division marched to near Lumpkin's Station, where they received orders to destroy the Georgia Railroad. The Second and Third Divisions marched on past them for a total of fifteen miles.

By the time Rufus and Tom made it back to the First Division, Joey and Robert had the campsite all set up. They had a nice fire going with hot water for Rufus and Tom to wash the pitch off their faces and arms. Robert even had supper ready.

Rufus looked at Joey and Robert. Both had a twinkle in their eye. Even Tramp looked happy. "All I can say is 'Thanks.' Tom and I are so tired, and to have the two of ya do our chores is a real blessin'."

"Well, we were back by noon and had all afternoon free. We felt we should try to help you. We even had time for a nap," Robert told them.

"I want to thank ya, too." Tom looked at the food Robert had cooked and felt much gratitude. He didn't feel like cooking tonight.

Later around the campfire, peeking through the tall pine trees, they could see the red sun setting. As shadows lengthened, a full moon rose in the clear night sky.

"It sure is a beautiful, warm evenin'," Rufus noted. "It's not like the December we know at all. Back home, this weather would mean summer, or at least late spring."

"Even so, I still like Michigan better," Joey replied. "At least Michigan don't have all them swamps." Since their units had spent day after day corduroying roads through wet lowlands and putting down pontoon bridges, the land in Michigan looked good to them.

Strains of music from a regimental band drifted to their campsite. The musicians were playing many popular songs, among them "Aura Lee," "Shenandoah," and the favorite song of the Confederates, "Lorena." Robert accompanied them on his harmonica. Enjoying the concert, Rufus, Tom, and Joey sang along with the familiar lyrics. Voices at other campsites could be heard as they joined in, too. The band signed off with "Stars in My Crown."

This lovely hymn made an appropriate introduction to their nightly time of prayer. All four men spent time praising and thanking God. Then they prayed for their families, for one another, for Simon, and even joined Joey in praying for Tramp before taps sounded—ending another difficult day.

December 5
Weather: Fair

Marched 6:30 a.m.

The First Division marched on the road toward the Savannah River, with the Second Division in front. Pine forests stood on both sides, as they had for the last three days. The area contained many swamps that required corduroying before they could be crossed, thus causing many delays.

Traveling within a mile of Jacksonboro, the troops marched sixteen miles. At 8:00 p.m. the First Division finally halted to bivouac on Buck Creek, six miles from South Carolina.

Joey and Robert once again had set up their tents while waiting for the First Division to arrive. A weary Rufus and Tom shuffled into camp after a much longer day's march.

Rufus knew when he looked at Joey that something was bothering him. "What's wrong, Joey?"

"I've lost Tramp. I can't find 'im anywhere." His lower lip trembled.

"We've looked everywhere for him. He just disappeared while we were foraging," Robert explained.

"Can . . . can ya help me look, Rufus? Maybe someone in camp has seen 'im." Joey just couldn't give up, even though he and Robert had searched thoroughly.

"Well, let's eat first. Then we'll see," Rufus told him. Each of them had only one bowl of rice for his meal. Robert had hulled the rice by pounding it between two rocks. Food had become scarce for the foragers to find. The swampland they were traveling through contained mostly rice fields; the corn and sweet potatoes they enjoyed before didn't grow in this part of Georgia.

During supper, they heard a dog barking off in the distance.

"That's Tramp!" Joey exclaimed.

"We don't know that for sure, Joey." Rufus tried to keep him from getting his hopes up. "There are other dogs in the camp."

"It's Tramp! I know it is," Joey insisted.

Rufus rose after supper to clean up the dishes. Joey hadn't been able to eat much and jumped up to help him. The work done, Rufus spoke to Joey. "Come on, we'll go look at the barkin' dog to see if it's Tramp."

Situated in a grove of evergreen trees, the camp was marked by hundreds of campfires burning pine knots that gave off their own pleasant aroma. Rufus and Joey made their way through those campfires toward the barking dog. Needles from the pine trees crunched beneath their feet. Threatening dark rain clouds floated across the night sky. They passed several campsites that were alive with chattering soldiers discussing the day's events.

"Everything all right, privates?" a voice asked from behind.

They turned around to see Major Eaton, the regimental commander of the Thirteenth Michigan Infantry. He wore a smile on his gentle face.

They both saluted the major. "Joey lost his dog today, sir. We keep hearin' barkin' over this way, and we're just checkin' to see if by chance it could be his dog," Rufus explained.

"I see," answered Major Eaton. "I heard the dog, too. I'll go along with you. I hope it is your dog, private."

They soon located the campsite where the dog kept barking. "Tramp!" called Joey. He ran and threw his arms around his dog. Around his neck Tramp had a rope that was staked to the ground. Joey started to untie it.

"What d'ya think y'er doin'?" a big man at the campsite asked in a surly voice, cursing Joey in the process. "He's my dog now. Git away from here!" He started moving toward Joey.

"Hold on there, private," Major Eaton ordered the big man, as he stepped between him and Joey. "Untie the dog. His rightful owner has found him."

Seeing the officer, the burly man jumped to attention and saluted the major, whom he hadn't noticed before. "Yes, sir," he answered, and finished untying Tramp. Once loose, the devoted little dog jumped into Joey's arms. Rufus and Joey then walked away alongside Major Eaton, leaving behind a disgruntled dog thief.

"Thank you, Major Eaton. I never would've gotten Tramp if ya hadn't been there."

"You're very welcome. It was my pleasure to see you find your dog." As he spoke those kind words, the major reached over and patted Tramp's head.

Back at their own campsite, Robert and Tom were overjoyed to see that Joey had found Tramp.

"I never woulda' gotten 'im if it hadn't been for Major Eaton. He sure is a nice officer," Joey told them. "I'm glad he's in command of our regiment."

"Yeah, we are, too," they all agreed.

"Ya know what?" Joey asked. "I'm hungry."

They all laughed. Tom brought out a bowl of rice he had put aside for Joey. He also gave Tramp a bit of the leftovers.

"Thanks, Tom. And thank ya, Rufus, for helpin' me look for Tramp. I sure have great messmates." Joey sighed.

"You're very welcome, Joey," they told him. "And you're a pretty great messmate yourself."

That night, Joey thanked God for sending Major Eaton along to help him get Tramp back.

Taps blew as they finished their prayer time.

December 6
Weather: Fair

As they neared Savannah, General Sherman ordered his four columns to march closer together. The Fourteenth Corps moved out on the River Road paralleling the Savannah River. Progress was not easy, for Rebels had delayed the march by obstructing the road with felled trees. Moving forward nevertheless, the Union troops spent the day traveling through the tidal swamp country between the Savannah and Ogeechee Rivers. After marching eighteen miles, they camped near Sister's Ferry, located on the Savannah River.

At the end of the day, Rufus and Tom marched past the almost empty forage wagons, looking for Joey and Robert. The area was home to few plantations, but the rice fields along the rivers helped supply what little food the foragers could gather for the hungry infantrymen. Not finding their two messmates, Rufus and Tom knew they must already be back.

Entering the encampment area, they quickly spotted Joey and Robert at the place near the road that those two had chosen as a campsite. Robert had hulled the rice and put the grain in a big black kettle. After adding water, he hung the pot over a smoldering fire, slowly cooking it. A bowl of rice would be their only meal again tonight. In this poor, sandy, swampy country they were fortunate to have even that. Tramp, too, had to be content with rice for his supper.

Following their meager meal, the four soldiers sat around the fire, enjoying a second cup of coffee made as usual from the grounds used that morning. The moonlight falling across the Savannah River created a beautiful scene. The clip-clopping of a lone horse's hooves caused the men to look toward the nearby road. There they saw Major Eaton, who turned into the encampment and, upon seeing Tramp, brought his horse to a halt.

"Well, hello there," he said to them all, as he dismounted. Each man saluted the officer. "How is everyone? Did you have enough to eat?"

"Yeah, we had rice tonight," Rufus answered. "We'll be all right as long as we have our coffee."

The major laughed. Looking at the coffee pot on the fire, he asked, "Can you spare a cup?"

"Of course. Why don't ya sit down and join us." Rufus took the cup the major handed him from his belt and filled it with steaming coffee. "I'm afraid we don't have any cream, but we have some sugar. Would ya like some sugar, sir?"

"No, thank you, I prefer it black," he replied.

The major turned toward Joey. "How's your dog doing, Joey? Will he eat the rice?"

"Yeah, he eats it, bein' there's nothin' else for him. But it's a hard job to gather the rice in all that swamp," Joey told him.

"Yeah, I know it is. I'm sure it was hard for the first German settlers to make a living on this soil. Do you know why they call this Sister's Ferry?" the major continued.

"No," admitted Joey, "why do they?"

"Well, from what I've been told, two sisters from one of the German families who settled here tried to cross the river in a canoe and drowned. It's a sad story."

"Yeah, that's a sad story all right," Robert said, and they all agreed. Soon the evening drew to a close, with only enough time left for devotions.

"We have a time of prayer every night, major. Would you care to join us?" Robert asked.

"Not tonight. I really must get to my own headquarters, but I would like to join you some other time, if I may." The officers in Sherman's army readily consorted with enlisted men such as the four messmates.

"You are always welcome, sir," Rufus assured him.

After prayer, the tired and still hungry troops crawled into their fly tents, hoping sleep would take their minds off their unsatisfied stomachs.

14

Ebenezer Creek

Death in the Creek ~ Bad Weather and Tough Going

DECEMBER 7
WEATHER: FAIR

MARCHED 6:30 A.M.

The Fourteenth Corps continued their march on the River Road. The column met little opposition from the enemy, except for numerous obstructions in the roadway and the destruction of bridges. Despite those difficulties, they still managed to march sixteen difficult miles and camped a few miles short of Ebenezer Creek.

That night the four messmates quickly performed their chores, keeping a watchful eye on the threatening clouds in the dark sky. They knew rain would soon be falling. After the tents were up, Joey and Robert gave Tom a hand in the arduous task of hulling rice. They wanted it ready when Rufus returned with water.

The rain held off through supper and still hadn't fallen as they gathered around the fire, having their evening coffee.

"How'd your day go?" asked Joey.

"Today was another rough day, what with clearin' obstructions, corduroyin' more swampy roads, and travelin' with the trains on narrow causeways," replied Rufus. "With these troublesome swamps, the Fourteenth Corps must be behind the other columns. Much of the time our wagon wheels are stuck in the mud. But I know, Joey," Rufus added, "that you and Robert have it just as hard gettin' rice in the straw and havin' to clean and hull it. We appreciate all ya do."

"I don't see how anyone could live on this swampy land," remarked Tom. "Some of the officers were sayin' that the owners of this land are the descendants of the original settlers. They never have been secessionists, and now want peace with the Union on any terms."

"I read something of the history of Ebenezer Creek while studying for the ministry," Robert told them. "It was settled by people seeking religious freedom, exiles from Catholic regions in Germany and from Salzburg in Austria, also predominantly Catholic. These early settlers followed the teachings of Martin Luther. The Roman Catholic archbishop actually expelled the exiles that came from Salzburg."

"When'd they come here?" Tom asked.

"If I remember right, they came here around 1734. At first, they settled inland, but they couldn't make a go of it there. So they relocated here by the Savannah River and did quite well until the Revolutionary War, when the British burned their town, something from which they never seemed to recover. Did you know the name Ebenezer means 'Stone of Help'?"

Joey laughed. "I have an Uncle Ebenezer. Was the two sisters who drowned at Sister's Ferry a part of this group?"

"Yeah, I think they were," answered Robert. "Major Eaton said they were from a German family. The first governor of Georgia also descended from these people."

"That's real interestin', Robert," Rufus commented. "I like to hear about Christians who stand up for what they believe, just like the Pilgrims did. They must be wonderful people."

"Yeah, they are. It's great that we live in a country that has freedom of religion, but there needs to be freedom of all kinds for everyone. All people need to be free. That's one of the reasons we're here right now."

Everyone agreed with Robert.

Suddenly, the clouds opened with a deluge of rain. The four troops, along with Tramp, scurried to take cover. They held their prayer time facing each other through the open ends of their tents. When taps sounded, they were all asleep.

December 8
Weather: Rained all night, fair on this day.

Marched 7:00 a.m.

Reveille awakened the camp before dawn. A heavy rain had pounded the fly tents all night, making it difficult for the troops to stay dry or to slumber peacefully.

The Rebels had succeeded in delaying the Fourteenth Corps by continuing to obstruct the Savannah Road with fallen trees and by destroying the bridge over Ebenezer Creek, which lay ahead.

Following a hurried breakfast, Rufus and Tom joined the other infantrymen in spending several grueling hours clearing the road and laying a pontoon bridge over the creek, a wide and deep stream, though they themselves did not yet cross it.

A Rebel's gunboat traveling on the Savannah River fired on the road where the trains were moving, then steamed away. No harm done.

The foragers once again searched all day, trying to find food for the soldiers. As usual, they mostly brought back rice from this swampy area. After marching three miles, the columns camped for the night, still short of Ebenezer Creek.

Following supper, the exhausted foursome made a shorter night than usual of their fellowship around the campfire. After prayer time together, they crawled into their fly tents, falling asleep before taps.

Around midnight Rufus awakened to hear a horse whinny and voices talking softly. He poked his head out of the tent to see Major Eaton riding into their campsite.

"We're going to march," the major said softly. "Pack up, making as little noise as possible. We don't want the enemy to hear us. I understand the Rebs fired on our division in the rear. We're moving across the creek. Pass the word!"

"Yes, sir," Rufus saluted the major, who returned it as he rode to the next campsite.

Rufus gently shook Tom. "Wake up, Tom. We're movin' out."

"We're what?" Tom had trouble waking up and understanding what was going on.

"We're crossin' Ebenezer Creek tonight. It seems the Rebs fired on the Third Division in the rear. We need to be real quiet, so the Rebs won't hear us."

Rufus moved over to Joey and Robert's fly tent. "Joey, Robert, get up. We're movin' out."

Joey jumped up, as did Tramp. "Is it mornin'? I didn't hear reveille."

Rufus laughed. "No, it's not mornin'. We're movin' out because the enemy has fired on us. We are to be very quiet so the Rebs won't know we're leavin'." Rufus spoke in almost a whisper. "Keep Tramp from barkin'," he added.

"I will." Joey put an arm around Tramp. "Don't bark, boy," he softly told him. Tramp looked at Joey with understanding eyes and remained still.

Upon hearing what Rufus told Joey, Robert got up immediately. "Is the pontoon bridge ready for us to cross?"

"It must be," Tom replied.

Quickly all four worked together, breaking camp. Soon they had the fly tents rolled up in their ponchos. After Tom put out the campfire, they picked up their rifles, threw their roll over their shoulders, and fell in with the column, ready to proceed quietly.

By 6:00 a.m., the entire Fourteenth Corps had gotten safely across Ebenezer Creek.

December 9
Weather: Fair

Marched 7:00 a.m.

The Second and First Divisions marched in the advance, encountering a small enemy force that used artillery, killing one soldier in the Second Division. Rebel gunboats on the Savannah River did more shelling. No harm done.

The troops marched seven miles and camped near Dr. Cuyler's plantation.

The mood at their campsite became somber that evening. Rufus and

Tom had not yet shared with Joey and Robert the news of an incident that had taken place yesterday at Ebenezer Creek. The First Division, in the advance, did not actually observe the scene firsthand, but heard about it from the Third Division, which, marching in the rear, passed over the creek last and witnessed what took place.

Rufus stood up to pour himself a cup of tea. Fond of the brew, he made a pot whenever possible, although his messmates didn't care for it.

Preparing to tell Joey and Robert what had taken place, he sat back down with his steaming cup, took a sip, and cleared his throat. "We heard some terrible news today about a tragedy that happened yesterday at Ebenezer Creek," he began.

"What happened?" asked Joey. He and Robert hadn't heard about it yet.

"Yesterday, under General Davis' orders, the slaves followin' our three divisions were turned aside by our Union guards when they neared the pontoon bridge over Ebenezer Creek. The guards simply forbade them to cross. General Jeff Davis felt the slaves followin' our troops hampered the movement of his men."

"But . . . but, they'd be captured," protested Joey.

"Yeah, some were. Once the Fourteenth Corps crossed over, they pulled the pontoon bridge away from the shore and abandoned the slaves. The blacks screamed in terror, and many jumped into the water. A few managed to swim across, but others were swept away and drowned."

"Couldn't anyone help them?" Robert asked.

"Yeah, some thoughtful Union troops threw trees and stumps into the creek for the slaves to cling to. Other troops quick cut down trees that bordered both sides of the road and threw them in, too. Some black men were able to tie a few of those trees together, buildin' a raft, which they then pulled with a rope made of blankets. They made several trips, towin' it back and forth. But it only held around six people. They kept takin' them across until Wheeler's cavalry caught up with 'em." Rufus's strained voice showed his feelings.

"There were around five hundred slaves, mostly women and children," added Tom. "They say over a hundred were recaptured. The rest either drowned or made it across. Some of the officers from the Third Division want to report General Davis. They want President Lincoln to hear about it and remove General Davis. I hope they do."

"We do, too," they all agreed.

The campsite grew silent, as each man grieved the fate of the slaves. Quietly the strains of "What a Friend We Have in Jesus" sounded through the still night air, as Robert played softly on his harmonica. One by one, the other three joined their voices to the melody, singing the encouraging words to the hymn, one line of which said, "What a privilege to carry everything to God in prayer."

That is what they would do tonight.

December 10
Weather: Fair

Marched 7:00 a.m.

The enemy had withdrawn last night after sundown. Today the column marched to within ten miles of Savannah, where it met the Twentieth Corps moving on Springfield Road, which intersected with the Savannah Road. Reaching the junction first, the Twentieth Corps took the advance, causing the Fourteenth Corps to go into camp somewhat disgruntled. Today's march totaled five miles, after which the troops bivouacked in Piney Woods.

The weather then turned cold and dismal, making the blazing campfire especially welcome at the end of their tiring day. The talk among the soldiers tonight concerned the safety of the troops. News had reached them that the Confederates had buried "torpedoes" in the road on which General Sherman was traveling with the Seventeenth Corps.

"Has anyone been killed?" Robert moved closer to the fire, holding his hands out to warm them.

"Not outright. One horse caught a fatal bullet, and several men were wounded—some seriously enough that they could die from their wounds." Rufus rose to pour himself another cup of coffee. "It was a squad of the First Alabama Calvary (U.S.) that rode over the land mines."

"How many mines was there?" Joey sat in his usual posture, his arm around Tramp. Robert and he, off doing their foraging, hadn't heard about the land mines. Rufus and Tom had been told about the buried torpedoes by some of the troops they worked alongside. News from other corps traveled rapidly.

"From what they said, Joey, I guess there were nine mines in all, and two exploded, injurin' our troops," Tom replied. "General Blair ordered a squad of Confederate prisoners to dig up the remainin' torpedoes. The frightened prisoners objected, but were forced to do it. Scared to death, they were able to dig up the other seven mines very carefully without anyone else being harmed."

"They said our officers were really mad over the Rebs layin' those mines. They thought it opposed the rules of war and that it was a cowardly thing to do," Rufus commented.

"Do ya think the Rebs will do that to our road?" Joey sounded nervous.

"No. I understand that one of the Rebel prisoners was sent to their lines to tell them that they would only harm their own Confederate prisoners if they planted any more mines," Rufus said, trying to assure him. "General Sherman was really angry about what had happened. He doesn't like anyone harmin' his troops."

Since Robert had joined their group, they enjoyed music nearly every evening. Tonight would be no exception. Robert played the old favorites and ended, as was customary, with a beautiful hymn.

"We really look forward to your music every night, Robert," Rufus told him. "You've been a real blessin' to our group." Tom and Joey agreed wholeheartedly. "You're gonna make a wonderful pastor when the Rebellion is over and you go back home."

"Thank you." Robert felt warmed by his messmates' words. "May I pray for you three tonight?"

Rufus, Tom, and Joey eagerly nodded.

After prayer, they wrapped themselves in their tattered blankets and crawled into the fly tents they had pitched to face the fire. All, including Tramp, were asleep before taps.

DECEMBER 11
WEATHER: FAIR

MARCHED 6:30 A.M.

The column of the Fourteenth Corps marched on the right of the Twentieth Corps, their trains following behind. As they proceeded, the corps encountered a swamp road that needed to be corduroyed. The First Division's head train stopped part way over the road and stayed until daylight. By sundown, the Fourteenth and Twentieth Corps were grouped together facing Savannah, having marched four miles.

Around all the campfires, an air of vigilance hovered over the troops tonight. Somewhere in the distance they could hear firing from the Rebels' heavy guns.

"I wonder if we'll have a battle," Rufus mused.

"Only if Uncle Billy feels it's necessary," answered Tom. "He would much rather outflank the enemy."

"He's been moving us toward Savannah real slow these last few days," Robert said, as he took his harmonica out of his shirt pocket. "Uncle Billy knows what he's doing. He's lining up his army where he wants us to be. We still need to take Savannah."

"Yeah, you're right," Tom and Rufus concurred.

Joey knelt beside Tramp. "Are ya all right, boy?" He petted his dog. "Tramp's sure gettin' thin. I can feel his ribs."

"I know, Joey." Rufus bent over and felt Tramp's bony sides. He too had noticed Tramp looking thin. "I'm sure he's hungry, like we all are. But we don't dare allow him to run and hunt for himself. Someone might steal 'm, or the Rebs might use 'im for target practice."

Joey nodded. "I know we can't let 'im run wild." The devoted dog always stayed near his master.

"I'm sure he'll be all right," Rufus tried to reassure Joey. "He'll have to get by on rice for a bit longer, just like the rest of us. But we should have more rations soon."

"I hope so." Joey's voice sounded worried.

Robert, wanting to bring a little cheer to the discouraged campsite, started playing his nightly concert, while his messmates, one by one, added their voices in song. The warm weather felt like summer to the troops from the north, like a clear June night with twinkling bright stars overhead. The friendly Michigan soldiers in the campsite next to theirs joined wholeheartedly in harmonizing with the melodies, including the favorite closing hymn, "Amazing Grace."

The day ended as usual with their devotions, the four of them praying for their families back home and for one another, including Tramp.

December 12
Weather: Fair

Marched four miles. Division stationary.

Led by their officers, the troops moved the trains from the Louisville Road to the Milledgeville Road and parked them about five miles from Savannah. The columns had now marched into country where the rice had already been harvested. The foragers found this rice in the straw, but the troops still needed to clean and hull it. All animals, including horses and mules, were forced to survive on that diet.

The four friends had just finished eating their rice supper when, from out of the shadows, Major Eaton rode into their campsite. The messmates all stood to salute him.

"At ease, men." After returning their salutes, the major took something out of his saddlebags.

"I have a present here for Tramp. Someone found a cow that had drowned in the mud. It was too long ago to be safe to eat, but I didn't think a bone for Tramp would hurt him. What do you think, Joey?"

"Oh, no, Tramp would love that."

The major threw the bone over to Tramp. They all watched with delight as Tramp growled and slobbered over his special present.

"Could ya sit down for a while, major?" Rufus invited.

"I'd love to." The tall major tethered his bay horse and joined their circle sitting around the warmth and light of the campfire. "Tomorrow the Fourteenth Corps should meet up with General Sherman and the other Corps," he informed them. "We'll soon be forming an effective siege line. The general is spending much time reconnoitering. Unfortunately, the approach to Savannah is protected by swamps and canals."

"And even bayous and rice fields," Tom added.

"That's right. If we have to attack the Rebs, this terrain will make it very difficult. There are only three wagon roads and two railroad lines leading into the city. Right now, General Sherman is in the process of forming a siege line across these routes. But knowing him, I'm sure we'll be successful in taking Savannah."

"That's somethin' we should pray about tonight," Joey stated, his freckled face showing his concern.

Major Eaton turned and smiled at Joey. "Yeah, we should do that. I'd like to join you, if I may."

"We'd love to have ya," Rufus quickly answered.

Robert reached into his knapsack for his Bible, opened it to Isaiah 2:3–5, and began to read.

> And many people shall go and say, Come ye, and let us go up to the mountain of the Lord, to the house of the God of Jacob; and he will teach us of his ways, and we will walk in his paths: for out of Zion shall go forth the law, and the word of the Lord from Jerusalem. And he shall judge among the nations, and shall rebuke many people: and they shall beat their swords into plowshares, and their spears into pruning hooks: nation shall not lift up sword against nation, neither shall they learn war any more. O house of Jacob, come ye, and let us walk in the light of the Lord.

"I thought this scripture would encourage us to think of a time when there will be no war."

"It blessed me, Robert," Tom told him.

Major Eaton, deep in thought, looked up. "It'll be a wonderful day when there is no more war—even no more of this war between the states, where brother is killing brother. I'm really looking forward to its end, as I know we all are. And I do believe this march is hastening that end."

They all agreed with the major.

Robert started to softly play "A Mighty Fortress Is Our God" on his harmonica. As usual, the other three messmates joined in harmony. The major quickly added his bass voice, completing the quartet.

After all five soldiers, including the major, had prayed for their families, they lifted up General Sherman and the capturing of Savannah. They prayed that Savannah would be taken with little bloodshed on either side and without much destruction of the city. They didn't want Savannah to become another Atlanta.

Immediately after their last "Amen," Major Eaton jumped to his feet. "I've really enjoyed spending this time with you," he told them, as he shook hands all around. "Now I need to hurry to my headquarters before taps." He untethered his horse, mounted up, and saluted before he rode away.

Joey stood watching Major Eaton as, guided by the light of many campfires, he made his way back to his own tent. As he rode along, pine needles snapped beneath his horse's hooves. A sliver of moonlight fell across the bay's black mane until mount and rider disappeared into the darkness. "He sure was nice to join us like this. Not many majors would do that."

"No, they wouldn't, Joey, but that's what makes 'im so special," Rufus replied. "We're blessed that he's our regimental commander."

Taps sounded. Tom put more wood on the fire as the four said good night and crawled into their tents. Tonight Tramp slept with his bone—outside the tent.

December 13
Weather: Fair

Moved at dawn.

The Fourteenth Corps arrived to join General Sherman and the other three corps by way of the Savannah Road, which runs along the Savannah River. The Fourteenth was to replace the Seventeenth Corps on the left center, pushing the Seventeenth farther to the right.

After getting an accurate position of the enemy lines, General Sherman arranged his men in a siege line.

Cannon fired from the Reb lines all day; no harm done. There was little fire from the Union side, which was not yet ready.

In camp, the troops, sensing that this would be home for a while, settled in, ready to make an entrenchment, if necessary. Rufus and his fellow messmates sat before a crackling pine fire, all wrapped up in their blankets, trying to keep the cold night breeze from chilling them to the bone.

"I don't think we'll be marchin' out in the mornin'," Rufus stated. "I think we've come to the end of the road for a while."

"I think you're right," Tom agreed. "There's nothin' but swamps, marshes, and the Rebels' fortifications ahead of us."

"Yeah, we have to take Savannah yet." Robert stood sniffing the air. "I think I can smell the ocean," he declared. "I'll be glad when we have a way clear to our fleet on the coast."

"Me, too," answered Tom. "Then we'll have supplies and won't be on half rations."

"Even better yet," added Rufus, "we'll have mail."

Each man sat quietly, thinking of the joy in receiving news from home once again. Most troops considered mail more important than their rations.

"Remember when we made camp a few nights ago near Dr. Cuyler's plantation?" Tom asked.

"Yeah, I remember," Robert replied. "And the Second Division camped right on his plantation."

"Yeah, they did. Well, the news from Uncle Billy's campsite is that he had Dr. Cuyler and his brother, R. R. Cuyler, as guests for supper. The brothers had somehow been taken prisoner by us from a train we captured on the Gulf Road. Uncle Billy knew R. R. Cuyler personally years ago. He's the Cuyler who is the president of the Georgia Central Railroad."

"That's interestin'. How'd they get along, after all the railroads we've torn up?" Rufus asked.

"Just fine, I hear," answered Tom. "Cuyler just took it as one of the fortunes of war. One thing Uncle Billy discussed with him was the many untrue accounts printed about us in Confederate newspapers, like reportin' that we murdered women and burned every dwelling in sight, as well as many other lies they wrote about us."

"What did Mr. Cuyler say to that?" Rufus inquired.

"Cuyler agreed it was lies. He said they don't believe these lies in Savannah."

"Savannah sounds nice," Joey said, sitting snuggled up to Tramp.

"I think those lies really bother Uncle Billy, though. Most of the burnin' that was not authorized was done by stragglers. I know Uncle Billy has no use for 'em," Tom added.

"I think you're right," Robert replied.

Shivering, the group decided to hold devotions and turn in early. Maybe the tents would help break the bite of the sharp wind.

15

Siege Line outside Savannah
A Long Wait and Sudden Victory: Praise God! We Made It!

December 14
Weather: Fair

Division stationary along siege line

General Sherman now sent an order to all the camps in every corps, notifying their troops of the fall of Fort McAllister on the west bank of the Ogeechee River. The Second Division, Fifteenth Army Corps, under General Hazen, had taken the fort the day before, December 13. The capture of Fort McAllister opened up communication with the Union fleet off the coast. Meanwhile, Sherman's troops formed siege lines.

Jubilant cheering resounded from camp to camp at the news about Fort McAllister. Flags waved, bands played, and batteries fired in the joy of the news. To the soldiers, this victory meant above all mail and supplies.

At Rufus's campsite all remained strangely quiet. Although overjoyed at the fort's capture, Rufus and Tom were anxiously awaiting the return of Robert and Joey. The two foragers had been sent out early this morning as part of a detail to go to the nearby plantations for rice. They were due back before now.

"I hope they didn't run into any Rebs," Rufus remarked for about the fifth time.

"Yeah, I know how you feel. We just need to keep prayin'." Tom raised his bowed head to encourage Rufus, when he suddenly received a wet, sloppy kiss from Tramp.

"Tramp! Where are they?" Tom shouted.

Robert and Joey soon came walking into the campsite, close behind the faithful dog.

"We were able to get some wagonloads of rice for our division," Robert told them. "Only it took longer than we thought it would."

"What's all the cheerin' about?" Joey asked.

"Fort McAllister has been captured. We'll be able to get mail and supplies," Rufus eagerly told them.

"The men from the division that captured the fort were truly brave," said Tom. "I really don't see how they did it."

"What outfit were they from?" asked Robert.

"They were from Uncle Billy's old outfit, the Second Division of the Fifteenth Corps. Now it's under General Hazen's command."

"And what'd they have to do to take the fort?" Joey asked.

"Well," boasted Rufus, "when the fifteen hundred men of the Second Division received their orders to attack, they paraded out from the cover of the nearby woods, flags flyin' high. Upon reachin' the bottom of the hill, they stormed toward their objective, movin' over many difficult obstacles. Yet they never stopped until they seized the fort at the top and our Yankee flag flew over the parapet."

"What kind of hard ob . . . obstacles do ya mean?" Joey wanted to know.

"Well, for one thing, the Rebels had planted mines and shells in the ground about four or five feet apart that were set to explode whenever someone stepped on 'em. In fact, they said that's what caused most of the casualties. But it still never stopped 'em. They charged straight forward. The Rebs had also planted tree tops with sharpened branches in their paths. Beyond these obstacles, they'd dug a ditch fifteen feet deep and about six or seven feet across, with five- or six-foot-high sharp stakes set in the bottom. The men threw logs across the trench and scurried over. They then mounted the hill and crept upward until the fort was ours."

"Weren't the Rebs shooting at them all this time?" asked Robert.

"Yeah, they were firin' at first," Tom answered. "But they said once the sharpshooters had the positions of the Rebel gunners, they were able to pick the Rebs off. I guess there was even a little hand-to-hand fightin' inside the fort at first, but they took it in only fifteen minutes. There were ninety-two casualties—twelve dead and eighty wounded. Of course, some of the wounded may die, but they were all heroes, all fifteen hundred of them."

"Wow!" Joey exclaimed. "They sure are heroes."

A reverent Robert just sat and nodded in agreement. "That they were. They knew that Uncle Billy never asks his boys to fight unless it's absolutely necessary, so when he does ask them, they give it all they have."

Suddenly he jumped up. "Well, let's join in the celebration!" He took his harmonica out of his pocket. The other three yelled and clapped, as Robert started playing "The Battle Hymn of the Republic" loudly. Even Tramp barked joyously. Other soldiers from nearby campsites sang along with the music, and everyone was jolly.

Long after the frivolity had stopped, troops continued to sit around their campfires, talking about the courageous soldiers' victory.

That night at bedtime, after praise-filled devotions, all four messmates went to sleep, dreaming about the long-awaited mail they now hoped to receive from home.

December 15
Weather: Fair

Division stationary along siege line.

The troops along the siege line spent their time preparing for the command to assault the enemy and take Savannah. The weather was beautiful, warm, and pleasant, like a summer day in Michigan.

"When d'ya think we'll hafta fight?" Joey lay on the ground beside Tramp, his arm dangling over the dog's back. He, like most of the troops, wondered when they'd be ordered to assault Savannah.

"We don't know, Joey," Rufus told him. "We just need to make sure we're ready. Uncle Billy won't ask us to fight unless it's absolutely necessary and we're prepared for it."

"I'm scared, Rufus," Joey confessed.

"We all are a little scared, Joey," Rufus admitted. "We don't want to destroy Savannah, which we'll do if we have to resort to an attack on the city. And we don't want to harm civilians, which would include children."

"Then why do we do it?" Joey sat up to face Rufus. "Why do we hafta assault them?"

"We have no choice, if the rebel forces in Savannah won't surrender. It's their decision."

"Oh," Joey's face looked sad, as he realized the situation.

"They say," Robert reasoned, "that the Rebs have only about nine thousand troops under General Hardee—mostly the Georgia militia. You'd think they'd realize they are greatly outnumbered and would surrender to save the town."

"Yeah, you'd think so." Tom believed as Robert did. They all thought that General Hardee should surrender his forces to avoid the destruction of Savannah and her residents. "We'll just have to wait and see what happens. It will be really difficult to attack the enemy over these marshes and swamps. Someone was sayin' that one of our outfits is makin' small one-man boats to use in the swamps when we do assault 'em."

The sound of Rebel cannon could be heard along the siege lines. Union artillery responded intermittently.

"Supper's ready," Tom said, as he dished up four small portions of rice, saving a bit for Tramp. After bowing their heads and blessing the food, everyone ate his scanty meal without complaining. Following devotions, the messmates once again went to bed hungry. Their meager supper of rice just didn't satisfy their manly appetites. For quite some time now, since entering the rice country, they had been on half and even quarter rations.

December 16
Weather: Fair

Division stationary along siege line.

The Fourteenth Corps now ordered a train to go to King's Bridge for supplies.

Rufus, Tom, Joey, and Robert enjoyed a summerlike evening at the end of the day, although the warmth made it too hot to sit next to the campfire. Beautiful moonbeams shone, despite the threat of a thunderstorm.

"When d'ya think the train will get back with the supplies?" asked Joey.

"When I went to fetch water, I was told they're back, but it's too late for them to start passin' out the mail," Rufus replied. "They left about 5:30 this mornin', and I heard they were at the bridge by 9:00. But no boats had arrived there yet. Later, two boats did come with mail. They said the water is so low in the Ogeechee River that the boats barely made it."

"I doubt many troops will sleep tonight, thinkin' about the mail they'll receive, or hope to receive, tomorrow," Tom mused.

"Didn't Uncle Billy also send some heavy guns to King's Bridge today?" asked Robert.

"Yeah, you're right. He wants them in position by tomorrow. The guns are so big, they'll be able to throw thirty-pound shells into the center of Savannah." Rufus's voice wavered as he spoke. "All communication is cut off from the city. Please God, may they surrender, for their own sake."

"Amen," the messmates answered together.

"Hey, Robert," one of the men from a couple campsites over called, "let's have some music!"

"Sure, what is your pleasure?" Robert called back.

"How about 'Lorena'? Let's give the Rebs a treat," he replied jokingly.

In response, Robert played the hauntingly beautiful song so well loved by the Rebs—and now by the Yanks as well. As he performed several additional lovely pieces on his harmonica, troops from nearby campsites sang along with Rufus, Tom, and Joey. Even Rebel soldiers on picket duty joined in the singing, and harmonizing Southern voices floated on the balmy night breeze from beyond the Union siege lines. Upon hearing the Rebels join in, Robert played louder, as an invitation for them to follow along.

As always, Robert ended the evening's music with a well-known hymn sung by everyone. Tonight he finished with "Nearer, My God, to Thee," a special favorite of all the troops, both North and South. Union soldiers suddenly became aware of a boy soprano from the Confederate ranks reverently singing the lyrics of the hymn. One by one, the awed Yankee troops ceased their singing in order to listen to the talented youth's clear voice.

No one spoke for a moment after the hymn ended. Rufus and his messmates fought back tears. Rufus looked at Joey and wondered about the age of the young vocalist. "Please, Lord," he silently prayed, "keep us from havin' to fight young boys whose voices haven't even changed."

They had just enough time to read and pray before taps. All four soldiers fervently prayed that there would be no battle for Savannah in addition to their nightly prayers for Simon.

December 17
Weather: Fair

Division stationary on siege line.

General Sherman sent over a flag of truce, demanding that General Hardee surrender Savannah. Hardee requested twenty-four hours to consider the summons.

Mail arrived today, along with rations of coffee and hardtack.

Heavy artillery sounded for a couple hours this afternoon.

"Mail call!" shouted the swarthy sergeant with the grimy beard.

Rufus stood among the men in his regiment, his eyes glued to the mailbag. He watched it become smaller with each piece of mail handed out. Happily he witnessed Joey, Tom, and Robert each receive letters from home. If they didn't call his name soon, the sack would be empty. For weeks he had looked forward to this very day, expecting many letters from Sarah. As yet, he had received none.

At last, he heard his name barked out.

"Rufus Seaman!" He ran up to get his letter, only to be disappointed by the penmanship on the envelope. It didn't belong to Sarah. The letter came from Sarah's pa.

Rufus shuffled over to a shady spot under a pine tree where he could be alone. He sat down on the ground and tore open his letter, anxious to see if Pa wrote because something was wrong at home.

"Where's Rufus?" Joey asked. He wanted to show him a letter he'd received from his mother.

"He's over there, sitting under the tree by himself. Leave him alone for now, Joey." Robert smiled kindly at the boy. "You'll be able to talk to him later."

"Why—why is he over there? What's wrong?"

"Rufus only got one letter toward the end of mail call. Tom and I don't think it was from his wife, Sarah."

"Oh, I'm so sorry. He's been waitin' and waitin' for a letter from her."

"Yeah, we know. We're real sorry, too."

Pa Walkley had penned a nice, newsy letter telling Rufus about Sarah and his two little girls. He wrote that they were all fine, but missed him very much. Pa told how much Sarah looked forward to his letters, and how she is now worried because she hasn't heard from him in over a month. Rufus smiled as he read that Dorothy wouldn't let anyone else trot her on his knee—only her Papa can do that. His eyes welled up with tears in reading that both Dorothy and Lucy kept asking, "When is Papa coming home?"

Pa briefly mentioned Thanksgiving Day. He and Ma had picked up Sarah and the girls to take them to church before they shared a nice Thanksgiving dinner with all the family. Even though he felt they had much to be thankful for, Pa claimed as long as Rufus and Wyllys's chairs at the table were empty, their holidays would always lack the complete joy they had with everyone home.

Pa closed by telling Rufus how proud he was of him and his being with Sherman. He enclosed newspaper articles about Sherman's march taken from the Grand Rapids newspaper, the *Daily Eagle*.

Rufus put Pa Walkley's letter back in the envelope. He silently bowed his head and thanked God. He knew he had so much to be thankful for, although he still felt sorry he hadn't heard directly from Sarah. Somehow, her letters weren't getting through. He knew other soldiers suffered the same disappointment. At least he had found out that Sarah and his little girls were fine. He thought of the many boys who had received letters from home today bringing sad news of illness, or even of the death of a loved one.

Relieved and grateful, Rufus got up and hurried across to join his messmates at the campsite—messmates who felt much better, noticing the smile on his face as he sat down beside them.

Rufus spoke to Joey. "I see you got some mail. Was it from your ma?"

"Yeah." Joey's face lit up. "My sister wrote it for her. You were right, Rufus. Ma's so glad I'm a Christian. She says she's proud of me." Joey flushed slightly.

"She has every right to be proud of ya. You're a fine boy, or I should say, man." Tom and Robert concurred.

Rufus wondered what had put the sparkle in Tom's eyes and the grin on his face. "Did ya have good news, Tom?"

"Yeah, Rufus, I sure did. I received a nice letter from Nellie. Her father mailed it up North. She said she doesn't hold what happened at Rome against me. She's lookin' forward to when we can meet again."

"Oh, I'm glad for ya, Tom. Nellie is a special girl. I think she's the one for ya," Rufus said, as he gripped Tom's shoulder.

"I think so, too," Tom muttered to himself under his breath.

Rufus turned toward Robert. "You're quiet. Did ya get bad news?"

"Well, I guess you could sort of say so. My ma wrote me a letter and in it mentioned a young lady I know who got married. It wasn't anyone I was interested in when I was home. Yet, since I've been in the army, I've thought about her a lot. I thought it was something I'd pursue when I got back home, and maybe she'd be the one for me. But, being she got married, she isn't the one God has for me."

"You're right, Robert," Tom told him. "God has someone else for ya, a fine Christian girl who will make a wonderful pastor's wife."

"I believe that, too," replied Robert. "And what about your mail, Rufus? Did you hear from Sarah?"

"No, I didn't, but I got a letter from her pa, and he wrote me all the news from home. Sarah and my little girls are fine, and that's what's important. He sent some clippin's from the *Grand Rapids Daily Eagle* about Sherman's march. Would you like to see 'em? I haven't read 'em myself, yet." Rufus took the articles out of the envelope and passed them around.

Pa had enclosed several different clippings, so Rufus had enough to share with all three of his companions. Each homesick soldier quickly scanned the particular article handed to him, anxious to read what the newspapers back home were publishing about Sherman and the march. Most of the articles in the *Grand Rapids Daily Eagle* came from Washington, D.C., or New York, which, in turn, often acquired their information from Southern newspapers, such as the *Richmond Whig*.

"This clipping is dated November 10," Robert stated. He laid aside a piece of hardtack and began to read aloud in his rich baritone voice:

> The Post's correspondent in the field, Ga., Nov. 10th, says: The latest yet heard from Sherman, says: This army, under the immediate

command of Gen. Sherman, now covering Atlanta, had been, for several days past, taking things easily, not that it has been idle, for there has been a healthy degree of activity, pretty much like that of a prize fighter undergoing his training. Transportation has been reduced to the simplest necessity of the occasion. The sick and wounded are sent to the rear. Unnecessary armaments are dispersed with, and extra tents and baggage removed. The army is literally stripped for the march and fight. Surgeons report the men in the healthiest possible state, and a more cheerful set cannot be imagined. They have faith in their leader.

"Oh, yeah," Tom responded. "That was an earlier report, before the march." He held up the article in his hand. "I have more news, dated November 18. This was taken from the *Richmond Virginia Whig* itself." Tom read to his fellow messmates what the Rebel paper had to say about Sherman. "Richmond papers of Wednesday are filled with speculations as to Sherman's movements, expressing the conviction that he is threatening Mobile. The *Whig* also demands the rebel authorities to send out a special force of seventy-three thousand to annihilate Sherman and Sheridan, and assails the rebel Congress for incompetency."

"And here's a small item attached from New York," Tom went on. "More about what the Rebel papers are sayin': 'New York, Nov. 18 – Rebel papers betray evident trepidation at the reported movement of Sherman's army, and anxieties concerning Augusta and Macon, where as well as at Columbus they have their most extensive powder mills, shops, and arsenals, and for the safety of which they evidently entertain great apprehensions.'"

"It is very interestin' to read how the Rebels felt," Rufus admitted. "But most of the news is over a month old. Oh, what do you have there, Joey?"

"This is supposed to be from a letter Uncle Billy wrote his father-in-law. I'll read it to ya. 'Another letter says: "General Sherman, a few days ago, wrote to his father-in-law, Hon. Thos. Ewing, that he was the leader of the bravest and best army that ever marched on American soil." (This was from the *Post* correspondent in the field, Ga., November 10).'"

Joey looked up after reading the clipping. "Do ya think Uncle Billy is really that proud of us?"

"Yeah, I think he is, Joey. He's proud of his army. What Uncle Billy doesn't like are the stragglers followin' us and not obeyin' orders. They're the troublemakers—burnin' when it's against orders, as well as lootin'," Rufus explained.

"You're right, Rufus. I heard that when the stragglers were sometimes caught and shot, Uncle Billy commented, 'It serves them right,'" Robert added.

"They're a bad lot," Rufus agreed. "Every army has good and bad in it, just like the Rebel deserters that are lootin' their own people. I don't think they represent the Confederate Army, either. They're more like our stragglers."

That night during devotions they discussed whether General Hardee would surrender or not.

"I certainly pray he will. Why would he cause a battle where many civilians could be hurt and even killed," wondered Rufus.

"We need to really go to the Lord about that—and also pray for the people of Savannah tonight," Robert hastened to say.

They were still deep in prayer when taps blew.

December 18
Weather: Fair

Division stationary along siege line

It was a quiet day. A flag of truce from General Hardee brought a reply to General Sherman's summons to surrender. General Hardee refused.

The Union Army received orders in the evening to hold itself in readiness to assault the enemy's entire line.

Just as Rufus and his messmates finished their meager rice supper, now accompanied with hardtack, Major Eaton rode into their campsite. All four stood and exchanged salutes with him. Somewhere he had found another bone for Tramp. After dismounting, he tossed it to the hungry, excited dog.

"Thank ya, major. Thank ya." Joey's glowing, freckled face showed his gratitude.

"You're welcome, Joey," the major replied. Then he turned and faced the four men. "I'm afraid I have bad news. General Hardee refuses to surrender. We're to keep in readiness for an assault on the enemy's entire line." His face showed the strain of the situation.

"Oh, no!" Rufus and his comrades felt like they had the wind knocked out of them.

"We've all been prayin' this wouldn't happen," Tom told him.

"I know. I have been praying that, too." Major Eaton removed his hat and with his handkerchief wiped the beads of perspiration from his brow. "I have to ride along the siege line and talk to the troops, informing them of our circumstances. I'd like to come back, if I may, to join you in your devotions." They all assured him he would be welcome. "And I'd like to hear more of your beautiful music, Robert," the major added.

"That would be a privilege, sir," Robert replied.

A short while later Major Eaton returned to enjoy an inspired hymn sing, with nearby campsites joining them. The singing carried along the siege line, with troops farther down the line adding their voices to the evening chorus.

After the last hymn, the major joined them in their devotional time and then rode back to his own campsite before taps.

December 19
Weather: Fair

Division stationary along siege line.

It was a busy day, as arrangements were made to assault the enemy's lines.

Five thousand Negroes were gathered and sent to King's Bridge to be shipped to Hilton Head, South Carolina, for their safety. The entire area was being cleared for action.

"I've noticed a large number of slaves marchin' past all day." Rufus removed the hardtack from his mouth to speak. "I wonder where they're goin'."

"Some foragers told me they're taking them to King's Bridge, where they'll ship them on to Hilton Head in South Carolina. They're moving them for their own safety. They also are removing any extra mules and horses," answered Robert.

Rufus nodded. "Well, we don't want 'em fired at and hurt, which they might be, if they kept 'em here."

"Why do so many of 'em look lighter-colored than others?" Joey asked. "Some look almost white."

"The lighter ones are what we call mulattoes. That is usually when one parent is white and one is black," Rufus explained.

"But . . . but how could the slaves have a white parent?" Joey wanted to know.

Rufus, Robert, and Tom exchanged glances.

"It's not a pretty picture, Joey. They usually are fathered by the master who owns them," Robert quietly explained. "The slave mother generally doesn't have a choice. Of course, in the end, she loves the baby and raises it."

"What about the father?" Joey inquired. "Don't he love it, too?"

"As a rule, to him it's just a slave like its mother. Quite often they even sell them to another plantation. The master's wives don't want slave children around that belong to their husbands. These children may even resemble their father."

"How sad." Joey hung his head in sympathy for the slave women and their unwanted children.

"Yeah, it is sad, Joey," Tom agreed. "Slavery is evil and a sin. It's true that some slaves love their white owners, the ones that were good to 'em. And some white children grow up lovin' their black mammies more than their own mothers. I heard General Sherman ran across a black slave woman who wouldn't leave the white children she tended. She felt they needed her, because they were so frightened by the soldiers."

"If we win this war, the slaves will be free, won't they?" Joey asked.

"Yep, that's one of the reasons we're fightin'. Almost two years ago, President Lincoln declared a proclamation givin' 'em freedom," Rufus informed him.

"I'm glad. I think a lot of President Lincoln, don't ya?" Joey looked into the faces of his messmates, who all nodded their love for President Lincoln, too.

"I want to pray tonight that those slaves will be all right," Joey decided.

"We'll all join ya, Joey," Rufus said.

That evening, after praying for their own families, each one prayed for the welfare of the slaves. They didn't forget to include prayers for the peaceful surrender of Savannah, which weighed heavily on their minds.

DECEMBER 20
WEATHER: WARM AND PLEASANT, FOGGY AT NIGHT

DIVISION STATIONARY ALONG SIEGE LINE.

During another quiet day all preparations went forward for an assault. Since sundown the day before, the Confederates had barraged Sherman's army heavily with artillery.

"Anyone ready for a refill?" Rufus rose to pick up the blue granite coffee pot from the smoldering fire. Each messmate held out his empty cup. All the troops now enjoyed coffee since receiving it when their rations arrived. Sherman's army needed their coffee almost as much as their food.

"Is there any more coffee left in that pot?" a voice inquired. They looked up to see Captain Roe ride into their campsite from out of the dense fog. The messmates all exchanged salutes with the officer. "I'm just stopping by to see if you're all set for the assault," he explained, alighting. Rufus poured coffee into the tin cup the captain took from his belt.

"I think we're as ready as we're ever going to be," Robert answered. "We were praying that General Hardee would surrender. We don't like assaulting Savannah with its civilians inside the city."

"No, none of us do. We all wanted him to surrender. I don't understand why he didn't. It's true; Rebel guns command all the roads or causeways that enter Savannah, but we have guns that can bombard the city from here. Savannah's completely cut off—we could just wait and starve them out. We know General Sherman won't sacrifice his boys' lives unnecessarily."

Captain Roe gulped his coffee down and then turned to go. Before mounting his horse, he paused to speak to Joey. "Try to keep your dog down in the trenches when the assault begins." He stroked Tramp's head. "Thanks for the coffee."

"You're very welcome," they answered.

The officer then swung into the saddle, disappearing into the smoky mist on his way to the next campsite.

Tom stood to rinse his cup before hanging it back on his belt. "I think we still should keep prayin' that we won't have to assault Savannah and that somehow God will change General Hardee's mind about fightin' us."

"We certainly will pray that, Tom. God can change things, as we've so often seen," Rufus told him.

During devotions that night they fervently prayed God would change General Hardee's mind.

December 21
Weather: Clear, fog lifted

Division stationary on siege line.

Before sunrise the Union pickets crossed the swamps to the enemy's outer fortification works. The rebels were gone. Savannah was evacuated!

General Hardee and his troops had escaped on the eastern plank road, the only exit left open, by crossing the Savannah River on a pontoon bridge they constructed. They then departed in last night's fog for Charleston, South Carolina, using a strong artillery barrage to cover the noise of their movement. Hardee left many heavy guns behind, although he had blown up his ironclads and navy yards.

At 4:00 a.m., General Geary had guided a New York Division from the Twentieth Corps down the Augusta Road, which led into Savannah. In the fog they could barely make out a group of men walking toward them. As the group approached, Geary's men noticed they carried a flag of truce. When the two groups met, the man with the flag introduced himself as the mayor of Savannah, Dr. Richard Arnold. Those with him were the city's aldermen, and the entire group had come to surrender their city to General Geary. They explained how they had ridden out of the city on horseback, but Confederate cavalry had stolen their horses, leaving them on foot. Mayor Arnold handed General Geary a formal request that read as follows: "Sir: The city of Savannah was last night evacuated by the Confederate military and is now entirely defenseless. As chief magistrate of the city, I respectfully request your protection of the lives and private property of the citizens and of our women and children."

General Geary received the request in the spirit in which it was made.

Upon entering Savannah, the general and his troops found a city in desperate need of law and order. Looters had broken into the stores, and mobs were fighting over the rice in the warehouses. Buildings had been set on fire. General Geary commanded a brigade of guards to stop the looting, and these Union troops soon restored order.

Tramp's barking woke Rufus and his messmates. Joey's dog, they had learned, never barked without a reason. They crawled out of their cozy tents to investigate, and heard troops cheering and yelling all along the siege line.

"Savannah is evacuated! She is ours!" An excited soldier from the campsite next to theirs cried out the joyous news to them.

"Praise God!" Robert shouted back.

For a minute, the four sat stunned, semidressed and not fully awake. They felt like men in a dream. Deep in thought, Rufus reached inside the tent for his well-worn boots. He shoved his calloused feet in, then said, his voice trembling with joy, "We have much to praise God for today. Our prayers have been answered. Now there will be no assault on Savannah."

"Also, Rufus, this ends our march to the sea," Robert said exuberantly, buttoning his shirt. "We made it!"

"You're right, Robert. Our long campaign is over." A deep sigh escaped Tom. With a spring in his step he gathered the wood for their morning coffee.

"Amen," added Joey, his freckled face creased with a grin under his tousled red hair.

For much of this glorious day all four of them kept remembering to thank God for answered prayer.

16

Christmas 1864 in Savannah
Sherman's Christmas Gift to President Lincoln ∼ Seeing the City

The sun filtered through the pine trees on the troops breaking camp. Once again they put their few possessions in their ponchos, rolled them up, and threw them over their shoulders. Picking up their rifles, they stepped out, ready to leave the siege line behind. The column of the Fourteenth Corps moved along the narrow causeway leading into Savannah. They jauntily marched to the beat of bands playing and troops singing. Rufus's First Division pitched its camp about a mile outside the city.

On the twenty-second of December General Sherman and his staff rode down Savannah's Bull Street into the city. They took up quarters in the Pulaski House hotel, where Sherman had stayed years ago while on duty in the area.

Many prominent local residents visited the general to show their respect, and he received them with great courtesy. One of his guests, an elderly gentleman named Charles Green, asked a favor of Sherman. Mr. Green, a wealthy banker, cotton merchant, and British subject, owned the finest house in Savannah. He urged General Sherman to make his quarters there. He preferred that the general occupy his home, rather than someone else. Sherman finally agreed to move there, if he and his staff could furnish their own army victuals. Everything settled, they wasted no time in making the beautiful home their headquarters.

General Sherman then sent President Lincoln a dispatch that read as follows:

> Savannah, Georgia 22d
> His Excellency President Lincoln:
> I beg to present to you as a Christmas gift the city of Savannah, with one hundred and fifty heavy guns and plenty of ammunition, also about twenty-five thousand bales of cotton.
> W. T. Sherman, Major General

The telegraphed message reached Lincoln on Christmas Eve. Union newspapers quickly published it, including Grand Rapids' own *Daily Eagle*. The great news brought joy to all who had loved ones in Sherman's army.

During the three days after pitching their camp on the outskirts of Savannah, Rufus's division drilled from morning to night, taking little time for breaks. In the evening the troops built campfires not for cooking, but only for keeping warm, as they now ate their meals in the mess tent. Since supplies were coming in slowly, the soldiers' portion of food was still limited to half rations.

Rufus and his messmates looked forward with enthusiasm to visiting Savannah today—Christmas Eve. They had heard so many wonderful reports about the city from the troops who already had the privilege of seeing it that they, too, were eager to tour the town. The messmates managed to receive the passes they needed to enter the city, knowing that all troops were required to be back in camp by the 9:00 p.m. curfew.

All four wanted to wait for the early afternoon mail before leaving on their sightseeing adventure. Rufus still hadn't heard from Sarah. A letter from her would be the best Christmas present he could ever receive or want.

The wait was over when Joey came running into their campsite, out of breath. "Rufus! Rufus! The mail is here!"

Rufus stood up. "I'm comin', Joey." He put his writing materials away. He had intended to write a letter to Sarah, but it could wait until tomorrow. It would be nice to write her on Christmas Day.

The four comrades walked over to where the mail was to be distributed. Rufus felt strange in the pit of his stomach. Each day that he stood there without hearing his name called became harder, as his disappointment grew.

The sergeant soon started shouting out the names on the letters he took from the mail sack. Each recipient raced up to claim his letter, smiling broadly.

"Rufus Seaman!" Rufus couldn't believe the sergeant had called his name. He rushed to get his letter. Letter in hand, he exhaled slowly. This time the penmanship was his precious Sarah's. After three long, lonely months, a letter from her finally had gotten through. He went back to his messmates for the rest of the mail call.

"Is it from . . . ?" Tom began to ask.

Rufus interrupted him. "Yeah, it's from my Sarah." The three friends slapped him on the back and wore smiles as big as his own.

By the end of mail call, they all had gotten letters: Tom from Nellie, Joey from his mother, and Robert from his parents—wonderful Christmas presents all. They hurried back to their campsite and sat around the fire. Each opened his mail. Engrossed in their reading, the soldiers' spirits no longer resided in camp. Their thoughts transported them home, if only briefly.

Rufus read Sarah's letter twice, then folded it and tenderly placed it in his shirt pocket. His hand lingered on the spot where it lay, while he paused to dwell on its blessed contents.

Sarah had rededicated her life to the Lord! She did this after receiving the letter in which he shared his need for God and asked her to return to the Lord with him. Upon reading his letter, Sarah had dropped to her knees and prayed for God's forgiveness in growing cold. She prayed to get back her first love for God and to regain the joy of the Lord she once knew. She promised Rufus that he would find her "praising the Lord" when he came home. She agreed with him that God might have allowed the two of them to be separated as a way to restore them to a closer relationship with Him. She believed He did it for their own good, because He loved them.

It tugged at Rufus's heart when he read how Sarah, Dorothy, and even little Lucy prayed for him off and on all day.

Tom, watching him, had to smile as he saw with what care Rufus handled Sarah's letter. Tom knew how he felt. A letter from home had value far above gold or jewels. He put his own letter from Nellie in his shirt pocket as well. He wanted it next to his heart.

Robert stood up first. "I think we're all about ready to start for Savannah, are we not?"

"That we are. That we are," Rufus answered in a carefree manner. The three comrades noticed his good spirits and felt the same.

The day turned out beautifully, a little chilly, but clear, with a deep blue sky hovering overhead. Mail call behind them, the four walked out of the camp and onto the road to Savannah. In minutes they entered the city to find the streets lined with oak trees covered with Spanish moss. These striking trees alone held the eyes of anyone from the North, who obviously had never seen them at home.

"Look at all that moss!" Joey exclaimed.

"Yeah, it's kinda pretty," Rufus commented.

"It looks like this is going to be the nicest Southern city we've seen," Robert decided, as they moved down the street. "Look at the red brick house over there." They all turned to look at the lovely home with a big fenced-in yard.

Tom noticed especially the white house with the picket fence around it that stood next door. It reminded him of Nellie's home in Rome.

Walking farther down the street, Rufus thought he heard children laughing. "Did you hear that?" he asked, looking up and down the street, trying to locate the source.

"What do you mean?" asked Robert. "I didn't hear anything, did you, Tom?"

"No, I didn't. What about you, Joey?"

"Tramp and me ain't heard nothin'," he laughed. They all laughed with him.

Rufus heard children's voices again, as they continued on their way. Then he saw the children themselves.

At the end of the streets were little areas much like miniature parks. Water from flowing fountains sparkled in the sunlight. Two curly-headed little girls about the ages of Dorothy and Lucy were playing on a swing in one of these park areas. Rufus heard them because his ear had been trained to hear his own little girls.

Seeing the children made him suddenly very homesick. How he longed to go over and talk to them, to push them on the swing and to play with them the way he used to play with Dorothy and Lucy. But he knew that would be wrong. He needed to stay away so as not to frighten them. It pained him to think that children would be afraid of him.

"Let's go see where General Sherman's headquarters are," Tom suggested. "We'll ask some troops to show us where it is." He had noticed the expression on Rufus's face, and guessed what he must be feeling about the children.

Union troops visiting the city generally behaved well, which General Sherman expected of them. The messmates stopped the first soldier they passed, a corporal who pointed them in the direction of Mr. Green's house.

Easy to spot, the home stood out from all others around it. The four appraised the structure. They knew nothing about architecture, yet they did recognize a fine dwelling when they saw one. Rufus, too, admired the mansion, though he personally believed the houses in the hill district of Grand Rapids, back in Michigan, were just as nice and possibly even statelier.

Then, to their amazement, the front door opened, allowing several raggedly dressed slaves to exit. When they saw Rufus and his friends, they shyly turned to go down the street. However, one older, white-haired man left the group and moved toward the four Union soldiers, bowing from his waist and thanking them for his freedom. "Thank ye! Thank ye! God bless ye!" were his grateful words.

Rufus reached out and shook the Negro's calloused hand. "You are very welcome. No man should be a slave. God bless ya."

"That's right," Robert told him as he, too, shook his hand. "It was never God's will for you to be a slave."

"Did ya visit General Sherman?" Tom asked, also shaking the work-worn hand.

"Yes, sir. The general always sees us. We prayed for him to come. God heard us." The old gentleman noticed Joey timidly standing back. He spoke to him, "Thank ye, too, boy. But ye should be home with your mammy."

"He has become a man on this march," Rufus explained.

The old man peered more closely at Joey. "Yes, sir, I see that he has."

Joey then moved nearer to respectfully shake the kind ex-slave's hand. "God bless ya," he shyly said to him.

"God bless ye, young man." He then stooped over to gently pat Tramp on the head before shuffling down the street to catch up with his friends.

An old city, Savannah offered Rufus and his comrades much to see. The earthworks still remaining from the Revolutionary War were of great interest to the Union soldiers, including the messmates. They also enjoyed viewing statues, monuments, and forts—and even visited a historic cemetery during their afternoon tour of the city.

As they slowly made their way out of the cemetery, Tom turned from reading the inscription on the last tombstone. "We probably should start back toward camp. We don't want to miss out on mess call."

"Yeah, you're right," agreed Rufus. "I think we've pretty much seen everythin' of interest there is to see."

"I understand the stores are going to be open soon. We'll have to come back when they are," Robert commented.

Walking back through the town, they noticed a few women and children on the streets who were passing Union troops without incident.

"How many people live in Savannah?" asked Joey.

"I heard the population is around twenty thousand," Rufus replied. "General Sherman offered the Savannah residents a choice. They could either remain here, or he would see them safely through the lines to wherever they wanted to go."

"That's right. I guess around two hundred did choose to leave. They say they were mostly Confederate officers' families," Robert noted.

"Where did they go?" Joey wanted to know.

"They took 'em to Charleston on a steamer. They sailed under a flag of truce," Tom added.

"Uncle Billy did all that for 'em?" Joey wondered. "I think that's mighty kind."

Everyone agreed with Joey.

"I also heard that quite a few Confederate officers contacted General Sherman to ask protection for the families they left behind here in Savannah," Rufus continued. "I understand one or two of the officers knew General Sherman from years ago. They must have felt they could trust 'im. General Sherman means no harm to anyone who remains peaceful and quiet."

"Yeah, they couldn't have believed all the lies the Southern papers printed about Uncle Billy, or they wouldn't leave their loved ones in his care," stated Tom. "You're right. He'll look after their families."

"Here's another church," Joey pointed out, as they passed a large red brick building adorned with a white wooden steeple. "How many churches have we seen?"

"At least five or six," Tom guessed. "I wonder if they'll hold services tomorrow."

"I hope so." Rufus knew he wouldn't be given another pass to attend services, as much as he wished he could.

"There's Captain Belknap!" exclaimed Robert, spotting a young soldier on the other side of the street, walking with two little girls. "He's the fellow forager who rescued those little girls we told you about."

Robert called to him, "Hello, captain."

The captain waved to Robert, and, with the little girls in hand, he started across the street to join him. After they all had saluted the officer, Robert introduced Rufus and Tom. "Rufus is from near Grand Rapids," Robert pointed out.

Captain Belknap smiled at Rufus. "You must be practically a neighbor. Grand Rapids is my hometown." They shook hands all around. He then turned toward Joey. "I think I already know this young man." Joey grinned. "Hello, captain." They'd met while foraging.

Joey took Tramp along as, hand in hand with the children, he strolled down the street to the park.

"How are things going with you?" Robert asked Captain Belknap.

"Not too well, I'm afraid. I've been to ask the Savannah city officials if they could find a home for these two little girls. They turned me away." The captain looked to make sure the children were out of earshot. "They told me they didn't have time for 'the little white trash.' I couldn't believe it."

Rufus looked at the young officer only a couple years older than Joey. "Are you serious? Doesn't anyone want 'em?"

"That's about it." The captain stood watching the girls romping with Tramp at the nearby park. He listened to their laughter. "Well, we're not giving up on finding them a good home. Maybe we'll have to take them up North to find them new homes there."

Robert shook his head in disbelief. "Yeah, I've noticed that here in the South the poorer whites are looked down upon almost as much as the slaves."

"I'd better take the girls back to camp. It's starting to get dark," the captain said, as he called the girls to come.

"We're leavin' now, also. We'll walk along with ya, if you'd like some company," Tom told him.

"Yeah, we'd like that, wouldn't we?" the captain asked the children.

The girls jumped up and down with joy to be able to spend more time with Tramp.

Leaving the city, Robert took his harmonica out of his pocket and started playing "Silent Night." His three comrades began singing the familiar carol, with the captain soon joining in to make the trio a quartet. The little girls had great fun singing their 'la, la, la.' Other troops traveling the road between Savannah and camp joined in as well.

With the setting sun, the weather became colder. A full moon rose slowly, providing some light on the road. Stars shone overhead, making a beautiful Christmas Eve.

Rufus noticed the younger child had stopped singing and worried she might be tired. "Would ya like me to carry ya, honey?" The little girl stopped, turned, and raised her fragile arms trustingly toward him. He gladly scooped her up and wrapped her in his coat.

All the way back to camp, Robert played one carol after another, with the soldiers adding their voices in singing the old Christmas refrains.

Christmas Day dawned dismal and rainy. Later in the morning many church bells pealed out, calling all to Christmas services. General Sherman and his staff attended the Episcopal church across the street from their headquarters. Following his lead, the Union troops flooded other church services all over town, worshiping alongside Savannah residents.

Rufus and his messmates had their own time of worship, huddled under their ponchos around a roaring campfire. Tom read about the birth of Christ from the book of Luke, and Robert gave a Christmas sermon. At the conclusion of this little service, each thanked God for the birth of His Son, Jesus Christ.

"That was an exceptional message, Robert." Rufus put his hand on Robert's drenched shoulder. "I was feelin' sad, because I couldn't go to church in town, but I enjoyed your sermon as much as any message anywhere."

Tom and Joey quickly agreed.

"Thank you." Robert looked pleased. "I think it's time to go to the mess tent. I wonder what we'll have for Christmas dinner."

After a steady diet of rice, they were looking forward to a special meal today. Most of the troops arrived early for their Christmas dinner, anxious to see what exceptional fare they'd be given. At last they served the holiday meal, but each man received only one slice of pork, thick meal gravy, one small cracker, and a cup of coffee. The troops sat silently and ate what had been set before them. The air was rife with disappointment, though no one voiced it. A number of the soldiers thought about home and the food piled high on the tables there this holiday.

The rain stopped by the time they left the mess tent. The air felt much warmer as they walked back to the campsite. As soon as they arrived, Rufus gathered his writing materials and began to pen a letter to Sarah. He wanted to request one thing in particular: to have a likeness of her and the children taken. To hold a picture of them in his hand, to look at now and then, would mean so much. When he finished writing his letter, he wondered if she would really receive it and how many of his letters actually got through to her. In any case, he knew he needed to write often.

The following day they again drilled for hours. The sergeant barked out orders to keep their ranks straight, eyes ahead, stay in step, pick up their feet, and on and on. By night they felt exhausted.

The next morning they understood the reason for yesterday's harsh drill. Today the Fourteenth Corps was to march down the streets of Savannah to be reviewed by General Sherman.

After breakfast, the sergeant ordered the corps to fall in. Rufus, Tom, Robert, and Joey lined up side by side, forming one rank in the same order in which they marched at drill. As unit commander, Major Eaton rode his mount at the head of their regiment, the Thirteenth Michigan Infantry in the First Division of the Fourteenth Corps.

When the corps entered the city, the troops stepped with a purpose. They marched erect, their eyes straight ahead. Rufus sensed the change. He, too, felt the pride the troops displayed in their marching. He threw his shoulders back, looked neither to the right nor to the left, and marched sharply down the street to the tune played by the regimental bands. The sturdy soldiers felt the wind from the Atlantic Ocean on their weather-beaten faces. The breeze toyed with their tattered flags, making them flutter proudly.

Toward the middle of one of the streets stood a general in a slouch hat, chewing on a cigar stub. He reviewed the Fourteenth Corps closely as they marched past. Even though they felt proud of themselves, no one felt prouder of them at this moment than Uncle Billy. General Sherman wanted the residents of Savannah to see his army, so each corps would have its own day to be reviewed.

The General needed to carry on, despite his grief at the personal tragedy he had read about in the *New York Herald* dated December 22. The paper told of the death of his six-month-old baby, Charles, the infant he had never seen. This was the second son he had lost.

The camp awoke the next day to a steady rain. Rivulets of water ran in every direction, making the campground a muddy lake. Returning from mail call, Rufus and his comrades picked their way around the puddles back to their tents.

Tom eyed the letters in Rufus's hand. "How many letters did ya get, Rufus?"

Rufus held them up. "Three. It looks like it's feast or famine," he laughed.

All four received mail today. Anxious to read their letters, they entered their tents to get out of the rain. Rufus and Tom still shared the same tent.

Having read all three letters, Rufus turned his back toward Tom. He clasped the written pages to his breast and kissed each one, wishing they were Sarah. Now, while he had time, he would answer her.

Drilling filled most of his days, leaving little opportunity for correspondence. Only the rain bought him time today. Rufus sat in his tent and penned Sarah a long letter. He asked her to send a box as soon as possible, with a half pound of tea, dried apples and blackberries, and some cakes, as well as needles and black thread. He assured Sarah that he was bearing up well, despite having only half rations—and sometimes only quarter rations.

Just as he finished the letter, he heard voices near the campfire. As he peered outside, smoke from burning pine knots drifted into the tent, stinging his eyes. He noticed the rain had stopped, and all his messmates, including Tom, were sitting around a cozy fire. He promptly joined them.

Tom looked up as Rufus sat down beside Joey and Tramp. "Did ya get your letter written?"

Rufus nodded.

"After the rain stopped, I quietly slipped out of the tent. You were so engrossed in your writin', I didn't want to disturb ya."

"Thanks, Tom."

"We were just sayin', Rufus, we'd like to build log shanties instead of havin' these tents. We'd have more protection from the weather—the wind and rain," Tom explained.

Rufus thought a minute. "That shouldn't be too hard. I helped build my own house back home. But where'd we get the logs?"

"We'll have to check into that. I don't think that will be a problem," Robert replied.

Tom stood to put more wood on the fire. "Then it's settled. We'll find some logs and build each of us a log shanty. They won't need to be very big."

The plan sounded good to everyone.

During the next few days the four of them spent every free moment searching the nearby fields and woods around the campground for logs. One day, Rufus ran across several neatly stacked piles that would be perfect, only he knew they couldn't afford to buy logs like those. On his way back to camp, Rufus passed by them again, and while doing so, he ran into an older, well-dressed gentleman wearing black leather boots. Two small dogs romped at his side.

Rufus stopped to admire the man's pets. "You have a fine pair of dogs there, sir." He bent over to pet the friendly animals.

"Thank you. I enjoy them. You must be from the army camp over there."

"Yeah, I am. My friends and I want to build a log shanty, and we're out lookin' for some logs like those." Rufus motioned toward the stacks. "Only we can't afford to pay for 'em. Do ya know where we might find some discarded logs or fallen trees no one wants?"

"You mean you want to build log shanties to live in while you're here?" He spoke in a low Southern drawl.

"Yeah."

"But when you move on, you'll leave them behind?"

"That's right."

"Then you're welcome to use these logs. I own them. They're logs from some slave shanties we tore down when I set my slaves free. We'll probably only use them for firewood. It won't hurt them to be made into shanties again. You may have them, as long as you leave them behind when you go."

"Oh, we will, sir, we will. Thank ya so very much." Rufus shook the man's hand before hurrying back to tell the others of his great find.

Tramp jumped up to welcome Rufus as he approached the campsite.

His three comrades were sitting around their fire, trying to keep warm. At times, the weather could turn quite chilly, especially after the sun went down.

Rufus looked at Robert. "Did ya find any logs?" The twinkle in his eye and the smile on his face revealed he had a secret.

"No, we traveled all over, each of us to many different places, but none of us found any. They're not as easy to find as I thought they'd be," admitted Robert.

Tom noticed the look on Rufus's face. "All right, what'd ya find? Ya look like the cat that swallowed the canary."

They all laughed, including Rufus. "Well, I didn't swallow a canary, but I did find us some logs." He went on to tell them about the Southern gentleman he had met and his offer to loan them some logs. Rufus sighed. "The only problem we have is haulin' 'em here."

"We'll work that out some way," Robert assured him. The others agreed.

After telling his messmates the good news, Rufus still had time to write a short letter to Sarah before evening mess. He needed to ask her not to send the box he had requested in his last letter. From the talk going around, he feared the box wouldn't arrive in time. Many soldiers believed they'd be marching quite soon.

When he finished his letter, Rufus and his three friends hurried to the mess tent for supper.

Later, back at the campsite, they sat huddled around the fire in their usual positions, with faithful Tramp at Joey's side, as always.

They looked up at the sound of snapping twigs to see Major Eaton approaching. They all stood and saluted as he alighted from his bay horse. He reached into his saddlebags to bring out another bone for Tramp. He unwrapped it and tossed it to the excited dog.

"Thank ya, Major Eaton," Joey gratefully responded. "I do appreciate ya bringin' Tramp another bone. He sure loves 'em."

"You're welcome, Joey. Tramp's a good dog and deserves a treat now and then."

Joey's freckled face beamed with pride over his "good dog."

Rufus then reached into his tent for his knapsack. He took out a lump of sugar, stepped over, and fed it to the major's horse, which was tethered to a pine shrub close by.

"Thank you, Rufus, that's very kind of you. I know you love horses."

"You're welcome, major. Your horse is a good one and deserves a treat now and then," Rufus said, echoing Eaton's words about Tramp. Everyone laughed.

"Do you have time to sit a spell with us?" Robert asked the officer.

"I'd like to very much." The major joined them as the four sat back down around the fire. Tramp stayed close by, growling over his bone.

"What's the news, major?" Tom inquired. "How much longer do ya think we'll be here in Savannah?"

"That's hard to say. To be honest, I really don't know. Sometimes the talk is that we'll be leaving soon, and other times it looks like we'll be here awhile."

"Major, I found some logs for us to make some shanties. Only we don't have a way to fetch 'em yet." Rufus explained how he came by the logs. The major appeared interested in the fact that a Southern gentleman had offered the logs to Rufus, a Union soldier.

"I'm not surprised the gentleman offered you the logs. Two delegates representing a large group of residents from counties west of here visited General Sherman a couple days ago. It seems they denounced the conspirators and declared their allegiance to the U.S. government. Many Southern citizens feel the war is lost."

"We'll all be glad when the war is over," declared Tom.

"That's for sure, North and South alike," Eaton said.

The officer then turned his attention toward Rufus. "So, you want to make a log cabin? Do you want to make shebang cabins, where you use your tent as part of the roof?"

"Maybe. We'll see how it goes."

"I'll leave word that you may borrow a wagon and team to haul the logs. I know, Rufus, you can handle a team well."

"Thank you, major. I'll take good care of 'em."

Tom took out his Bible. "Would ya like to join us in our nightly devotions again, major?"

"Yes, I certainly would. I was really blessed the last time." His kind face showed the pleasure he felt at Tom's invitation.

Tom chose to read Philippians 1:21: "'For me to live is Christ and to die is gain.' What does this verse say to ya?" he asked.

Robert, always the pastor, answered first. "Paul did not fear death, just as we Christians shouldn't fear death either. God has a purpose for each of our lives. When we die, it is the end of that particular purpose. Then we start a new, wonderful life with Christ in heaven."

Rufus listened intently to every word Robert spoke before he voiced his own feelings. "I've thought a lot about this very thing. I just want to make sure I'm ready to die, whenever that time comes. I don't know if I was ready or not when I first entered the army. I felt like I had lost my first love for God, the love I had when I was saved at seventeen. But I know I'm ready now, for I've rededicated my life to Christ. Because of my daily relationship with Christ now, I'm sure I would experience that glorious life with Jesus in heaven that Paul is writin' about."

"I know exactly what you are saying, Rufus," the major said, moving closer to him. "I'm sure other soldiers have gone through the same experience of making certain they're ready to die." He looked away for a moment. "I know I have," he quietly shared.

Tom spoke up: "If we've repented of our sins and asked Jesus to be our Savior, we've nothin' to fear in dyin'. We'll be with Jesus."

"You're right, Tom. That's just what I did," Rufus explained.

"Just like I did, too, huh, Rufus?" Joey asked.

"Yeah, Joey, just like ya did, too."

After they joined in prayer for all of their families, the major rode back to headquarters, guided only by moonlight.

Five days later found Rufus and his messmates snug in their newly built log cabins. True to Major Eaton's promise, Rufus had had no trouble in borrowing a wagon with a team of horses to haul the logs to their campsite. Every evening all of them worked together, building the cabins until almost taps. With the fine quality of the logs, the huts went together easily.

During the daylight hours, the messmates drilled. But when night came and they occupied their cabins, they discovered they needed a candle for light.

All four received passes into Savannah for the day. The sergeant dismissed drill at noon, which helped them to get off on their shopping excursion right after mess. On this trip into town they planned to browse in the many stores now open, in order to buy the needed candles.

Tom looked at Rufus's hand as they jaunted along the road to town. "How does your thumb feel, Rufus? I notice it looks red."

Rufus had injured his thumb yesterday while finishing the final touches on his cabin. "It kept me awake all last night. I think it's developed into a felon—quite a bad one—but I prefer to keep active, so I won't think about it. It should be better soon."

"Maybe ya should see the doctor," advised Tom.

"Yeah, I will, if it ain't better by tomorrow." Rufus slowed his step. He turned and looked at his three comrades. "After we finish our shoppin', how would ya like to go down by the harbor to view the ocean? Maybe we could even get some of those oysters I keep hearin' about."

"Yeah, I'd like that," Robert quickly replied. "Wouldn't you?" He turned to Tom and Joey.

"We sure would, wouldn't we, Joey?" Tom asked.

"Yeah, me and Tramp sure would."

They had pleasant weather for walking into town, cool but not cold. The sun kept them from feeling chilly.

Reaching Savannah, the four Yankee soldiers enjoyed the city's stately homes and buildings once more—almost as much as they had the first time. The paved streets, with beautiful parks and flowing fountains on every corner, gave everyone's eyes a sight to behold.

Strolling down the main street, they browsed in every shop they passed. Tramp sat and waited patiently outside each store. Joey or one of the others always kept him company.

One of the last stops on the block happened to be a mercantile store. When they set foot inside, they saw that the shop seemed to carry anything anyone would ever need.

Robert found candles and candlesticks in the back of the store. "The candlesticks only come in pairs. I suppose we could buy two pair and split them so we'd each have one."

"Yeah, that should work out." Rufus picked out candles, while Robert and Tom chose two sets of candlesticks.

Rufus saw many items he wished he could buy for Sarah. In one corner of the store he noticed sheet music displayed on a rack. Thumbing through the various pieces, he came across "Lorena." Even though it cost ten cents, he decided to buy the tune for Sarah.

The high cost of the merchandise in all the shops surprised him, especially the price of food. Flour sold at fifteen to twenty-five cents a pound. Upon making his purchases, Rufus went outside to stay with Tramp, allowing Joey to visit the store.

Their shopping finished, they went to the harbor, as planned. A stiff ocean breeze braced their faces as they approached the rolling waves. A Union vessel lay anchored at the dock, its precious cargo being unloaded. This ship had brought supplies for Sherman's army and food donated by compassionate Northerners for the residents of Savannah. Understandably, some of the Southerners did not appreciate this food. One Rebel lady estimated that Sherman's army had taken more food from just one plantation than all the Northerners put together had sent. General Sherman, aware of the shortages in the city, initiated emergency food supplies for the residents.

The sailors on the docked vessel waved a friendly greeting. Farther along the coast, small groups of soldiers from camp were gathering oysters. Rufus and Joey walked over to watch them shovel the saltwater delicacy into buckets to carry back. They could see beds of shellfish in areas of shallower water.

"I guess we should have brought a pail or somethin' to fetch the oysters to camp," Rufus noted.

"We can fill our pockets," Joey suggested, standing behind Rufus.

One of the soldiers looked up from his shoveling. "You need a pail? I have an extra one you can borrow." He handed an empty bucket to Rufus.

"Thanks, private." Rufus accepted the pail and motioned for Tom and Robert to come over. All four removed their boots and socks, rolled their pant legs up to their knees, and waded over to the oyster beds, the frigid water quickly numbing their feet. They then bent down and with bare hands started scooping oysters into the bucket, soon filling it to capacity. Carrying their catch, they then went back on shore and walked to near where the ship was moored. Today being the first time any of them had ever seen the ocean, they sat on the dock, quietly admiring the sea. It even had a different smell.

Rufus broke the silence. "I can't get over how vast it is."

"All I can think about," Robert shared, "is how this ship will soon be up North. It makes me homesick."

"It would be nice to be able to go home on it." Tom spoke for them all.

Reluctantly, Rufus put his socks and boots back on and stood up. "We'd better start back to camp, so we can fix the oysters." The other messmates jumped up and put their footgear back on, too. They wended their way toward camp, taking turns carrying the heavy bucket.

As they walked, a horse and rider pulled up.

"Captain Belknap! How nice to see you." Robert said. All four saluted and greeted the officer.

"How are the abandoned little girls?" Rufus asked.

"They're fine and on their way up north. A wounded lieutenant was leaving on furlough, and he offered to take the little ones with him to his home."

"That's wonderful!" Rufus exclaimed. "I'm happy for 'em." All the men expressed joy.

"I knew you would want to know about them. That's why I rode up." The captain smiled, waved, and went his way.

That evening at the campsite their supper consisted of food they'd never tasted before. Joey questioned whether the strange, slippery morsels should be eaten or not.

"Are ya sure we're supposed to swallow these?" he asked, just before gulping one down. Whether they liked the oysters or whether they didn't, it at least gave them a break from their half rations of rice.

Right after devotions, Rufus said good night and retired to his log shack. His thumb, now more red and swollen, pained him too much for sitting around the campfire tonight. He would see the doctor first thing in the morning.

Rufus lit his new candle, put it in the new candlestick, and set it on the floor by his bed. Removing his boots, he lay down on the poncho he had spread over a bed of pine needles and moss. He pulled his blanket over him and blew out the candle.

In the dark, he lay awake for hours. The throbbing pain in his thumb made sleep impossible. Feeling extra lonesome throughout the night, he thought of Sarah. He found himself worrying about exactly how she was faring at home. At 2:00 a.m., he lit the candle, got up, and composed a letter to her, asking her all the particulars he needed to know. He then lay back down until reveille.

"You should have come to me sooner with this." The doctor examined Rufus's thumb carefully. "I'm going to have to lance it. There's nothing more painful than a felon."

"Yeah, it has kept me awake for two nights."

The doctor quickly cut the thumb open and dressed it with a bandage. It alleviated Rufus's pain almost at once. Rufus thanked the surgeon.

He then walked back to his cabin to get Sarah's letter for mailing. He'd wait to send the music until next time. As tired as he felt right now, he needed to report for drill. He certainly would sleep tonight.

A few days later Rufus found time to write Sarah another letter. He wanted her to get word from him at least once every week. With this letter he enclosed the sheet music he had bought, and imagined her playing and singing "Lorena." How he wished he could be there to sing with her.

Remembering his last letter to Sarah, Rufus felt a twinge of conviction in his heart. Written during the night that the painful felon on his thumb had kept him awake, he recalled the anxious concern he had suffered all that night for his family. He knew worry was a sin. In his new recommitment to the Lord, Rufus wanted the grace to trust Jesus more. He needed to release Sarah and his children completely into the care of God.

Rufus sealed the letter and bowed his head. "Dear Lord, please forgive me for my sin of worrying, and please help me to have the faith to trust you with my family. I now surrender Sarah, Dorothy, and Lucy into your protective care. And I give my own life, and whatever may lie ahead for me, completely into your hands. I love you and praise you with all my heart. Thank you for your loving care. Amen."

Feeling a weight lift from his shoulders and a peace come into his heart, Rufus picked up his letter containing the song and went to mail it. Once the army started the march into South Carolina, there would be no mail.

17

Casnovia, January 1865
Lonesome Letters from the Front

The sound of sleigh bells drew Sarah to her frosty kitchen window. She looked out to see King and Prince prancing into her driveway, puffing smoke in the frigid air. Ma and Pa Walkley's heads were barely visible, snuggled under heavy lap robes. Sarah never expected to see them on such a cold day. She quickly added a few sticks to the kitchen range to keep the room warm.

Pa stopped the horses and helped Ma out at the back porch, then drove the sleigh onto the upper barn floor between the haymows. They always parked their teams there, out of the cold wind, so that the animals could enjoy their feedbags in relative warmth.

Ma burst into the kitchen, a big grin on her rosy face. With one look, Sarah knew she brought good news.

"What is it, Ma?"

"You have three, Sarah. Three letters! I told you Rufus would write when he could." She held them out. "Just look, honey."

Hand trembling, eyes moist, Sarah gently took the letters. It had been two months since the last one.

Ma pulled out a chair to sit close to the stove. She took off her gloves and blew on her hands, then held them over the heat. Sarah realized how cold she must be.

"I'm sorry you've gotten so chilled, Ma," she said, carefully putting

Rufus's letters in her apron pocket. "I'll fix you and Pa a cup of hot coffee. It's already on the stove."

She took three cups with saucers and three dessert plates down from the cupboard. She filled a serving plate with molasses cookies from a jar.

Pa stomped the snow off his feet at the back door, removed his boots, and took them into the house. He placed them near the range. He and Buster, who had followed him from the barn, entered the kitchen together just as Sarah finished setting the table. She poured steaming coffee and they all sat down. Buster lay in front of the stove next to the boots.

Sarah looked at her father. "How are you, Pa? I really want to thank you and Ma for coming out on a cold day like today to bring me the letters."

Pa reached over and covered her warm hand with his cold one. "It was our pleasure, honey. We know how concerned you've been about Rufus."

"That's right," Ma agreed. "If you want to go into the parlor and read your letters, go right ahead. We'll be all right."

"As long as you leave the molasses cookies here," Pa joked.

Sarah laughed. "No, I think I'd like to read the letters aloud right here. I'm sure Rufus wouldn't mind."

"We'd love it," they said.

She took the letters out of her pocket and removed them from their envelopes. "Let's see the dates. I want to read them in the order Rufus wrote them in. One was written on Christmas Day, December 25, another on December 28, and the last one on December 31."

"See, Sarah, he wrote you three letters in less than a week." Ma knew he'd write when he could.

"I'll read the Christmas Day letter first." Sarah began to read in a clear, soft voice.

Savannah the 25 in 1864
Of December

Dear Wife,
Tis with pleasure that I take my pen in hand to write you a few lines to let you know that I am well and hope these few lines will find you enjoying the same blessing. Sarah I received a letter from you

yesterday dated the 21 and was glad to hear that you was well and more than glad there was 8 postage stamps in it.

Sarah I would like to be at home today to hold Christmas with you. I hope you will have a good time and plenty of good vittles to eat. Sarah my Christmas dinner consisted of one small cracker one slice of pork cup of coffee and meal gravy thick as puddin.

Sarah you wrote that everybody was dunning you. I would pay no attention to them for they can do without it as well as you can and as for Bill Person tell him that I was not to pay him til next October for that cutting box I owe him three dollars to be paid as soon as I could handy on rames account but don't sell no wheat unless it is for yourself for your need of it. When you have three dollars that you don't want you can pay Bill. I owe him seventy pounds of corn in the ear that I promised to let him have seed corn for so weigh him out seventy pounds of ears of corn and don't let him have anything else of any kind only three dollars when you have it and don't want to use it for that is all I owe him.

Sarah I was in Savannah yesterday. It is a nice place. We are camped about a mile from town. Sarah you wrote you looked for a letter the day before you wrote and did not get any in November. You didn't get any for I could not write any until we got here. I wrote one the other day as soon as I could send it. I hope I can write so you can get one every week.

Sarah I would be glad if you would get your likeness and the children's taken and send them to me.

Sarah my captain's name is George M. Roe general's name is Jeff C. Davis.

Sarah I wish I could send you a Christmas present but I have nothing to send only my love to you. My trust is in Him Who says believe in Me and ye shall be saved. Sarah trust in the Lord thy God and remember me.

Sarah I have a poor place to write set on the ground and a board in my lap so you can guess how a soldier has to do everything in proportion. The weather is very warm. I haven't seen any snow yet. I suppose there is good sleighing there. Sarah I hope you have got plenty of wood to keep you warm. I hope you have got moved before this time where you can be taken care of and where you won't be so lonesome and where you can go to meeting.

Sarah I want you to get Warren to let you have trade so you and the children can have what clothes you want. I want you to clothe yourself well get good clothes and plenty of them. Don't be afraid to get them.

So no more at present this is from your affectionate husband,

Rufus W. Seaman
To Sarah E. Seaman

After Sarah had finished reading the letter, she folded it and returned it to its envelope. The three sat in silence, all deep in thought, pondering Rufus's written word.

Pa spoke first. "What was it that Rufus wrote about someone dunnin' you, Sarah?"

"It's true, Pa. Rufus owes Bill Person for a cutting box. He was supposed to pay him for it next October, after he gets out of the army. I ran into Bill in Casnovia, and he asked me for the money now. He doesn't want to wait until October. I wrote and asked Rufus what I should do about it."

"I'll pay him for you, honey." Pa reached into his pocket for the money.

"No, thank you, Pa, I have three dollars to pay him with. It would help, though, if you could weigh out seventy pounds of ears from our corncrib for Bill. Then, according to Rufus's letter here, that's all I'd owe him."

"I'd be glad to do that. I'll come by sometime next week."

"Rufus didn't have much of a Christmas dinner, did he?" Ma felt sorry for him. "And we had so much food."

"I know, Ma, yet it can't help but be difficult to find food for that large an army," Pa reasoned.

"I didn't receive the letter he said he wrote before this one." Sarah pointed to the envelope in her lap. "And I write and write to him, but he's only gotten one of my letters."

"Rufus couldn't write in November, because that's when they were marchin' through Georgia. They must have marched for at least a month," Pa explained. "The papers have been full of General Sherman and his campaign. He's a pretty popular man right now, since sendin' Savannah to President Lincoln as a Christmas present." Pa's face showed the pride he felt in Rufus's being a member of Sherman's army.

Ma reached over and patted Sarah's arm. "You really should get a likeness taken of you and the children to send him. It would mean so much to him."

Sarah nodded. "I know, Ma, I'll try to do that."

"And it's so sweet the way he wants you to get new clothes for yourself and the children." Ma sighed. "He's always thinking of his family."

"The best part of this whole letter is where Rufus says he's trustin' in God. That's what we want to hear!" Pa exclaimed.

"I agree, Pa." Sarah stood to refill their coffee cups. "Everybody ready for the next letter?"

Pa and Ma nodded their heads. Sarah picked up the letter of December 28 and began to read.

Savannah
December the 28 1864

Dear Wife,

I take my pencil in hand to write a few lines to you to let you know that I am well and hope these few lines will find you enjoying the same blessing. Sarah I have received three letters from you one with five dollars in and two with postage stamps and was glad to receive them for the money I needed very much.

Sarah you may think I am getting very foolish as I tell you that I kiss the letters and wished it was you. Sarah I would like to know how you get along and you fare whether Warren pays you as according as he agreed to.

Sarah I would like to have you send me a box of things. I want some black thread needles pins and a casing to put them on half pound of tea some dried fruit of some kind. I would like some dried apples and blackberries and a few cakes get a box about as large as a raisin box and put the things in to send and if you send it send it right away the sooner the better. If you can't send it right away you had not better send it at all but I need the things. If you can't send them as well as not let them go.

Sarah when the rebs left this place they left 388 cannon. Sarah I was out on review before Sherman yesterday. Sarah I haven't had only half rations since we left Tilton and some of the time only quarter rations but I have stood it very well.

Sarah it rains today and I set in my tent and write you a letter and wish I was at home with you while it rains. It would be so much pleasure for to see you and tell you what I have seen and to trot the children on my knee.

Sarah I think the rebellion is very near played out. I don't think it will last longer than spring for the way the rebs left here shows they are getting discouraged and evacuating and leaving things as they are. The talk is that we will go to Louisville from here that is the 14 corps but we will stay here about 60 days without doubt before we leave. Anyhow time enough for you to send me those things if you send them right away. Sarah everything is very high here flour from 15 to 25 cents a pound and everything in proportion and scarce at that.

Sarah am in good spirits and courage trusting in the Lord in confidence believing that He will deliver me from this bondage so I can come home and comfort and cherish you.

Write as soon as you get this and let me know how you get along and how all the rest of the folks do. Give my respects to your folks and all the rest of my friends. Tell Hull that he don't know anything about soldiering but he may be glad he don't. The old soldiers say this is the hardest campaign in the whole war and I guess it is so for it is hard enough.

This is from your husband goodbye

Rufus W. Seaman
to Sarah E. Seaman

As soon as Sarah finished reading Rufus's second letter, she and Ma started making plans to prepare the box he requested.

Sarah walked over to look in her cupboard. "I just bought some tea the last time I went to the store." She reached up and took it from the shelf. "I can send this, and we have dried fruit in the root cellar. I'm sure I can find a small box somewhere. I feel that a box may reach him now, since he finally received three letters from me."

"If you can get it ready, Pa and I will take it to the post office on our way home," Ma told her. "Don't forget the thread and needle. Do you have some small cakes?"

Sarah nodded. "I would love to send him some johnnycake, too."

Pa looked at the two women. "Aren't ya gonna read the third letter?"

Sarah sat back down at the table. "I'm sorry, Pa. Ma and I are just anxious to fix the box for Rufus. I'll read the last letter now."

She took it out of its envelope. "It's much shorter than the first two—only one page."

After a sip of coffee, she began to read.

December the 31st in 1864
Savannah, Georgia

Sarah, I take my pen in hand to write a few lines to you to let you know that I am well and hope these few lines will find you the same.

Sarah, I wrote to you to send me a box of things but if you get this before you send it, don't send those things I never will get. So don't send them.

I have nothing much to write this time and if I had I haven't time. I would love to see you and the children. The report is Sarah here that Sherman says he will in the course of three months, he will give the boys a campaign that they will like. If that is so, I don't know what it is unless it is to send them home and I think myself the war will end in that time so no more at present.

from your husband
Rufus W. Seaman
To Sarah E. Seaman

After putting the letter back in its envelope, Sarah sighed with disappointment. "Well, I guess we don't need to get the box ready after all. But I so enjoyed the thought that at last maybe I could do something for him."

Ma slipped her arm around Sarah's shoulder. "I know you did, honey, but he doesn't think he'd ever get it. And he did get money and stamps from you. That's helping him, too."

Pa cleared his throat. "It's good news that Rufus believes General Sherman thinks the war might be over in three months. We pray that's true."

"Grandpa! Grandma!" Dorothy and Lucy burst into the kitchen after waking from their afternoon nap.

Both grandparents reached for the girls and gave them big hugs. Sarah poured two glasses of milk for her daughters to enjoy, along with a molasses cookie.

When Dorothy and Lucy had finished their milk and cookies, Pa stood up. He kissed each girl on her soft pink cheek. "I'm sorry, little ones, but Grandma and I need to start for home. We'll be back to see ya in a few days."

Ma rose to join him. "Grandpa's right. We do need to leave, but your Mama has some wonderful letters to read to you."

Both girls looked at Sarah through shining eyes. "Are they from Papa?" they asked in unison.

Sarah smiled. "Yes, they are. I'll read them to you after we say goodbye to Grandpa and Grandma."

Pa put on his warm boots from beside the stove. He buttoned his coat and put on his hat and gloves before slipping out the back door to bring the team and sleigh from the upper barn. Pa always picked Ma up at the back door. While waiting in the kitchen for him, she bundled herself up in her coat, hat, and gloves.

"Here, Ma. Wrap this around you," Sarah said, as she held out a wool scarf for her mother. "It should help keep you warm. Put it over your face."

"Thank you, honey. I think I will."

"I hear sleigh bells, Grandma!" Dorothy exclaimed.

"So do I!" echoed Lucy.

Both girls ran to the window. "Grandpa's here," Dorothy announced.

Pa pulled up to the back steps in the sleigh, and Ma gave hugs all around. "Grandpa and I will stop by again very soon," she promised, as she left the cozy kitchen to brave the bitter, cold ride home.

A few days later, as Sarah and her daughters were leaving the barn, Dorothy and Lucy skipped ahead of their mother. They romped with Buster in the newly fallen snow along the path to the house. A snowball tapped Dorothy on her back. She jerked around to see who had thrown it.

"Uncle Ed!" she squealed. Both girls ran into his open arms.

Sarah joined them. "Hello, Ed."

"Good morning, Sarah."

"I didn't hear you drive in. We were in the barn. I just finished doing the chores."

"Queenie's still dry, isn't she?" Ed asked.

"Yeah, and it makes my chores much easier when she doesn't need to be milked. How is Mariette? I keep hoping she'll come with you for a visit. I would love to see her."

"She's right in the middle of quilt making, but she plans to come the next time." Ed's face lit up with a smile. He reached in his pocket. "I stopped by to bring you this." He held out a letter from Rufus. "I picked it up at the post office."

"Thanks, Ed. I appreciate you bringing it all the way out here." Sarah eagerly took the letter from his hand.

"You're very welcome. Why don't you go in the house so you can read it? I'll play with the girls for a while. I have something I want to make for them with this nice, fresh snow."

"Will you have time for a cup of coffee when you're through?"

"I'll make time." He bent over and started rolling a snowball.

Sarah ran up the back steps and into the house. She put a fresh pot of coffee on the range before sitting down at the kitchen table.

As she took the letter out of its envelope, her eyes hungrily searched its pages for news from Rufus.

Savannah, Georgia
January the 5 in 1865

Dear Wife,

Tis with pleasure that I sit down to write you a few lines to let you know how I am. I am well with the exception my thumb. I have a felon on it. It is a milling bad one. It kept me awake all night last night and tonight it is nearly two o'clock and I have not slept a wink so I thought I would write you a few lines to pass the time away. I have a comfortable log shanty to stay in. I bought a candle so I can read or write. For day times, I don't have much time to write for I have to drill.

Sarah, I am a little lonesome tonight for everything seems to bother and worry me. It seems to me that you are not provided for as you should be. It seems as if you were left to take care of yourself. It seems as if everybody is trying to rob you instead of helping you as they should. It seems as if you had no friends at all.

Sarah, write as soon as you get this whether the folks do try to help you or rob you and whether they charge double what it is worth when they do help you. Write all the particulars and how you fare, whether Warren pays you as he agreed to or not and whether you get money enough to get things with and whether you have wood plenty to burn to keep you and the children warm. Sarah, write the whole particulars and how the weather is for I don't know what cold weather is for there has been no cold weather here this winter yet.

Write how things are, how much wheat brings, oats, hay, corn, pork, potatoes, and whether you have fodder enough to keep the cow and how much corn you have and whether you kept that sow pig or not and if you did, I want you to keep corn enough to keep her good all summer.

Sarah, you may think I am making a great many inquiries about things but you will excuse me for I feel as if I would like to know something how things are to home for I know little about it at present.

Sarah, I don't know but your folks think hard because I don't write to them but I can't help it if they do for I told them that I would not make any promises. Sarah, you tell them that I only have time to write to you and not have time at that for I would like to write every day if I could. I would write to you Sarah if I had time as often again as I do.

Sarah, can you get Ed to plant the orchard to corn in the spring and sow the oat—them patches of oats—if you can't, try somebody else for I would like to have them put in.

Sarah, my thumb hurts me so I will have to close by saying goodbye.

From Rufus W. Seaman
To Sarah E. Seaman

After perusing Rufus's letter, Sarah sat deep in thought. It bothered her that he seemed so worried about his family. He deserved an answer to all the "particulars" that concerned him, so she immediately jumped up from the table to get her stationery. She wanted to write Rufus at once to reassure him of their well-being.

She had just finished the letter when Dorothy opened the kitchen door.

"Oh, Mama! Wait till you see what Uncle Ed made. Do you have an old hat we could use? And a scarf, too?"

Sarah went over to the coat hooks by the door. She took down one of Rufus's old hats and a scarf she never wore and handed them to her waiting daughter.

Dorothy took the hat and scarf with a warning to her mother. "Don't look out the window, Mama, until we call you."

"I won't, honey, but what do you say for the hat and scarf?"

"Thank you, Mama."

"You're welcome."

Dorothy shut the door, leaving the kitchen silent once again.

Sarah addressed the envelope of her letter, sealed it, and put a stamp in the upper right-hand corner. Now Ed could take it to the post office for her on his way home.

Shortly Dorothy opened the kitchen door a crack. She poked her head in.

"We're ready, Mama. You can go to the window now and look. See the snowman Uncle Ed helped us make."

Sarah moved over to the window to see exactly what Dorothy and Lucy had made with their uncle. Her surprised eyes beheld a man-sized statue made of huge snowballs and wearing Rufus's hat and her scarf.

"Oh! He's marvelous! You made a wonderful snowman."

Ed entered the kitchen, carrying Lucy on his shoulder. Buster slipped in through the door behind him to lie in his favorite spot in front of the range.

Sarah turned toward her brother. "Where did you learn to make those, Ed? Do you call them snowmen?"

"Yeah, that's what they're called. I saw them in New York and other northern states where there is snow. I thought it would be fun for the girls."

"I'm sure it was. I've never seen one before."

"No, I haven't seen any around Casnovia, either."

"Thank you for playing with Dorothy and Lucy."

"Oh, it's nothing. I really enjoy them, and I know how much they miss their papa." He put Lucy down and took off her coat, hat, and overshoes. Lucy hung her own coat and hat on the hooks near the door and placed her overshoes and mittens behind the stove to dry.

After helping Lucy, Ed turned to do the same for Dorothy, only to find that she already had hung up her hat and coat.

"You can help me with my overshoes, Uncle Ed," Dorothy told him.

He bent down and helped her remove them.

"Thank you, Uncle Ed."

"You're welcome."

Then Dorothy put them, together with her soaked mittens, next to Lucy's.

With those small tasks completed, Sarah took cups from the cupboard for the coffee that she poured for Ed and herself. She filled glasses of milk for her daughters and placed a plate of johnnycake and oatmeal cookies on the table.

While she was preparing this little coffee treat, Ed, Dorothy, and Lucy stood huddled together at the kitchen window, admiring their snowman in the backyard.

"We can all sit down, now," Sarah said softly, almost sorry to call them away.

Both girls wanted to sit next to Uncle Ed, so he took his place between them.

Dorothy looked at her mother. "I'd like to say grace, Mama."

"Of course, Dorothy." Sarah proudly smiled at her.

They all bowed their heads while Dorothy thanked God for their food. "And thank you, God, for Uncle Ed making a snowman with us," she added, before saying "Amen."

Lucy added her usual extra loud "Amen" to that ending. They all laughed.

"Won't you have some johnnycake, Ed?" Sarah asked, passing the plate.

He chose a big piece. "Thank you. No one can make johnnycake like you, Little Sister."

"I thank you for those kind words, Big Brother."

Ed looked around the table. "I heard that someone sitting at this very table has a birthday next week. Is that you, Dorothy?"

Lucy giggled. "You know it's me, Uncle Ed."

"Oh! Is it you, Lucy? How old will you be?"

Lucy held up three fingers. "I'll be three."

Her uncle bent over and whispered to her. "Is your mama going to bake you a birthday cake?"

"Uh huh. She's gonna make me a chocolate cake, 'cuz I like that best."

"I like that best, too. Do you think I could have a piece?" Ed smiled at Sarah.

"Oh, yes! I want you and Aunt Mariette to come and have cake on my birthday."

"Thank you. We'll try to do that."

The week before, Sarah had already invited Ed and his wife Mariette, along with other Walkley family members and some of the Seamans, to come for cake on Lucy's birthday.

Ed saw Rufus's letter lying on the table beside Sarah's cup. "How is Rufus doing?"

"He has a felon on his thumb that is very sore. It's kept him awake for two nights."

"What's a felon, Mama?" Dorothy asked.

"A felon is a sore that is very painful," Sarah answered.

"Oh, does it hurt Papa?" Lucy asked, her face about ready to cry.

"Yes, it did hurt Papa, but it's much better now. Papa wrote this letter over a week ago. The felon has had time to heal," Sarah explained.

"You may read the letter, Ed," Sarah said, pushing it toward him. "I've already answered it. Would you be able to mail it for me on your way home?"

"Sure. That'll be no problem." Ed sipped his coffee while he read.

Sarah wanted Ed to go through the letter silently, because she didn't want to discuss the deep concern Rufus felt for his family in front of the children.

When Ed finished, he handed the letter back to Sarah. "I can see why you answered it right away. It's good that you did. And you can tell him I'll be happy to put in the corn and oats he wants planted this spring."

"I know, Ed, but you'll have work of your own to do, come spring."

"That's okay. I haven't forgotten how Rufus helped Mariette with my farm work when I was away in the army. He's always been there if anyone needed him."

Sarah nodded proudly. "He enjoys helping people."

Ed stood to leave. "I'd better get going, or Mariette will wonder what happened to me."

"Thanks for bringing me the letter and for the snowman. I think I also know someone else who is always helping others." Sarah patted his shoulder.

Ed gave them all a hug and, with Sarah's letter to Rufus in his pocket, walked out the back door to the barn to pick up the team and sleigh he had left tethered inside.

Dorothy and Lucy stood at the kitchen window and waved to him as he drove past their snowman out to the road and toward home.

18

Casnovia
A Birthday Party without Papa

The big day came. Sarah stood bent over, frosting the chocolate cake she had made that morning for Lucy's birthday. Lucy, whose blue eyes were level with the top of the kitchen table, stood on tiptoe to peer at the luscious pastry her mother had just finished icing.

"Ooh, Mama! Can I lick the spoon?"

Sarah smiled down at her daughter. She allowed only a little of the frosting to remain on the spoon before handing it to Lucy.

"Here, you may have a taste."

Seeing what was happening, Dorothy came from across the room. "Can I have a taste, too, Mama?"

"Of course." Sarah took a clean spoon from the silverware drawer and also gave Dorothy a small dab of the chocolate icing.

"Now I'd like you both to take your nap early today. You don't want to be tired when the family is here."

"All right, Mama," Dorothy answered.

"I will, too, Mama," Lucy agreed.

With the girls down for their naps, Sarah sat in Rufus's chair to read her Bible. Since coming back to the Lord at Rufus's urging, she again hungered for God's Word and tried not to miss her daily time alone with the Lord.

Ma and Pa Walkley arrived just as Sarah closed her Bible. Pa dropped Ma off at the back step and then, as usual, took his team to tether them on the barn floor. Sarah's younger brothers and sisters jumped off the sleigh to play in the yard.

Ma quietly shut the kitchen door behind her. "Are the girls sleeping?" she whispered.

"They are down for their naps, but will be getting up soon," Sarah answered. "I put them down early."

"I thought you would."

Sarah took the cake Ma held in her hands and set it on the table. "What kind is it?"

"I made a burnt sugar cake. I knew you would make Lucy her favorite, which would be chocolate, but I thought we could use two cakes."

"And you're right; with the twins, Alfred and Ursula, turning six next week, and Emily becoming thirteen on the twenty-ninth, we can certainly use two birthday cakes. By the way, where are they? Is Oliver with them?"

"Yes, he is. They had to go look at the snowman Edwin and your girls made. It's beautiful. I've never seen a snowman before."

"It's the first one I've seen, too. I do appreciate Ed so much."

"Edwin doesn't have children of his own yet, and he loves Dorothy and Lucy." Ma reached into her pocket. "I almost forgot. I have another letter for you from Rufus. It's a thick one. That's why we came early."

"Thanks, Ma. Have you heard from Wyllys lately?"

"Yes. We got a letter from him today, too. I read it aloud to Pa in the sleigh as we were on our way here. He's doing fine and seems to enjoy being a medic. It was his birthday on the seventeenth of January."

"Yes, he turned nineteen. I wrote to wish him a happy birthday. I hope he received it."

"Sarah, you go read your letter before the rest get here. I'll finish getting things ready in the kitchen."

"All right. I'd like to read it right away."

Sarah walked into the parlor and sat down in Rufus's rocker. She opened the envelope to find a piece of sheet music folded around his letter. She glanced at the title of the music, "Lorena," but decided she would read the letter before she looked at the song.

Savannah
January the 10 in 1865

Dear Wife,
I take my pen in hand to write you a few lines to let you know that I am well and hope these few lines will find you enjoying the same blessing. Sarah I sent you a book last week and today I will send you a song that I paid ten cents for. You may think I am foolish but I thought it was worth it. To send home the book I sent to you cost me nothing for this the boys confiscated a lot of them.

We lay here yet but don't know how long we will stay. The talk is that we will go to Wilmington North Carolina from here but it is uncertain where we will go.

Sarah I have no news to write to you this time there is nothing new. My thumb is better. The doctor cut it open so it don't pain me so much as it did when I wrote to you before.

Sarah I have not got only four letters from you since I left home and I am afraid I shan't get one a month for is on the fourth month now and I would like to hear from you oftener if I could I would be very happy. Sarah write often write two or three and send them at once. Write two or three a week and send them out Saturday if you can't send them before. Sarah I don't know what else to write. Sarah I would like to have you send me some more postage stamps for mine is mostly gone and no money to get any more with.

Sarah if you can sell the farm for the money sell it sell it at first chance you can get for we'll go to Illinois as soon as I get out of this for it is the place for me. I can get good land there for ten dollars per acre. So I think I shan't stay in Casnovia long after I get out of the service. So sell out if you can and get the money and you and I will go where we can take comfort the rest of our days. I hope I will try to make up for the days of sorrow. They say the darkest time is just before day and I hope it is for I hope the day will break soon for your sake. The day is coming soon I think for they have sent peace negotiators to Richmond and I hope they will come to some kind of a settlement.

Sarah write often my mind is scattered this morning so I can't write much and my ink is poor and together I make bad work of it. Sarah I will have to close by saying goodbye may God bless you Sarah this is from your husband.

Rufus W. Seaman
To Sarah E. Seaman

Sarah read Rufus's letter twice before putting it back in the envelope. Then she picked up the song and noticed its lovely lyrics. "It will be fun to play it later," she thought, "when everyone can sing along."

Sarah rose and placed the music on the piano before rejoining her mother in the kitchen.

At that moment Pa came in from the barn, where he had stabled Prince and King, his prize Morgans.

"Hello, Pa," Sarah said. "Thank you for coming early to bring me Rufus's letter."

"You're welcome, Sarah. Your mother and I know what it is to wait for letters from a loved one in the war."

"Ma said you received a letter from Wyllys, too."

"Yeah, Ma read it to me on our way here."

"That's what she told me. I'm glad he's doing all right."

"How is Rufus?

"He's fine."

The back door soon opened, admitting Sarah's four young siblings, who were covered in snow from head to foot.

Sarah chuckled when she saw them. "It looks like we have four live snowmen in the kitchen." She hung their wet coats on pegs behind the stove, where she also put their boots. "How did you like our snowman?"

"We loved him!" Oliver answered. "We'd like to build one at our house, too."

"Could I ask you girls for your help?" Sarah asked.

Ursula and Emily nodded. Both sisters resembled Sarah, with their brown hair and blue eyes—like those of their mother. Alfred and Oliver, her younger brothers, looked more like their redheaded father.

"Emily, could you take the grownups' wraps and carefully lay them across my bed?"

Sarah turned toward her youngest sister. "Ursula, could you take their scarves, hats, and gloves, and put them on my bed, too? The children's coats you can hang on the pegs by the back door."

Both sisters were pleased to be asked to help.

Before long the sound of stomping feet on the back porch announced the arrival of their guests. Edwin and Mariette Walkley entered first, followed by the Seaman family, which included their daughter Silence and her three small children. Silence and Sarah's friendship had begun in grade school. With Silence's husband, Charles Russell, also away while serving in the Union Army, the former school chums now had even more in common.

Sarah welcomed Rufus's family members with a warm embrace. "Hello, Ma and Pa Seaman. I'm so glad to see you. I received a letter from Rufus today. He's fine."

Ma Seaman's face lit up. "I'm so glad to hear that."

Sarah bent over to look at each of Silence's children: Will, six years old; Rose, four; and baby Frank, two. "Silence, your little ones are really growing. They're wonderful children."

Silence beamed proudly. "I didn't know if we were ever going to get them to come in the house. They were so taken with the snowman."

"Yes, it is quite an attraction," Sarah admitted. "I owe it all to my brother Edwin."

Emily took the grownups' coats into the bedroom, while Ursula hung the children's on the pegs by the back door.

"Let's all go into the parlor and be seated," Sarah invited them.

"Mama, can we get up, now?" Dorothy stood in the doorway of their bedroom, her hair tousled from sleeping. Lucy followed close behind. The jingle of sleigh bells announcing the arrival of their company had awakened them just in time.

Sarah stepped toward them. "Yes, of course you can. Just let me run a comb through your hair first," she said, as she gently unsnarled the light brown curls of each daughter. She then brought out two boxes from under the bed and from the larger box lifted out a lovely blue dress just Lucy's size. "This is your birthday present from Papa and me. Papa asked me to get you children some clothes." Sarah then looked reassuringly at Dorothy. "You will get a new dress on your birthday, just like your sister."

"Ooh, Mama." Both girls' eyes gleamed, as Mama slipped the dress over Lucy's head. "I can hardly wait for my birthday, too, Mama," Dorothy exclaimed. "But I wish Papa could be here to see me in my new dress."

"Me, too!" Lucy wished her Papa could look at her right now.

Then Sarah opened the smaller box and took out a pair of shiny new shoes.

"Ooh, ooh, Mama, new shoes, too?" Lucy reached out to touch them.

"Yes, new shoes, too. But these are your birthday gift from Uncle Warren and Aunt Mary and Uncle George and Aunt Sarah. They said a pretty new dress called for pretty new shoes," Mama explained, as she slipped them on Lucy and buttoned them up. "They can't come to your party today, but we will see them after church on Sunday, and then you can thank them."

Lucy looked down at her feet. "I will thank them, Mama. I love my new shoes."

After using the commode in the corner and washing their hands in the washbowl, Dorothy and Lucy merrily raced out of the room to greet their grandpas and grandmas, aunts, uncles, and cousins. Everyone called out "Happy Birthday!" to Lucy and presented her with gifts.

"Say, 'thank you,' Lucy," Sarah reminded her.

"Thank you," Lucy shyly responded.

"You're welcome, Lucy," they replied.

"You may sit down and open your presents," her mother added.

Lucy sat on the floor in the parlor and opened each gift. She unwrapped the package from Uncle Edwin and Aunt Mariette first, it being the biggest. Aunt Mariette had made a beautiful quilt for her bed. Lucy loved the pretty colors and wrapped the quilt around her.

One by one, she opened the other gifts. Grandma and Grandpa Seaman gave her a warm, knitted red sweater, and Lucy liked it so well that she could hardly wait to wear it the next day. She also loved the knitted slippers from Aunt Silence and Uncle Charles. Last of all, Lucy unwrapped Grandma and Grandpa Walkley's present to find knitted clothes for her rag doll, Katie, which Grandma Walkley had made her earlier. Dorothy, Rose, and Ursula all wanted a turn at dressing Katie in her new outfits. Lucy would have to share her doll today.

"What's this, Sarah?" Edwin sat on the piano stool, holding a sheet of music in his hand.

"That's a song I received from Rufus just today. It's called 'Lorena.'"

"Yeah, I've heard this song. It's especially popular in the South."

Sarah approached Edwin. "I like the song's words. I thought it might be fun for all of us to sing it around the piano."

"I'm game. Are the ladies going to lend their voices also?" Edwin asked.

"We'd love to," Silence and Mariette said, as they both jumped up to join Edwin and Sarah.

Sarah sat on the piano stool, and Edwin took his place behind her. She examined the song closely before starting to play the haunting melody. The three standing behind her blended their voices in harmony, joyfully singing verse after verse of the lovely lyrics.

Ma and Pa Walkley, along with Rufus's parents, preferred to sit and listen to the younger people sing. Being old neighbors of many years, they were happy for an opportunity to chat with one another.

The children, for their part, kept on playing and paid little attention to the music.

After the musicians had finished singing all the song's many verses, Sarah excused herself to go finish her work in the kitchen. "I'm sorry, but I need to get back to fixing the refreshments. This was fun. Let's do it again soon."

"Sarah, could we have just one hymn?" Pa Walkley asked, as she was preparing to leave the room. Since Sarah had rededicated her life to the Lord, the family enjoyed singing hymns around the piano again, as they once had done.

Sarah played the introduction to Pa's favorite, "Amazing Grace," and they all joined in and sang the hymn before she went back to the kitchen.

Silence and Mariette went along to help.

Grandpa Seaman called Lucy over to where he sat and pulled her up on his lap.

"You ought to see what we have on the back porch for your birthday," he whispered in Lucy's ear. He put his finger over his lips. "Shh, don't tell anyone. Come, I'll show only the birthday girl."

Grandpa Seaman took a coat from the peg near the back door and wrapped it around Lucy. With her hand in his, they went together onto the back porch, where Lucy saw a large tub. Grandpa took the top off a tall, round container packed in the middle of ice. He allowed Lucy to stick her tiny finger into the cold freezer to sample the ice cream made especially for her birthday.

"Mm." Lucy loved the taste. "More, Grandpa." Grandpa's blue eyes twinkled.

"We'll have more later with your birthday cake," he explained to her, as he put the top back on the ice cream. "Remember now, this is our secret," he reminded her before they reentered the kitchen.

Lucy then ran off to play in the parlor with Dorothy and the other children. The girls always looked forward to a visit from their cousins and their mother's younger siblings, who were only a few years older than they.

Meanwhile, Pa Seaman kept a close eye on the preparations taking place in the kitchen. When he saw Sarah start to cut the cakes, he decided the time had come to bring in the special treat.

No one noticed him go out onto the porch, but all eyes were on him as he brought in the freezer amid a chorus of oohs and aahs.

"Pa! You made ice cream!" Sarah exclaimed.

"Yeah, we made it for Lucy's birthday and all the other January birthdays present." Both Pa and Ma Seaman wore beaming smiles, pleased over the special surprise they had brought.

First, Sarah sat only the children around the kitchen table because it wasn't large enough to accommodate everyone; the company would eat in shifts. After Grandpa Seaman said grace, the children began to eat their ham sandwiches, cake and ice cream. They were given hot cocoa to drink, and the older children helped baby Frank so he wouldn't get burned.

The adults enjoyed visiting in the parlor while waiting for Lucy, Dorothy, and their friends to finish eating. Sarah sat in the doorway of the kitchen to supervise the children.

"What did Rufus have to say in his letter, Sarah?" Pa Seaman asked. "How is his thumb?"

"His thumb is much better. He thinks he would like to move to Illinois when he comes back home," she added. "Land sells there for $10.00 an acre. He told me to sell the farm, if I get a chance."

The room suddenly became quiet. Although everyone knew the Seamans were an adventuresome family that moved about easily, this news took them by surprise.

"How do you feel about that, Sarah?" Mariette finally inquired.

"I'll go wherever Rufus feels it's best for us. But we can talk it over when he comes home. He'd never ask me to go somewhere I didn't want to go. Maybe Illinois would be better for us."

"Well, I know it has wonderful farmland," Ed commented. "I've seen some of it."

"Ma and Pa heard from Wyllys today, too," Sarah said, wishing to change the subject. She didn't care to discuss moving to Illinois just yet, although she knew she could trust Rufus's judgment as to what would be best for them.

"How is Wyllys, Ma?" Ed asked.

"He's doing fine. As I told Sarah, he really enjoys being a medical corpsman."

"Yeah, he always was good at helping cows deliver their calves when there was a problem. And the sight of blood never bothered him," Ed replied. "I'm sure he does a good job, even though he just turned nineteen. There are many boys in this war even younger than Wyllys."

"I think we're all done eating, Mama," Dorothy said and looked at Sarah. "Can we go play?"

Sarah rose from her chair and walked over to the kitchen table. It did look like the children were finished, including baby Frank. "You may all go play," she answered Dorothy.

The children quickly left the table, except for Frank. Sarah looked at baby Frank's angelic face with his blond curls and big blue eyes. She bent over to kiss the top of his head, remembering another little boy who was very dear to her heart. After wiping off his face and chubby hands, she lifted him onto the floor. He quickly scooted after the other children to go play in the parlor.

In no time at all, the table was cleared and the adults were all gathered where the children had been sitting just moments before.

Sarah poured everyone a hot cup of coffee, while Ma Walkley served the ham sandwiches and cake, and Ma Seaman dished up scoops of ice cream. The grown-ups were as excited over the ice cream as the children.

"Uncle Ed?" Lucy called from the parlor.

"Yes, Lucy," Ed answered.

"Don't forget to have my cake. You said you like chocolate best."

"I'm having a piece, Lucy. Thank you."

The conversation continued around the table. Each one found contentment in being together as a family, though they sorely missed Rufus, Wyllys, and Charles.

Lucy felt that the time came all too soon for the company to start home—while it was still daylight. The Seamans left first with Silence and her family, as they had the farthest to go.

Lucy went up to Grandpa Seaman. "Grandpa, I liked our secret."

He bent down and gave her a big hug. "I liked it, too." With hugs all around, they were off. Ma and Pa Seaman went home that night knowing their surprise had brought pleasure to all.

Edwin and Mariette prepared to leave next. "I'll be stopping by soon, Little Sister. Is there anything you need done?" Ed asked.

"Not right now, Big Brother. Thank you for asking, and thank you both for coming. The quilt is beautiful, Mariette." "You're welcome." Mariette put on her coat. "We enjoyed ourselves. It was such fun to sing your new song, 'Lorena.'"

"Hey, I like that song, too. We'll have to do that again," Edwin suggested.

After making sure everyone received a hug, Mariette and Edwin started on their way.

Only Ma and Pa Walkley, with their young children, remained. "I'll help you do the dishes, Sarah," Ma said, as she started clearing the table.

"No, Ma, I can do these. You'll want to get home before dark."

"It won't take us that long," Ma insisted.

Ma proved right; the dishes took only a short time. Pa had left for the barn when they started, and now he pulled up to the back steps with his sleigh and team just as Ma finished drying the last dish and hung up the towel.

"Come on, children. Pa's out there waiting for us." Ma handed them their coats, taking them from the pegs. She then put on her own coat and scarf.

"Thank you, girls, for your help," Sarah said, as she gave her little sisters a hug.

She gave Alfred a quick squeeze and ruffled Oliver's hair as she said, "I hope you boys do make a snowman in your own yard."

"Thank you, Ma, for all your help and for bringing me the letter." Sarah put both arms around her mother and held her tightly.

"You're very welcome, Sarah." Grandma bent over and hugged Dorothy and Lucy. "Has this been a happy birthday, Lucy?"

"No, Papa wasn't here to see me in my new dress and my new shoes."

Grandma clasped Lucy one more time and looked at Sarah. "We all wish your papa could have been here, honey." Ma stood up. "We'll see you very soon." Ma shooed her young ones out the door and followed close behind.

Sarah and her daughters stood at the window to wave. As they watched the last sleigh move out of sight, pangs of loneliness gripped them. Sarah's thoughts wandered to Rufus. She wondered when he would be on the march again—this time the march toward home.

19

South Carolina and Casnovia
Sloshing through Rainy Lowlands ~ Illness ~ Snowy Memories

The pummeling of heavy raindrops on the tin roof of his makeshift cabin awakened Rufus before reveille. Today, January 17, was the day scheduled for his First Division to start its march through the Carolinas. He lay on his wooden cot, listening to the hammering of the rain, knowing what it meant to any troop movement—wagon wheels sunk in mud to their axles and troopers marching in water to their knees.

Except for the rain, Rufus felt excited about starting the move northward. This time he would be marching toward home, not away from it. He knew each step he took would bring him closer to Sarah, Dorothy, and Lucy. Sherman's army would be homeward bound.

Reveille sounded. Rufus jumped up and quickly dressed himself in his tattered uniform. He shoved his feet into his well-worn boots after shaking them out to make certain nothing had crawled into them during the night. Bending over, he laced them tightly for the march. He rolled his few belongings, including his tent, into his blanket. Because of the heavy rain he needed to wear his poncho. Pulling his slouch hat firmly down on his head, he shouldered his rifle on his right and his blanket roll on his left. He then stepped out onto the puddle-laden field to join his three messmates in line for roll call.

As soon as it was completed, the sergeant dismissed the troops to fix their own breakfast in the rain. Rufus and his messmates prepared a bowl of rice, a roll, and coffee flavored with milk. On their last visit in Savannah a couple days ago, they had pooled their money to buy some rolls and canned milk. This morning they cooked their food outside over the campfire, then entered Rufus's cabin to eat out of the rain. They even brought the coffee pot inside. Joey fed half of his roll to Tramp, who lay at his feet. In addition, Tramp, as usual, had a bowl of rice along with the messmates.

"This is sure awful weather to start marchin' in." Tom sat on Rufus's cot, finishing his mug of coffee.

"It couldn't be worse," Rufus agreed.

"I think it would be good for us to pray together before we start on this march," Robert suggested.

They all thought the same.

"Could ya read the part in the Bible that ya gave Simon?" Joey asked. "I like that."

"Do you mean the Ninety-first Psalm, Joey?" Robert asked.

"Yeah, that's what I mean."

Robert took out his Bible and read the psalm. Then they all took turns praying that all would go well on the march.

"I'm concerned about how our troops are going to behave in South Carolina. They feel different toward South Carolina than they did toward Georgia. They blame South Carolina for this terrible war," Tom said, as he stood to refill his coffee cup.

Rufus nodded. "I've been worried over that, too, Tom. You're right. Our boys really have it in for South Carolina."

"Shouldn't they forgive?" Joey asked.

"That's the Christian thing to do," Rufus answered, "only many of our boys have seen their comrades blown to pieces in this war that never shoulda been. We need to pray for 'em."

"Columns fall in!" the sergeant barked. Tom grabbed the coffee pot and emptied it outside. He loaded it on the nearby pack mule, along with the pot of cooked rice he had prepared in advance for their dinner and supper. The four fell in line with the other troops in the column. Rain was still coming down in torrents.

At the command to march, the left column stepped out, and the troops proceeded along the Savannah River towards Sister's Ferry. At times they marched four across; at other times, only two, depending on the condition and width of the road. Hour after tedious hour, they sloshed through the rain. Their ponchos offered little protection from a downpour of this magnitude. Over and over they had to put their shoulders to wagons mired in the mud.

At noon the columns halted to break for dinner. Rufus, soaked to the skin, couldn't stop shivering. All the soldiers were wet through, but it affected Rufus the most.

Tom and Robert, along with Joey, hurriedly searched for some dry wood to build a fire to warm Rufus. They found a large pine knot that they hoped would burn. After several tries, it finally ignited and flared up into a nice blaze.

"Come by the fire, Rufus," Tom called. "I think we have it goin'. I'll quickly heat our rice."

"Thanks, Tom and Robert—and you, too, Joey." Rufus's teeth chattered as he spoke. "I h-hate to b-be a bother."

"You'll never be a bother, Rufus," Tom assured him.

"That's right, Rufus. Don't ever start to think that way," Robert told him. "You'd do the same for us. Wouldn't he, Joey?"

Joey nodded. "Yeah, he sure would."

"I think I'd be fine, if I could just get warm and dry," Rufus managed to say.

Joey, concerned about Rufus, moved over to sit close by him. Rufus noticed, and understood how he felt. He reached over, patted Joey's knee, and forced a smile at him through his trembling lips.

"We aren't makin' many miles today," Tom stated. "The river sure is swollen."

"Yeah, we're marching back to Sister's Ferry, where we'll cross the Savannah into South Carolina—that is, if it's not too swollen for us to pontoon it," added Robert.

Rufus didn't eat much of his bowl of rice. He took some tea out of his knapsack and had Tom make everyone a hot cup, which they all needed.

All too soon, the time came for the column to resume marching. On and on they slowly plodded through the mud that sometimes reached the top of their boots. The rain never stopped. It beat unmercifully down on them, and the river continued to rise.

Around 4:00 p.m., the commanding officer of the First Division ordered the column to bivouac. Rufus and his three messmates found a spot under some pine trees to set up their camp. Joey, determined to do

Rufus's chores, grabbed the buckets off the pack mule and went searching for water. Tramp followed him. Tom found drier wood under a pile of brush and started a fire. Robert worked at setting up the tents, and Rufus tried to help him. They pitched them to face the fire Tom had built. Rufus crawled into his tent, trying to escape the heavy rain.

Major Eaton rode into their campsite when Tom, Robert, and Joey were finishing their supper. The three saluted their officer.

"I'm just riding throughout the campground to see how all the boys are doing. Where's Rufus?" the major asked.

"Rufus is in his tent. He's ailin' and didn't want any supper," Tom told him. "He became soaked to the skin and couldn't stop shiverin'."

"That's too bad. If he isn't better in the morning, have him ride in the ambulance," Major Eaton told them. "You should get into your tents out of this rain or you'll be sick, too." He saluted them and rode to the next campsite.

After they had cleaned up the supper dishes, they did as the major suggested. All three ducked into their tents, and Tramp too.

The next morning, Rufus shuffled over to the ambulance wagon and attempted to climb in. The driver, a burly, bearded man, recognized Rufus and jumped down from his seat to assist him. He remembered when Rufus had helped him drive his team of Morgans through the mud one rainy day a few weeks back.

"Do ya remember me, private?" he wanted to know. "My name's Jeremiah Jones." He spit out a wad of tobacco. "Ya showed me how to gentle my team to get 'em to pull through the mud."

Rufus stood and studied Jeremiah's face. He smiled weakly and nodded. Not having slept all night, he suffered from what seemed to be a bad cold, with pressure in his chest. He felt shaky all over. Until the teamster spoke to him, Rufus failed to recognize him. He then slowly recalled the Morgans and the day he showed Jeremiah how to drive a team when it's muddy.

Jeremiah helped him to a cot in the wagon. Rufus now lay in the ambulance that was hitched to the very team he had wanted to drive when he first saw the horses in Atlanta before the march began. The rest of the way to Sister's Ferry he marched when he could manage it, and rode in the ambulance with Jeremiah when he couldn't.

A few days later, after a combined, exhausting, nearly forty-mile march, the First Division reached Sister's Ferry. Their trek had taken much longer than expected, because of the difficult, muddy conditions. They arrived to find the river swollen to a width of almost three miles on the South Carolina side—too wide to put a pontoon bridge across. They would have to lie in camp until the water receded.

Rufus's health showed no improvement. He still felt a deep pressure in his chest and suffered from cramps and diarrhea. He mostly sat in his tent, day after day, feeling miserable, while he waited with the other troops for the water to go down.

"Rufus," Tom said, as he stuck his head into the tent they shared, "they're gonna take mail back to Savannah. Do ya want to write a letter to send home? Are ya up to it? If not, I can write it for ya."

"Thanks, Tom. I can write a short one to Sarah."

Rufus reached for his knapsack to get pen and paper. Although he didn't feel up to writing a long letter, he managed to write one page for Tom to send with the outgoing mail. It might be the last chance he would have in a while to send Sarah any mail and to tell her how much she meant to him.

Four days later, the swollen water had receded enough for the pontoon bridge to reach across the Savannah River. The First Division proceeded into South Carolina, but too weak to march, Rufus reluctantly followed in the ambulance. It concerned him that his weight might slow the wagon down. He knew that trains, stationed three quarters of the way back in their division, struggled to keep pace with the troops in the advance.

Once in South Carolina, Robert and Joey, along with the other foragers, started the search for food again, and Tom went back to tearing up the railroad. Except for Rufus, the messmates quickly fell into their old routine. Rufus often rode in the ambulance, but tried to march whenever possible. He didn't want to give up, but on February 20, Colonel Eaton assigned him strictly to the ambulance, no longer requiring him to fall in for roll call.

The march through South Carolina proved more strenuous and difficult than the march through Georgia. The Thirteenth Michigan Regiment, as part of the Fourteenth Corps's column under General Slocum, marched mostly to the south of General Sherman and endured South Carolina's worst-flooded lowlands. The troops waded in water to their knees and could scarcely find relatively dry ground on which to pitch their tents and sleep. Almost daily they needed to slog through rivers, swamps, and creeks, cutting down beautiful large magnolia trees to use for bridges and for corduroying the roads. Sometimes the soldiers were even forced to wade through freezing water as high as their shoulders, carrying their rifles and boots over their heads to keep them dry. Some sang hymns to give them courage while crossing such frigid streams. The rain never ceased for long.

Whenever the divisions halted to bivouac for the night, they searched for dry areas where water didn't cover the ground. Rufus's messmates wanted to make camp near the ambulance train to stay close to him, but the wet conditions seldom permitted it. The wagons, including the ambulances, were usually parked in puddled areas, since they could stand the water better than the tents could. The friends missed Rufus during their evening devotions around the campfire.

Sick and lonely as he was, one day just rolled into another for Rufus, as he rode along. Jeremiah tried to take care of him, but he used such profanity that it made Rufus cringe. Whenever Rufus tried to talk to him about the Lord, Jeremiah changed the subject.

The two corps of the left wing were to cross the Catawba River at Rocky Mount. The Twentieth Corps, with General Sherman, arrived there first and laid their pontoon bridge. Soon after Sherman's corps had crossed the bridge on February 23, heavy rains washed it away, leaving the Fourteenth Corps stranded behind. General Sherman halted the Twentieth Corps to camp at Hanging Rock, while waiting for the Fourteenth Corps to cross the river.

General Davis had a difficult time constructing another bridge. It took days to finish the tremendous task. While they were held up, the weather cleared one evening, making it possible for Rufus's messmates to set up camp near the wagon trains. What a happy time they had, being together once again. Robert and Joey helped Rufus out of the ambulance so he could sit over by their campfire. Joey sat down beside him, his freckled face beaming with joy. The four messmates invited Jeremiah to join them, but he declined, preferring to spend time with some of his teamster friends.

Robert looked Rufus in the face. "Hey, Whiskers, I think you're gonna have quite a beard before long," he kidded.

"Yeah, I haven't shaved since Savannah. But Whiskers, yourself, Robert; ya look like ya haven't shaved either." Rufus glanced over at Tom. "And that goes for ya, too, Tom." They all laughed. The three friends were letting their beards grow again on this march.

Tom made chicken and rice soup especially for Rufus's supper. It tasted good, and Rufus did eat more than usual. After supper, they held their devotions. It meant so much to Rufus, who had missed this time with his Christian brothers.

"We need to pray about all the devastation goin' on. It's just as we feared, Rufus; our troops are wreakin' vengeance by burnin' everythin' in their way but churches." Tom regarded Rufus, whose head hung in sorrow, as he huddled by the fire. Riding in the ambulance, he didn't know how bad things really had become.

During their time of devotions, they all prayed that there would be no further destruction and that their troops would learn to forgive. They prayed for forgiveness on both sides, Union and Confederate. Each, then, prayed for his own family, and Tom, Robert, and Joey concluded by praying for Rufus's health.

When they finished, Robert reached into his shirt pocket for his harmonica. He started playing the old familiar hymns. Tom and Joey sang along, while Rufus tried to find the strength to join in. Soldiers from campsites around them added their voices in the still night air. It was a beautiful, starry, moonlit evening, and everyone kept singing along with Robert's harmonica until taps.

The following morning dawned clear, but with a hint of rain on the far horizon. Rufus ate breakfast with his messmates before they moved back toward the front of the column to resume their work on the pontoon bridge.

"Goodbye, Rufus." Robert bent over to shake hands with his sick messmate, who was sitting in front of the fire. He looked up at the sky. "I hope this lovely weather holds, so we can camp by you every night."

"Goodbye, Robert. I hope so, too."

Joey shyly extended his hand to Rufus. "Goodbye, Rufus. I sure miss ya."

"Goodbye, Joey, I sure miss ya, too. I miss all three of ya," Rufus said, as he weakly shook Joey's hand.

Robert and Joey walked away, with Tramp following close behind. Rufus sadly watched them go. Tom would soon follow.

Suddenly Joey, with Tramp nipping at his heels, turned around and ran back, as if he'd forgotten something. Joey threw his arms around Rufus and embraced him. Rufus returned his hug. Then, without a word, Joey jumped up and raced back to rejoin Robert, who was waiting for him. They then continued on their way to forage.

Tom sat down beside Rufus. "That boy really misses ya."

"Yeah, I know, and I really miss 'im, too. He's such a good boy."

"Yeah, I know he is."

"Tom, would ya kinda look after 'im?"

"Sure, Rufus. Ya don't even need to ask. I love Joey, too."

"Thanks, Tom, I know ya and Robert both love 'im."

Tom helped Rufus up and walked him over to the ambulance, where they shook hands. "Goodbye, Rufus. I hope we can get together more often and that ya stop ailin' soon."

"I hope so, too, Tom. Goodbye, and thanks for everythin'." Tom then turned and started running to catch up with Robert and Joey, while Jeremiah boosted Rufus up into the ambulance.

By noon, Rufus heard the raindrops bouncing off the canvas top of the wagon again. There would be no get-together with his messmates that night.

Rufus, back in the ambulance, noticed a change in Jeremiah. He hadn't heard him swear or seen him spit his tobacco all morning. He even spoke calmly to the team.

At dinner, Jeremiah prepared some vegetables and rice for the two of them over an open fire. He then climbed up into the wagon with their meal in his hands and sat on the vacant cot across from Rufus.

"Here, Rufus. Ya should eat somethin'." Jeremiah handed him a plate of food, as Rufus sat up.

Rufus didn't feel hungry, but he knew he should try to eat a little, as Jeremiah suggested. He bowed his head and silently prayed a blessing over his food. Jeremiah respectfully waited to eat until Rufus looked up.

They ate in silence, but Rufus sensed that Jeremiah felt ill at ease. "Everythin' goin' all right with ya?" he managed to ask.

"Sure, I'm fine," he answered. Then he cleared his throat and, without looking at Rufus, spoke. "Rufus, you're a Christian, ain't ya?" he asked.

"Yeah, I am." Rufus answered.

"How do ya become one? What makes ya a Christian?"

Rufus, feeling weak, handed his plate to Jeremiah and lay back down on his cot.

"Well, Jeremiah, we're all sinners. The Bible is very clear on that. When someone comes to the place where he realizes he is a sinner and wants to be forgiven, he needs to repent of his sins and be washed in the blood of Jesus. Jesus Christ's blood is all that can wash our sins away. He shed his blood on the cross for us—you and me—everyone. He died in our place."

Jeremiah listened intently. He did not change the subject this time. "How do ya repent? What does that mean? Does it mean you're sorry?"

"Yeah, but it means to be sorry enough to turn away from our sin—to stop sinnin'—not just to be sorry alone."

"How . . . how is someone washed in the blood?"

"He prays a sinner's prayer to ask Jesus to forgive 'im and to come into his heart as his Savior. He needs to believe Jesus is the Son of God and that he died on the cross and arose from the dead on the third day."

A single tear rolled down Jeremiah's cheek. "Rufus, would ya help me pray the sinner's prayer? I want to be a Christian. I don't know how to pray."

"Of course I'll help ya pray. Just repeat after me."

Jeremiah knelt in front of his cot and repeated a short sinner's prayer after Rufus, whose feeble voice almost gave out from sheer exhaustion.

Fatigued as he was, Rufus felt quietly elated over Jeremiah coming to the Lord. He now knew why he had noticed a change in him. He wondered what had brought this change about, but didn't have the strength to ask. Maybe he could do that later.

Almost as if Jeremiah read Rufus's thoughts, he told him what had happened last night.

"Ya know, Rufus, when all of ya were singin' them hymns last night, it carried me back to when I was just a little boy and my grandma took me to church. She was a fine Christian and wanted me to be one. My ma and pa ain't Christians, just my sweet Grandma. She always prayed for all of us to become Christians. The words of the hymns seemed to speak to me last night. I wanted to be like Grandma and serve Jesus, too."

Rufus tried to smile at him as he nodded. "Ya are now," he said, his voice barely audible.

Jeremiah's face glowed. "Yeah, I know."

Early the next morning, on February 27, the Fourteenth Corps moved out and crossed the Catawba River. Rufus's bumpy ride in the ambulance over pontoon bridges and corduroyed roads caused him great pain. His sick body suffered punishment from the jarring caused by the deep ruts and potholes along the trail. Instead of improving in health, Rufus grew steadily worse. He now ran a high fever most of the time and slipped in and out of delirium. Jeremiah sent word to the ambulance surgeon, who examined Rufus.

"You are much sicker than someone with a bad cold," he told him. "You have an illness with fever. It may be typhoid or yellow fever. You should really be in a hospital."

The weather had not permitted Rufus's messmates to camp near the wagon trains again. All of them missed one another badly.

Despite the hardship the unceasing rains produced, Sherman's army persevered in making its way northward through South Carolina. No swollen bayous, rivers, swamps, or streams could stop them when they faced homeward.

After the Union forces had finished crossing a particularly difficult, overflowing river, even the revered Confederate general Joseph Johnston observed, "I made up my mind that there had been no such army since the days of Julius Caesar."

* * * * *

Sarah stood at the kitchen table, busily kneading bread dough, while Dorothy and Lucy took their afternoon naps. The howling wind outside alarmed her as it rattled the back door. She knew the all-too-familiar sound of a blizzard.

"I'm glad Edwin came this morning and helped with the barn chores," she thought. "And that he also filled the woodbox. I won't need to go outside anymore today."

She gave the dough one last punch before putting it aside to rise and then wiped the flour off her hands onto her apron.

Amidst the noise of the wind, she couldn't believe she heard the faint sound of sleigh bells. She rushed to the window to see her parents pulling up to her back porch. A gust of wind almost tore the door out of her hands as she opened it to greet Ma. Out of breath from hurrying, Ma embraced Sarah.

"We can't stay, honey. Pa is turning the team around so we can quickly go to the school and pick up the children before they start to walk home in this weather. It's terrible out there. Don't you go outside! Do you have plenty of wood? What about the animals in the barn?"

"It's all right, Ma. Edwin came early this morning and took care of everything," Sarah assured her worried mother.

"I'm glad. Oh, here's a letter for you." Ma took the letter out of her pocket and handed it to Sarah. "That's why we stopped by on our way to the schoolhouse. We just wanted to drop off your mail from Rufus. Goodbye, dear."

Sarah clutched the letter. "Thanks, Ma. Goodbye." She waved at Pa through the window as he picked Ma up at the back step. She could barely see the barn, with the snow coming down heavily and the wind blowing in every direction. Everyone would be snowbound by nightfall.

Sarah laid more wood in the kitchen range and shoveled a couple scoops of coal into the potbellied stove in the parlor. She shivered just looking at the windows freezing over with ice, and pulled Rufus's rocker closer to the stove before sitting down. She opened his letter and quickly read it.

Georgia February the 4 in 1865

Dear Wife,
I sit down to write you a few lines to let you know I am still alive but have been sick for two weeks ever since we left Savannah. I marched part of the time and part of the time I rode in the ambulance.

We are laying in camp waiting for the water to fall so we can cross the river into South Carolina. We will march soon for the water is going down. I had a chance to send a letter out today so I write to let you know how I am. I don't feel like writing much.

The day we left Savannah, it rained all day and night so I got wet through. I caught a violent cold and left me in the cramps and a heavy pressure in my chest and I get no relief yet.

Sarah, direct your letters to
Savannah Georgia via New York to Company G 13 Michigan VV Infantry 14th AC

Tis from Rufus Seaman
To Sarah Seaman

Oh, Sarah, my wife, you are more dear to me than my life.

Sarah folded the letter and put it back in its envelope, disappointed to read that Rufus had another bad cold and didn't feel well enough to write more. Her heart went out to him—sick and away from his family. If only she could be the one to nurse him. She bowed and prayed that Rufus would soon be well.

She then went into the kitchen to check on the bread. It had risen, so she opened the oven door and placed the pan on the middle rack. With the added wood, the oven temperature had become hot enough to nicely bake the bread.

Listening to the blizzard outside, Sarah became increasingly anxious for her parents and siblings. She kept praying that they would make it home safely.

The fearful weather outside took her back to another blizzard years ago, when she happened to be one of the children in the schoolhouse. Sarah smiled as she recalled that memory . . .

. . . It was 1852, some thirteen years ago, when Miss Elliot, an attractive blonde woman in her late thirties, sat at her oak desk at the front of the one-room Cambria Township School in Hillsdale, Michigan.

She frowned as she looked through the school's narrow windows to the scene unfolding outside. She surely didn't like what she saw. How could the weather create a beautiful winter wonderland one moment and then change so quickly, she must have wondered. Oh yes—Michigan in February, she reminded herself.

The cold wind blowing the large snowflakes into white mounds and drifts could prove treacherous, Miss Elliot realized. As the squalls kept whipping the snow against the school building, the windows started to ice over.

"Bobby, would you please put some coal in the stove?" she asked.

Bobby quickly got up and did as she asked. His freckled face glowed with delight that the teacher had called on him to feed the potbellied stove that stood near her desk and heated the school. The older students, Bobby among them, felt it a privilege to take turns putting coal on the fire.

The clock on the back wall struck 2:00 p.m., usually too early for school to be dismissed, but Miss Elliot knew she must act. The welfare of the students, ages six to fourteen, was her responsibility, and she really cared about them.

She gently tapped her desk to get their attention. "Boys and girls, because of the stormy weather I'm dismissing school early. Most of you live close enough to walk home. But the farm children, the Seamans and the Walkleys, must stay here at the school with me. It wouldn't be safe for you to try walking that distance in this weather."

A low murmur could be heard in the room as the children softly talked to one another, while they put away their books, papers, and pencils.

Miss Elliot rose from her desk and walked to the cloakroom. The dozen or so children who lived nearby followed her. She made sure they buttoned their coats tightly and pulled their hats down over their ears.

She then gave the smaller children a hug and patted the older children on the shoulder.

"Go straight home," she cautioned them.

"We will, Miss Elliot," they replied in unison.

After the teacher had seen each child out the door, she walked over to the frosty windows and blew on the glass of one of the panes, rubbing her hand across it to make a circle through which she could see outside. Looking through that circle, she watched the children walk safely to their homes down the street.

Before turning away from the window, she caught a glimpse of a sleigh and team of horses driven by two young men still in their teens, as it pulled up outside the school. After they came to a stop, the older boy jumped down and walked up the steps. Before he rapped on the school door, he took his hat off to reveal a mop of unruly blond hair and slapped his snowy cap against his leg, stomping the snow from his boots at the same time.

Miss Elliot immediately opened the door and invited him in. Hat in hand, he entered, his smile shining out from a wind-beaten, red face. Crystallike snowflakes clung to his eyelashes, and snow covered his clothes.

"I'm Rufus Seaman, ma'am," he told the teacher. "My ma sent us to pick up our brother and sister, Lafayette and Silence Seaman; our neighbor, Mrs. Walkley, also wants us to pick up the Walkley girls. They're worried about the storm," he explained.

"Yes, I'm worried about it, too. I didn't want to dismiss the Seaman or Walkley children to go home; it would be too dangerous," Miss Elliot replied.

When Rufus walked into the schoolroom, his sister, Silence, stole a glance at Sarah, sitting across the aisle from her. When she noticed the beaming smile on Sarah's face, she understood the reason behind it. She and Sarah, being best friends, shared many secrets. Silence knew Sarah had a crush on her older brother, Rufus. But Rufus only thought of Sarah as a little girl—his sister's friend whom he enjoyed teasing. Just then, Sarah turned and looked at Silence, her blue eyes twinkling. Both girls clasped their hands over their mouths to keep from giggling.

The teacher turned to face her remaining students. "You children come with me into the cloak room and get bundled up to go," she instructed. Again, as she had done with the children who had left for home earlier, she made sure the three Walkley girls—Sarah, 11, and twins Sofia and Maria, 8—along with Lafayette Seaman, 12, and Silence Seaman, 11, had buttoned their coats and pulled down their hats to cover their ears. She held the twins' bright scarves in her hand.

"Here, Sofia, let me tie your scarf around your face. That wind will sting," she said, as she reached out toward the twin nearest her.

When she noticed the girls snickering, she knew she had mixed them up again. She laughed and gave each twin a hug. She couldn't always tell them apart; with their long auburn braids and their mischievous blue eyes, they looked exactly alike. They often played tricks on good-natured Miss Elliot by sitting in one another's desks, purposely confusing her, though she was a teacher they loved and someone who understood them and loved them in return.

Waiting patiently for the children to get bundled up, Rufus took off his gloves and tucked them under his right arm, then held out his palms towards the potbellied stove to warm them.

The children, all bundled up, started filing past him to go out the door. When Sarah walked by, Rufus pulled the light brown pigtail hanging below her hat. Sarah, feeling her face blush, turned away so he couldn't see. She didn't want him to guess how she really felt about him.

Before Rufus turned to go out the door, he spoke to Miss Elliot. "Would ya like a ride home, ma'am? It's lookin' worse out there all the time."

The teacher already had her coat and hat on. "No thank you, Rufus. I just live across the street."

She turned the damper on the stove to help smother the fire, put on her gloves, and moved out the door with Rufus. After locking up, she walked down the steps.

Recognizing Martin all wrapped up in a robe and sitting in the sleigh, she called a greeting to him.

"Hello, Martin! You're really brave to be out in this."

"Hello, Miss Elliot," Martin answered. "It's gettin' pretty bad."

Rufus had graduated from the eighth grade four years ago, before Miss Elliot came there to teach, but his brother Martin had been her student last year as he finished school, so they knew one another well.

"Be careful going home," she told Rufus, and started across the street.

Rufus stood and watched her, barely able to see through the blowing snow, until she arrived at her door, where she turned and waved before going inside.

Approaching the sleigh, Rufus met a disgruntled Lafayette. "I'm not sittin' in back with those gigglin' girls," he stated.

Rufus put his hand on his shoulder. "Ya can sit up on the seat between Martin and me, but it will be colder," he warned him.

"That's okay with me," Lafayette muttered. "Anythin's better than back there with them." He looked at the four girls huddled together under warm robes, who stopped their giggling long enough to stick their tongues out at him.

Rufus and Martin laughed. "Let's get started. We need to get home and out of this weather," Martin said, his teeth chattering as he spoke.

Rufus took Lafayette's arm and helped him up to the seat next to Martin. Then he sat down next to Lafayette, rewrapped the robe across their three laps and tucked it securely around Lafayette before he took the reins. He clucked to the horses, and they started their laborious trip homeward. Even though they lived only two miles from school, in this weather it would be an arduous journey for them.

The blankets the horses wore protected their bodies a little, but the wind whipped the snow into their exposed faces. After they had traveled about a mile, Rufus stopped the sleigh and handed the reins to Martin before jumping down and brushing the ice crystals off the horses' noses and eyes. He then climbed back up, and Martin started to hand the reins back to him.

"No, ya drive the rest of the way, Martin. Ya can do it," Rufus told him.

Even though Martin had just turned fifteen, he had a way with horses, just like his brother Rufus.

The storm seemed to be getting worse, and the horses strained to pull the sleigh through the deepening snow. The temperature kept dropping, and visibility grew steadily worse. Rufus and Martin kept the team on the road by using the trees along the sides as guideposts. In stretches with no trees, Rufus got out and, grasping the bridle of one of the horses, guided them forward. Needless to say, they passed no other sleighs.

The talking and giggling from the girls in the back had long since ceased, as Silence and the twin Walkley girls, Sofia and Maria, grew frightened. Lafayette felt afraid as well, though he would not admit it, but Sarah remained calm. She trusted Rufus to get them home safely. In her eyes, he could do anything.

At last they reached the Walkley farm, located just across the road from the Seamans. Mrs. Walkley stood in the doorway of the home as the sleigh pulled into the drive. She hurried her daughters into the house, thanking Rufus and Martin over and over again for bringing the girls home safely. Sarah, the last one to enter, first turned and shyly waved at the sleigh. They all waved back, but in Sarah's heart she meant the wave for Rufus, her hero. Martin then drove the team across the road and into the Seaman driveway.

After Sarah and Rufus were married, Rufus told her the rest of the story. After dropping off Lafayette, Silence, and Martin at the house, Rufus took the team and sleigh to the barn. He unhitched the horses and led them to their warm stalls, where he took off their soaked blankets and gave each one a rubdown. After feeding and watering them, Rufus knelt in the hay. He wanted to thank God for bringing them home safely. He had been praying all the way home, and he knew God had answered his prayer.

20

North Carolina

A Bumpy Ambulance – Gentle Deserters – Costly Battles

On March 4, 1865, the Fourteenth Corps crossed the state line into North Carolina's tall pine forests. The weary troops still marched in a steady downpour, knee-deep in mud, as they advanced northward. As they entered the state, they stopped most of their destruction and burned few houses, since the Federal soldiers did not hold North Carolina responsible for the start of the war.

The Morgans' muscles rippled as they strained to pull Rufus's ambulance over the bumpy, treelined roadways, which sometimes still sank away into the soggy ground. At the end of the day, one could hardly tell the color of the mud-spattered team. Jeremiah handled the pair gently and tried to find time to give the cherished horses a rubdown every evening.

Teams of six mules pulled the wagons loaded with heavy artillery.

The Federal soldiers marched relentlessly through the rural countryside with its pine foliage. General Sherman ordered the Four Columns to close in around Fayetteville, one of the larger North Carolina towns situated on the Cape Fear River. The general wanted to destroy the U.S. arsenal located there, since the Rebels had seized it in 1861 and had used it to supply arms for the South ever since.

The Fourteenth Corps, under General Slocum, crossed the Pedee River at Sneedsboro and marched directly toward Fayetteville in order to enter and occupy it ahead of the other columns. Sherman's army camped at Fayetteville from March 11 to March 15, awaiting supplies and preparing to destroy the arsenal.

Meanwhile, Rufus, confined to the ambulance toward the rear of his regiment, knew little of what was going on around him. His health still hadn't improved; the chronic diarrhea sapped his strength, and each day he grew weaker. Now that the columns had halted for a few days, he enjoyed a respite from being jarred in the wagon as it traveled over terrible roads. He missed his messmates, but Jeremiah proved to be a good Christian friend in caring for him.

On their last day at Fayetteville Jeremiah left the wagon to tend to the horses. The morning rain gradually ceased, but the gray sky still held ominous clouds. Rufus lay dozing on his wooden cot, when he suddenly awoke to a rough tongue licking his face.

"Tramp!" he cried, quickly looking around for the dog's master, for he knew Joey would not be far behind. Joey ran over, climbed into the ambulance and fell to his knees by the cot to shake Rufus's hand. "Joey!" What a welcome sight that freckled face was, for he loved the boy like one of his own kid brothers. Tom and Robert jumped up into the wagon together. Rufus didn't catch the look exchanged between them, but they had noticed the dark circles under his eyes and his gaunt face. His health clearly had failed since they had last seen him. He and his messmates shook hands and warmly greeted one another.

"We brought ya some coffee. Would ya like a cup? We brought some sugar, too, and some oats for your horses." Tom held up a sack. "A boat came from Wilmington up the Cape Fear River with a few supplies. We were afraid ya might miss out on receivin' anything, travelin' back here at the tail end."

"Coffee does sound good," admitted Rufus. "Thanks, fellas."

"You're welcome," Robert said, as he sat down facing him.

Just then Jeremiah returned from tending the horses and warmly received the surprise visitors. He jumped in to help Tom build a fire to brew a pot of coffee, and after filling everyone's cup, they left the coffee pot on the fire for refills. They also heated a kettle of water for washing their tin cups.

Soon the five soldiers sat in the snug wagon, sipping steaming coffee. Some even took sugar.

Tramp suddenly growled and got up. But when he stalked over to look out the doorway of the wagon, his tail started to wag.

"Any coffee in this pot out here?" a familiar voice called. Tramp jumped down to greet the voice he recognized as that of a friend. The three messmates, along with Jeremiah, were not far behind the dog. The soldiers saluted Colonel Eaton, who stood bent over with both arms around Tramp. He soon straightened up to return their salutes and to shake hands with each one.

"We didn't hear ya ride up, Colonel." Tom picked up the coffee pot and filled the colonel's cup.

"I guess this muddy ground muffles the sound of my horse's hooves," he said. "How's Rufus doing? I came to see him."

"He's still not well. He's growin' weaker every day, ridin' in the ambulance," Jeremiah quietly answered.

"I'm sorry to hear that. It doesn't sound good. When we reach Goldsboro, I hope something more can be done for him. I'll go see him right now."

He took his coffee and walked over to the ambulance, where he rapped on the back entrance. "Hello, may I come in?"

"Yeah, come on in," Rufus replied.

Colonel Eaton stepped up into the wagon and moved to the back, the messmates behind him.

"Hello, Rufus," he greeted him.

"Hello, Colonel." Rufus saluted him without rising to his feet.

Eaton understood and returned his salute before sitting down on the cot opposite where Rufus lay. He took a sip of the steaming brew from the cup in his hand. "This is good coffee."

"Yeah, it is." Rufus finished his own cup. "Tom, Robert, and Joey brought us some today, and Tom made a pot."

"How are you feeling?" the colonel asked, his eyes showing concern.

"Not the best, sir," he replied. "I feel very weak and just sick all over."

The colonel reached over and squeezed his shoulder. "I'm truly sorry, Rufus. I dropped by to let you know we move out tomorrow for Goldsboro. Maybe we can get you more help there. I'm hoping we can send you North to a real hospital."

"I'd like that, sir."

"We'll see what we can do. Thanks for the coffee."

"You're welcome. Thank ya for comin', sir."

Standing to leave, Colonel Eaton reached over and shook Rufus's hand. "I'll see all of you at Goldsboro," he told everyone. He quickly left the ambulance and rode off.

"I still think he's the best major there is," stated Joey.

"We all agree with you, Joey, but he's a colonel now," Robert reminded him.

"I didn't get a chance to ask him if he'd seen anything of the Rebel deserters. Have ya seen any?" Tom asked.

Rufus looked puzzled. "What deserters do ya mean? We haven't seen any."

"Many of the Confederate troops have deserted and attached themselves to us. We think they're comin' from the trenches of Virginia," Tom answered. "They've brought their families along. Our men are sharin' what little food we have with 'em. They mostly stay around the trains at the rear. I'm surprised ya haven't seen any."

Rufus shook his head. "No, I haven't, but I don't leave the wagon very much."

"We hope it will be better for them when we reach Goldsboro. We hope they can get supplies there, so they can travel north," Robert added.

Joey looked at Rufus. "Are they cowards to desert?"

"Not necessarily, Joey," Rufus answered. "I think they're just men tryin' to take care of their families. We don't know what we'd do in their place."

"Yeah, I didn't think about that," Joey said, flashing a big grin.

"How are things goin' with you boys up in the front?" inquired Jeremiah. "Do ya ever have to fight the Rebels?"

"Yeah, a couple weeks ago our regiment was engaged at Catawba River back in South Carolina," answered Tom. "We had a skirmish with 'em a day or so after we saw ya. But mostly I work at tearin' up the railroads, while Robert and Joey forage."

"I'm glad no one was hurt," murmured Rufus. "Travelin' back here we don't always know what's goin' on." Rufus spoke in a low voice that was barely audible.

"It's hard for the trains to keep up with the troops in all this mud," added Jeremiah. "Even with the corduroyed roads, the wagons can still sink to their axles."

"Shall we have our prayer time together?" asked Robert.

"I think we all need that," Rufus softly replied.

Jeremiah looked over at Robert. "Do ya still play your harmonica?"

Robert's handsome face lit up. "Yeah, I do. After we pray together, would you like me to play some hymns?"

"I sure would. I love those hymns." Rufus smiled knowingly at Jeremiah, who returned his smile. Rufus understood what the hymns meant to him.

Robert took a small Bible from his coat. "Does anyone have any scripture he would care to share?"

"I do, Robert," replied Tom, turning the pages of his own Bible. "Lately I've been meditating on 1 Corinthians 13." Robert opened his Bible to 1 Corinthians and read the first three verses of chapter 13.

> Though I speak with the tongues of men and of angels, and have not charity, I am become as sounding brass, or a tinkling cymbal. And though I have the gift of prophecy, and understand all mysteries, and all knowledge; and though I have all faith, so that I could remove mountains, and have not charity, I am nothing. And though I bestow all my goods to feed the poor, and though I give my body to be burned, and have not charity, it profiteth me nothing.

Robert paused in his reading. "I always enjoy this chapter, too, Tom. It is very powerful. Would you like to read more of it?"

"Yes, I'd like to read the next four verses explainin' what charity is really like."

> Charity suffereth long, and is kind; charity envieth not; charity vaunteth not itself, is not puffed up, doth not behave itself unseemly, seeketh not her own, is not easily provoked, thinketh no evil; rejoiceth not in iniquity, but rejoiceth in the truth; beareth all things, believeth all things, hopeth all things, endureth all things.

Tom paused after finishing the text.

"Is there a reason, Tom, you've been thinking about this particular chapter lately?" wondered Robert.

"Yeah, I've been thinkin' a lot about when the war is over. Our country, both North and South, will need a lot of healin'—healin' that will call for charity on both sides."

They all agreed with him.

"Ain't we showin' charity when we share our food with the deserters and their families?" Joey wanted to know.

"If it's done with the right spirit, Joey," Rufus answered. "It needs to be done in love."

"You're right, Rufus. And we have been praying for them ever since we knew they were following our trains," Robert explained. "Shall we pray now?"

Each man prayed heartfelt prayers for his own family first. Even Rufus managed to huskily verbalize a special prayer for Sarah and his little girls. Next, they prayed for the Confederate followers and for the war to end. When they prayed for one another, Rufus's three messmates and Jeremiah prayed an especially fervent prayer for Rufus. Joey prayed his heart out for Rufus to get well. When he finished, hot tears brimmed his eyes. He felt awkward.

Rufus looked up at Joey. "Thank ya, Joey," he whispered. "That really blessed me."

After they finished their prayer time, Robert took out his harmonica and softly started to play hymns. Rufus lay back to listen to the inspiring music. Too weak to sing, he gladly rested, as Tom and Joey sang. Jeremiah's dark eyes softened as he joined them. A new Christian, he relished every moment of their fellowship. The big, burly man possessed a deep bass voice that blended in harmony with the other two voices to form a trio.

They had sung a couple hymns when, on the chorus of "Abide with Me," they heard a beautiful soprano voice, along with another baritone, join them in their singing. Robert kept on playing, while the trio stopped, hoping to hear the two singers more clearly. As they listened, they could hear that both voices had decidedly Southern accents.

Tom rose from his seat and hopped down from the wagon to try to locate them. Following their voices, he found the couple huddled under one of the wagons. The baritone belonged to a young man whose scruffy blond hair and beard needed trimming. He wore a tattered Confederate uniform that had seen a great deal of duty. Beside him sat the soprano, a raven-haired young woman holding a little girl in the lap of her faded dress. The child had a torn blanket wrapped around her.

"Hello there," Tom called, as he approached them. "Ya have nice singin' voices. Come on over and join us."

"Do . . . do . . . ya know who we are?" stammered the man, his eyes cast downward.

"Yeah, I think I do. You're still welcome to come join us." Tom put his hand out. "I'm Tom Shafer."

The man stood and shook Tom's outstretched hand. "I'm Bobby Shore. This is my wife, Elizabeth, and our little girl, Mary Jane. We'll join ya if ya really don't mind. We love singin' hymns." He looked over at his wife. "I used to lead the singin' in our Baptist church, and Elizabeth played the pump organ."

Tom escorted the little family over to the ambulance, where Joey and Jeremiah still were raising their voices in song. "We have company," he announced, as he helped Elizabeth and Mary Jane up into the wagon. He and Bobby followed close behind.

Elizabeth stood frozen with fear. She found herself facing four Union soldiers gathered at the rear of the ambulance. Three sat on one cot, and across from them lay an apparently ill soldier on another. She knew these soldiers belonged to Sherman's army—an army of devastation to the South. She picked up her daughter and clasped her to her pounding heart. Even Bobby's reassuring hand on her shoulder didn't take away the terror she felt.

Robert recognized the fright in Elizabeth's dark eyes. He bounded up from his seat to assist in allaying her feelings of panic and gently guided her to his place on the cot across from Rufus. Jeremiah moved over to make more room, and Joey sat on the floor with Tramp. After Elizabeth had sat down with Mary Jane on her lap, Robert leaned over and whispered to her, "You don't have to be afraid, ma'am. You're safe with us." Elizabeth looked into Robert's kind eyes and knew he told her the truth, so she nodded her head to show she believed him. Satisfied, Robert sat down on the end of Rufus's cot.

Tom made all the introductions. First, he introduced their guests. "Fellas, this is Bobby and Elizabeth Shore, and their daughter, Mary Jane. This couple really loves to sing hymns. Bobby led the singin' in his church, and Elizabeth played the organ."

All the soldiers except Rufus graciously stood to their feet and spoke a greeting. Rufus nodded to them from his cot.

Then Tom introduced his comrades to the Shores. "This is Robert Turner, who is the harmonica player. He's a pastor. And this is Joey

Thorpe, our youngest member, and his dog, Tramp. This is Jeremiah Jones, who is the team driver for this ambulance." Bobby shook hands with each one.

Tom walked over near Rufus and introduced him last. "And this is our dear friend, Rufus Seaman, who we came to visit today. He became ill after bein' soaked in the rain. Because he's too sick to march, he rides in this ambulance, but we're sure he'll be back on the march soon." Bobby bent over and shook Rufus's hand.

"Where are ya'll from, private?" Elizabeth asked Rufus.

"Michigan, ma'am. All of us in this regiment are from Michigan," Rufus replied. "And please call me Rufus."

"Do you have a family back home, Rufus?"

He looked at Mary Jane sitting on her mother's lap. "Yes, ma'am, I have a wife and two little girls like your Mary Jane. Dorothy is five now and Lucy is three."

"I'm sure they miss their papa," Elizabeth told him.

"Not as much as their papa misses them."

"Would you like a cup of coffee?" Robert asked their guests. "We have some left in our pot."

"Yes, please. That would be very nice," Elizabeth shyly answered.

Tom took his tin cup and Robert's outside to the campfire and washed them. He poured two cups for Bobby and Elizabeth.

"Do ya take sugar?" he asked, handing them their coffee.

"No, thank you," they both replied. "This is fine. Thanks."

"Do we have any of the goat's milk left, Jeremiah?" Rufus asked. "Is there enough for a cup for this little girl?"

"Yeah, I think there is. I'll get her a cup."

Jeremiah took his own cup outside to wash it. From a box under the wagon he took out the jar of goat's milk and filled the cup. He had managed to get the milk from one of the several goats that traveled along with the train, hoping it would be good for Rufus. Back inside, Jeremiah handed the cup to Elizabeth, who gently held it to her daughter's lips. Mary Jane eagerly gulped every drop.

Rufus looked away. Anyone could tell the child was suffering from hunger. He thought of his own Lucy, who would be only slightly older than this little girl. Jeremiah noticed, too, and refilled the child's cup. After Mary Jane had finished her second cup, although more slowly this time, she grew sleepy and rested her curly head on her mother's shoulder. Soon her long eyelashes lay closed on her cheeks, as she slept in her mother's arms.

"Y'all have been so kind. Thank you," Elizabeth drawled, her eyes becoming misty. "She was too hungry to sleep well last night."

"You're very welcome," they all answered.

"Where are you from?" Robert asked.

"Our home is here in North Carolina, but we want to go north," Bobby answered.

"We should have more supplies to share with ya when we get to Goldsboro," Tom told him. "Food is pretty scarce now."

"We know. We are thankful for whatever ya can do," Bobby assured them. They all knew Bobby had deserted, but no one mentioned it.

Robert started playing his harmonica once more. All but Rufus blended their voices in praise and glory to the Lord. Rufus felt privileged to be able to lie there and listen to them. After they had sung several of the old hymns, they concluded their time of fellowship with the song "Blest Be the Tie That Binds." No eyes were dry as they sang this one. Each knew of a tie that bound them together—His Name is Jesus Christ.

Reluctantly, Tom stood up. "I hate to break this up, but we'd better start back toward higher ground to pitch our tents for the night."

Joey's face showed his disappointment, for he hated to leave Rufus. "C'mon, Tramp," he said. Tramp got up from sleeping in the corner of the wagon, his tail wagging.

"Thanks for comin'." Rufus tried to sit up a little. "I really miss ya."

"No more than we miss you," Robert smiled down at him.

"I hope to see ya again, soon." Rufus's voice cracked as he spoke.

"We'll see you for sure when we arrive at Goldsboro," Robert promised.

"Yeah, I'll see ya for sure when we get to Goldsboro, Rufus," Joey echoed. Everyone laughed.

Rufus looked up at Joey. "I'll hold ya to that promise, Joey," he teased.

"I'll be there, Rufus. I promise," he answered seriously.

"We should arrive at Goldsboro in a week," Tom figured.

"Then we'll be expectin' a visit from all three of ya at Goldsboro about that time," Jeremiah replied.

"We'll be there," Tom said. After making plans for meeting Rufus and Jeremiah again, the three messmates bade them a fond farewell and were on their way.

Rufus felt exhausted but blessed by their visit. He looked forward to seeing them again at Goldsboro. He missed each of them so much, especially Joey.

"I think we'd better leave, too," Bobby told Elizabeth. She agreed.

Bobby hopped down from the ambulance, followed by Jeremiah. Elizabeth handed sleeping Mary Jane to her father before she descended from the wagon, with Jeremiah's assistance.

"Do ya have a special place ya stay?" Jeremiah asked, before the family started to walk away.

"No, usually under one of the wagons, so it will be a little drier," Bobby answered. "We just got here yesterday."

"Jeremiah!" Rufus's raspy voice called from inside the wagon.

"Yeah, Rufus," Jeremiah answered.

"Get my tent from under the cot. They can borrow it. I won't need it. They can use my poncho, too."

"Good, Rufus, and I'll give them my tent, too, so they can hook 'em together."

Jeremiah went about gathering the tents and ponchos. "Which wagon do ya think will have the driest dirt around it?" he asked Bobby.

"The one we were under earlier today," Bobby said, as he led them over to the spot. About an inch of water covered the ground around the wagon. Near most wagons the water ran three to six inches deep.

"We can help fix that," Jeremiah told Bobby. "Let's find some tree limbs." The two went searching and soon had three or four armloads of limbs. Jeremiah carefully placed them in rows near the wagon and tied them together with a rope. He laid the poncho over the limbs, and then he and Bobby pitched the two tents they had buttoned together on top of this makeshift campsite. Bobby and Elizabeth were very pleased to have a tent; when Bobby deserted, he had to leave his behind.

"Thank ya, Jeremiah, for all you've done. And thank Rufus, too, for his tent and poncho. You've all been so kind." Bobby shook his hand.

Before he left them, Jeremiah helped Bobby, who didn't have any matches, build a campfire of pine knots near the tent. He hoped it would give them some warmth. He left his matches with them for future use, as he had more.

"I can't promise ya much," he told Elizabeth, "but I'll try to keep Mary Jane in goat's milk."

"Oh, that would be wonderful," she drawled. "Thank you."

"You're very welcome." Jeremiah hurried back to the wagon, knowing Rufus needed help to get to the latrine.

March 15 found Sherman's entire army across the Cape Fear River, marching in the rain toward Goldsboro. The Fourteenth and the Twentieth Corps traveled north on the left, with the Twentieth Corps on the extreme left. The cavalry, under General Kilpatrick, guarded the Twentieth's left flank. General Sherman ordered General Slocum to send his wagon trains on a separate route under heavy protection. Acting on those orders, General Slocum placed those trains on a centrally located road between the left and right wings, thus freeing the divisions for combat.

Bobby, Elizabeth, and Mary Jane still followed close to Rufus and Jeremiah's wagon. Mary Jane, wrapped up in Jeremiah's poncho, rode on the seat beside him, or else inside with Rufus. She behaved very well for a toddler confined to a wagon, and her light weight never bogged down the ambulance. Her parents traveled along behind—Elizabeth wearing Rufus's poncho to protect herself from the rain, and Bobby marching wrapped up in a blanket.

After covering several miles, the trains halted to make camp. Rufus and Jeremiah gladly stopped for the night. Progress had been difficult; many times during the day the continuous rain and muddy roads forced the troops guarding the trains to push the wagons out of the mire to keep them moving. Bobby always put his shoulder to the ambulance to assist the soldiers.

Jeremiah, wearing his slouch hat pulled down against the rain, took his and Rufus's fly tents from the bed of the wagon to help Bobby pitch them for the night. Next, Jeremiah struggled to build a campfire and to somehow keep its wet wood burning. Willingly doing her part, Elizabeth helped him fix the meal that had to feed the five of them, peeling sweet potatoes, cooking rice, and making a pot of coffee. Mary Jane sat inside with Rufus and her papa, who helped Rufus to the latrine when needed.

Most of the troops were kind about sharing their food with the Shore family, contributing sweet potatoes and rice when they could. They even helped Jeremiah get Mary Jane more goat's milk, for she had stolen the heart of each soldier who met her.

Preparations completed, the five of them sat in the ambulance to eat their supper out of the rain. Elizabeth prepared Rufus a plate with mashed sweet potatoes and a helping of rice. She also handed him a cup of coffee with a large amount of goat's milk to flavor it, the very way he liked it. "Here, Rufus, you should try to eat this." Rufus could only pick at his food, despite Elizabeth's urging, but drank the coffee right down.

"Boom!" They heard firing again in the distance. Fear gripped Rufus's heart for Joey, Tom, and Robert over with the First Division.

"Are those our guns?" Jeremiah asked. "I've been hearin'em all afternoon."

"I don't know," Rufus replied, as they kept hearing heavy artillery. "It sounds more like a battle than skirmishes," he noted.

"I hope it isn't a real battle," Bobby stated, his head down. "We don't need more men killed on either side."

"Seepy, Mama, seepy." Mary Jane crawled into her mother's lap. After eating her supper and drinking a cup of goat's milk, she felt drowsy and soon fell asleep.

Earlier, Jeremiah had helped Bobby pitch their tent. Everyone felt tired from a long march and now wanted to turn in.

"Would ya like to lay Mary Jane in the corner of the wagon on a blanket?" asked Rufus in a feeble voice. The ambulance carried extra blankets.

"Thank you, Rufus," Elizabeth nodded. "Bobby, would you put the blanket down for Mary Jane to sleep on, please?" She tenderly kissed her daughter's cheek and laid her on the blanket, covering her with part of it for warmth. Then she and Bobby left to bed down in their tent.

Rufus lay awake all night, listening to the firing of the rifles and artillery, and kept praying for his messmates.

The noise of the battle continued all the next day, March 16, until sundown. In the evening, Jeremiah walked along the wagon trains, trying to find out if the First Division with the Thirteenth Michigan had taken part in the fighting. He knew Rufus's concern for Joey, Tom, and Robert, and found that some information had drifted over to the wagon trains.

"I heard it's mostly General Kilpatrick's cavalry and two divisions of the Twentieth Corps that's involved in the fightin'," Jeremiah told Rufus when he returned. "It seems General Hardee with a small corps of Rebels attacked General Kilpatrick's cavalry. The Rebs put up quite a scrap until the two divisions of the Twentieth got there to help Kilpatrick."

The day had been difficult. General Hardee had dug in with a strong line of resistance near Averasboro, North Carolina. General Sherman personally instructed one Union brigade to circle behind the Rebels and hit them from the rear, a tactic that succeeded in routing them. The Confederate troops fled, only to regroup into another line of resistance soon after. When the Federals endangered this second line as well, the Rebs moved back to form a third line, which withstood many Union attacks, until the enemy finally fell back at sundown. By the next morning General Hardee had retreated, and the Rebels were gone. But it had been a bloody day: the Battle of Averasboro had cost the Union forces 682 casualties and the Confederates 865.

Union troops had carried 68 wounded Rebel soldiers to a nearby house, where Union surgeons performed all necessary surgical procedures before they were to move out. The Federals eventually left the wounded with as much food as could be spared and in the hands of five Rebel prisoners whom they released—an officer and four enlisted men.

Before they left, General Sherman visited the Rebel wounded in the house, where he heard someone whisper, "Are you General Sherman?"

At the sound of his name, Sherman paused and turned to look into the ashen face of a young Confederate captain lying on a nearby bed. Union surgeons had just amputated his arm in an effort to save his life.

"Yes, I am General Sherman," he said, speaking gently to the wounded soldier.

"I remember you visiting my father's home in Charleston before the war," the captain whispered. "My name is Macbeth."

General Sherman recalled the visits he'd made to the Macbeth home in Charleston. "Would you like me to write a brief message to your mother?"

"Yes, please." The young man spoke with great effort.

The general sat down and assisted him in writing to his mother. He mailed the letter later, when they reached Goldsboro.

Turning east from Averasboro, the Fourteenth Corps led the left wing toward Goldsboro. While the left wing had continued to engage in combat at Averasboro, the right wing had marched on northeastward toward Goldsboro. This movement had widened the gap between the two wings, isolating General Slocum's wing and putting it in jeopardy.

General Sherman still traveled with the left wing, as it tramped through the swamps and lowlands, where the terrain held them back even more.

They marched all day under canopies of billowing black smoke from burning turpentine stills. Late in the day, General Slocum's column stopped to camp near the village of Bentonville.

Reports of Rebels being sighted in the area reached General Sherman, but did not disturb him. He and General Slocum were convinced the Rebels who had been seen were only a small cavalry group.

The morning of Sunday, March 19, dawned sunny and clear. General Sherman rose early and, believing no danger lurked nearby, rode across the countryside to join General Howard's right wing.

Rufus and Jeremiah realized their wagon was traveling far back from the rest of their regiment, the Thirteenth Michigan. Unable to keep up because of the roads, the wagon trains were spread out for miles.

Their own First Division, under General Carlin, marched in the advance. The Third Division escorted the wagon train to protect it. The trains had been on the road for only a few hours when off in the distance they heard a loud boom. All the wagons stopped, and the teamsters sat looking at one another, dumbfounded.

"That was cannon!" one teamster finally yelled. Before anyone could answer, there came another boom.

"That's not the cavalry!" another teamster cried.

Bobby walked up to Jeremiah, who was sitting on the wagon seat. "I'm afraid that's the Confederate cannon."

The noise frightened Mary Jane, as she sat beside Jeremiah, and she started to whimper. Bobby reached over and picked her up.

"But . . . but if they have cannon, it won't be just a skirmish," Jeremiah stated. He knew the First Division, which included his regiment, had the advance.

Jeremiah turned around on his seat and looked back in the wagon at Rufus. "Did ya hear that boom, Rufus?"

"Yeah, I heard it. They must be fightin' again."

"Yeah, that was cannon. We need to really pray."

"You're right. I've been layin' here prayin' since I first heard the cannon. Our division is in the lead."

"I know. I've been prayin' for 'em, too."

The train remained stationary for the rest of the day, while the sound of cannon continued until nightfall.

"If we just had a way of findin' out what happened," an anxious Rufus said to the others at supper.

"I did ask around, but no one seems to know anything yet. We're so far from the action now," Jeremiah explained. "I'll try again in the mornin'."

Bobby sat with his eyes cast downward, listening to Jeremiah and Rufus. He noted the fear and concern in their voices. "It's all so useless," he thought. Finally, he raised his eyes and spoke. "Ya have never mentioned anything about me being a deserter. But I want to try and explain to ya why I deserted."

Rufus put his hand up. "Ya don't need to explain. We aren't judgin' ya."

"I know ya aren't. That's why I want to tell ya." Elizabeth gave her husband a smile of encouragement. "I'm not a coward," Bobby went on to say. "I've fought in many battles, includin' Gettysburg. But I deserted for two reasons. My family needed me, and I simply did not want to kill anyone or be killed when the war is already lost. The Confederates should surrender. Think of the lives that were taken on both sides just today," Bobby continued. "And think how useless it all is. No one can beat this army. It's all wrong to keep fightin' for a lost cause that's costin' so many lives."

After Bobby finished speaking, everyone sat without saying a word. Rufus and Jeremiah agreed with him on the futility of it all. They understood his feelings.

Sporadic fighting could be heard for the next two days, Monday and Tuesday. Tuesday night Jeremiah walked along the trains, inquiring if anyone knew what actually had happened. This time he got information to take back to Rufus.

Jeremiah entered the wagon and looked down at Rufus lying on his cot. "Rufus! The cannon we heard was General Johnston's Confederate army attackin' our corps!"

"Oh, no!" Rufus painfully rose to a sitting position. "What happened to our division?"

"I was able to learn a little about 'em. As we feared, they was in the lead and took the brunt of the surprise assault. Just hordes of Rebels charged Carlin's brigades on the left flank and swept them back to the rear."

"Then what happened?" Rufus asked breathlessly.

"They regrouped behind the line of the Twentieth Corps, who thankfully had just got there. The enemy continued to launch several more attacks against our left flank, but all failed. The Rebs couldn't push 'em back again."

"What about the Second Division?"

"Morgan's division held the right flank. They was surrounded on three sides, but still held their ground."

"Good for them!"

"One thing they said that made it harder for our soldiers, was some of the Rebels wore Union uniforms. Our troops didn't know who to fire on."

"What's goin' on now?"

"I guess these last two days there's been mostly skirmishin'. The right wing got to the battlefield yesterday. Johnston's outnumbered now, so we're only waitin' for 'em to skedaddle."

Jeremiah paused and looked away. He spoke softly: "I heard there was heavy casualties. I ain't been able to find out anythin' about Joey, Tom, or Robert. We'll have to wait until we reach Goldsboro."

Rufus nodded. "Yeah, when we all meet at Goldsboro." The tremor in his voice showed the anguish he felt and the fear that maybe they wouldn't all meet at Goldsboro as planned.

During the night of March 21, General Johnston with his Confederate forces slipped away in the rain toward Smithfield. General Sherman, anxious to meet up with General J. M. Schofield and General A. H. Terry at Goldsboro, allowed Johnston and his army to escape. When General J. A. Mower pursued the retreating enemy, Sherman ordered him back to his own corps.

The Battle of Bentonville had resulted in heavy casualties. A total loss of killed, wounded, and missing amounted to 1,604 for the Federals and 2,343 for the Confederates—not mere numbers, but husbands, sons, fathers, and brothers. Many a table, North and South, would suffer an empty chair because of this battle.

By noon the next day, March 22, the wagon trains began to roll toward Goldsboro. The rain clouds cleared, leaving a mild but windy day. Gusts of wind buffeted the canvas coverings on the wagons transporting the many wounded from the battles of Averasboro and Bentonville. Accompanying soldiers heard the cries of their injured comrades as they bounced over the bumpy, corduroyed roads.

21

Goldsboro, North Carolina
A Sad Loss ~ Typhoid Fever in a Field Hospital ~ General Sherman's Visit

General Sherman rode his horse Sam into Goldsboro on March 23, 1865, to keep his rendezvous with General Schofield and General Terry. Their combined forces now totaled ninety thousand troops.

Following him, on March 23 and 24, Sherman's army streamed into Goldsboro to join their beloved general. The rugged troops had marched 425 miles from Savannah, Georgia, to Goldsboro, North Carolina, in 50 days. They had tramped in the rain over countless swamps and rivers and had corduroyed miles and miles of muddy roads.

As soon as the wagon train entered Goldsboro, the surgeons gave orders to set up a field hospital. Medical corpsmen pitched large tents at once and lined up cots to accommodate the wounded arriving in the wagons. The small town bustled with activity.

The First Division moved on and picked the designated field for the Fourteenth Corps. Jeremiah pulled his team up in preparation to camp. His eyes surveyed the ground to see how wet it would be for tents. Hopefully, Joey, Tom, and Robert would be able to join them. He turned and peeked into the wagon behind him. "Rufus, the ground here ain't covered with water. They could pitch their tents here."

"Oh, good!" Rufus exclaimed, knowing to whom Jeremiah referred. "I'm anxious to see 'em and know they're all right."

"I am, too."

Captain Roe rode his horse up and down the train, checking on the troops from his regiment, the Thirteenth Michigan. He stopped when he came to Jeremiah's ambulance. Jeremiah and he saluted each other. The captain noticed Bobby standing next to the wagon and little Mary Jane seated beside Jeremiah. Bobby respectfully saluted the officer, and Captain Roe returned his salute and smiled at Mary Jane.

"How is Rufus?" the captain asked Jeremiah. "Is he any better?"

Jeremiah shook his head. He didn't want to speak so Rufus could hear him.

Captain Roe dismounted and stepped up into the wagon. After returning Rufus's salute, he spoke to him. "We prepared a field hospital for all the wounded coming in. You are to go there, too. They plan to send the wounded north to a hospital in New York Harbor. I want you to be able to go with them."

"Thank ya, sir."

Captain Roe shook Rufus's hand, jumped down from the ambulance, and mounted his restless horse. He looked at Jeremiah, still seated and holding the reins.

"Jeremiah, I want you to drive Rufus over to the field hospital and see that he gets settled in."

"Yes, sir, I'll take 'im over there at once." They exchanged salutes, and the captain rode away.

Bobby reached up and took a tired Mary Jane from the wagon seat. Elizabeth joined him as they stepped over to the open end of the ambulance to tell Rufus goodbye. They had heard what Captain Roe told Jeremiah about moving Rufus to the field hospital.

"We want to thank ya for all you've done for us, Rufus. We'll miss ya, but we hope you'll get better care. You'll be in our prayers," Bobby told him.

"I'll miss ya, too, Bobby. Take good care of Elizabeth and Mary Jane. Your family's what's important to ya, now. And most of all, keep servin' the Lord."

"You're right there," Bobby hastened to agree.

Elizabeth, too, said her goodbyes and thanked him. Bobby wouldn't attempt a visit to the hospital in his Confederate uniform, so they wouldn't be seeing Rufus again.

Mary Jane squirmed until her papa put her down in the wagon. She hurried over to Rufus and hugged him.

"Bye, Unca Wufus."

"Bye, honey, I love ya."

She toddled back to her papa. "We'll get the camp set up while you're gone," Bobby promised Jeremiah, as he picked up Mary Jane.

Jeremiah got the ambulance in line, following the wagons carrying the wounded. They reached the Fourteenth Corps's field hospital situated on the Neuse River opposite Goldsboro. A medical corpsman guided Jeremiah to a bed for Rufus. The surgeon had arranged for the diseased soldiers to share tents away from the wounded. After assisting him to the cot, Jeremiah saw to it that Rufus was comfortably positioned on it. He covered him with a blanket, for the weather was pleasant, but a bit chilly.

"Be sure and tell Joey, Tom, and Robert where I am," Rufus reminded Jeremiah in his raspy voice. He didn't like the thought that he might miss seeing his messmates tonight. They had all promised to meet in Goldsboro, so he knew they'd be looking to camp by the ambulance.

"I will, Rufus. I'll tell 'em you're here, and I'll come and see ya every day myself."

"I'll like that, Jeremiah. Thank ya for lookin' after me. I don't know how I'd have managed without ya."

"Ya did more than that for me. Ya led me to the Lord. I'll be forever grateful."

"I didn't do anythin'. Jesus did it all."

"I know He did, but someone needed to point the way for me. I'd better get back to camp. Sleep well, Rufus. See ya tomorrow."

"Good night, Jeremiah."

All the patients in the field hospital had soup for their supper, but Rufus could not eat. Nothing tempted his appetite anymore.

That night he slept very little. Moans from the wounded in nearby tents kept him awake. His heart ached for each one, especially for the young boys in pain who were calling for their mothers. He prayed off and on most of the night.

Rufus looked up early the next morning to see Tom and Robert enter the hospital tent. They moved from cot to cot, searching for him. Their faces were drawn and sober. When they located Rufus, who was motioning to them, they found it difficult to make eye contact.

"What's wrong," Rufus managed to whisper. "Where's Joey?"

Robert walked over to his cot and put a hand on his shoulder. "I'm sorry, Rufus, but we have bad news. Joey was killed at the Battle of Bentonville."

"It's hard for us to bring you this news," added Tom.

Rufus never said a word. Tears started pouring down his sunken cheeks. He didn't have the strength to hold them back. "Oh, no, not Joey, who was so young. He had his whole life to live," he thought. He also remembered Joey's widowed mother back on the farm in Michigan. What a terrible loss for her.

Tom and Robert cried with him. They gave him a few minutes before they continued. "We tried to keep Joey between us, but when the enemy charged, it wasn't possible," Tom went on to say. "Everything happened so fast, and there was smoke everywhere from the artillery."

"After we pulled back and the smoke cleared, we looked for Joey, and he wasn't with us," Robert explained. "Then we spotted him about thirty feet away, lying on his stomach. He wasn't moving. He'd been hit. We couldn't get to him because the Rebs were still firing and had us pinned down."

Tom moved over and sat down gently beside Rufus on the cot. He spoke softly. "Joey commanded Tramp to stay on the side of the field away from the battle. Tramp obeyed until he saw Joey lyin' out there. Then almost as though he sensed somethin' was wrong, he bolted for Joey and ran right across in front of the firin'. When we heard him yelp and saw him jump, we knew he'd been hit. The shot knocked him down for a minute. We helplessly watched Tramp crawl on his belly, inch by inch across the whole battlefield, until he reached Joey, to lie at his side." Tom became too choked up to go on.

"We did see Joey reach out and put his arm around Tramp," Robert continued. "We knew then that Joey was still alive and that he was aware that Tramp had come to him."

"But when Robert and I were finally able to crawl out to Joey, he and Tramp were both dead, lyin' there side by side, with Joey's arm still around his beloved Tramp," Tom concluded. "We wrapped each of them in a blanket and buried them together; we thought Joey would like that. Then Robert held a graveside service for him." Rufus lay there, numb with grief, listening to all that Tom and Robert told him about Joey's death. He knew they loved Joey and had done their best to protect him.

"His poor mother," Rufus murmured.

"I know," Robert's voice grew husky. "I've already written her, telling her what a fine boy Joey was and how much he loved the Lord. I knew you'd want me to do that."

"Yeah, thank you. That was kind of ya, Robert." Rufus tried to manage a smile, but couldn't.

"We lost another friend—and fine officer—at Bentonville," Tom continued. "Colonel Eaton was also killed. He died leading our regiment in a charge against the enemy."

Rufus just shook his head. "Oh, how terrible. He was truly a fine officer, and Joey was really fond of 'im," Rufus replied.

"Yeah, we all were," Robert stated. "We'd like to pray with you now before we go." Robert and Tom joined in prayer for Rufus, asking God to comfort him and all the suffering patients around him.

"We shouldn't stay any longer," Tom stood up. "We hated to bring ya such bad news, but we wanted to be the ones to tell ya."

They shook hands with Rufus. "Goodbye, Rufus, we'll try and see you tomorrow."

"And Rufus, we should get mail soon," Tom added.

"I hope so. Thanks for comin'."

All tents had been set up, and the field hospital at Goldsboro admitted a total of 1,368 patients, which included all the Federal wounded from the battles of Averasboro and Bentonville, as well as all soldiers with diseases. The surgeons performed 88 amputations. Within 48 hours, 131 of the wounded died.

Rufus's messmates, numbering two now instead of three, tried to visit him often. Though always glad to see them, Rufus still felt a pang of sorrow whenever they entered the hospital tent without the redheaded Joey at their side. He deeply missed seeing his freckled face and big grin and kept remembering how Joey promised he would see him in Goldsboro.

Jeremiah kept his word and visited Rufus daily. "How's the Shore family?" inquired Rufus. "How's my little darlin' Mary Jane?"

"They're all right. Mary Jane gets cuter every day."

"Are they still gonna follow the columns?"

"Right now there's some uncertainty about where they'll go."

"I hope they'll be all right. They're a nice family."

One morning a few days later Tom and Robert entered the tent with wide smiles on their faces. Tom held up an envelope. "Look, Rufus! Ya have a letter from home." He handed it to him.

"Thanks." Rufus's heart pounded as he took it and recognized Sarah's handwriting. He lay there stunned, with the letter in his hand.

"Go ahead. Read it," Robert urged.

Rufus feebly opened the envelope. His hand shook as he removed the letter. He scanned the pages first, and then reread the letter more slowly. Sarah had written to tell him not to worry about them. She assured him she and the girls were doing fine; the letter contained only good news from home. When he finished reading, Rufus looked up at his two friends. "It's from Sarah, and she writes everythin's fine at home."

"We're glad to hear that," Tom told him. "We also received a letter from Simon Foster. He's been a prisoner and was just paroled the end of February. He sent the letter to all three of us—you, Joey, and me. He wrote from Camp Chase in Ohio, where he is now. Would ya like to read it?" He handed Simon's letter to Rufus. "He didn't say much, but just wanted us to know he was alive and safe." Tom looked away for a moment. "Joey would've been so happy. He never gave up hope for Simon and prayed for him faithfully every night."

"Yeah, I know," Rufus spoke in his raspy voice. "And I'm really glad to learn he's safe. But I must admit, I didn't think Simon had much of a chance. From all the killed foragers that were found—many with their throats slit and others hangin' from trees . . ."

"No, I didn't think he stood much of a chance, either," Tom admitted. "Only Joey believed he was a prisoner and still alive. Simon writes he was held at Belle Island."

"Oh, no," Robert exclaimed. "That's a terrible prison camp. How long was he there?"

"It must have been about three months," Tom figured.

"Ya didn't know Simon, did ya, Robert?" Rufus whispered.

"No, I didn't know him, but I remember seeing him in our regiment. He was rather short with brown hair, wasn't he? I recall him as nice-appearing. I'm glad he survived."

"I'll answer Simon's letter and write him about Joey." Tom took the letter back from Rufus to keep Simon's address. "Did ya have time to read it?" he asked.

"Yeah, it's a short letter with wonderful news."

"Oh, say, Rufus, guess what they're building not too far from here." Robert sounded excited.

"I dunno. I did hear some light poundin'. What are they buildin'?"

"They're setting up an outdoor meeting place with a pulpit, an altar, and benches to sit on."

"Who's doin' this?"

"It's the Christian Association of the First and Second Brigade of the Twentieth Corps. It's nondenominational. I hear they held meetings during our time in the Carolinas, too. Three chaplains are involved."

"When will they start their services?"

"Tonight. Robert and I plan to go." Tom sounded excited as well.

"I wish I could, too. I think Robert ought to preach."

"So do I, Rufus," Tom agreed, "and play his harmonica."

Robert laughed them off. "We should be getting back. We'll pray with you before we leave." Together they prayed for Rufus, but also included the other sick and wounded, as they always did. Then they left.

Following supper, strains of music drifted into the hospital tent on the balmy night air. It sounded like the regimental band was playing hymns for the camp service. The frail, dark-haired private on the cot next to Rufus weakly tried to sing along with the three preservice selections, but sheer exhaustion forced him to give up before he had finished the first song.

Rufus longed to be able to sing the Lord's praises as he once did, but he knew he no longer possessed the strength. When the music stopped, it became strangely quiet, except for the braying of mules nearby. Because of the distance between the hospital tent and the service, Rufus and the soldier on the neighboring cot were not able to hear the chaplain's message.

After catching his breath and resting a few minutes, the private looked over at Rufus, his brown eyes questioning. "Do ya know why the band played hymns, Rufus?"

"Yeah, George; they're holdin' nightly revival meetin's, beginnin' tonight. I wish I could be there."

George sighed. "I'd like that, too."

Because the soldiers in Rufus's tent suffered from debilitating diseases, they didn't feel well enough to develop camaraderie with one another. They might know the name of the soldier in the next cot, but wouldn't know much else about him.

"Are ya a Christian, George?" Rufus asked.

"Yeah, I am. You are too, ain't ya, Rufus?"

"Yeah, George, I'm a Christian, too."

A little later that evening, they heard the band playing the invitational hymn, "Just as I Am."

"They're havin' the altar call," Rufus murmured.

"Yeah. I . . . I . . . hope it's a big one," George stammered.

"So do I. I'm gonna pray that it will be."

"I'll pray with ya."

Both soldiers bowed their heads and silently prayed for those needing Jesus as their Savior to answer the altar call and accept him into their hearts.

A few minutes later, the band closed the meeting with "Nearer, My God, to Thee." George didn't try to sing. It took all his strength to speak. "I like that hymn. Think . . . think how wonderful that will be, Rufus, when we are with God."

"Yeah, George, it will certainly be wonderful when we see Jesus."

"Good . . . good night, Rufus."

"Good night, George."

When Rufus woke the next morning, George's cot lay empty. He wondered if the corpsman had taken him out to the latrine. He remembered hearing movement there during the night. He asked about George when they brought breakfast.

"I'm sorry, private, but George Adams died in the night," the medical corpsman explained, never taking his eyes off of Rufus's breakfast tray.

"Then he's with God, now," Rufus replied. "He's seein' Jesus."

Around 3:00 p.m., Tom and Robert burst into the tent, faces aglow. They rushed to Rufus's side.

"We wish you could've been there, Rufus." Tom's eyes shone with enthusiasm. "The revival meetin' was unbelievable. Hundreds attended, and several answered the altar call."

"They didn't have near enough benches," Robert joined in. "Many troops stood all around the back. And did you know the regimental band played for the service?"

Rufus nodded. "We could hear the music from here, but not the message." He told his friends all about what he and George had done last night during the meeting. Then he shared with them how after the service, sometime in the middle of the night, George had slipped away to be with Jesus. "The last thing George said to me," Rufus went on to say, "was what a wonderful day it will be when we're with God. Last night George experienced his wonderful day. He's with God. He's seein' Jesus."

The three fell silent, but not with sorrow. Each rejoiced in his heart for George.

The revival meetings took place every night and continued to draw large crowds. Hundreds accepted Jesus as their Savior—some for the first time, while others recommitted their lives.

Lying on his cot, Rufus kept hearing rumors from the medical corpsmen, who told the patients they would soon be transported to a hospital in New York. A higher authority soon substantiated this.

"Uncle Billy! Uncle Billy!" a soldier cried out.

Rufus looked up to see a man standing in the middle of the tent. He wore a slouch hat and chomped on a cigar. Rufus recognized him at once as General Sherman. He had on a much cleaner uniform than the last time Rufus had seen him.

The general removed the cigar from his mouth as he looked up and down the rows of cots where the soldiers lay ill. "I just came to tell you boys how proud I am of each one of you. Tomorrow, we'll be leaving Goldsboro at dawn. I'll be marching out with the army north to Raleigh, but you boys will move out the following day. You'll travel by train to Morehead City, where a ship will be waiting to take you to De Camp General Hospital in New York. God bless each of you."

He saluted and turned to walk away, pausing to greet the soldiers as he passed by their cots. When he got to Rufus, he stopped abruptly and stood beside him. His piercing eyes studied Rufus's face. "Don't I know you, private? You're Rufus, aren't you?"

"Yes, sir, I am."

The general put out his hand. Rufus shook it weakly.

"I remember you from Georgia. You kept the fires hot to bend the rails. You were anxious to get mail, if I remember correctly. Did you hear from home?"

"Yes, sir, I heard from home. My family is well. Did ya hear, too, sir?"

The general looked away for a moment, remembering the news from home: the newspaper had told of the death of his baby son. He turned toward Rufus. "Yes, private, I heard from home. Have a safe trip to New York." He put his cigar back in his mouth and slipped out of the tent.

Later that day, when Tom and Robert visited, Jeremiah accompanied them. Rufus told them about General Sherman's visit.

"He said all of ya will be pullin' out for Raleigh tomorrow." Rufus's trembling voice revealed the sadness he felt.

"Yeah, that's what we hear. We came to tell ya goodbye." Tom reached over and squeezed Rufus's foot. An awkward moment of silence followed. All of them found it hard to say farewell.

"General Sherman even remembered me," Rufus said, in an effort to break the mood.

"That's what they say about him, Rufus. Once he's met someone, he doesn't forget him. There are those who claim General Sherman knows the names of all his troops," Tom chuckled.

"He told us we'll be leavin' for a hospital in New York soon. Maybe Sarah could come and visit me," Rufus said wistfully.

"I'm sure she can." Robert tried to encourage him. "We'll really miss you, Rufus, but we want what's best for ya."

Tom and Jeremiah agreed.

"Robert, do ya have your harmonica with ya?"

"Sure. Would you like me to play something?" Robert and Jeremiah both sat down.

Rufus cleared his throat. "Could ya please softly play 'Amazing Grace' for me just one last time?"

"Of course, Rufus." Robert took his harmonica out of his shirt pocket and tenderly started to play Rufus's request.

Many of the occupants on the cots raised their heads to watch Robert. Their serene faces showed how the song of faith calmed them.

"Louder! Louder!" those positioned farther away called out to Robert, wanting to hear better. After Robert had played the song through twice, he stopped.

"Thanks, Robert." Rufus found it difficult to form the words to express how much he enjoyed hearing his favorite hymn. He could only manage to say "Thanks."

"You're always welcome, Rufus."

"Play more! Play more!" the patients cried out.

Robert looked at Rufus. He wanted to spend this time with him, but Rufus understood and nodded for him to go ahead and play on for the other patients.

After Robert had gone through several more hymns, they needed to go.

Tom, Robert, and Jeremiah shook hands with Rufus. They had much they wanted to say. They bowed their heads as Robert spoke a final prayer.

"After the war, Rufus, I'm gonna look ya up in Casnovia," Tom promised.

"I'd like that," Rufus weakly answered. "But first, ya need to look up a certain young lady in Rome, Georgia."

"That I will. Maybe I'll bring her with me."

"I hope ya do. Sarah would love that."

Robert put his harmonica back in his pocket. "I'd like to come and visit you and Sarah, too, if it's all right."

"Me, too," Jeremiah quickly spoke.

"Of course, it's all right. We'd love to see all three of ya."

After making promises that they'd all meet again, Rufus's three messmates reluctantly left the field hospital and Rufus behind. At the doorway, Jeremiah whirled around and hurried back to Rufus's side. Tears in his eyes, he shook Rufus's hand again. "I just wanted to thank ya one last time, Rufus, for leadin' me to the Lord. If it wasn't for ya, I wouldn't know Jesus Christ. Thank ya, Rufus."

"I've told ya, Jeremiah, I didn't do anythin'. Jesus did it all. But I'm really glad you're saved. Thank ya for takin' such good care of me."

"Tweren't nothin', Rufus." Jeremiah turned to go. Rufus touched his arm.

"And Jeremiah, we will meet again."

Jeremiah looked deeply into Rufus's dull eyes and nodded. A tear escaped from one eye and rolled down his right cheek. He knew what Rufus meant.

At daybreak, April 10, 1865, General Sherman and his reinforced army left Goldsboro, moving north toward Raleigh, North Carolina, in pursuit of Confederate general Joe Johnston and his troops. They marched out with flags waving and regimental bands playing.

Rufus heard them leave and never felt more alone in his life. His friends were gone. He prayed God would take care of them.

That evening, the corpsmen started packing up any extra medical supplies that wouldn't be needed during the night. "We'll leave at the crack of daylight," one corpsman explained to Rufus.

The day for transporting the patients from the field hospital dawned sunny and clear. They were to travel by the Atlantic and North Carolina Railroad from Goldsboro to Morehead City, where they would board a steamer to take them to New York Harbor.

As soon as the train pulled in, the sick and wounded were carried out onto a field near the railroad tracks, where they waited to be taken aboard. Almost immediately, the corpsmen started moving the patients onto the train. Those who could sit up, they placed in coaches. They laid the others on mats of straw on a flatbed car.

Two corpsmen came with a stretcher to pick up Rufus. "It's your turn, private. We'll load you now."

The corpsmen carried him to the train, where they laid him in a row with other men on a flatbed car. One by one, they loaded all of the patients from the field hospitals. The medical corpsmen themselves boarded last. It was their task to escort and tend their patients on the stressful journey to the hospital in New York Harbor.

The engineer blew the whistle, and the train jerked into motion, moving down the track and leaving a trail of smoke coiling upward to the cloudless sky.

22

Davids Island, New York
In Transit ~ De Camp General Hospital

Rufus found riding on the train's flatcar more comfortable than bouncing in the ambulance over corduroyed roads. Lately he sometimes suffered from chills. The warmth of the sun beaming down on him as he lay on the open platform chased the shivers away.

The ninety-mile train ride from Goldsboro to Morehead City would take several hours. Always exhausted, Rufus decided he'd try to sleep part of the way. Much later, the harsh scraping of the train's wheels on the track when braking awakened him. They had arrived without incident at New Bern, the largest city in North Carolina, about sixty miles southeast of Goldsboro. Rufus couldn't believe he had slept all the way.

"We stopped here because the engine needed to take on water," the corpsman explained. "Wouldn't you boys enjoy a drink yourselves?" He brought the bucket up the row, offering each man a drink. When necessary, he assisted some of the troops to the latrine.

Before long, the engineer blew his whistle, and the train started creeping down the track to finish the last thirty-six miles to their destination. After traveling for nearly an hour and a half, Rufus and his companions noticed seagulls circling overhead, so they knew they must be close to the Atlantic Ocean. Soon billows of steam spewed from the engine, as the engineer brought the train to a stop at Morehead City.

The *Clarion*, a steamer, lay moored in the harbor, waiting to take on her passengers. Captain Morac, a man of about forty, with a face weather-beaten from the salt air, stood on her deck. His stance showed an officer in command. In his hands he held the orders to take the sick and wounded from General Sherman's army to New York Harbor.

The medical corpsmen soon began the job of transferring their patients from the train to the ship. For Rufus, traveling on the water was something new; he had never been on a boat before.

The beautiful weather made it a perfect day for an ocean voyage, but Rufus's illness prevented him from being excited about the trip. He just wanted to get closer to Sarah. It didn't matter what the mode of transportation was—the faster the better.

"How 'bout something to eat?" one of the wounded cried out.

"I know you boys are hungry, but we feel you'll travel better with empty stomachs," one of the corpsmen explained.

With everyone on board, Captain Morac could no longer hold back the sensational news he wished to share with the troops. His dark eyes glistened as he spoke. "Men, I don't believe you've heard the latest war bulletin. General Lee surrendered to General Grant at Appomattox two days ago. The papers up north are full of the story."

The sick and wounded who felt well enough to shout, shouted. Others lay quietly on the deck, with tears streaming down their hollow cheeks. They knew the war was virtually over. Only General Johnston remained, and surely he would now surrender.

"No more war," Rufus thought. "No more war. No more troops, North or South, will die. It's finally over." He silently offered a prayer of thanksgiving to God.

Captain Morac cast off at 4:00 p.m. He steered the *Clarion* into the outside route on the Atlantic and steamed north toward New York Harbor. The pitching and rolling of the ship soon caused the soldiers to understand why they hadn't been fed. Almost everyone, including Rufus, became seasick. Even though he hadn't eaten, he suffered dry heaves throughout the passage. The entire voyage became only a blur to him. He vaguely remembered medical corpsmen coaxing him to eat and drink. After they had made many stops at ports along the way to take on food and coal, he began to think they'd never arrive at their destination.

Finally Captain Morac blew the ship's whistle, as he guided his vessel among the score of boats and freighters in New York Harbor. He cautiously maneuvered the steamer up to the dock at Davids Island, the location of De Camp General Hospital.

De Camp Hospital, with Assistant Surgeon Warren Webster in charge, consisted of twenty-two buildings with the capacity for housing over twenty-five hundred occupants. In the beginning, around 1861–62, it was used for the treatment of Federal soldiers only. After Gettysburg, Davids Island became both hospital and prison camp for Confederate prisoners. The Federal authorities allowed healthy Rebel captives freedom to roam about and to fish for their own food, since the barrier formed by the water prevented escape.

The medical corpsmen started unloading their wounded and diseased passengers as soon as the ship docked. Other corpsmen hurried from the hospital to assist them. Two of them carried Rufus on a stretcher to the sixth pavilion. When he entered the building, a sickening odor greeted him. He covered his mouth and nose with a trembling hand. One of the corpsmen noticed. "You'll get used to the smell, private. They all do in time."

The corpsmen toted Rufus into a long, narrow room, where twenty cots lined the walls, in two rows facing each other. The spotless wooden floor looked worn from many scrubbings. A mild spring breeze gently floated in through a row of open windows, dispelling the pungent odor.

After carefully lowering Rufus's stretcher down onto one of the few vacant cots, the corpsmen helped him slide over onto his new bed. "Is there anything we can do for you, private?" the tall one named Paul asked, after they had positioned Rufus comfortably.

Rufus shook his head. "No, thanks." His parched lips longed for a drink, but his stomach still suffered from the boat trip. He wanted to wait a while longer before drinking or eating again.

"There'll always be one of us around to care for you," Paul continued. "You'll also be examined by a doctor, probably tomorrow."

"And we have a couple nice chaplains. I'm sure one will visit you soon," Ray, the other corpsman, hurried to add. "We'll also be on duty and will be seeing you again. Goodbye for now."

After giving Rufus reassuring smiles, the two corpsmen picked up the stretcher and returned to their other duties.

Rufus lay there that night, trying to fall asleep, but the strange sounds around him prevented it. He could hear men moaning, coughing, retching, praying, and even crying. He knew he needed time to get accustomed to the misery in this place.

Just as Rufus began to nod off, he heard shouts of anguish coming from the hallway outside. "Oh, no! Oh, no!" a voice cried, horror-struck.

The corpsmen on duty rushed out of the ward to see the reason for the disturbance in the hall. They closed the door behind them.

When they returned a few minutes later, their eyes glistened with tears. One of them cleared his throat to speak to the concerned patients. "I have some very bad news, boys. President Lincoln has been assassinated. An actor shot him at the theater where he had gone to see a play. He died yesterday morning. Someone brought a *New York Herald* newspaper to the island, and they just read the story."

Except for some sniffling, no one made a sound. Everyone felt nothing but shock and sorrow.

Long afterward Rufus lay there wide awake, thinking about President Lincoln. "How could anyone do this to such a good man?" he wondered. He thought about how everyone had rejoiced just last week at Lee's surrender to Grant at Appomattox, which ended the War of the Rebellion. With the war over, President Lincoln—not a vindictive man, but a generous one—would have been the best friend the defeated South could have. Rufus slept little that night, as he mourned his wonderful president.

Two corpsmen on night duty cared for the soldiers in the ward. As the darkness deepened, they shut the tall windows, one by one, to protect the room's feverish occupants from the cool night air. One of the corpsmen's main duties was emptying slop jars. Many of the diseased, like Rufus, suffered from chronic diarrhea.

The following morning after breakfast, a man about Rufus's age with dark hair, sideburns, and a beard entered the room and walked up to Rufus's cot. He examined the chart that hung at the foot of his bed.

"Private Seaman? I'm Dr. Webster. How are you feeling this morning?"

"Not very well. I always feel so weak. And I can't seem to stop my diarrhea."

"Did you eat your breakfast?"

"Not much. I mostly drank my coffee."

The doctor began to examine Rufus. First, he listened to his heart and lungs. Then he pressed on his abdomen in different places. "Does it hurt anywhere I press?" he asked.

"It's tender in the lower part," Rufus answered.

"I imagine you've lost weight?"

"Yes, sir, I have."

"Just how long have you been ill?"

"About two and a half months."

The doctor shook his head. "Can you tell me how it started?"

"I got soaked marchin' in the rain when we left Savannah. I came down with what I thought was a bad cold. My chest hurt, and I had cramps and diarrhea."

"Did you have a fever?"

"Yeah, I've had a fever at times, or at least my skin felt hot."

"Were you ever examined by a doctor?"

"Yes, sir, I was. He thought I must have one of the fevers, typhoid or yellow fever."

"He was probably right, but now you are suffering from chronic diarrhea. You may even have had pneumonia at first. We can't tell now." The doctor noticed that Rufus's frail condition didn't allow him the strength for much talking, so he stopped asking questions. "We'll try to treat your diarrhea the best we can, private. I'll leave some pills for you with the corpsmen. But try to eat." He smiled, laid a hand on Rufus's shoulder, and walked on to the next cot.

Later that afternoon Rufus had another visitor when a handsome man walked up to his cot and introduced himself. "Hello, Private Seaman, I'm Chaplain Rogers," he said, as he reached out and shook Rufus's weak hand. "Do you mind if I visit you for a few minutes and pray with you?"

Rufus looked at the young, red-haired man who didn't appear to be any older than twenty-five. "A grown Joey," Rufus thought. "I would love that," he told the chaplain.

"I'm glad. We have a little book titled *Provisions for Passing over Jordan* that we hand out to all the occupants in the hospital. It's a book of uplifting scriptures. Would ya like one?"

Rufus nodded. "Thank ya, I would." The chaplain handed him a small book, only about two and a half inches by three. Rufus held it in his hand. "I'll enjoy readin' it. Thank ya very much."

"Are you a Christian, Rufus?" the chaplain asked.

"Yes, sir, I am." As tired as talking made him, Rufus still wanted to share his testimony with the chaplain. "I believe, chaplain, that God allowed me to be drafted for a purpose—for my own good. I believe God used it to draw me and my wife, Sarah, back to a closer relationship with him again. We went through a deep sorrow in our lives, and it caused us to lose our first love and the joy of the Lord. We have that back now."

"Do you still feel that way, Rufus, even when you're sick?"

"Yes, sir, I do. I'd rather"—he stopped to swallow—"I'd rather die havin' a close relationship with Jesus than live without Him." Rufus could only speak in a whisper now.

The tears in the chaplain's eyes revealed how much Rufus's testimony blessed him. "I know you'll love that book, Rufus. I'll pray for you now. I heard you call your wife Sarah. Do you have children?"

Rufus nodded and feebly held up two fingers. "Dorothy and Lucy," he whispered.

The chaplain prayed a beautiful prayer for Rufus and his family. "I'll see you again tomorrow, Rufus. I'm really happy to meet you. You've blessed me greatly." He then shook his hand and walked away.

Rufus enjoyed reading *Provisions for Passing over Jordan*. The author's desire was for the reader to "experience a sweet, spiritual repast" in reading the passages. Rufus received exactly that.

Chaplain Rogers visited Rufus daily. They discussed the little book at length. "Is there a particular passage that blessed you the most, Rufus?" the chaplain asked.

"I like 'em all," Rufus answered, as he thumbed through the book to a certain page. "But this passage I sincerely pray daily." He read, "May the last sound on my expiring lips be 'Hallelujah to the Lamb,' and with this song may I enter the Canaan of rest."

The chaplain could only answer, "Amen."

Dr. Webster visited Rufus one morning about a week later. "How are you coming along, private?"

"About the same, I guess."

Dr. Webster noticed that Rufus looked more frail than he had a week ago. "I think what you need is a visit from your wife. Would you like that?"

"Oh, yes, sir, if she could come."

"Some of the wives visit their husbands here. Now that the war is over, even Confederate wives will be visiting. I'll send word to your wife right away."

"Thank ya, sir."

That afternoon the chaplain found an excited Rufus. "Dr. Webster's goin' to write Sarah and ask her to come!" he exclaimed.

"Wonderful, Rufus! I'll look forward to meeting her after all the nice things you've told me about her." On visits when Rufus felt strong enough to chat, he'd talk to Chaplain Rogers about Sarah and his children.

"How long do ya think it'll take for her to get here?" Rufus wondered.

The chaplain sat down in the chair by the cot. "I don't know, but Dr. Webster's letter will take a few days to reach her. It will probably take longer for the letter to get there than for Sarah to come here on the train."

Rufus's face showed concern. "I hope she doesn't come alone. I don't think it would be safe for her to travel alone on the train."

"Does she have a sister who could travel with her?"

Rufus brightened. "Yeah, she does. She'll probably travel with one of her sisters—or even with one of mine."

As the last week of April slipped by, Rufus talked and read less and less. Chaplain Rogers still visited him and sat beside his bed. He often read to him from the Bible or the little book. Sometimes he just sat quietly, praying for him.

Rufus lay with his eyes fixed on the doorway, expecting Sarah to walk into the ward any moment.

"She should be here soon," the chaplain assured him. "We'll keep praying for her safe arrival."

Rufus nodded, but never took his eyes from the doorway.

23

Casnovia

Happy Memories ~ An Ominous Letter

Spring finally came to Michigan, and thus to Casnovia. Much warmer temperatures gradually melted the deep winter snowdrifts, making the once icy roads more easily traveled. The merry sound of sleigh bells on cutters gliding over the snow gave way to the rumbling noise of buggy and buckboard wheels on bare dirt roads.

Trees budded with new leaves. Colorful blossoms decorating a variety of fruit trees promised apples, pears, and peaches to come in the late summer and fall.

The lilting song of red-breasted robins could be heard once again, as they migrated back to Michigan from their more southerly winter home.

The spring brought with it a blessing for the country. The War of the Rebellion had come to an end with Lee's surrender on April 9. Peace called for much rejoicing, as steam whistles blew, shops closed, and flags flew high. Red-white-and-blue decorations adorned many buildings, celebrating the end of all the sorrow and agony of war.

The spring also brought a tragedy to the country with the assassination of the Union's beloved President Lincoln on April 14. "Vale! Vale!" cried the *Grand Rapids Daily Eagle* of April 15. "The wine of life is spilled. Treason has done its worst. The President is dead, the greatest, purest, kindest soul." Grand Rapids's Mayor Comstock decreed that "all places of business be closed and draped in mourning, that flags fly at half mast, and church bells be tolled for three hours."

In Sarah's heart, spring had not come. She rejoiced in the news that the war had ended, and she mourned over the tragic death of President Lincoln. Overshadowing it all, however, and keeping her emotionally numb was her concern over not hearing from Rufus for several lonely weeks. She anxiously waited, day by day, praying to receive word from him.

On a particularly beautiful spring day Sarah sat on the top wooden step of their back porch, letting the warm sun soak into her weary bones, while she watched Dorothy push Lucy on the rope swing hanging from the old maple tree. The girls loved the swing their papa had fixed for them last summer.

"Look, Mama! See how high I can push Lucy," Dorothy called to her.

"Yes, honey, I can see, but don't push her too high," Mama cautioned.

"I can go high, Mama. I can go high," Lucy squealed.

Mama smiled at her and nodded.

"Yes, you can go real high, Lucy."

Buster snuggled beside Sarah on the porch, sniffing the letter she held in her hand to read once again. The lonesome dog whined his sorrow, looking at her with mournful brown eyes.

"I know, old boy. We miss him." She gently put her arm around her faithful friend, talking softly to him.

Sarah looked down at Rufus's precious, well-worn letters in her lap. She had saved each one to read over and over again. She picked up the last, dated February 4. It contained only one page, because he said he was suffering from a bad cold and didn't feel up to writing more. As she took it out of the envelope, her eyes fell on the last sentence. "Oh, Sarah, my wife, you are more dear to me than my life." Her eyes misted as she read it again. She thought back to the church picnic so long ago where it all began . . .

. . . Getting ready for the church picnic back then, Sarah looked at her reflection in her bedroom mirror. "Is that really me?" she whispered.

Her sister, Mary Louise, had arranged Sarah's hair in an upsweep with a bun on top, a style most girls didn't wear until their teens or even twenties. Mary Louise, several years older than Sarah, had worn her red hair piled on top of her head for a long time.

Mary Louise laughed. "Yes, that is really you. And you do look pretty."

"Do you think Ma will let me wear my hair like this to the church picnic? I'm still quite young. I want . . . ah . . . Silence to see me like this."

"Maybe Ma will let you; you can always ask her." Mary Louise's green eyes lit up as she smiled to herself. She knew who Sarah really wanted to see her. "And after three years," Mary Louise thought.

Three years ago the Seamans had moved to Casnovia from Hillsdale. And just last week, the Walkleys, much to Sarah's delight, had moved to Casnovia as well.

Pastor Wheeler from the Baptist church had called on the Walkleys, inviting them to the church picnic. The Seamans attended the same church. With the two families unable to arrange a visit as yet, they would love this opportunity to see one another at the picnic.

Sarah decided to leave her hair up for the rest of her family to see at supper. She and Mary Louise went back to their job of helping Ma unpack boxes from the move. They finished in the bedroom they shared and then went out into the kitchen.

The aroma of freshly baked bread and supper on the stove greeted them. Their mother, standing at the hot wood range, her face flushed from the heat, turned and smiled at her daughters. Ma, a small woman who had become slightly plump in later years, had a kind face with an engaging smile. Her light brown hair showed only slight traces of gray. Petite Sarah, with the same hair color, and blue eyes, favored her mother in looks.

"Supper's ready," Ma told them. "Call your brothers and sisters."

Eight siblings plus Ma and Pa sat around their large supper table. Oliver Walkley, a good-natured man who loved his family, sat at the head. He said grace as they all respectfully bowed their heads.

Afterwards Pa leaned back in his chair and looked around at each one. A slightly balding man with bushy, dark red eyebrows, he appeared more formidable than the kind person they knew him to be. "Where's Sarah, Ma?" he asked, his brown eyes twinkling. "And aren't you going to introduce your friend, Mary Louise?" All the siblings snickered. Sarah and Mary Louise laughed, too.

"You look mighty pretty, honey," Pa said seriously. "All my daughters are beautiful."

Ma looked at Sarah and nodded in agreement. Sarah now knew it would be all right for her to wear her hair up for the picnic.

Early the next morning Sarah stood at the stove, browning white sugar in a cast-iron skillet. "Is the sugar burnt enough, Ma?"

Ma, busy at the kitchen table rolling out piecrusts, took a peek at the sugar in the pan. "Yes, that should be just about right for your cake."

Sarah wanted to help Ma with the food preparation and had volunteered to make a burnt sugar cake for the church picnic tomorrow. Mary Louise entered the kitchen carrying two-year-old Emily on her hip. "What may I do to help, Ma? I can give the baby to Maria and Sophia. They won't mind tending her."

Ma reached over and patted the rosy-cheeked cherub's head. Her hand left traces of flour on Emily's golden curls. "It would help if you could slice the ham for sandwiches," Ma told Mary Louise. "You may find Maria and Sophia on the front porch. They asked me for scraps of material for sewing."

Mary Louise took her littlest sister outside to look for the twins. They found the look-alikes, with their auburn hair in pigtails, sewing doll clothes on the wooden porch steps.

"Will you girls watch Emily?" Mary Louise asked, putting the toddler down beside them. "I'm going to help Ma in the kitchen."

Sophia reached out and circled her arm around Emily. "We'd love to." Maria smiled and nodded and laid aside her sewing. Everyone loved the baby of the family. As the youngest member, she held a special place.

As she sliced ham, Mary Louise looked over at Sarah, assembling the pastry. "Do you think he'll like your cake, Sarah?" she teased. Sarah felt her face turn red. She decided to try to ignore the remark.

Ma heard Mary Louise's comment and observed Sarah's red face. "Who do you mean? What are you saying?"

Mary Louise suddenly felt sorry she had said anything. She didn't want to embarrass Sarah. "It's nothing, Ma. I shouldn't have teased Sarah."

"Who is the boy that Sarah likes?" Ma persisted.

"When we lived across the road from the Seamans in Hillsdale, and Sarah was friends with Silence, she had a crush on Silence's brother Rufus."

"Rufus?" Ma asked in surprise. "He's too old for you," she stated firmly.

"No, he isn't," thought Sarah, but she remained silent.

"Who's too old?" Pa had entered the kitchen through the back door without being noticed. Apparently he had heard Ma's statement.

"Rufus Seaman is too old for Sarah," Ma answered.

Pa walked over to the water pail on the cupboard and took a big drink from the dipper. "Rufus is a fine Christian man. Sarah could do worse." He glanced at Sarah and winked before he went back outside to finish his chores.

The three women, working together, bustled about in the kitchen all afternoon, preparing food. Ma made a variety of six fruit pies, while Sarah baked and frosted her cake and made large jars of lemonade and cold tea. After Mary Louise finished making the ham sandwiches, she baked a batch of molasses cookies. There would be plenty to eat at the picnic. The Walkleys made sure of that.

The next day dawned overcast. A strong hint of rain hung heavily in the air. Disappointment showed on Sarah's face as she joined the rest of the family at the breakfast table.

Pa reached over and patted her arm. "Don't look so discouraged, Sarah. It's still three hours before the picnic. The weather could go either way—rain or shine."

Sarah managed a smile.

After breakfast, she and Mary Louise did the dishes. As Sarah washed off the oilcloth on the kitchen table, a sunbeam danced across it. She quickly glanced out the nearby window, overjoyed to see the sun flooding the sky again; it would be a beautiful day for a picnic.

When the time to leave came, they loaded the buckboard with all of the food, blankets, and utensils that would be needed. The children huddled on robes in the bed of the wagon, while Ma and Pa sat up on the driver's seat, with little Emily on Ma's lap. Pa clucked to his team—a beautiful pair of young bay Morgans who performed very well together. They arrived at the churchyard in no time at all.

Putting planks over sawhorses, two men worked at making a long table solid enough to hold all of the foods. When they were finished, some of the women covered the boards with checked tablecloths. Edwin, Mary Louise, and Sarah, as well as the twins, began unloading their wagon. Other picnickers also started bringing over their contributions to put on the makeshift table.

Peals of laughter rang out, as the children enjoyed a rousing game of tag. Sarah's younger siblings—Wyllys, age 9 and Oliver, now 5—ran off to join in the fun, while Emily played on the grass near Ma.

John Seaman, Rufus's father, passed by the picnic tables. Catching sight of Pa, he walked over to meet him and shake his hand. "Glad to see ya, Oliver"—he nodded politely to Ma—"and ya, Parthenia."

Pa clasped John's hand in both of his. "I'm glad to see ya, too."

The two former neighbors began to fellowship at once, eager to renew their past friendship.

Lucretia Seaman followed her husband over to greet the Walkleys. Happy to meet each other again, she and Ma chatted away as though they had never been apart.

Sarah decided to take a stroll around the grounds. "Ma, do you need me for anything? If not, I think I'll take a walk to look for Silence."

"No, honey, I don't need you right now. Go and find your friend," Ma answered.

"She's around here somewhere," spoke up Silence's mother.

"Yes, go and look for ... uh ... you did say Silence, didn't you?" teased Mary Louise.

Sarah opened her parasol with a snap, flipped it over her shoulder and, without looking at Mary Louise, sauntered away. Sarah wanted to rush off to find Silence, but now, with her hair up, she had to walk with dignity. Her new hairdo even changed the way she selected her clothing. Mary Louise had loaned her a long white dress to wear today, along with a matching bonnet adorned with blue ribbons. Black buckled shoes and a white parasol completed her outfit.

Sarah hadn't gone far when she saw another younger woman watching two men playing horseshoes. Sarah admired her appearance, noticing that she wore her hair up, tucked neatly under a pink bonnet that matched her dress. When she drew close enough to see the girl's face, Sarah gasped as she recognized her former school chum, Silence Seaman.

Silence turned around. "Sarah!" she cried. "Is that really you?"

The girls rushed into each other's arms. Three years of absence from one another immediately melted away.

"I've been watching Rufus and Charles play horseshoes. I'll introduce you to Charles," Silence told her, after they had had a moment to collect their thoughts. Sarah noticed the way Silence's cheeks turned rosy pink when she mentioned Charles.

The game of horseshoes over, the men walked up to the two young women. Sarah's heart pounded so hard when she looked at Rufus that she thought the others must hear it.

Rufus smiled at Sarah. "Hello, Sarah. It's nice to see you again."

"Hello," Sarah replied, her mouth too dry to say more. He looked steadily at her for a moment, taking in her loveliness, and then spoke to Charles. "I'll see you all later," he said before he departed.

Silence took Sarah by the arm to draw her closer to Charles, so she could introduce them. "Sarah, this is Charles Russell. And Charles, this is my very best friend, Sarah Walkley."

"It's nice to meet you, Sarah. Silence has talked a lot about you," Charles told her.

"I'm happy to meet you, too, Charles," Sarah replied.

After the introductions, Charles excused himself to go help with the children's activities. "I'll see you after the games, Silence." Silence smiled.

The two friends walked around the grounds arm in arm. Silence looked at Sarah. "You still like Rufus, don't you?"

"Yes, I do," Sarah admitted. She never could keep a secret from Silence; they always shared everything. "And you like Charles, don't you?"

"Yes, in fact, he calls on me now and then. Did you like him?"

"Yes, I liked him very much. He's nice. I'm glad for you. Rufus doesn't know I'm even alive. Does he have a girlfriend?"

"No, he doesn't have any particular girl he likes. You felt hurt when he walked away like that, didn't you?"

"Yes, I did. I got more attention from him when he used to pull my pigtails."

"Don't worry about it. He noticed you. I know he did."

The girls stopped to watch the boys' three-legged race, joining other spectators standing in the shade of an old oak tree. A gentle summer breeze rustled the leaves. Overhead the blue sky showed no threat of rain—an ideal day for a picnic.

Sarah saw her brother Wyllys enter the race. Soon his leg was tied to the leg of a new friend, Andy Harland. After each contestant had his leg properly bound to that of his partner, Charles carefully lined them all up on their marks. He blew the whistle—they were off. Sarah cheered for Wyllys and Andy, as did Silence.

"Come on Wyllys! Come on Andy! You can do it!"

Many of the contestants fell down, but scrambled to their feet again. Despite taking a fall, Wyllys and Andy still managed to hobble across the finish line first, just moments ahead of the pair behind them. Everyone cheered when they received their prize of two sacks of stick candy. Both boys quickly shared the candy with others who had been in the race.

The girls moved on to watch more games and contests. As they wandered about, Sarah watched Rufus mingling with his brothers and other young men. He never looked her way. She felt deeply disheartened. For three years, her young girl's dream had been to see Rufus again. Now that she had reached the age to wear her hair up, she had hoped he would show some interest in her.

Walking along, Sarah and Silence passed him talking to her pa. She wondered what they were conversing about so seriously. Rufus turned his head in time to catch Sarah looking their way. He smiled at her, but she turned away and walked on.

Sophia and Maria came running up to Sarah and Silence. "We're going to have ice cream!" they exclaimed. "We saw them making it."

Silence laughed. "Yes, my folks brought their ice cream freezer. We still have some ice in our icehouse, so my ma made ice cream as a special treat. I wanted it to be a surprise for you," she explained. "My brothers are taking turns working the crank on the freezer. It should be almost ready now. Let's go see."

The twins led the way to where the ice cream makers were busy at their task. Sarah and Silence followed close behind.

Maria and Sophia rushed up to Warren and George, Rufus's twin brothers, who had taken over this stage of the ice cream production. The freezer sat packed in a wooden bucket of chopped ice that had been sprinkled with salt. Warren worked hard at cranking the ice cream paddle, barely able to turn the outside handle. He and George always tried to outdo each other.

"Is it ready yet?" asked Maria. Warren groaned. "As hard as it is to crank, I'd say it's very close to being ready." He looked up and noticed Sarah. "Hello, Sarah, how are ya?"

"Hello, Warren and George—how are you two?" Sarah replied.

"I'm hungry for ice cream," Warren laughed. "Aren't ya, George?"

"Yeah, and I still say I get the paddle. Oh, hello, Sarah."

"Hmm. We'll see about that," Warren mused.

Sarah looked at Silence. "The paddle—what do they mean?"

"Oh, they always like to eat the ice cream off the paddle after it's been pulled out of the maker," she laughed. "The boys always argue about who's going to get it."

Pastor Wheeler stood up and called all the people over to the food table. "It's time for us to eat, so let's bow our heads for grace." After the pastor had blessed the food, the families spread their blankets out on the ground. All got in line, moving along the long table to fill their plates with a variety of scrumptious food. At the end of the table, ice-cold lemonade awaited them. Tubs of ice from icehouses had kept the foods and lemonade cold. With a plate piled high in one hand and a glass of lemonade in the other, each person made their way to join family and friends on their blankets.

Sarah and Silence joined Mary Louise on a blanket between the Walkleys and the Seamans.

"Do you mind if we sit here, Mary Louise?" Sarah asked.

"No, please do," she replied. "I'd love to have you."

Silence kept looking for Charles. Then she saw him walking with Rufus, heading their way. Each carried two dishes of ice cream. As the young men reached the girls, Charles handed a dish to Silence.

"Oh, thank you, Charles."

Rufus handed one dish to Sarah and one to Mary Louise.

"Thank you, Rufus," both girls responded.

"You're very welcome. May I sit here after I fill my plate?" Rufus asked, looking at both of them.

"Of course," answered Mary Louise.

Charles got up with Rufus to get his food, too.

"Now I know," thought Sarah. "Rufus likes Mary Louise. That's why he's ignored me." She loved Mary Louise, but she still felt tears well up in her eyes. She just wanted to go home, but she knew she couldn't. Silence remained quiet, afraid she might have made a mistake about Rufus liking Sarah. Maybe he liked Mary Louise instead. Mary Louise, acting uncomfortable, quickly ate her meal.

When Charles and Rufus came back, Mary Louise stood up. "Will you please excuse me? I need to help Ma with Emily." She immediately disappeared.

Rufus looked at Sarah. "Do ya want to run off, too?" he teased. Then he noticed her red eyes. "Are ya all right, Sarah?" he whispered, his voice showing concern.

Sarah nodded. She couldn't speak. Rufus moved closer to her. "We can't have anything happen to my girl." He grinned at her. "You'll be my girl, won't ya?" He spoke seriously now. "I talked to your pa about it today. He gave his permission for me to court ya. I didn't want to show ya much attention until I had talked to him."

Sarah understood everything now. "Yes, Rufus, I'll be your girl always," she whispered. Her dream had come true.

"I'll always be here for you, Sarah," he promised, as her heart overflowed with joy and thanksgiving.

During the following months of courtship, Sarah's schoolgirl crush blossomed into a woman's love, and Rufus's caring for Sarah deepened into a love that would never fade.

Sarah's father, a newly elected justice of the peace, performed their marriage ceremony on April 6, 1856, in the Walkley home . . .

The rumbling of a buckboard on the road interrupted her nostalgic thoughts and brought her back into the present. She looked up, and her heart started racing as she recognized Edwin's familiar buckboard and team. Maybe he was bringing word of Rufus.

As Edwin drove quickly into the driveway, waving an envelope in the air, squawking chickens scurried out of the wagon's path. When Sarah saw what he held in his hand, she scooped up Rufus's letters from her lap and bounded down the steps to meet Edwin in the drive.

Edwin brought the sweaty team to a halt, jumped down from the buckboard, and handed Sarah the piece of mail that had come for her at the post office.

"It's not from Rufus," he quickly warned her. "The return address shows it's from a Dr. Warren Webster, assistant surgeon in charge at De Camp General Hospital on Davids Island, New York Harbor."

Sarah's hands trembled as she struggled to open the official military document. When she finally managed to get at its contents, tears filled her eyes as she read the sad news. Rufus was suffering from a lingering case of typhoid fever causing severe dysentery and wanted to see her. Dr. Webster advised her to come as soon as possible.

Sarah handed the heartbreaking message to Edwin. "Read this. I need to go to him immediately," she hoarsely whispered.

Edwin took the letter and quickly scanned the brief message. He noticed the letter had been written on April 23—8 days ago. He knew Sarah, indeed, needed to hurry.

"Of course you do," he answered. He pulled out his red bandana handkerchief and noisily blew his nose and dabbed at his eyes. "I thought it must be word of Rufus with such an official military envelope, so I brought it out as soon as the mail arrived at the post office." Edwin gently put his arm around his sister. "You go pack right now, while I tend to my horses. Pack for the children, too. We'll take care of them while you go to Rufus."

"Mama, are you going away?" Dorothy asked, her lower lip trembling.

Unnoticed by Sarah and Edwin, Dorothy and Lucy had run from the swing to see Uncle Edwin. They had overheard enough of Mama and Uncle Edwin's conversation to realize their Mama needed to go away.

Upon hearing Dorothy's quiet question, Sarah quickly dabbed her eyes, turned, and looked down at her precious daughters. She saw concern and fear in their sad little faces. Both of them had tears rising in their large blue eyes. They knew what it meant for someone to go away. They no longer had their papa at home, and they definitely needed their mama.

Sarah bent down, reached out, and drew them to her.

"Yes, I am going away, but only for a little while," she explained. "I won't be gone long. Papa is sick, and I'm going to go visit him. You will stay with Grandpa and Grandma Walkley. You'll be fine with them."

"Can I go, too, Mama?" Dorothy asked. "I want to see Papa."

"And I want to see him, too," Lucy pouted.

Sarah couldn't tell them the truth about the seriousness of Rufus's illness—that their papa might be dying.

"No, I'm sorry. I wish I could take you both, but it's too far," Mama said, as she sadly rose.

"Come. Let's go into the house. I need some helpers to help me pack my suitcase. And we need to pack your clothes, too, to take to Grandma's."

Reluctantly they went into the house with their mama. Sarah led the girls into their bedroom and began taking clothes out of their dresser drawers for them to pack.

"Put your clothes in here," she instructed them, as she pulled a box from under the bed. Soon the girls' lively chatter could be heard, as they busily packed the box with clothes to take to Grandma's house.

Quietly Sarah slipped away into the bedroom she shared with Rufus, closed the door behind her, and knelt down on the rag rug beside Rufus's side of the bed. She reached for his pillow to bury her face in, to muffle the sobs she could no longer restrain. She knew what it meant when a soldier became seriously ill in this war. A great many of them had died of disease. She allowed her pent-up tears to flow as she talked to her Lord, asking him to watch over Rufus, to heal and to comfort him. Through prayer she sought strength and courage for the difficult journey she faced, not knowing what she would find at the end.

Rising from her knees, she sensed the Lord's presence with her. It brought to her mind the verse, "I am with thee always." She felt renewed strength as she walked back to the girls' room. She knew the Lord would go with her—she wouldn't be alone. Passing through the parlor, she stopped by the maple end table to pick up her worn leather Bible. The cherished book, God's Word, had become a dear friend, a friend she needed with her now above all else.

After they had finished packing, Uncle Edwin carried Sarah's satchel and the box of clothes for the girls out to the buckboard. He carefully placed them in the wagon bed, then lifted Dorothy and Lucy to sit beside them on a bearskin robe. The girls seated, he helped Sarah up to the seat beside him.

"Do you want me to take you to the folks?" Edwin asked. "Else the children are welcome at our house, too. And I can take you to the train."

"Thank you, Edwin, but I would like to go to the folks. I need them right now. I've already told the girls they're going to their grandparents. Can you do the chores here? I appreciate all you are doing to help us. Thank you for coming right away with the mail."

Edwin reached over and patted her arm. "I just wish I could do more," he huskily mumbled to her.

He then flipped the reins, clucked to his team, and started rumbling out of the driveway. On the porch a forlorn-looking Buster watched them leave. He stood with his tail between his legs, whining at being left behind.

Sarah put her hand on Edwin's arm. "Do you mind if we take Buster?" she asked. She simply couldn't leave him behind. Buster had been only a wee puppy when Rufus first brought him home shortly after they were married. Now the old dog seemed like a part of their family.

"Why, no, of course not." Edwin stopped the team.

"C'mon, Buster," Sarah called.

Buster, his tail now wagging, lumbered down the porch steps and over to the buckboard. Edwin jumped down from his seat and gently lifted the dog into the bed of the wagon, putting him on the bear robe between Dorothy and Lucy, much to their delight.

Sarah and Edwin conversed very little on the short, brisk drive to their parents' sprawling farm home. The warm, early-May sun had hidden behind a cloud, leaving a chilly breeze to take its place.

Edwin and Sarah had deep thoughts of their own—thoughts of Rufus. Both realized the significance of the foreboding word Sarah had just received. Thinking of Rufus lying ill in a military hospital far away left them with heavy hearts and deep concerns. "Do you know the train schedule, Edwin?" Sarah meekly asked, as she drew her shawl more tightly around her shivering shoulders.

"No, I don't. But I think if you can go into Grand Rapids today, you could catch the train in the morning."

"I hope so," Sarah mumbled. She only knew that somehow she had to get to her Rufus. She'd travel any way she could in order to arrive there, but she knew the train would be the speediest mode—faster than the stagecoach.

When they entered their parents' circular dirt driveway, she spotted her mother at the side of the house, hanging up Monday's wash on a rope clothesline. As soon as Edwin brought his frisky team to a complete stop, Dorothy and Lucy jumped down from the back of their uncle's buckboard, accompanied by Buster, and ran to see their grandma.

"Mama's gonna see Papa, Grandma," Dorothy excitedly exclaimed. "Mama's gonna go on the train!"

Puzzled by what Dorothy had just told her, Sarah's mother turned to look at her daughter walking haltingly toward her. She knew by Sarah's pale, drawn face that she had received bad news.

"Did you hear from Rufus, honey?" Ma softly asked her.

"No, Ma. Edwin brought me word from a doctor at De Camp General Hospital near Brooklyn, New York. He wrote to say Rufus is very ill with typhoid fever, and I should come at once." Sarah's tone of voice revealed her despair.

Ma looked around to see where Dorothy and Lucy had gone. Finding they had run off to play with Buster, she took Sarah in her arms, and both women cried on each other's shoulder.

"I'm so sorry Rufus is sick, honey," Ma said through her tears. "We must get you on that train. But I don't like you making the trip alone. Maybe Mary Louise could go with you."

"No, Ma. I'll have to go alone. We don't have time to go and see Mary Louise. She's an hour from here, and every minute counts. We should try to get to Grand Rapids before dark," Sarah explained.

"You find Pa, while I go inside the house to fix the two of you a lunch to take along. He'll gladly take you to Grand Rapids right now," Ma told her.

Mother and daughter pulled away from one another, wiped the tears from their eyes, and walked arm and arm to the back of the house. Ma went inside to prepare a lunch, while Sarah hurried toward the barn, looking for her father. As she neared it, she could see Edwin hitching Pa's team of Morgans to his buggy.

Edwin turned toward her, looked up, and shaded his eyes from the capricious sun, which had come out again. "I told Pa everything, Sarah. He has gone into the house to get cleaned up to take you. I'm just helping him by getting the rig ready. Your satchel is in the buggy, and you'll soon be ready to start," Edwin explained.

"Oh, I see. Thank you, Edwin."

Sarah quickly went to find Dorothy and Lucy so she could tell them goodbye. She located them in the back yard, still playing with Buster.

"I'm going, girls—come give me a big hug and a kiss. I love you." Sarah reached her arms out toward her daughters.

Both girls flung themselves at their mother as she clasped them to her. After countless hugs and kisses, Sarah gently pulled away from them.

Grandma then came down the back steps carrying a nice lunch all wrapped up, which she handed to Sarah.

"Thanks, Ma," Sarah said as she took the food.

"Be sure and obey Grandma," she reminded the two now solemn little girls.

"Oh, they'll be fine. They always obey me," Grandma assured her.

"Sarah! We're ready to go," Pa called. Sarah quickly slipped away as she heard Pa's voice.

Grandma, holding each child by the hand, followed closely behind Sarah to say goodbye to her and Pa.

"I'll be back tomorrow, Ma," Pa told her. He reached out to hug and kiss his wife goodbye.

"Please be careful," Ma answered. She hugged her daughter one last time. "We'll be prayin' for you, Sarah."

"Thanks, Ma."

Sarah and her father would have to spend the night in Grand Rapids, if she were to board the first train out in the morning. Before she climbed into the buggy, she went up to Edwin to thank him once again for all his help.

"I'll tell Rufus how much you've helped me, Edwin. He'll be very grateful, I know. Thank you!" She knew his heart ached for his brother-in-law, too.

"Give Rufus my love," Edwin told her. "Goodbye."

Pa assisted Sarah into the buggy before climbing in himself. He picked up the lines and gently snapped them over the horses' rumps. The Morgans started moving slowly out of the drive.

Suddenly, Dorothy broke away from Grandma's hand to run after the buggy.

"Mama! Mama!" she shouted. "My kiss! My kiss!"

Pa stopped the horses and Sarah climbed down from the buggy to see what Dorothy wanted. She ran up to her mother, grabbed her around the legs and looked up at her with tear-filled eyes. "One more kiss, Mama," she breathlessly pleaded. "One more kiss for you to give to Papa from me."

Sarah swallowed the lump in her throat, as she bent down so Dorothy could give her a kiss to take to her papa.

"Of course, honey. You may give me a kiss for Papa."

Lucy ran up to give Mama a kiss for Papa as well. "Give my kiss to Papa, too," she told her.

"I will, Lucy, I'll give Papa a kiss from each of you," Mama promised them.

As Sarah and Pa started for Grand Rapids, Sarah loosened her bonnet, settling back in the cozy leather corner of the buggy, with the lap robe folded as a pillow beneath her head. The sun had come back out, kissing her cheeks with warmth. She knew she had a long, tedious ride before her. Her anxious thoughts kept going to Rufus and back to the letter from De Camp Hospital—the letter she kept reading over and over. Each time she read it, the word TYPHOID jumped out at her, bringing back memories of a similar tragedy she had faced over two years ago. Only, then she had Rufus to stand beside her and comfort her. Now he lay far away, seriously ill with typhoid himself.

24

Casnovia to Grand Rapids
Sad Memories ~ Getting Underway

As the buggy moved onward, Sarah's thoughts of Rufus's illness brought back memories of two years ago and another illness . . .

. . . All morning buckets of rain had poured down, bringing respite from the summer heat wave. The gray skies turned a hazy blue, as a hot sun peeked out again, quickly drying up the raindrops on the ground.

When five-year-old Oliver and two-year-old Dorothy awoke from their afternoon naps, Sarah let them go outside to play in the backyard under the maple tree.

"Keep an eye on Dorothy, Oliver," Sarah called to her son, as she stepped out on the back porch to check on the children. "Don't let her wander off."

"I'll watch her, Mama," Oliver quietly answered.

At the dull sound of his voice, Sarah turned to take another look at him. As she did, she noticed how pale he was, so she walked down the wooden steps over to the children. Dorothy, much to her delight, had found a little mud hole to play in, but Oliver just sat quietly under the tree with his arm around their dog Buster, who loyally sat beside him.

"Do you feel all right, Oliver?" Sarah asked.

"My head hurts, Mama," he wearily replied.

"Then wouldn't you like to come inside with me, honey?" Mama kindly asked him.

Oliver sighed. "No, Mama. I just want to stay here."

"Well, all right. Supper will be ready soon. Maybe you'll feel better after you eat." Mama tried to encourage him.

Less than a half hour later, Sarah came back out on the porch to ring the dinner bell calling her family to the supper table. The distant clanging was a welcome sound to Rufus, who was hard at work hoeing in the cornfield. He wiped his beaded brow with his red bandana handkerchief and started for the house.

Oliver and Dorothy, with freshly scrubbed faces and hands, sat at the table, waiting for their papa to come and say grace.

Dorothy happily clapped her small hands together, giving her tired papa a big smile as at last he entered the kitchen and took his place at the table. Papa returned her smile, and as each bowed their head, he said grace.

"Dear Lord, for what we are about to receive make us truly thankful. And most of all, we thank thee for Jesus. Amen."

Mama dished up steaming food on Oliver's and Dorothy's plates. She gave each a small scoop of mashed potatoes, a crispy fried chicken leg, a helping of green beans, applesauce, and a slice of johnnycake slathered in freshly churned butter.

"Rufus, could you keep an eye on Dorothy with her piece of chicken, please? Maybe you should just cut the meat off the leg for her," Sarah suggested.

Then the once cooing baby, lying on a colorful, thick, patchwork pallet on the floor, suddenly interrupted the meal, crying with pangs of hunger.

Mama laughed. "Someone else wants to be fed, too." She quickly got up from the table, picked up a hungry seven-month-old Lucy and carried her into the bedroom to nurse.

A few minutes later Sarah brought the contented baby back to the kitchen table and handed her to Rufus, who had finished eating. When she sat back down, she noticed Oliver hadn't touched his food.

"How is your headache, Oliver?" Mama asked. "You haven't eaten your supper."

"My head still hurts, Mama. I'm not hungry," he answered.

"He complained of a headache this afternoon," Sarah informed Rufus. "You try to eat a little, honey. It may help your head," Mama coaxed him. "Can't you eat some mashed potatoes? They're your favorite."

Rufus reached over and felt Oliver's forehead. "He feels warm to me."

Oliver took a few small bites of mashed potatoes. "I can't eat, Mama. My stomach hurts," he moaned, bent over in pain. "I have to go to the outhouse."

Rufus got up to put Lucy back on the pallet. He led Oliver by the hand to the outhouse. After several minutes, he carried him back inside, whimpering.

"He's really sick," Rufus told Sarah. "He threw up and has bad diarrhea. We need to put 'im to bed." He carefully carried his fragile son into the bedroom and gently laid him on his bed. Sarah quickly followed them.

"He probably has bad summer complaint," Sarah suggested.

Rufus agreed. "Yeah, you're probably right. But if he's not better in the mornin', I'll go fetch Doc."

Together, Sarah and Rufus undressed their ill son and tucked him into bed. They knelt beside him and prayed fervently for his recovery. Afterward, Rufus brought in a slop jar for Oliver to use, so he wouldn't have to endure any more strenuous trips to the outhouse.

Rufus quickly went to the barn to do the evening chores. Once finished, he rushed back to the house and entered Oliver's room. He stood by the bed and stroked his son's feverish brow.

"Ya go take care of the girls, Sarah, and after they're in bed, ya get some rest yourself. I'll sit up with Oliver."

Sarah shook her head. "No, Rufus. I'll take care of the girls, but after they are in bed, I'll sit up with Oliver. You worked ten hours in the field today and you need your rest. Besides, I couldn't sleep anyway."

Oliver's sickness did not let up, with both vomiting and diarrhea all night. Rufus, unable to sleep, kept checking on him with Sarah. He had not improved by daybreak.

Rufus hurried in from the barn when finished with the early morning chores.

After looking in on Oliver hopefully one more time, he sighed as he spoke to Sarah. "He's no better. I'm goin' to fetch Doc."

"Yes, Rufus please go. Now . . . now he even has blood in his diarrhea," she said with trembling lips.

Rufus looked at Sarah's anxious face as he reached over and put his arms around her. "I'll get the doctor. Don't worry, honey. I'll ride Colonel instead of takin' the buggy. It'll be much faster."

He turned and rushed out to the barn, saddling the horse within a few minutes. Soon Sarah heard the clip-clopping of Colonel's iron shoes, as horse and rider galloped away.

Dr. Shelliday lived two miles down the road from Rufus and Sarah's farm. After yesterday's rain, the sun had baked the muddy road into a hard, level surface, making a fine track for horses. Colonel carried Rufus at a full gallop a good deal of the way. Having arrived at his destination, Rufus reined his mount into the doctor's driveway and rode him to the side door.

Dr. Shelliday's office opened onto the side porch. Rufus jumped off Colonel, dropping the reins to the ground to tether the sweaty horse. He walked up the steps, hoping the office would be open, but the locked door wouldn't budge. Desperately, he started pounding on the door to get the doctor's attention. Finally, Dr. Shelliday appeared.

"Rufus!" he exclaimed. "What is wrong that causes you to be here so early?"

"It's Oliver, Doc," Rufus answered. "He's terrible sick. We thought it might be summer complaint at first, but he seems sicker than he'd be with that. Now he even suffers from bloody diarrhea."

At the mention of Oliver having bloody diarrhea, Dr. Shelliday quickly turned and took his medical bag off the nearby table in the hallway. "Let's go," he told Rufus, as he compassionately gripped him on his drooped shoulder. "You may ride with me in my buggy. Just tie your horse onto the back."

The drive back to the farm seemed to Rufus to take an eternity. Kind Dr. Shelliday tried to keep up a conversation with small talk, but Rufus's mind only held the picture of Oliver so pale and so sick.

At last they pulled into Sarah and Rufus' driveway, with Buster barking a greeting and Sarah meeting them at the door. Throwing his reins over the hitching rail, Dr. Shelliday picked up his medical bag and hurried into the house, following Sarah into the sickroom. Rufus jumped down from the buggy, quickly taking Colonel to the barn to give him a rushed rubdown.

Dr. Shelliday washed his hands at the commode before examining Oliver. He knew by looking at him that he had something more serious than the many cases of summer complaint he treated so often this time of year.

When he finished his exam, he shut his medical bag and called Sarah and Rufus, who had just tiptoed out into the sitting room.

"I'm sorry," he told them, "but Oliver is very sick. I'm afraid he has typhoid fever. When there are bloody stools with typhoid fever, it's not good. Don't allow him to move more than necessary. He may perforate his bowel if he moves around too much. Feed him only milk in small quantities several times a day. Sponge him down with cool well water. It should help lower his fever and make him more comfortable. I'll stop back this evening."

The country doctor knew there would be sad days ahead for Sarah and Rufus. He squeezed Sarah's arm before he turned and, with his medical bag in hand, walked back out to his buggy in the driveway.

In the days that followed, little Oliver showed no improvement. Each day, his fever rose higher and he became weaker and more emaciated.

The parson, along with many friends and relatives, stopped by to see if they could help in any way, but no one could be allowed to enter the sick room. Rufus and Sarah especially kept their little girls away from their big brother.

"Please, Papa, can't I see Oliver," Dorothy asked. "I won't hurt him."

"I know ya wouldn't, honey, but we don't want ya sick, too," Papa explained.

The doctor faithfully visited Oliver every morning and evening. Sadly, the dreaded morning came when he needed to inform Rufus and Sarah of the tragic news. Oliver would not recover. He stopped on his way to their farm to speak with Parson Wheeler. As a result of their conversation, the parson made plans to arrive soon to stand with Rufus and Sarah through this roughest of storms.

Dr. Shelliday continued to Rufus and Sarah's home and hurried straight into the sickroom. After examining Oliver, he came back to the sitting room and spoke to the anxious parents.

"I'm sorry, Rufus and Sarah, but Oliver only has a few hours to live. There is nothing more that can be done for him."

Sarah crumpled into Rufus's arms, as a sob escaped her lips. They stood crying and holding one another while Dr. Shelliday embraced them both. "I'll stay here with you until the end," he assured them.

As soon as they could compose themselves, Rufus and Sarah went back in to be with Oliver. One sat on one side of his bed, and the other on the other side. They wanted to spend every last moment with him.

The summer showers during the night had helped cool his stuffy bedroom, but an odor of sickness still permeated the air. Oliver remained barely conscious for a while longer. Looking up at his parents sitting beside him, he slowly turned his head toward Sarah.

"Mama, sing," he whispered. "Sing about heaven." Oliver loved to hear his mother sing the old hymns.

Sarah swallowed, cleared her throat, and, with God's help, softly started singing.

> I am thinking today of that beautiful land
> I shall reach when the sun goeth down;
> When through wonderful grace by my Savior I stand,
> Will there be any stars in my crown?

Rufus joined her on the chorus, blending his baritone with her soprano.

> Will there be any stars, any stars in my crown
> When at evening the sun goeth down?
> When I wake with the blest in the mansions of rest,
> Will there be any stars in my crown?

As they finished singing the chorus, Oliver motioned with his hand to stop them.

"Mama, Papa. What is heaven like?" he huskily asked.

Rufus and Sarah quickly stole a startled look at each other, their heartache showing on their faces.

"It's a beautiful place, son. It's a place where no one cries, no one is sick or hurtin'. Everybody's happy there," Rufus answered.

"Are there many children there?" Oliver wanted to know.

"Yes. Many children," Sarah told him.

"What do they do there?" he questioned further.

"I imagine they play games together and play with Jesus. Jesus really loves children like ya. I'm sure he holds 'em on his lap and talks to 'em," Papa explained.

Oliver sighed. "Heaven sounds like such a nice place," he drowsily murmured. Soon he fell into a deep sleep from which he never awoke. Sarah and Rufus sat holding his hands, when suddenly they went limp. Oliver had slipped into the arms of Jesus.

Rufus and Sarah cried most of the day—a day that became a blur to them. Many relatives, neighbors, and friends came to give them their condolences. Their parson stayed with them, comforting them with Scripture and prayer.

At bedtime they had only each other. Grandma Seaman had taken the girls with her to care for them. Rufus enfolded Sarah in his arms.

"Do ya know, honey, what I keep thinkin' that helps me?"

"No, Rufus. What?" she sobbed.

"I keep thinkin' about one of the passages Parson Wheeler read from the Bible." Rufus reached over to the table for their Bible and, quickly opening it, turned to 2 Samuel 12:23. "Here it is. David said this after his baby son died. 'I shall go to him, but he shall not return to me.' I keep thinkin' that I now have one more reason to look forward to heaven. I shall go to Oliver. I've always looked forward to seein' Jesus and I still do, but I now have a second reason to look forward to heaven—I'll see our own Oliver."

Sarah blew her nose on her soggy handkerchief and wiped her eyes. "We will see Oliver again, won't we, Rufus. We'll see him someday—I know we will." That assurance in God's Word did much to comfort her.

"Yes, Sarah," Rufus agreed. "We will see Oliver again. I'm lookin' forward to it. We're only pilgrims in this world. Heaven is really our home. Oliver is home now . . ."

"Sarah! Did ya hear me?"

Pa's voice startled Sarah out of her despairing thoughts of Oliver's death and brought her mind back to the present heartache.

"I'm sorry, Pa, what did you say?"

Reaching over to pat her hand, he told her, "I said that not everyone who gets typhoid fever dies. Many people live."

"I know, Pa. I know," she whispered, as she weakly smiled up at him.

Pa knew where Sarah's thoughts had wandered. He understood the deep sorrow Sarah and Rufus had lived with since the death of their son, his grandson and namesake, Oliver, two years ago. Having lost two children of his own, Pa was well acquainted with the agonizing pain the loss of a child brings and the toll it takes on any marriage. All that sustained him and Ma was the blessed hope of one day being reunited with their precious daughters, Lucy and Martha. Pa realized that grief draws some couples closer together while others are pulled farther apart. It causes some to draw nearer to God, whereas others turn away from Him in anger.

Rufus and Sarah's grief had drawn them closer to one another, but sadly, Pa had witnessed them pulling away from God. Yet Rufus, after a taste of rough army life, had seen his need for his Heavenly Father and had rededicated his life to the Lord. When by letter he persuaded Sarah to join him in turning back to God, Ma and Pa rejoiced. Knowing Sarah feared she may be facing another tragedy, Pa silently prayed that her new re-commitment to God would help carry her through whatever may lie ahead.

The warm sun once again floated behind a cloud, bringing back the chill in the air. Sarah took the lap robe from behind her head, wrapped it around her, and tied her blue bonnet on more securely. Pa buttoned his coat up and pulled his hat down on his head.

"I hope it don't rain," he muttered. "If it does, we'll never make Grand Rapids by tonight. Muddy roads will slow the horses down."

"Oh, no!" Sarah thought. "I must get to Grand Rapids today if I'm going to catch the train tomorrow."

Midway through their journey they made their usual stop along the familiar babbling brook to rest, feed, and water the horses. After taking care of the Morgans, Pa opened Ma's lunch, hoping to get Sarah to eat something.

"Won't ya eat a sandwich, daughter? You'll feel better."

"Not now, Pa. Maybe later," she answered.

Pa quickly ate his lunch, and soon they were on their way again.

When they came to the outer limits of Grand Rapids, they drove east to Cyprus Avenue, which would take them south to Leonard Street.

After they had traveled all day and into early evening, the fickle sun came back out from behind the clouds for the last time, slowly making its descent in the red western sky and creating a breathtaking sundown as they entered the city limits at Leonard Street.

"We'll take Leonard to the railroad depot. Near the railroad station there's a new hotel, the Sherman House, built just last year to serve the train passengers," Pa told Sarah. "I think we can get rooms there, but it will be very expensive."

"Oh, Pa," Sarah muttered.

"It's all right, honey. I'll take it out of my emergency fund." Pa always had an emergency fund for unexpected expenses. He had just replenished it by selling his prize sow to their nearest neighbor down the road.

Driving his pair of bay Morgans, with their tails held high, down Leonard Street, Pa couldn't get over how much Grand Rapids had grown.

"Look at the new buildin's, Sarah." He pointed them out to her as he wove his way through the traffic caused by many fine horse and buggy rigs carrying their occupants home after work. "Grand Rapids is really bustlin'."

Pa knew the ten-year census figures had shown the population of Grand Rapids to be less than 3,000 in 1850 but more than 8,000 in 1860.

"I wonder what the population is now," he mused. "With the war over, it will mushroom."

But Sarah didn't notice her surroundings. She had her mind on only one thing: reaching Rufus.

In less than a mile they came to the Leonard Street Bridge, which spanned the Grand River, Michigan's longest river. After paying their one cent toll, they drove across the long bridge with the shingled roof. On the east side of the bridge the city had not grown toward the railroad station.

Pa slowed Prince and King to a walk as the street became mucky; Leonard Street had given way to mud.

Shortly he pulled up in front of the Sherman House Hotel. He jumped down, tethered the horses to the hitching rail, and went around to assist Sarah out of the buggy. He reached over to pick up both their satchels from behind their seat.

Pa and Sarah carefully stepped onto the swept boardwalk. Slowly walking up the few wooden steps to the hotel's entrance, they heard faint voices and soft laughter coming from the wide veranda that encircled the building and overlooked the flowing Grand River. Guests were still seated in comfortable chairs behind the safety of the spindled railing, where they had been privileged to watch the gorgeous sunset over the gurgling rapids.

As they entered the hotel's spacious lobby, the warm light from a large, gas-lit chandelier invited them in. Softly shutting the door behind them, they walked to the desk and spoke to the man behind it.

"My daughter and I would like two rooms with a connectin' door," Pa told the hotel clerk, a balding, overweight man with thick glasses. "We'll only need 'em for one night."

"Yes, of course," the clerk answered, pushing the registration book toward them. After they had signed their names, the clerk called for a young man to take their satchels and to escort them to their rooms.

The porter escorted them to their rooms, unlocked their doors and handed the keys to Pa. He then entered the rooms before them, turned up the gas on the globe lamp, and quietly left.

Pa saw Sarah comfortably settled before leaving the hotel. "There's a livery stable nearby, so I'll put the horses and buggy away for the night. Don't allow anyone to come into your room," he cautioned, as he handed her the key. "No one! I'll be right back."

While Pa drove the rig across the road to the livery stable, Sarah took off her bonnet and hung it on a hall tree in her room. She walked over to the black walnut commode. A sigh escaped her lips as she looked into the mirror and saw her weary face gazing back at her. Pouring water from the pitcher into the bowl, she started freshening up. Finished with her toiletry, Sarah pulled back the blue bed cover, took off her shoes, and lay down to rest until Pa came back.

Meanwhile, Pa walked down the hotel steps into the chilly twilight. Bullfrogs croaking their springtime melody broke the silence of the night. A pair of twinkling gas lamps set on posts burned in front of the hotel, giving off a yellow light that dispelled the darkness.

Carefully tiptoeing through the mud to untie Prince and King from the hitching rail, he climbed into the buggy seat and drove the tired team down the sloppy street to a nearby livery stable.

Pa pulled up the team at the end of the stable, where a gas lantern hung on each side of the open doorway. He jumped down from the buggy and walked over to the young man spreading straw in the horse stalls.

"Hello, my name is Oliver Walkley," he told him, extending his hand. "My name is Levi," the young man answered, as he firmly grasped the older man's hand. "I'm the stable attendant here. What can I do for ya?"

"Do ya have a place for my team and buggy?" Pa asked.

"Sure," the attendant answered. "Bring 'em on in. I'll put your horses right here. I'm sure you'll want 'em to have a rubdown. It's part of our service."

"Yeah, I'd like that," Pa agreed. "They're a special team."

"I can see that. Morgans, ain't they?" Levi asked.

"Yeah, they are. We drove in from Casnovia. My daughter is takin' the train tomorrow, so I'll only need to leave 'em here one night. I'll be goin' back home after she departs."

After stabling the horses, Levi suggested, "Let's put your buggy over here." Following his suggestion, both men pushed it off to the side.

Pa looked around the stable. The pungent smell of horses filled the air, but Levi kept the stalls clean and well bedded with fresh straw; he also had stocked the mangers with hay. This would be a good place to leave the horses.

Pa turned toward Levi, who had begun the laborious task of brushing the mud off King before starting on Prince. "Nice talkin' to ya. I'll see ya in the mornin'."

"Good night," Levi answered.

A gentle rapping at her bedroom door woke Sarah from a restless nap.

"Honey, it's me," Pa softly called to her. She quickly rose to unlock the door.

Pa gingerly stepped into the room, balancing a silver tray of steaming victuals in his hands.

"I've brought us a little supper from the dinin' room," he told her, slowly making his way over to set the large tray on a marble-topped table near her bed. "I didn't think you'd feel up to goin' downstairs, but ya do need to eat to keep up your strength for the trip," Pa cautioned.

"Thank you, Pa. I'll try and eat," she promised. "I know you're right."

Pa carefully moved the table next to where Sarah was sitting on the side of the bed. He drew the chair from near the door over to the table for himself.

Seated, they bowed their heads while Pa said grace.

Sarah poured the tea. On the tray were also two hot bowls of savory potato soup, crackers, two roast beef sandwiches, and for dessert, two pieces of spicy apple pie, still warm, fresh from the oven.

True to her word, Sarah finished all of her soup and sipped some of the fragrant tea she had poured. She nibbled on a cracker, but didn't attempt one of the thick sandwiches, though the aroma of the warm apple pie spiked her appetite to where she managed to eat a few bites.

"Ain't ya gonna finish your pie, Sarah?" Pa asked. "It's mighty good."

"I know it is, Pa, but I'm too full. I've eaten all I can," she replied. "You may have it."

"Yeah, you've done well," Pa complimented her, reaching for her pie so he could finish it. "Were ya able to get some sleep?"

"Yes, I dozed when you were gone, but I kept having terrible dreams," she answered. "Almost like nightmares."

"That's too bad. I'll pray that ya do better tonight. And remember, I'll be in the next room," Pa reminded her. "I hate to see ya makin' this trip alone, Sarah," he added.

"I'll be all right, Pa. I'll be very careful. I just want to see Rufus. He needs me." Her lips trembled and her eyes brimmed with unshed tears.

Pa put a comforting arm around her shoulder. "I know he does, honey. You'll be the best medicine he could have."

After Pa finished the pie, they neatly stacked the dishes back onto the tray for the maid to pick up in the morning. Sarah blotted her mouth with the white linen napkin before folding it and placing it on the tray. Pa laid his napkin alongside hers.

"Keep your sandwich to take with ya on the train," Pa suggested. "Ya don't know when you'll have a chance to eat again."

Sarah took his advice and wrapped the sandwich in a clean handkerchief. She stifled a weary yawn by covering her mouth.

"Well, ya have a long way to go tomorrow," Pa pointed out. "We'd better turn in."

Pa walked slowly across the blue paisley rug to the door that separated their rooms. Upon opening it, he turned in the doorway to look at Sarah with a father's eyes of compassion. His heart felt heavy for the forlorn, pale figure sitting slumped on the bed. If only he could do more to help the daughter he loved so deeply. He would surely pray.

"Now remember what I told ya," he reminded her once again. "I'm right in this room next door."

"I know. Good night, Pa," Sarah quietly replied.

"Good night, honey," he answered, carefully closing the door.

After a fretful night of tossing, Sarah rose early to do her toiletry and to dress for her train trip. She donned a wool gray suit for traveling and brushed her hair up into a bun on the back of her head. The curly, wispy hair at her temples and forehead refused to be tamed, framing her drawn face in charming ringlets.

All dressed and ready, she walked over to the connecting door between her room and her father's. She had heard movement earlier, so she thought he must be awake.

"Pa," she called, knocking gently on the door. "Are you up?"

The door opened to reveal Pa fully dressed and prepared to leave. Carrying his satchel, he entered her room. "I'm all set. I think we should stop and have breakfast downstairs. We have time before your train leaves at eight. The restaurant opens at seven."

"All right, Pa, if you wish."

"But first, let's pray together," he proposed, putting down his bag. "I want to pray for ya to have a safe journey."

"And we'll pray for Rufus, too, Pa," Sarah hastened to add.

"Yeah, of course. We'll always pray for Rufus."

They stood facing each other, holding hands, with heads bowed. Pa prayed in his deep voice, reverently talking to his heavenly Father. Sarah always felt that her father's prayers went straight to the throne of God. By the time Pa said "Amen," a sense of peace had come over her.

Pa bent over to pick up their bags. Together they exited her room and walked downstairs to the lobby. Leaving their baggage by the desk, they went over to stand in line at the entrance to the crowded dining room. Service being good, the host shortly seated them at a table.

Round tables covered with white linen cloths filled the large dining room, and a matching napkin was folded neatly at each place setting. The chairs were upholstered in red velvet, the color of the carpet. Waiters dressed in white shirts and black trousers scurried back and forth from tables to kitchen, trying to serve their customers as quickly as possible.

One such waiter, a young man, approached their table. "Good morning," he said, smiling as he handed them a menu. He stood, politely waiting, with his pencil poised to take their orders.

Sarah didn't look at the menu. "I would just like toast and coffee," she told him.

The waiter wrote it down and then looked expectantly toward Pa.

"I'll have a stack of pancakes with scrambled eggs and coffee," Pa ordered.

"It'll only take a few minutes," the waiter promised, as he finished writing Pa's order. He left, heading for the kitchen, where orders were stacked high.

While they waited for their food, Pa glanced around. The dining room held a variety of people—men, women, children, and even Union soldiers.

Before long, their waiter returned, carrying a tray with their hot breakfast. Pa and Sarah unobtrusively bowed their heads, as Pa softly said grace.

Even though Sarah had ordered only toast, the slices were extra thick and spread with melted butter. On the side of her plate lay an assortment of jams and jellies. The coffee tasted as good as it smelled.

Pa's order of hot cakes came with maple syrup and honey. The meal was delicious.

After breakfast, they picked up Sarah's baggage and walked out onto the veranda. The rain that had muddied the streets before now came down in torrents, turning the street into a sodden thoroughfare.

"Ya wait here," Pa advised Sarah. He slipped inside the lobby to borrow an umbrella from the rack the hotel provided for its guests.

Coming back out, he opened it, hunched under it, and made his way across the slippery street to the Detroit and Milwaukee Railway ticket window, where he purchased a round trip ticket to Detroit for Sarah.

"Is the train on time?" he asked the elderly, white-haired agent.

"Yup. It's due in about seven minutes."

"How are the connections between Detroit and New York?" Pa wanted to know.

"Oh, they're very good. Several trains a day."

Pa hurried back to Sarah waiting on the veranda. "Here's your ticket, honey, and some extra money I want ya to have," he explained, handing her the small white ticket and several crumpled bills.

"But I have some money, Pa," she informed him.

"I know ya do, but I still want ya to take this money, too" he insisted. "If ya don't need it, ya can give it back. Come, we need to hurry. The train will arrive any minute."

Pa hurried Sarah along as he picked up her satchel, held the umbrella over her head, and guided her safely to the train platform, where a group of people had gathered. Horses and buggies were lined up on the side of the depot in an attempt to stay under the protection of the eaves.

A stir went through the waiting crowd as puffs of smoke could be seen coming down the track toward them. The train was on time.

As the engine chugged up to the depot, it let off steam, frightening the horses. Their nostrils flared as they threw their heads back and reared up on their hind legs. The drivers kept a firm hand on the lines, gentling them down with soothing talk.

The smell of wood smoke filled the air, and sparks flew everywhere, looking like fireflies on a summer's evening. The iron horse had arrived.

"All aboard! All aboard!" the conductor's bass voice alerted the passengers. Standing in front of the entrance to the train car and dressed in his black Macintosh, he looked protected from the inclement weather. He already had the heavy bottom step in place for boarding.

Sarah turned and threw her arms around Pa's neck. She hugged him and held on tightly. How she wished he could go with her.

"Let's get ya on the train, honey," Pa quietly said to her, gently freeing himself from her embrace.

Sarah let go without protest, for she needed to go to Rufus. "Rufus is all that matters," she thought. She walked with Pa along the platform down to where the conductor stood, ready to assist her up the steps. Pa handed her valise to her.

"Goodbye, Pa. I'll be all right," she assured him, looking at his worried face.

"Goodbye, honey. I'll be praying for ya and Rufus," he once again promised.

After climbing aboard, Sarah slowly walked to the back of the car and sat in the last seat by a window. There were windows along both sides, and a brown rug runner ran the full length of the aisle. The smell of the engine's wood fire saturated the air.

The conductor had witnessed Pa's painful goodbye to Sarah as she boarded the train and noted the despair in his face.

"Is your daughter going very far?" he gently asked.

"Yes, she's travelin' to Brooklyn, New York, to visit her husband, a Union soldier. He's very ill in De Camp Military Hospital on Davids Island in New York Harbor," Pa answered. "I don't like her travelin' so far alone."

"I understand how you feel. I have a daughter about her age. I'll try to look after her and help her all I can when we get to Detroit," the conductor told him. "What is her name?"

"Her name is Sarah Seaman," Pa replied. "And I thank ya so very much."

"You're welcome. I'm happy to do it."

The conductor put the bottom step back after everyone had boarded. He then climbed the stationary steps, leaned over, and gave the engineer the signal to depart.

Pa waved at Sarah as the train pulled out. "Be with her, God," he softly prayed.

Sarah tried to look out of the steamy train window but found it useless. Taking her handkerchief, she prepared to dry the pane, when a hand holding a large man's handkerchief reached across her and wiped the moisture from the glass. Sarah only nodded toward the helpful figure behind her, quickly turning back to wave to Pa. "Thank you," she managed to murmur.

"Don't mention it," a somewhat familiar voice answered.

Sarah, her mind set on seeing Pa, didn't pay it any notice.

Pa's face, peeking out from under the umbrella, brightened at the sight of Sarah at the window. They kept waving until they couldn't see one another anymore.

25

Grand Rapids to Brooklyn, New York
A Long but Hopeful Trip

Settling back in her seat, Sarah realized the man who had dried the window was sitting beside her. She stole a glance in his direction to discover that her seatmate was a young, bearded Union soldier no older than her brother Wyllys. The left sleeve of the lad's uniform hung empty at his side—his arm another casualty of the war.

Seeing Sarah look his way, the soldier politely tipped the brim of his hat and nodded to her. "Are you traveling alone, ma'am?" he asked.

"Yes . . . yes, I'm traveling alone," Sarah answered hesitantly. She didn't care to call attention to the fact that she was by herself.

"I only asked because I didn't want to take this seat away from someone who might be traveling with you," he explained.

Their short conversation was interrupted by the train conductor with his call for "tickets, tickets," as he walked down the aisle to check each passenger and then return to them their little white stub. His wet shoes squeaked at each step he took.

Approaching Sarah's seat, he smiled broadly at her. After returning her stub he spoke to her. "Mrs. Seaman, I'm Conductor Baker. When you arrive in Detroit, wait right here in your seat for me. I'll go with you to find your best connection to New York. I told your pa I would help you."

Sarah returned his smile. "That is very kind of you, but I don't want to cause you a lot of bother."

"You won't," he assured her. "It'll be my pleasure."

Secretly, she felt very relieved.

As the conductor walked back down the aisle, the soldier, having heard Sarah referred to as "Mrs. Seaman," suddenly sat up straight in his seat. Turning toward Sarah, he carefully examined her face—searching for someone he knew.

"You're Sarah Seaman, Wyllys Walkley's sister!" he exclaimed.

"Why, yes, I am. Do you know Wyllys?" Sarah looked more closely at the haggard young man on her right.

"Wyllys is one of my very best friends. I'm Andy—Andrew Harland. Don't you remember me, Sarah?"

Sarah's sad face brightened for a moment when she heard his name. "Of course I do, Andy, but it's been a while since I've seen you. And back then you didn't have a beard. When I knew you, you and Wyllys were just boys running three-legged races."

Andy smiled, remembering the Baptist Church picnic where he had first met Wyllys and the Walkley family over ten years ago.

But Sarah knew the main reason she hadn't recognized Andy: her mind was only on Rufus and reaching him.

"How is Wyllys?" Andy asked. "I saw your father-in-law last week and asked about him. He said he thought he was all right."

"Yes, he's fine. My parents regularly hear from him. He's still in the army, serving as a medical corpsman."

"That's wonderful! I owe my life to the medical corpsmen. If they hadn't crawled out on the battlefield under fire when I was wounded, and put a tourniquet on my arm, I would have bled to death. The corpsmen saved a lot of lives by their bravery."

"I'm happy to hear that. But I . . . I'm sorry about your arm, Andy."

"Thank you, but according to the doctors, I'm one of the fortunate ones. Among the wounded, it was mostly the amputees that lived. Few of the other wounded survived."

"How sad," Sarah thought, "for all those poor wounded men."

"I'll be fine," Andy continued. "I've always wanted to be a school teacher. That's why I went to see John Seaman. There are several grade schools in Casnovia Township, but I knew he serves on the board of the Seaman School. As it turned out, they will need a teacher for that school this fall. Mr. Seaman promised to do all he can to get me the contract."

"I'm glad, Andy; I think you'll make a fine teacher," Sarah said in a tired voice.

"I'm on my way to Camp Blair at Jackson, where I'll be mustered out, so I'll certainly be home to stay by this fall."

Sarah only nodded in agreement.

Andy suddenly wondered why Sarah was alone. "How is Rufus, Sarah? Why isn't he traveling with you?" Sarah leaned toward the window and pressed her hot forehead against the cool glass, watching the raindrops stream down the outside of the pane. She swallowed, and with tears glistening in her eyes, turned to answer Andy. "Rufus is very ill in a military hospital near Brooklyn. I'm on my way to see him," she replied with a shaky voice.

Andy looked stunned. "I . . . I'm really sorry. I didn't even know Rufus was in the army, and his pa surely didn't say anything about a hospital."

"They don't know yet. We received word only yesterday. Ma and Pa Seaman won't hear about it until my parents or my brother Ed gets word to them." Sarah's voice kept growing fainter.

"Is there anything I can do?" Andy inquired. He felt terribly sorry for Sarah, as he took note of the dark circles under her eyes.

"No, thank you, Andy. If you'll excuse me, I'm going to try to rest." Even though she felt exhausted, she knew she wouldn't be able to sleep.

"Of course, you go right ahead," Andy urged her.

Laying her head on the back of the seat, she kept listening to the sound of the train's wheels going clickety-click over the rails, carrying her nearer to Rufus.

Hour after hour passed with Sarah and Andy quietly sitting side by side, seldom talking, each lost in their own thoughts.

Andy was sensitive to Sarah's grief. No stranger to tragedy, he had seen the same pain on the faces of wives and mothers who came to visit—and often to bid a final farewell to—their loved ones in the military hospital where he had been a patient. He silently kept praying for God to give Sarah the strength he knew she needed.

Finally, in the middle of the afternoon Andy broke the silence by offering to share his lunch with Sarah. "Wouldn't you like a sandwich? My ma fixed me a huge lunch."

"No, thank you, Andy. I have a sandwich from the hotel, but I'm not hungry. I'll try later."

Sarah did try to eat later, shortly before they arrived in Detroit. Pulling her white handkerchief with the sandwich out of her valise, she slowly managed to eat most of it by thinking of Rufus. She knew she needed to eat to have strength for her journey.

Meanwhile, the train kept moving steadily along at speeds up to twenty miles per hour as the engineer in the cab drove it toward its destination—Detroit.

As the train arrived at the bustling Detroit Station, the engineer slowed to a complete stop. They were on time; it was 5:00 p.m. Conductor Baker opened the side door. Putting the bottom step down, he stood once again at his post, ready to assist the passengers off the coach.

Andy got up to make his departure with the other passengers. "I heard the conductor tell you to stay in your seat, so I know you won't be getting off just yet."

"No, I'm to wait here."

Andy pushed his lunch toward Sarah. "Here, I want you to take the rest of the food my mother gave me. You have much farther to travel than I do."

"But, Andy . . ."

"I won't take 'No' for an answer."

"Well, thank you very much. You've been so kind to me, Andy." Sarah put the lunch in her valise.

"I'm so glad I got to see you, Sarah. You'll be in my prayers. God bless you and Rufus."

"Thank you, and God bless you."

Andy then turned and walked down the aisle to the side door. Sarah was gratified to see the respect his Union uniform earned him. With smiles on their faces, passengers stepped aside to allow him to go ahead of them. One man even slapped him on the back as he told him, "Well done, soldier." Most of the people didn't even seem to notice he was an amputee.

"Rufus wore the same uniform," she thought. "Only I've never seen him in it."

After all the other passengers had left the coach, the conductor hurried back to get Sarah, quickly picking up her valise.

"Come with me," he urged her. "We'll check the schedules to see which train will leave for New York earliest."

The sun shone brightly. The showers had cleared, leaving a beautiful rainbow. Looking at the multicolored arc in the sky, Sarah felt blessed, remembering that God's promises are new every morning.

The kindly conductor guided Sarah into the station thronged with people, where they joined the long line at the ticket window. Finally their turn came. Once they found out which train Sarah needed and that it would leave in just a half hour, she quickly purchased her ticket and followed her helpful conductor to the boarding area. There he gently took her by the arm to escort her to where she could meet the train's young conductor, whom he immediately recognized.

"Bill, this is Mrs. Seaman, who is traveling alone. I would like you to look after her on your run, if you would, please."

Conductor Bill Warren, a smartly uniformed man of medium build, was assisting passengers into the coach. His congenial eyes crinkled when he smiled at Sarah. "It's nice to meet you, Mrs. Seaman. I'll be happy to look after you," he answered gently.

"Thank you, it's nice to meet you," Sarah said.

She then turned toward Conductor Baker: "Thank you for all your help. I don't know what I would have done without you."

"You're welcome, Mrs. Seaman. It's just part of doing my job. I know you are anxious to get to Brooklyn to visit your ill husband. The train you are boarding now is one of our fastest passenger trains. You'll arrive at your destination by tomorrow evening! I hope the rest of the trip goes well for you and that you find your husband much improved."

"Thank you," she replied, taking her valise from him before boarding the train.

Sarah entered the coach. As she sat, she noticed a middle-aged, well-dressed man sitting across from her who seemed to be engrossed in a book. Looking closer, she saw that he held a leather Bible. She immediately felt the tension in her body ease.

The conductor made his way down the narrow aisle, checking each person's ticket before tearing it and handing back the stub. He checked the ticket of the gentleman across the aisle before he took Sarah's. After returning her stub, he spoke to the two of them.

"I see you both are going to Brooklyn. Do you know each other?"

Although Conductor Baker of the Grand Rapids–Detroit run had introduced Conductor Warren to Sarah, he hadn't told him her destination. Wanting to look after her, the conductor wondered if she had run into an acquaintance on the train.

"No," Sarah answered.

The gentleman smiled and agreed. "No, we're not acquainted," he said, but as soon as the conductor moved on, he introduced himself. "I'm Reverend DeYoung, and I live in Brooklyn. Do you live there, too, or are you just visiting?" he asked.

"I'm Sarah Seaman," she replied. "My husband is a patient at De Camp Military Hospital on Davids Island. He's very ill with typhoid fever, and I'm on my way to visit him." Her voice quavered as she spoke.

Compassion flooded the parson's gray-bearded face. His eyes filled with sorrow.

"What is your husband's first name, Mrs. Seaman?" he inquired. "When I'm home in Brooklyn, I visit De Camp Hospital to talk and pray with the soldiers. Maybe I've seen him, although I don't remember visiting anyone named Seaman."

"It's Rufus," Sarah excitedly replied. "Have you met him?" she anxiously asked, leaning forward.

"No, I don't remember that name. How long has he been there?"

"The letter I received said he had been admitted to the hospital on April 15, not quite three weeks ago," she answered.

"Well, that explains it. I haven't been home since then. When your husband was admitted I had just traveled to Chicago to listen to a young evangelist some friends told me I should hear. His name is Dwight L. Moody. He's a much-anointed preacher, and I'm sure he'll reach many people for Jesus. Have you ever heard of him?" he asked.

Sarah hesitated, trying to remember the name. "No, I haven't," she thoughtfully answered.

"You will someday, I'm sure," he emphatically stated.

They rode on for a few miles without talking, the only sound being the clicking of the train wheels rolling steadily eastward. The parson continued reading his beloved Bible, while Sarah sat hunched over in her seat, silently praying for Rufus.

Reverend DeYoung, glancing over at her, noticed the despair in her drawn face. After all of the pain and suffering he had seen at that hospital, he truly understood her anxiety.

"Are you a Christian, Mrs. Seaman?" he delicately inquired.

Sarah's eyes suddenly brightened as she answered. "Yes, I am. My husband and I both have a personal relationship with the Lord," she assured him.

"Oh, how wonderful. I'm so glad to hear that!" he exclaimed. "How long has it been since you accepted Jesus as your Savior?"

"I accepted Jesus shortly after my tenth birthday, and Rufus accepted him at seventeen. But just recently we both recommitted our lives," she confided.

"That's wonderful," he exclaimed. "You're very brave to be traveling so far alone. Please be careful. It's not always safe," he went on to caution her.

"The conductors have been watching out for me as much as they can because I'm alone."

"That's good. Since we are both going to Brooklyn, you should always take a seat next to mine if we have to transfer trains," he advised her. "Then you won't be traveling alone. Where are you going to stay when you get to Brooklyn?"

"Someone told me to find a rooming house," she replied. "They said it would cost less."

"Yes, it would, but as I told you, I visit De Camp Hospital. You could stay with my wife and me, and I could take you to the hospital. My wife would appreciate the company, and we both would enjoy having you as our guest. Our two daughters are married, leaving us with two extra bedrooms."

"Oh, but I would be imposing on you and your wife. You don't even know me," she protested.

"But Christians are family, are we not?" he reminded her.

"Yes," she quietly agreed. "All right, I'll stay with you and your wife, if she doesn't mind."

"Then it's settled, because she won't mind. She'll be delighted, Sarah," he assured her. "Oh, may I call you Sarah?"

"Yes, please do, after all, we are family," she smiled.

Sarah could now rest in the company of this kind, paternal parson as she traveled on to Brooklyn. Not only had he generously offered her his assistance; he had even invited her to experience the hospitality of his home when she went to visit her beloved Rufus.

"Brooklyn! Brooklyn!" the conductor called. As the train pulled into the station at twilight, Sarah's heart beat rapidly at the thought of soon seeing Rufus. Though she was drained by fatigue, the excitement gave her strength to go on. Reverend DeYoung ushered her off the train car onto the crowded platform. Multitudes of people from all walks of life gathered alongside the trains—some coming, some going. Sarah's attention was caught immediately by some weary Union soldiers in the throng. With the war over, she wondered if they were on their way home. She hoped so.

The parson hailed a driver from the row of black carriages waiting to be hired. He helped Sarah into the horse-drawn cab and, once they were comfortably seated, turned to face her. "I'm sorry," he kindly said, "but it's too late to take a ferry over to Davids Island tonight. You'll have to wait until morning."

Sarah knew he told the truth, but disappointment surged through every bone of her body. She couldn't stand being this close to Rufus, yet not being able to see him. She blinked away the painful tears that welled up in her tired eyes.

Under different circumstances, Sarah would have enjoyed the sights as the spirited team of shiny bays strutted down Flatbush Avenue. At this hour lamplighters could be seen igniting the gas streetlights that cast a yellow glow over the warm springtime evening. The rapidly growing, young industrial city showed many styles of architecture, including that of its Dutch founders. Little tulip heads peeped up in front of houses that had room enough for large families.

Turning up a side street lined with maple trees, the driver, sitting high on his box, slowly brought his rig to a stop in front of a neat red brick home. Flickering lights radiating from the tall windows on the first floor welcomed them.

The parson jumped out of the cab, happy to be home. He reached up to pay the driver, then turned and helped Sarah down from the carriage. He picked up their baggage, and with a spring in his step hurried Sarah to the front door. Before he could get his latchkey out of his pocket, the door burst wide open, and a short, slightly plump lady with gray hair and kind brown eyes stood there with arms outstretched. Reverend DeYoung at once dropped the baggage and embraced the woman. He held her tight before introducing her to Sarah.

"Sarah, this is my wife, Grace." Then turning to Grace, "This is Sarah Seaman, a young woman I met on the train. Her husband is a Union soldier at De Camp General Hospital. She traveled all the way here from Grand Rapids, Michigan, to visit him, so I invited her to stay with us. I told her you wouldn't mind."

"Of course I don't mind," Grace answered, putting an arm around her guest and drawing her into the house. "I'm really happy to meet you, dear."

"I'm so happy to meet you, too," Sarah answered with warm gratitude.

Grace proved to be all that Reverend DeYoung had said about her during their long train ride. She happily escorted Sarah up the brown-carpeted open stairway to a lovely bedroom.

"We have two married daughters," she explained, "and this room belonged to Sally, our younger. Please make yourself at home. I'll get you warm water for your toiletry," she added, picking up the empty pitcher from the cherry commode. "I'll be right back."

Grace came back shortly with the warm water, saying, "Supper will be ready soon. I'll call you, dear." She then shut the bedroom door behind her and went back downstairs.

Sarah took off her bonnet, laying it on the dresser. Her eyes scanned the pretty room with its floral wallpaper and white ruffled curtains gently fluttering in the May breeze. Her thoughts turned to Rufus and their family and the hope that someday her little girls would have a room like this. Standing there, Sarah thought she caught a delightful whiff of lilacs. She moved to the window, looking down on the yard in search of her favorite flowers. She located the bush just below. The lilacs were early this year and even more beautiful than usual.

Sarah removed her blouse to do her toiletry, being very thankful for the warm water for washing off the grime of the dusty, sooty train ride. She put on a clean white blouse and combed her hair. Just as she finished, she heard a soft tap on the bedroom door; it was Grace calling her to supper. She walked with her hostess down to the kitchen, where the mouthwatering aroma of delicious food filled the air.

Set with places for three, a medium-sized oak table with four matching chairs occupied the center of the room; on it was a pot of steaming stew. Grace picked up two hot pads before opening the oven door of the cookstove to take out freshly baked biscuits.

"Sit down, Sarah and Jacob," Grace said.

"You may sit here, Sarah," Jacob told her, pulling out a chair, then holding Grace's chair for her before he sat in his own place.

When all three were seated, they folded their hands and bowed their heads for grace. Reverend DeYoung said a prayer of thanksgiving, not only for the food, but for their safe arrival as well. Each one at the table agreed with a hearty "Amen."

During the tasty meal of hot stew and melt-in-your-mouth biscuits, the parson spoke to Sarah about De Camp Hospital.

"There are also Confederate prisoners on Davids Island," he explained to her. "If they are well enough to walk around, some of them fish for their food. They're allowed freedom because they can't get off the island. Food is scarce for them; some New Yorkers who are Confederate sympathizers bring them provisions. I take them rations myself, but not because I am a Confederate sympathizer. I do it because I know that's what our Lord would want me to do."

Sarah readily nodded. "Yes, Jesus would want you to feed the hungry."

"Now, with the war over, I'm sure those healthy enough to travel will go home," the reverend said.

"Oh, I hope they can. I'm sure many of them have wives and children waiting for them," she said with deep feeling.

"Yes, I'm sure they do. Some of their wives may also come to visit them now."

Grace spoke up. "I thought you could take the rest of the stew to them, Jacob."

"Thank you, honey. I will."

Sarah's head suddenly jerked as she almost fell asleep. Grace noticed and realized how exhausted she must be—too exhausted to talk anymore.

"Come, you go to bed, dear," Grace told her.

The parson pulled Sarah's chair out for her so she could rise from the table.

"Thank you, Parson DeYoung. Good night," she quietly said.

"Good night, Sarah. Sleep well."

Grace, with her arm around Sarah's waist, escorted her up the stairs to her bedroom. Entering the room, she turned down the bed.

"You need your rest. I'll call you in the morning for breakfast." She patted Sarah's arm before quietly exiting.

Waking off and on throughout the night, Sarah found herself praying. She rose very early, taking extra time for her toiletry after Grace brought her hot water. She wanted to look especially nice for Rufus. The aroma of perking coffee and frying bacon drifted up the stairway.

Shortly, there came a soft rap on the door. "Breakfast, dear," Grace called.

"Thank you, Mrs. DeYoung." Sarah quickly descended to the kitchen. Although too excited to eat, she still politely sat with her hosts and managed to drink a cup of coffee.

26

De Camp Hospital, Davids Island

The End of the Journey ~ Crossing Safely

Finally ready to depart, they started on the last leg of Sarah's journey. Her pulse raced wildly as she and Reverend DeYoung rode along in the carriage he had hired to take them to the Davids Island ferry.

It seemed to Sarah that the time for seeing Rufus would never come. The parson calmly sat beside her, holding in his lap the pot of leftover stew that his compassionate wife was sending for the Confederate soldiers.

The weather couldn't have been more beautiful; it was a perfect, sunny spring day in May. Green leaves budded on the trees, where birds merrily chirped as they built their nests. Here and there, brightly colored flowerbeds bloomed.

Sarah sat quietly, dealing with strong, mixed emotions. In her excitement she longed to see Rufus and nurse him back to health, and yet, somehow, she felt anxious about what she might find. Reverend DeYoung, a sensitive man, imagined what she must be feeling. He silently kept praying for God to give her strength for whatever she might face.

The taxi driver, sitting in his carriage box, drove the team of chestnut horses down a number of streets until they safely arrived at New York Harbor. At the dock, passengers were boarding the island ferry.

Reverend DeYoung handed Sarah the stew and biscuits. "Would you hold these for me, please, while I pay the driver?"

"Of course." Sarah took the food and balanced the covered pot on her knees. After paying the driver, the parson reached into the carriage for the victuals, placed them in the crook of one arm, and with the other assisted Sarah out of the taxi. Taking her by the elbow, he guided her over to the ticket booth. Tickets purchased, they boarded the ferry that would at last take Sarah to Rufus.

Benches lined the deck along the boat's railing. "There's room for us here, Sarah," the parson said, ushering her to some empty seats. While the boat was leaving the dock, fog horns continued to bellow their warning, even though the harbor's thick white clouds were lifting, leaving a thin mist in their place—a mist that felt cool to Sarah's flushed face.

Seated, the reverend viewed the other passengers. He knew most of them were coming to visit loved ones. His shepherd's heart went out to each one. He particularly noticed a young woman standing off by herself, apart from the crowd, carrying a large basket of food on her arm. Although her clothes appeared to be far from new, she was neatly dressed in a gray suit, with her blond hair tucked under a pink bonnet. "I wonder who she intends to visit," mused the parson. He especially noted her sad expression, one worn by too many women these days.

Sarah trembled. "Are you cold, Sarah?"

She smiled. "No, just excited about seeing Rufus. I can't believe I'm really here."

Their short voyage at an end, the captain edged his vessel alongside the dock on Davids Island. Passengers stood to disembark. The parson and Sarah went ashore with the others.

"I'll walk you over to Dr. Webster's office before I drop off the stew for the Confederates. The buildings over there house the infirmaries." The parson nodded toward a long row of narrow wooden structures.

"Oh, is Rufus in one of them then?" Sarah breathlessly asked, as she eyed the buildings.

Parson DeYoung sensed her excitement. "Yes, that's where he is." He knew the suffering Sarah had experienced while traveling to get here. He only hoped . . . well, he would walk her over to the office.

On the way they passed a soldier on crutches wearing a tattered Confederate uniform. His dark hair needed a trim, as well as his bushy beard. He carried a fishing pole tucked under his arm.

The parson greeted him. "Good morning, do you think they'll bite today?"

"I hope so, sir," the soldier drawled.

"I brought some stew for you boys. I'll bring it over shortly."

"I appreciate that, sir."

"Are there many of you still here?"

"A few, but now, with the war over, most have gone home." His face brightened. "I'll be goin' home next week myself."

Parson DeYoung gently put his hand on the weary soldier's shoulder. "I'm glad to hear that, son. I'll see you later."

Sarah and the parson walked on, soon arriving at the assistant surgeon's office. An orderly stood on the stoop, about to enter the building. Rev. DeYoung spoke to him as he guided Sarah up the steps. "Would you be able to help this lady? She wants to see her husband, who is a patient here."

The orderly smiled broadly. His broad face and curly hair made him look even younger than he probably was. "Yes, I'll help her, sir." He politely opened the door for Sarah.

The parson walked back down the steps. "I'll be back in a few minutes." He wanted to see Rufus, too, but felt Sarah needed to be alone with her husband when she first greeted him. He would meet Rufus later, after he had delivered the food.

Sarah stepped past the orderly into a dimly lit hall. Sudden waves of nausea washed over her from the unexpected stench emitted by the infirmary. Without even noticing it, she put a handkerchief to her mouth.

The orderly stopped in front of the first door on the right. "This is Dr. Webster's office." He rapped lightly on the thin wooden door.

"Come in," a pleasant voice called.

The young man held the door for Sarah before following her into the room. Dr. Webster was sitting at a large oak desk facing the door. Behind him, the curtains at three open windows blew gently in the May breeze.

"Doctor, this woman wants to see ya about visitin' her husband, a patient here."

Having done his duty, the orderly excused himself. Sarah thanked him.

"Won't you be seated, ma'am?" Dr. Webster smiled as he directed her to a chair facing him. "What is your name?"

Glad for the invitation to sit down, Sarah eased herself into the straight-backed chair. She looked at the man sitting across from her. He appeared too young to have the position of assistant surgeon. He didn't look any older than Rufus.

"My name is Sarah Seaman," she answered. "I received a letter from you informing me that my husband, Rufus, is suffering from typhoid fever. I believe he is in the sixth pavilion. I would like to see him. How is he?"

She didn't like the dark cloud that passed over the doctor's face when she told him about Rufus. He kept his eyes averted as he shuffled papers on his desk before looking up at her. The compassion in his eyes told her everything.

"I'm sorry, Mrs. Seaman. We did all we could, but Rufus passed away two days ago."

Sarah's shoulders slumped. "Oh, Rufus, Rufus," she whispered, before bursting into uncontrollable sobs. She grasped the arms of her chair tightly as the room started spinning. She cried out to God. Numb with grief, she could no longer be brave.

Dr. Webster jumped up from his chair and came around the desk to her side. He awkwardly placed a hand on her shoulder in an attempt to comfort her. "I'll get the chaplain, Mrs. Seaman. He spent a lot of time with your husband and remained at his side until the end."

The young doctor went out into the hall to look for the orderly. Finding him, he sent him to bring the chaplain. Back in his office, he didn't know how to comfort Sarah. No matter how many times he broke the news to someone about the loss of their loved one, it never got easier. He would much rather fight on the field of battle than bring these sad tidings.

Shortly, the door opened. Chaplain Rogers entered, and Dr. Webster introduced Sarah to him. "This is Mrs. Seaman, Rufus's wife."

The chaplain knelt beside her. "Mrs. Seaman, I'm Chaplain Rogers. I knew Rufus. I sat with him when he went home to Jesus."

Glancing at him, Sarah desperately tried to control her sobs. Even in her fresh grief, it helped to meet someone who knew Rufus, someone who cared enough to stay at his side when he was dying.

"Do you feel strong enough to walk outside for some fresh air?" the doctor asked. "I think it would do you good."

"I . . . I . . . felt faint for a minute. Maybe some fresh air would help me," she sniffled.

"We'll support you," the chaplain assured her. With the help of the doctor and the chaplain, Sarah made her way outside, down the steps, and over to a nearby park bench. The air smelled fresher outside—free of the stench—and the morning sun felt warm on her face.

"Are you feeling all right, Mrs. Seaman?" Dr. Webster asked. "I must make my rounds at the hospital. If you need anything, please let me know." Once again showing his compassion, he briefly patted her arm. "I'm really sorry about Rufus." He hurried off to tend the many sick and wounded left in his care—both Union and Confederate soldiers.

Chaplain Rogers sat down on the bench beside Sarah. "Rufus talked so much about you that I feel I know you," he told her. "He talked of you and your daughters all the time. He loved all of you dearly. Being a godly man, he didn't fear death. Christians shouldn't fear death," the chaplain gently said. "After all, it's really the beginning of life—not the end."

"Yes, I know," Sarah managed to say.

"I know you do," the chaplain replied. "Rufus told me that you now serve the Lord, too. He shared with me how the two of you came back to the Lord after Rufus entered the service. He truly believed God allowed him to be drafted to bring the two of you back to him. He felt only God's love in all that happened. He actually would rather have died in Jesus than to have lived without him. He believed that all God did was for the benefit of both of you."

"Yes, I believe that, too," she whispered.

"Did you come to Davids Island alone?"

"No, Reverend DeYoung brought me," she whispered.

"I'm happy to hear that," the chaplain told her. "He's a good friend of mine."

Sarah later learned that the chaplain and the parson had become well acquainted as they ministered side by side to the soldiers at De Camp General Hospital. They both willingly gave of their time to pray with them and to show them the love of Jesus. But right now it was Sarah to whom they were called to show that love.

Reverend DeYoung was ambling along the narrow dirt path leading back to the infirmary, where he planned to rejoin Sarah. Beside him strolled Susannah Fuller, the young woman he had noticed standing alone on the ferry that morning. He then saw the chaplain and Sarah sitting on a park bench near the entrance to the building. Alarmed at finding Sarah outside, he quickened his pace to approach her.

"Sarah, are you all right?" One look at her pale face told him things had not gone well. Chaplain Rogers quickly got to his feet. He gently pulled Reverend DeYoung aside and in a low voice explained how Sarah had just found out that Rufus had died two days ago, that she had arrived too late to see him.

Susannah overheard their mumbled conversation about Rufus. Her own husband had died the same day as Rufus, except that she had arrived in time to be with him. For this she felt thankful. Her large brown eyes misted as she looked at Sarah sitting on the bench so forlorn.

Their conversation ended, the chaplain and the parson turned back to the ladies. The chaplain, upon seeing Susannah, spoke to her. "How are you doing today, Susannah?"

"I think I'm doing a little better, thank you, chaplain," she drawled.

"Oh, do you two know each other?" the parson asked. "I just met Susannah—Mrs. Fuller—when I visited the Confederate prisoners with some food. I wanted her to meet Sarah."

"Yes, they have much in common," the chaplain agreed. "Susannah's husband was a Confederate prisoner, and he died the same day as Rufus. Her brother is also a prisoner here, and he's the reason she's stayed on. He will soon be well enough to be released, and she'll go back South with him to their home in Georgia. Like Sarah, she's also a fine Christian," he added.

Reverend DeYoung introduced Sarah and Susannah to one another.

Sarah looked up at Susannah with sympathy in her already sad eyes. "I'm so sorry, Susannah, about your husband," she managed to say.

"Thank you," Susannah replied. "And I'm so sorry for you, too." She sat down on the bench next to her, putting her hand over Sarah's.

"When you feel up to it, Sarah, I think we should go back to my house, where you can rest," the parson suggested. "Where are you staying, Susannah?" he asked.

"I'm staying at a boardinghouse near here," she answered.

"I would like you to come home with Sarah and me. There's room for you to stay with us, too. My wife would love it. We can stop and pick up your satchel on the way."

Sarah smiled weakly at Susannah, trying to encourage her with what strength she still possessed. It would be nice for Susannah to accompany them; she had already grown to like her very much. After briefly hesitating, Susannah agreed to go home with the parson. She felt so alone and longed to have a friend like Sarah, who shared the same grief. But would his wife really be receptive to having a Southerner stay with them? She prayed so.

"If you can wait a minute, I have something for Sarah in my office. I'll be right back," the chaplain said, hurrying off.

Presently he returned with a small brown book the size of his palm. "Sarah, this book is called *Passing over Jordan* and was given to Rufus. It brought him much comfort as he read it; it's the kind of book that would comfort any person facing death. He wanted you to have it."

With trembling hands Sarah took and held close to her heart the little book Rufus had held close to his just a few days before. "Oh, thank you, chaplain."

"Sarah, I'm sure you would like to visit Rufus's grave, wouldn't you?" the chaplain asked.

"Yes, I would. Where . . . where . . . where is he buried?"

"He's buried in Cypress Hills Cemetery in Brooklyn. Part of that cemetery is set aside for Civil War soldiers, both Union and Confederate. Susannah's husband is buried there as well. Maybe she would like to go with you, so she could visit her husband's grave again."

"Oh yes, I would like to go again," Susannah readily said.

"I can take them both tomorrow," the parson offered. "I think it would be too much for Sarah right now."

"I agree," replied the chaplain. "I would like to meet you there, if I may."

"Of course, shall we make it nine o'clock tomorrow morning?"

Everyone agreed.

Hospitality and warmth overflowed from the DeYoung home as Grace greeted them at the door. The parson introduced Susannah to Grace, explaining that he had told her she could stay at their home. "Her husband was a Confederate prisoner of war," he continued. "He died the same day as Rufus." Grace winced at this news, even though the parson had confided to her the possibility of Rufus being dead when Sarah arrived. She simply hadn't been able to believe that could be possible. Before turning to Sarah, Grace gave Susannah a big hug. "Of course she may stay. We'll put her in Mary's room."

All fear of not being accepted melted away in Susannah's heart. She knew God had brought these people to help her during this most trying of times in her life.

Grace then looked at Sarah, and her heart broke at the sight of her.

She encircled Sarah with her arms, and the two women wept. Susannah stood to the side, softly crying alone. Grace drew her in. She held both young widows to her heart as all three released their sorrow.

Grace gradually pulled away. "I think Sarah needs to go to her room and lie down."

Sarah nodded. She felt drained.

Grace once again put her arms around both Sarah's and Susannah's waists. They mounted the wide stairway together. At the door to Sarah's room, Grace paused. "Is there anything you need, honey? Would you like a cup of tea brought to you?"

"No, thank you. There is nothing I need. I'll be all right," Sarah answered in a subdued voice. When Sarah opened the bedroom door, a shaft of sunlight flooded the hall. Grace entered the room ahead of her, walked over to the windows and pulled the shades. "There, that should help you rest better," she said to Sarah, and left.

"Thank you," Sarah replied.

Grace then took Susannah farther down the hall to Mary's room. "Is there anything I can get you?" she asked. "We'll bring your satchel up. You may stay here and rest, or, if you'd rather come downstairs with me, I'd love the company, dear."

"Thank you, there's nothing I need. I'll rest a little. I may come down to you later, if you don't mind."

Meanwhile Sarah unbuckled her shoes and removed them before flinging herself across the bed. She longed to escape into a dreamless sleep. Her thoughts turned to Dorothy and Lucy. How could she tell them their father would never be coming home again? She remembered the sweet kisses they had sent to their beloved Papa—kisses for her to deliver. Recalling this scene with her daughters brought forth a new wave of tears to her eyes.

A gentle rap on the door awakened Sarah with a start. She wondered how long she had slept after crying herself to sleep. The soft rap came again.

"Sarah, are you all right?" asked a sweet Southern voice, as Susannah gently pushed the door open.

"I'm all right, Susannah," Sarah drowsily replied. "I fell asleep. What time is it?" she asked, as she sat up in bed and then swung her feet onto the floor.

Susannah entered the room and sat down beside her. "It's almost supper time. Grace sent me to invite you to come down to eat."

"Oh, that is gracious of her. I just don't think I could eat a thing. Please thank her for me."

Susannah briefly patted her hand. "I know you aren't hungry. I'm not either, but I told Grace I would try some tea and biscuits. Would you try some with me? If you like, we could probably eat together here."

"Yes, I would like that. Thank you."

Before Susannah left to go downstairs, she walked over to pull the window shades back up. Late afternoon sunlight filled the room.

Alone once again, Sarah turned to look for Rufus's little book, Passing Over Jordan. She found it in the middle of the bed where she lay clutching it during her nap. She picked it up and walked over to one of the velvet chairs by the window where there would be more light. She sat and browsed, wondering what words of wisdom and comfort Rufus had found there.

She began with the author's introduction. It was his desire, she read, that those reading it would "meditate on the glorious character of Christ, connected with praises to His adorable name—gaze upon the Son of Righteousness in all the brightness of His Father's glory." The result, he hoped, would be that "His beauty will hide your deformity." He encouraged the reader to "ponder over the passages" and to "commit to memory some of the more prominent parts of the little work—for when you cannot have access to the book itself." He went on, "I would hope that you may, with the divine blessing, have many a sweet spiritual repast, especially should you be called to lie upon a protracted death-bed."

Thumbing farther into the book, Sarah came across a quotation from the the Apostle Paul: "I have fought a good fight, I have finished my course, I have kept the faith: Henceforth there is laid up for me a crown of righteousness, which the Lord, the righteous judge, shall give me at that day: and not to me only, but unto all them also that love his appearing." (2 Timothy 4:7-8)

Sarah also noted passages on love and forgiveness. "A new commandment I give unto you, That ye love one another; as I have loved you, that ye also love one another" (John 13:34).

Toward the end of the book, Sarah found other passages of comfort for the dying:

Father, I will that they also, whom Thou hast given me, be with me where I am; that they may behold my glory. (John 17:24)

"Oh what transport will seize my admiring soul, when I find myself on the shores of the heavenly Canaan—when I find myself safely there, free from all possibility of being lost—when the first beams of the glories of my reconciled God and Saviour shall burst upon my soul. How will the arches of Heaven ring with my hallelujahs."

To die is gain. (Philippians 1:21)

O death, where is thy sting? O grave, where is thy victory? Thanks be to God which giveth us the victory through our Lord Jesus Christ. (1 Corinthians 15:55)

Welcome, welcome, welcome death! Hallelujah to the Lamb!

As she continued to read, a deep peace began to settle in her heart. Sarah felt pleased with "the little word." It contained appropriate Bible verses with wise comments to comfort a dying Christian, as well as showing a sinner the way of salvation. Since it was a small book, only two by three inches, a soldier could easily carry it on his person.

She never doubted Rufus had gone to heaven. These passages of Scripture must have been a great comfort to him.

27

Cypress Hills Cemetery, Brooklyn

Safe in God's Arms ~ United in Peace

Hearing the bedroom doorknob rattle, she walked over to open the door. Susannah stood there with a large yellow tray. She entered and carried it over to the round table nestled between the two velvet chairs in front of the window.

"We can sit here and eat," she said.

"Yes, this will be nice. I've been reading in this little book while you were gone."

The tray held a steaming pot of tea, cream and sugar, and warm biscuits and honey. The two bowed as Susannah said grace.

"What do you take in your tea, Sarah?" she asked as she poured.

"I'll just take a little of this cream," Sarah answered, helping herself to the tiny pitcher.

Each of them took a biscuit, poured honey on it, and began to nibble.

"You have been so kind, Susannah. After all, you lost your husband the same day I lost mine."

"Yes, I know. But I got here in time to be with Jimmy before he died. Also, I've had a couple more days to accept his death. Today you were met with a terrible shock."

"Yes, it's a shock I'll never get over. It helped to meet you, because you are going through the same thing. As the parson says, when we are Christians, we are family. You've been a wonderful sister in Christ to me."

"Thank you, Sarah. You have been to me as well, by accepting me as your friend instead of your enemy. Not everyone here up North has taken to my Southern accent. I felt so alone until I met the parson and you."

"I felt alone, too, until I met him on the train coming out here. He's been a real blessing."

"When are you leaving to go back home, Sarah?"

"That depends on what time the train leaves for the West. I think the parson knows the schedule. I'll check with him. I dread having to go home and tell my daughters and Rufus's family about his death. His parents already lost one son in the war, and now . . . now Rufus."

"Where is your home?"

"Casnovia, Michigan. It's a very small place north of Grand Rapids. We own a farm there."

"We own a small farm, too. Jimmy worked so very hard on it, from sunup to sundown."

"Didn't you have slaves?" Sarah wanted to know.

"Oh, no, we couldn't afford slaves. Only the rich plantation owners had them. They were very expensive. Besides, neither of us believed in slavery."

"Then why did Jimmy become a Confederate soldier?"

"Because he believed in states' rights."

Sarah nodded her head. She understood how a man could believe in states' rights, just as Rufus believed in the Union.

"Where is your home, Susannah?"

"Our farm is near Savannah, Georgia."

"Savannah, Georgia!" Sarah exclaimed. "Rufus wrote me from there. They were camped about a mile outside of the city. That's where he spent Christmas. In one letter he wrote he had gone into Savannah, and that it was a nice town."

Susannah's face clouded. "Then he marched with Sherman through Georgia?" The tone of her voice indicated that she meant it more as a statement than a question.

"Yes . . . yes, he did." Sarah had momentarily forgotten that she and Susannah were on opposite sides during the war.

"Sherman devastated Georgia," Susannah declared. "He's a hated man for all his destruction. He even boasted he would make Georgia howl."

Without looking at Susannah, Sarah slowly picked up the teapot with a steady hand and poured tea into both empty cups. After adding cream to hers, she took a sip. Setting the cup down, her misty eyes met Susannah's. She liked Susannah and understood her feelings. She didn't want to say anything to hurt her or to spoil their new friendship. Yet she felt the need to defend Rufus's service to his country.

Sarah spoke gently and calmly. "I'm truly sorry for you and anyone on both sides who has suffered loss of any kind in the war. But I'm not ashamed that Rufus marched with Sherman. I would rather have him destroy property than kill someone's brother, son, or husband on the battlefield. To me," she continued, "true devastation has to do with all the lives lost at places like Antietam and Gettysburg. I have nothing but the highest respect for each brave soldier who ever fought, and for the many who died in battles like that. They were truly courageous and honorable men. You can rebuild railroads, towns, and property, but nothing will bring back Rufus or Jimmy or all the other lives lost." Sarah's voice dropped to almost a whisper as she added, "And if Sherman's march helped end that terrible war sooner, so more lives weren't lost on both sides, then I'm proud of Rufus."

The cloud began to slowly lift from Susannah's face. Tears coursed down her cheeks. "I know what you say is true, Sarah. Lives are more important than property! Yet, it's still hard to accept Sherman's march."

"Oh, I would never expect you to accept it. Sherman was definitely your enemy and did a lot of harm to your state. Still, maybe you can understand a little better how I feel about Rufus being with him."

"Yes, I do understand about Rufus. Only . . . Georgia is my state, and I've always been proud of it."

"Of course, and you should be." Sarah reached over and touched Susannah's knee. "If the people of Georgia are like you, they will rebuild everything—and make it even better than before, for it will be free of slavery."

"I believe that, too."

"Now there needs to be healing throughout our land. I was just reading about forgiveness in Rufus's little book." She reached for *Passing over Jordan*, lying on the table beside her, turned to the page that had the passage from passage from Ephesians 4:31-32, and read it aloud: "Let all bitterness, and wrath, and anger, and clamor, and evil speaking, be put away from you, with all malice: And be ye kind one to another, tenderhearted, forgiving one another, even as God for Christ's sake, hath forgiven you."

When she finished reading, Susannah spoke. "Thank you for sharing that familiar passage. That is one of my favorite verses. We all need to work at forgiving one another."

"Yes, we do."

The next morning Sarah awakened to the chirping of birds outside her window. Sleep hadn't come until almost 4:00 a.m., and even then she kept having disturbing dreams—dreams of Rufus dying without her present.

She quickly got out of bed, anxious to do her toiletry and to be ready to go to Cyprus Hills Cemetery. Standing in front of the commode, she glanced at the face in the mirror above the washbowl—a drawn face with dark circles under the eyes. Could it have been only yesterday she stood in the same spot in this room, doing her toiletry in anticipation of seeing Rufus? Fresh tears welled up in her eyes, but she fought them back. The water in the pitcher at room temperature would be fine with her; it'd be more refreshing. She didn't need Grace to go to the trouble of bringing her hot water. After washing up, she put on a crisp white blouse with her dark blue suit. Her hair neatly arranged, she now would be ready for whenever they wanted to leave.

The scent of lilacs again floated through the open window. She walked over to look down on their beauty. Rufus had loved lilacs, too. Sarah wished she could . . . Maybe Grace and the parson wouldn't mind . . .

She took her bonnet off the dresser and walked out into the hall, where she met Susannah coming out of her room. Sarah noticed how lovely she looked in the fresh white blouse she had put on to wear with her gray suit. They warmly greeted each other, and then, linking arms, descended to the kitchen.

Grace had set the table for the four of them and was standing at the stove, busily frying eggs and bacon and making toast in the oven. The aroma of coffee perking filled the room. Tom, their brown tabby, lay stretched out on the rug in front of the stove near his mistress's feet, purring his contentment. Grace turned from her cooking, her face red from the heat. "Good morning, girls. Breakfast is ready." She smiled as she spoke. "Just sit down at the table. The parson will be here shortly."

"Good morning, Grace," the girls replied.

"Isn't there something I can do to help?" Sarah asked.

"Yes, I would like to help, too," Susannah added.

"No, thank you. Everything is ready." Grace dished the bacon and eggs onto a platter and put it on the table.

The parson entered the kitchen. "Good morning, Sarah and Susannah."

"Good morning, parson," they answered.

Pastor DeYoung stopped by Grace to plant a kiss on the top of her head before sliding into his chair at the head of the table.

Grace poured coffee into each cup, put a plate of toast on the table, and sat down. All four of them bowed their heads while the parson said the blessing.

Sarah took an egg and one slice of toast from the platter Grace passed. She knew she needed to keep up her strength. Susannah followed her example. Both of them enjoyed the coffee most of all. Sarah noticed the pleased expression on Grace's face as she watched her guests eat a little breakfast.

"I've hitched up my own rig to take us to the cemetery. Then we can spend as much time as we want without keeping a cab waiting," the parson explained.

"That does sound good," Sarah agreed. "How large is the cemetery?"

"Cypress Hills is a large, private cemetery where they set aside about three acres for the Civil War dead. That area is known as Union Grounds, and that is where Rufus is buried." The parson turned to Susannah. "And I'm sure that's where you found Jimmy buried, also."

Susannah nodded.

"It's a beautiful, sunny, warm day, as far as the weather goes," the parson commented. "The trees have even budded."

"I wondered if you would care if Susannah and I each picked a bouquet of your lilacs to take for Rufus's and Jimmy's graves?" Sarah asked. "They are a favorite flower of Rufus's and mine. I can smell their fragrance coming through the window in my bedroom upstairs. I noticed your bush is right down below."

"No, of course we wouldn't care," Grace answered. "I'll pick some for both of you. I think that's a wonderful idea." She jumped up from the table and hurried outside to the lilac bush. Sarah and Susannah followed close behind. Soon all three had their arms loaded with the fragrant, lovely flowers.

The parson then drove his rig into the driveway, ready to leave for the cemetery. When Sarah and Susannah saw him, they ran inside the house to get their bonnets and hurried back out. Rev. DeYoung stepped down to help them both into the carriage. Seated comfortably, their laps filled with lilacs, Sarah and Susannah appeared ready to embark on a visitation journey whose poignant memory would linger with them for the rest of their lives.

After they had traveled about an hour, the parson drove onto Jamaica Avenue. "It won't be long now. The cemetery is just up this street." The nearer they came to their destination, the more the traffic thinned out. Few rigs passed them now.

They went about six blocks farther down the avenue. "I think that's the entrance over there, parson," Susannah pointed out. "I remember it from when I was here with the chaplain." She looked at Sarah. "The chaplain did a small funeral service for Jimmy, even though I was the only one present. Maybe he and the parson would do that for Rufus."

"Yes, we'd be glad to do that, Sarah," the parson assured her.

"I would like that very much," she replied.

The parson turned his dappled gray onto the dirt road winding through the cemetery. Before going very far, they met a parked rig. The chaplain was sitting in the carriage waiting for them. He hopped down and walked over as the parson pulled to the side of the road.

"Hello, everyone. How are you feeling today, Mrs. Seaman?" the chaplain asked.

"I'm better, chaplain. But please call me Sarah."

The chaplain assisted both women out of the carriage. "What beautiful lilacs you have. They'll be very nice for the graves. I thought, Sarah, that we could have a small service for Rufus, if you would like that. The parson could assist me."

"I would really like that. Susannah told me how you held one for Jimmy, and the parson has already agreed to join you in holding a service like that for Rufus."

"Right over here is Rufus's grave." The chaplain took Sarah by the elbow as he led them over to a mound of fresh dirt. Not too far from Rufus's grave they could see a similar mound—Jimmy's grave.

"I want to talk to you, Sarah, about your husband, and also remind you, Susannah, of what I said about Jimmy at his funeral. I happened to be with both of them when they died. You and I, Susannah, were together with Jimmy, and I was alone with Rufus when he passed on. The two were Christian, godly men. Under different circumstances, Rufus and Jimmy could have been the best of friends, because they were brothers in the Lord. I'm sure they are together in heaven, no longer enemies."

In their hearts Sarah and Susannah knew the chaplain was right. There are no enemies in heaven.

"Jacob, would you lead in prayer as we begin the funeral service?" the chaplain asked.

As the parson prayed, Susannah moved over and put her arm around Sarah.

Chaplain Rogers conducted a beautiful service. He shared much about Rufus from the conversations they had held during the weeks Rufus lay ill at De Camp. The chaplain had visited his bedside many times before he died.

He described how Rufus's love for his family came second only to his love for God and how in his thoughts he always put his wife and daughters ahead of himself.

The message warmed Sarah's heart. She realized how well the chaplain had come to know Rufus in such a brief time. He had cared enough to call on her husband often. He told how Rufus felt God had allowed him to be drafted as a means to draw him and Sarah back to a closer relationship with him, their precious Savior. Rufus thought no sacrifice too great to have that close relationship.

The chaplain ended the service by honoring Rufus for giving his life on the altar of sacrifice for his country. Reverend DeYoung closed with an appropriate prayer.

Sarah wiped the tears from her eyes and thanked both pastors. "Thank you, Reverend DeYoung and Chaplain Rogers. I appreciate what you said. Your words of comfort blessed me."

"It was our privilege to do it," Chaplain Rogers answered, and the parson quickly agreed.

Chaplain Rogers shook hands with Sarah and bade her goodbye. "I need to get back to the hospital," he explained. "Since I won't be seeing you again, I wish you a safe journey back home. You have my deepest sympathy."

"Thank you," Sarah whispered.

He then turned to Reverend DeYoung and Susannah. "Goodbye, Jacob," he said, as the two parsons shook hands. "And I'll see you tomorrow, Susannah."

"Yes, goodbye, chaplain," Susannah replied.

Going over to his rig, the chaplain untethered his restless, pawing horse. Back in the driver's seat, he gently snapped the lines over the bay's back. The frisky steed quickly picked up a trot, moving out of the cemetery.

"Take all the time you want, ladies. I'll wait in the buggy," the parson told them, as he walked over to get into his carriage. He smiled as he noticed the camaraderie the two women shared. Both widows experienced a fellowship beyond this world. Each felt proud of her husband, even though the men had fought on opposite sides. As sisters in Christ, they had a bond stronger than the division caused by war. It reminded the parson of the old hymn, "Blest Be the Tie That Binds."

> Blest be the tie that binds
> Our hearts in Christian love;
> The fellowship of kindred minds
> Is like to that above.

Sarah stepped up to the grave and bent down to arrange the lilacs like a bed across it. Susannah walked over to place her lilacs where Jimmy's body lay.

Sarah knelt at the head of Rufus's grave, kissed her fingertips and pressed the kiss into the grave's soil. She did this three times; a kiss from Dorothy, a kiss from Lucy, and a kiss from herself. Looking at Rufus's grave, plot 2660, Sarah returned in her thoughts to a small grave in another cemetery in Michigan, a spot also dear to her heart. "If only Rufus and Oliver could lie side by side in the same cemetery," she mused.

Of course, she knew Oliver and Rufus now lived together in heaven, not in their graves. She recalled the comforting words Rufus had spoken to her when Oliver died. "Yes, Sarah, we will see Oliver again. I'm looking forward to it. We're only pilgrims in this world. Heaven is really our home. Oliver is home now."

"And so are you home now, Rufus, my husband," she murmured.

Rufus had come to the end of his pilgrimage. He had sacrificed his life on the altar of freedom—freedom for all people in his country.

She rose and moved a little ways away from the grave. She wanted to have a clear view of the cemetery to hold in her memory for the rest of her life. Susannah joined her. They stood arm in arm, one blue arm entwined with one gray, surveying the beauty around them. The ribbons on their bonnets fluttered in the gentle breeze. Trees were budding and birds were singing their bright melodies on this sunny spring day. April rains had turned the ankle-high grass a rich green. Sarah's eyes lingered on the brown mounds that dotted the serene landscape.

Before leaving, she silently prayed for the families represented by these graves. She asked God to heal her country and prayed there would never be another war like this—brother against brother.

>Fallen heroes, North and South
>Lie buried beneath this sod.
>Not enemies, but comrades,
>Home safe in the arms of God.
>
>If they now dwell together,
>Then all enmity should cease.
>We who are left to follow
>Must unite to live in peace.

The End

Author's Notes

FACTS ABOUT MY NOVEL: All of Rufus's Civil War letters are genuine. The spelling and punctuation have been corrected; otherwise they are copied exactly as Rufus wrote them to his wife, Sarah. The characters that are members of the Seaman and Walkley families were all real people; Rufus's younger daughter, Lucy, became my grandmother. Rufus and Sarah did lose a five-year-old son, Oliver. The small book Passing Over Jordan was given to Rufus at De Camp General Hospital and is now in our possession. Sarah took the train to Brooklyn, N.Y., to visit Rufus but arrived too late, just as in the story. Captain Belknap actually rescued two little abandoned girls and found them a loving home up North. After returning home to Grand Rapids, Michigan, Captain Belknap rose to become a prominent citizen serving as that city's mayor from 1889 to 1893. The revivals mentioned in the story really did take place in Sherman's army, as they did in the Confederate Army, as well. After the war, General Sherman saw Captain MacBeth again in St. Louis, where the former Confederate officer was employed as a clerk in an insurance office.

Original Christmas Letter

The following is a reproduction of the original letter Rufus wrote to his wife, Sarah, on Christmas Day, 1864, one hundred fifty years ago. He used one large sheet of stationery and folded it in the middle, thus making four pages on which he could write. The text of the letter appears in its original form; its spelling and punctuation have not been altered. The corrected version of this letter is found on pages 188-189 of the novel.

Savanah the 25 in 1864
of December
Dear wife tis with plesure
that I take my pen in hand
to wright you a few lines to
let you know that I am
well and hope these few lines
will find you the same blesing
Sarah I received a leter from you
yesterday dated the 27 and was glad
to here that you was well and more
then glad thay was 8 postagage
stamps in it Sarah I wold like
to be at home to day to hold
crismas with you I hope you will
have a god time and plenty of
god vitels to eat Sarah my crismas
diner concisted of one smol craker
one slise of porke cup of cofey
and meal gravy thick as podon
Sarah you wrote that evry body
was duning you I wold pay no
atintion to them for thay can

do with out it as well as you
can and as for bill person tel
him that I was not to pay
him til next october for that
cuting box I oe him three dolars
to be payed as sone as I cold handy
on ranes acount but dont sel
no wheat unles it is for your self
for your nead ol of it when you
have three dolars that you dont
want you can pay bill I oe him
seventy pounds of corn in the ear
that I promest to let him have
seat corn for so way him out
seventy pounds of ears of corn
and dont let him have eny thing
elce of eny cind onley three dolars
when you have it and dont want
to use it for that is all I owe him
Sarah I was in Savanah yesterday
it is a wnise plase wee are
camped a bout a mild from town

Sarah you wrote you loked
for a leter the day before you
wrote and did not get eny now wonder
you didnot get eny for I cold not
write eny untill wee got heare
I wrote one the other day as son
as I cold send it I hope I can
write so you can get one evry
weake Sarah I wold be glad if
you wold get your liknes and the
childrons taken and send them
to me Sarah my captins name is
gorge M Roe general name is
jef C Davis Sarah I wish I cold
send you a crismas presant but
I have nothing to send only
my love to you my trust is
in him ho see beleve in me and
ye shel be saved Sarah trust in
the lord thy god and remember
me Sarah I have a pore plase
to wright set on the ground

and a bord in my lap so
you can ges how a solger
hafto do evry thing in proporton
the wether is very warm I hant
sean eny snow yet I sopose
thay is good sleyang thare
Sarah I hope you have got plenty
of wood to ceap you warm I hope
you have got moved before this
time whare you can be taken
care of and whare you wont
be so lonsom and whare you
can go to meating Sarah I want
you to get woren to let you have
trade so you and the children
can have what close you want
I want you to clothe your self
well get good close and plenty of
them dont be afrade to get them
so no more at presant this is
from your affectionate husban
   Rufus W Seaman
 to Sarah E Seaman

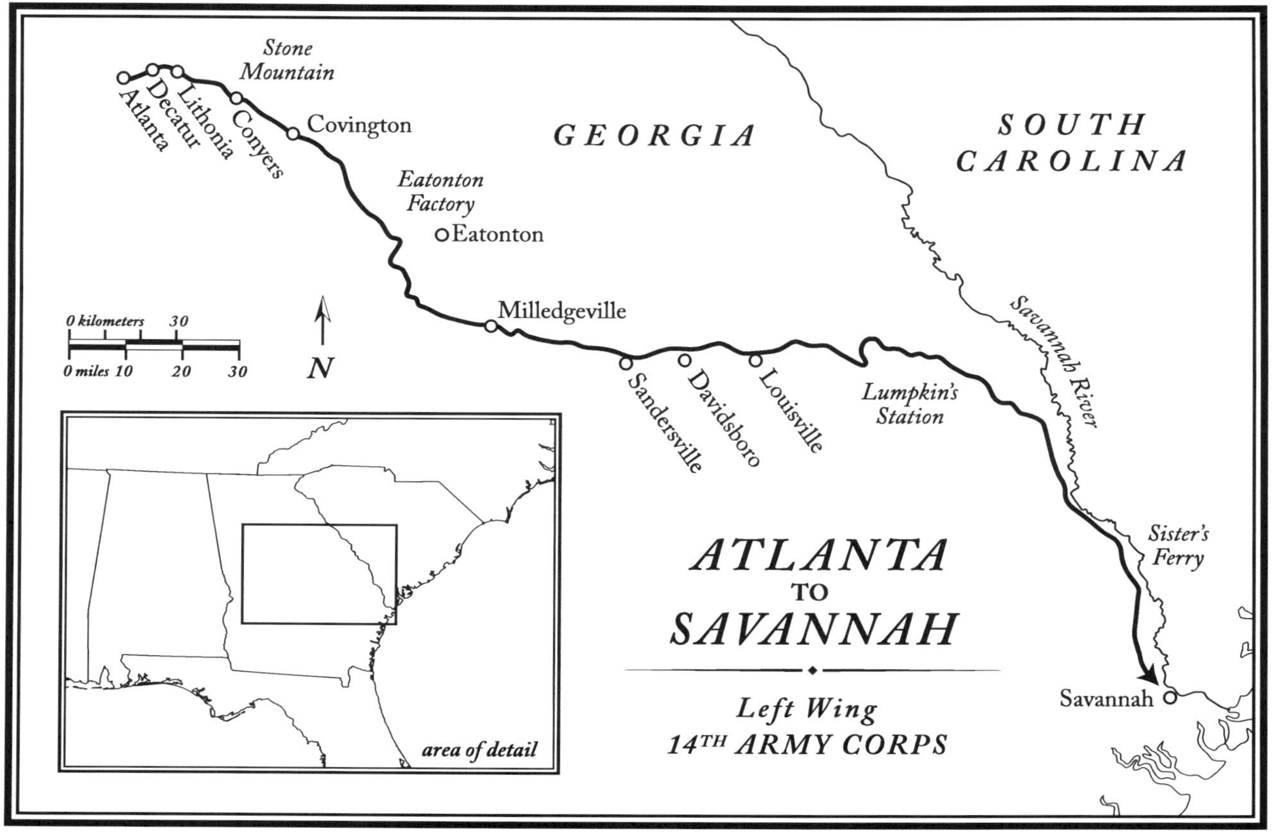
Stone Mountain
Atlanta
Decatur
Lithonia
Conyers
Covington
GEORGIA
SOUTH CAROLINA
Eatonton Factory
Eatonton
Milledgeville
0 kilometers 30
0 miles 10 20 30
N
Sandersville
Davidsboro
Louisville
Lumpkin's Station
Savannah River
Sister's Ferry
Savannah
area of detail
ATLANTA TO SAVANNAH
Left Wing
14TH ARMY CORPS

Made in the USA
Charleston, SC
29 January 2015

A MICHIGAN YANKEE

MARCHES with SHERMAN